THE

RUIT

OF HER

ANDS

THE RUIT OF HER ANDS

THE STORY OF SHIRA OF ASHKENAZ

MICHELLE CAMERON

POCKET BOOKS

New York   London   Toronto   Sydney

Pocket Books
A Division of Simon & Schuster, Inc.
1230 Avenue of the Americas
New York, NY 10020

"My heart is in the East," by Yehuda ha-Levi, translation reprinted by
permission of zionism-israel.com and zionismontheweb.org.

First Pocket Books hardcover edition September 2009

POCKET and colophon are registered trademarks of Simon & Schuster, Inc.

For information about special discounts for bulk purchases,
please contact Simon & Schuster Special Sales at 1-866-506-1949 or
business@simonandschuster.com.

Designed by Claudia Martinez

Manufactured in the United States of America

10   9   8   7   6   5   4   3   2   1

Library of Congress Cataloging-in-Publication Data
Cameron, Michelle
The fruit of her hands : the story of Shira of Ashkenaz / by Michelle Cameron. — 1st
Pocket Books hardcover ed.
p.   cm.
1. Jewish women—Fiction.   2. Rabbis' spouses—Fiction.
3. Jewish families—Europe—Fiction.   4. Jews—Europe—History—Fiction.
5. Antisemitism—Europe—History—Fiction.   6. Middle Ages—Fiction.
7. Jewish Fiction.   I. Title.
PS3603.A453F78 2009
813'.6—dc22   2009007217

ISBN 978-1-4391-1822-1
ISBN 978-1-4391-6438-9 (ebook)

For my mother,
who always said we could trace our
family roots back to the thirteenth century.

GIVE HER OF THE FRUIT OF HER HANDS; AND LET HER WORKS PRAISE HER IN THE GATES.

—*Proverbs 31:31*

ART I

FALAISE, 1224–1230

BLESSED ARE YOU, LORD OF THE UNIVERSE, FOR HAVING MADE ME ACCORDING TO YOUR WILL.
    —*Women's morning prayer*

NE

Childhood is a garland of roses.
—THE TALMUD

ONE OF MY FIRST COMPLETE MEMORIES, when I was about three or four, was sitting nestled on my father's lap in the classroom, answering questions just like the young boys in the Falaise seminary that was my home. A thrill swept through me as my father proclaimed, "My little songbird has given us the correct response! Do you see why her answer is right, boys? She is equal to any one of you!"

I looked at him, delighting in the proud glow on his thin face. But, peering shyly at the boys in the classroom for approval, I saw dour expressions instead. They muttered to one another, a whisper of complaint that made me clutch my father's arm, alarmed and confused.

Perhaps I combine two early memories into one, but it seems I looked away from the aggrieved students to the long, narrow windows of the *yeshiva*, where several of the neighborhood wives peered in. They clucked their tongues dolefully, shaking their heads at this girl seated where she should not be, studying with boys. Their disapproval made me shrink back against my father's chest.

But as my glance moved up to my father's smiling face, I ignored the undercurrents of irritation swelling around me. My papa was pointing to those passages in the Talmud that confirmed my correct answer, flipping pages, showing me here, here, and here. Following his finger as it moved across the illuminated pages, I remember how my cheeks flushed in pride, my joy at his attention overshadowing every other emotion.

———•———

Like so many of my orphaned playmates, I could barely remember my mother. Pressed in among the women at prayer, there were moments when I caught a familiar scent or heard a melody in someone's chanting that brought me to the edge of memory, envisioning a hazy white face looking fondly down at me, smoothing my hair, singing a wordless tune. But I could not penetrate the fog that misted my thoughts when I tried to conjure my mother's face, the softness of her dress when I rested my cheek against her chest.

My mother had persevered despite many futile pregnancies. Trying desperately to fulfill the biblical commandment to be fruitful and multiply, she suffered time and again through prolonged childbirth, four times enduring hours of pain only to deliver dead babies. Three others died in the early days of infancy. The midwife pulled each of these keening, wizened beings forth and shook her head at the anguish in my father's questioning eyes. My own birth was considered nothing less than a miracle by my long-suffering parents, who took enormous pleasure in my fat limbs, clear, dark eyes, and healthy cry.

The last baby, the boy who took my mother's life, was the gravest of my father's many disappointments. My father was, after all, Rabbi Shmuel ben Solomon, the great Talmudic scholar of Falaise—a man who hungered for a son. My mother was his second wife. My father's first bride died from a lingering fever mere months after the young couple wed. Engrossed in his studies, Papa let several years pass before he discharged his duty to the community and married again.

I remember huddling in a dark corner of the long, gloomy synagogue hallway at the age of four, waiting for my father. I sat with my knees pressed to my chest, my arms wrapped around them on that cold, wet, melancholy afternoon. The sound of steady rain on the rooftop made me recall a child's tale in which mourning angels wept teardrops of sadness, drenching the earth.

Unseen in my corner, I overheard the mother of one of my friends whispering to a bride newly come to our community, "That's her. That's the rabbi's daughter."

"He has only one?"

"Her mother was brought to bed just yesterday—lost another child. Her third or fourth, I forget how many. A sad thing. But the rabbi is always so kind, where other men might complain and beat her . . . oh! Good evening, Rabbi."

My father emerged from the door of one of the antechambers. A small group of older students was huddled around him, but the men dispersed when the housewives approached, laughing and talking as they walked off.

"Good evening," my father said solemnly, but with the smile that always made people beam back at him—what I used to call his white smile.

"Rabbi, Floria was just telling me about your poor wife. I hope she's well," said the new bride.

My father's smile dissolved. "Thank you, Ruth. She is weak yet. We hope for better luck next time."

"I was telling Ruth how kind you are, despite her many miscarriages. Not every man in the community would be so gentle, you know."

My father's shoulders hunched. But he laughed disparagingly, "Well, I act as my Talmud instructs. That's all."

"The men should take a lesson in patience from you," Floria said, balling her fists on her stout waist. "We women always tell them so."

My father laughed again, but I detected a bitter tinge to his mirth. Even as young as I was, I knew he yearned for a son. It was something I had always known.

Later I would learn how a boy might have continued the unbroken line of scholarship that stretched back to his ancestors, who were students and teachers in the great Babylonian schools. My grandfather Solomon had had three other sons, each of whom was blessed with boys. My father consoled himself that the family name and its revered scholarly tradition would not disappear altogether. But he felt incomplete despite his pride in the Jewish seminary he had founded—a *yeshiva* similar to those where he had studied as a boy and a young man in France and Germany, the area of Europe we Jews called Ashkenaz. Whenever the family gathered, he watched his nephews growing into thoughtful, intelligent men and must have longed for sons of his own.

My mama died when I was nearly five and Papa had only me to care for. Perhaps that was why he indulged us both, putting me on his knee when he studied from the sacred book of the Talmud long after I should have been banished to the kitchen to learn more womanly skills.

———•———

Bella Tova, our good and pious neighbor, walked up the path through our kitchen garden one spring morning carrying a covered kettle of stewed beef, still bubbling and warm. She rapped on the heavy oak side door. Our family maidservant, a straw-haired Christian girl named Jeanne, came to the door to greet her. Bella Tova, wearing the high-necked gown and hair covering of the modest Jewish wife, would later recall how taken aback she was by Jeanne's unlaced bodice and the way her blond hair was tied back with just a thin ribbon, loose curls escaping around fire-flushed cheeks.

Jeanne was my wet nurse, hired by my parents to place their children to her ample breasts to suckle. Her own baby had died of a fever and Jeanne's husband, Pierre, a foot soldier under the command of a local baron, had perished fighting in the arid desert during one of the Crusades. Jeanne told me endless stories about her husband's bravery and beauty, how he was pledged to rid the Holy Land of infidels. I was too young to understand Jeanne's measuring glance as she spoke of the unbelievers living in Jesus Christ's homeland—and for years I confused Jesus Christ, Jeanne's son of God, and the baron her beloved Pierre had served.

Had my mother lived, Jeanne's stories would have dissipated in the vapors of infant memory. But after she weaned me, Jeanne's milk dried up. She complained she had been robbed of her livelihood. Partly because her claim was just and mostly because he needed someone to care for me, Papa retained Jeanne as my nursemaid and the family's sole servant.

I adored Jeanne as the one warm constant of my life. When I scraped my knee, her cornflower eyes welled with tears. I fell asleep to the music of her lullabies. She sang of a cradle that, perched in the boughs of a tall tree, smashed into the green ground when the branch snapped. Curiously, the song always made me feel warm inside, knowing Jeanne would catch me if I fell. Jeanne taught me to sing the romantic ballads of the age, songs of great chivalry such as "La fille du roi d'espagne" and the lighthearted "Aucassin et Nicolette." As soon as I could talk, music and poetry were always on my lips, prompting my father to bestow upon me my baby name—Songbird.

It was not unusual back then for Jewish households to hire Christian servants. From time to time, fresh laws put forth by the Pope in Rome or by our own local rulers tried to prevent too much familiarity between Jew and Gentile. We Jews were careful not to confide too greatly in the Christians we hired. We harkened to scandalous whispers of Gentiles bringing priests to back doors in the dead of night to baptize new babies. Stories circulated of servants collecting cakes of *matzo* made for our Passover feasts, offering them as evidence that we murdered Christian children to use their blood in the recipe. Less sensational but almost as terrifying was the prospect that the Gentiles in our homes might befoul our food or undo our careful observances of the Law.

What happened that day when Bella Tova visited our house would be the subject of much outraged discussion in our small community. Bella Tova watched in horror as Jeanne, thanking her for the stew, propped it on the far hob in the great stone kitchen fireplace and stirred it with the spoon already in her hand. A pot of milk warmed on the hearth. Bella Tova gasped as Jeanne removed the spoon from the meat, wiped its curved back carelessly on her apron, and put it into the milk. The Christian girl, hearing the neighbor's intake of breath, stepped back hastily. Perhaps she recalled my father's instructions to always, always keep milk and meat dishes separate. But Jeanne could be stubborn and she squared her shoulders and stood her ground.

"Jeanne, where is the rabbi?" Bella Tova's flinty tones staked a claim of duty.

Jeanne raised her chin, her eyes narrowed, and—according to my neighbor—her ample bosom heaved with insolence. "With his students, of course," she retorted. "I will not disturb him."

"And where would young Shira be?" Bella Tova persisted. She was glad to see Jeanne's insubordination begin to crumble. The rabbi might refuse to see her during study hours, but I could not.

"With him, I believe," Jeanne faltered.

"Bring her here," demanded my neighbor.

Bella Tova gleefully recounted how Jeanne left the warm kitchen. She watched as the servant reluctantly turned down the narrow hallway leading to the large front room filled with long, wooden tables that served as our school.

I had been allowed inside the classroom ever since I had toddled in one day on my own. My father often told me fondly how he was about to usher me out when I reached one chubby hand up as if to ask for a book, crowing in delight. He could not deny me the room when it gave me so much pleasure, he explained, stroking my hair.

The schoolroom held our most precious treasures. My father's leather-bound books were carefully stored on a high shelf. These were painstakingly copied by hand by scribes who illuminated them with rich colors and intricate designs. Our few silver objects, perched on a second shelf located in an alcove toward the back of the room, shined in the flicker of the fire. There was a pair of candlesticks that we lovingly brought down every Friday evening, a cunningly wrought spice box my great-grandfather had purchased in a bazaar in faraway Constantinople, and a wine cup we used only on Passover, in which the prophet Elijah's magical portion of wine glowed red as a gemstone.

The rest of the room was given over to boys and young men. The same scene was repeated every day of the week except for Saturday, the holy Shabbat. At the back, the older students sat on wide benches at the longest table. They studied on their own, breaking off their solitary muttering to argue a point with their tablemates. My father sat among them, though sometimes he would move to the front of the room to help the tutor, the *melamed*, urge the youngest boys, aged three to five, through the simplest of studies—the Hebrew *aleph-bet*, the prayers, and stories from the Torah.

On the day in question, I sat on a stool in the windowed corner of the study, one of my father's precious books on my lap and a large tablet of wax that I used to make notes at my elbow. Though I was only nine years old, I had already begun to master some Talmud, keeping pace with the boys my own age. My father, however, realizing he could no longer keep me in the circle of students as he had when I was four or five, placed me to one side of the room, where I could listen to the lessons and learn from them but not interrupt. Even so, the scholars muttered that I was a distraction, disturbing the sanctity of their studies.

I glanced up from my book when Jeanne entered. My father glared at her, annoyed at the interruption.

"Sir Morel?" Jeanne said, addressing my papa by the name he was called in town. "One of your neighbors wishes to speak with Shira."

Papa looked at me as I bent in concentration over my book. He sighed. I often felt his conscience pricked him when he reflected on how he treated me—almost as though I were a son.

Watching me put the book down carefully on my stool to obediently follow Jeanne, he sighed once more, then seemed to forget me altogether as he turned his attention back to the boys in his care.

———•———

I stood bewildered in the kitchen as Bella Tova told me how to prepare the beef stew for my father and his students. Jeanne stood, glowering, in the corner of the room, her arms folded over her chest.

"You'll need to take it off the fire if it starts to bubble too much," my neighbor instructed. "So you have to keep a close eye on it. It will scorch otherwise."

"Jeanne will watch it," I said, itching to get back to my book.

The corners of Jeanne's mouth turned up in a smirk. Bella Tova pursed her lips.

"You need to take charge of the kitchen, Shira. You're old enough now."

I could feel the heat creeping up my neck. "Jeanne's always prepared our meals," I said.

"So there's no need for you to put your long nose into this household's affairs," Jeanne said from her corner.

"Do not talk back to me, girl!" Bella Tova snapped. She took three long strides across the room and picked up the spoon that Jeanne had thrown onto the sideboard, brandishing it in my face. "Shira, do you see this spoon?"

I stared at it. It was just a long, carved, wooden spoon. I shifted uncomfortably from one foot to another. "I see it."

"When I arrived today, Jeanne was using this spoon to stir the milk."

"Which boiled over and was wasted, because of your interference," Jeanne griped.

"Shira, forbid her to speak!"

Both women looked at me. I could not understand why they were fighting or why I had been pulled from my beloved classroom to witness their argument. There was a long, tense silence. "I see the spoon," I finally admitted, an irritated tone creeping into my voice. "What of it?"

Bella Tova started, "I brought the stew—"

"Half-cooked, like all your messes," Jeanne interrupted.

"Jeanne!" I admonished. My nursemaid stuck out her chin defiantly.

"Jeanne put the milk spoon into the meat." Bella Tova emphasized every word, waving the implement in the air. She flung it disdainfully onto the floor and stepped back, surveying my face, making sure I felt the full horror of what she was telling me.

I stared at the servant. This was serious. If my father knew, it would mean a week of scouring and cleaning the entire kitchen. The spoon itself would have to be buried in the earth for a month and prayed over before it could be used again. Even worse, if any of the parents of Papa's students found out, the boys would be pulled from the seminary. If others found out, no new students would be sent. No one would study in a school where the rules of *kashrut* were not observed. Jeanne's careless action could mean the end of my father's *yeshiva*.

Jeanne tried to bluster past my expression of dismay. "It's a foolish rule anyway," she said. "You Jews care about the oddest things!"

"No less strange than what you Gentiles believe!" Bella Tova retorted. "Shira, I will return this evening to speak with your father. Until then, you stay in the kitchen. Do not return to the schoolroom. Promise me!"

Looking at her stern frown, I felt forced to agree. I swallowed and nodded.

Not until the evening arrived was the full force of Bella Tova's visit made clear to me. She returned as promised, accompanied by her husband. They closeted themselves with my father upstairs in his solar. Jeanne sat, rigid and unhappy, at the kitchen table, the wretched spoon clenched tight in her hand. She hunched a shoulder when I pleaded with her to be more careful in the future.

After my father bid his visitors farewell, he drew me into his study and told me that I couldn't join him and the boys in the classroom any longer. I would have to stay in the kitchen, to take on the duties of a housewife. I thought about the book I had left behind me, about all the books I would no longer be able to study from. I cried, promising wildly to make sure the kitchen rules were obeyed if only, only, I could still study with him and the boys. I remember how he stroked my wet cheeks and looked wretched in the face of my pain. But I couldn't change his mind.

I ran upstairs, to fling myself on my bed and cry. I never did hear what he and Jeanne discussed after I stormed off.

———•———

About a week later, straw baskets over our arms, I collected early raspberries with my friends in the shadow of William the Conqueror's imposing keep. In later years, William the Conqueror's square castle would serve as the emblem of my childhood, rising majestically in my memory. My nursemaid often told my friends and me about the noble king, born and raised in our local keep. William the Bastard! Perhaps he meant so much to us, the children who were set apart by our faith, because William overcame the stigma of bastardy to gain mythical status. It was something we Jews could only dream of.

"Shira," my friend Miriam said, startling me as I brought a sun-ripened berry to my lips, "tell us. Why is your father called Sir Morel by the Gentiles of the town and Rabbi Shmuel by us Jews?"

The rest of my friends circled around me, clamoring for an answer.

But I didn't know why. I had heard him greeted so ever since I was a young child, clutching his hand as we walked through Falaise. It was the name that most often appeared on the letters he received from other Jewish sages. Yet none of the congregation of Falaise called him by that name.

At home, I asked Jeanne. But she was in a foul mood, as she had been all week, her eyes smarting as she stirred together the fat and lye that she used to make our household soap. She had been curt with me ever since the incident with Bella Tova. Every night I was startled from sleep, the bed beside me empty in the cold darkness. There were raised voices downstairs. One night, I woke to find the pillow we shared wet with tears and Jeanne's cheeks cold and damp. I could not understand what was happening.

"Go away, Shira!" she snapped now, her face flushed from the soap fumes and the fire. I slunk away, bewildered.

I decided to ask Papa directly. I approached him after our evening meal. He sat at a table in the front room, a pile of books stacked before him, writing to one of his fellow scholars in Germany. These letters traveled, as though borne by the blessed angels, back and forth between my father and the other scholars who lived in exile in Christian and Mohammedan lands. By such means, great Jewish questions of the day were resolved.

I wished I could read those important writings. But Papa was careful never to leave the sheets of paper on which he shaped and sharpened his arguments lying about, for fear, he said, only half joking, of provoking the evil eye. He gathered the remnants together and locked them away. When he no longer needed them, they were buried outside by one of his most diligent students.

I asked once if it would not be easier to burn the pages.

"Burn the pages, Shira? It is forbidden to burn the name of the Lord," he had said, handing the casket and key to a waiting student, who snickered at my ignorance under his breath.

I was glad to see my father was alone now. I boldly came closer to him, and my shadow, flickering in the candlelight, fell upon his letter.

"What is it, sweetness?" He flicked my cheek with a forefinger in a quick gesture of fondness.

"Papa, may I ask a question?"

My father turned his paper over and put down his pen. "I am struggling with an idea, Shira, one that stirs just outside my grasp. If I ignore it for a while, perhaps it will choose to edge a little closer, so I can catch hold. While I wait, I might as well hear your question." He sat back and smiled at me.

"The people in town call you Sir Morel. Many of your letters are addressed to Sir Morel rather than Rabbi Shmuel ben Solomon. When Jeanne tells me bedtime stories, "sir" is a title for a noble—Sir Knight. Are you a nobleman? A knight? Can a Jew—and a rabbi—be a nobleman?" My voice rose excitedly as I asked the final question. I was dancing on tiptoe, hopping up and down.

Papa laughed and reached out to grasp my elbow, pulling me down into the half circle of his arms. "And just what would it mean to you, little songbird, if you were to discover your father was a nobleman?"

I cuddled into the warmth of his chest, still bobbing a little in enthusiasm. "Why, just think, Papa! Nobles live in castles like William's Keep and common people bow to them. They dress in velvet in the winter, linen in the summer, eat partridge and oranges no matter what season, and never, ever work."

Papa's arms tightened around me as he shook with suppressed amusement. "It's clear you think nobles have a fine and easy life for themselves. And perhaps it is so. But what kind of life do Jews have, then?"

I fingered the despised golden O sewn to the front of my gown, the cloth badge that marked me as a Jew whenever I left the house and went to market. We called it a *rouelle,* a gold wagon wheel badge that circled endlessly upon our breasts. It felt enormous pressing against my chest, showing the townsfolk I was different. Papa's question had changed my mood. I sat still, pensive.

I faltered, then said, "When I go to town, the boys taunt me and call me 'Jew girl.' They say I killed their Christ—that I will go to hell when I die for something that happened more than a thousand years ago."

"So while being a noble is splendid, being a Jew is . . . not, Shira?" My father let his arms drop. His voice sounded gritty. I glanced uneasily at his face, where I saw raised eyebrows and thin lips. I searched for words to please him.

"Every Friday evening we light the Shabbat candles. I would miss that if we weren't Jews. Or hearing you and the boys chanting when I walk past the study. I love the chanting."

The angry creases in my father's face relaxed. "I am glad, daughter, for you will remain a Jewess all of your life. And you are not, I regret to say, a noblewoman."

I sighed. I could imagine myself wearing the blue velvet dress of a lady. "Then why *are* you called Sir Morel, Papa?" I persisted, pulling playfully at his tunic sleeves.

My father hesitated. I had often seen him pause that way before. As I grew older, I would recognize how he would take a difficult concept and reshape it so the young minds in his care could grasp it. But even at the age of nine, listening to his carefully chosen words, I realized he might not be telling me the entire truth.

"I did a favor for an English prince before I came to Falaise. The prince needed some information that was buried deep in Spain and I supplied it to him through a fellow scholar. When I reflect on it, it is not something I am proud of. But the prince wanted to reward me for my service. Not having ready funds at that time, and since the laws of his country prevent him from offering a Jew land, he bestowed upon me a worthless title. So I became Sir Morel."

I sat back to think for a moment. My father watched me, gently smoothing my dark hair with his hand.

Finally I asked, "If it means nothing, why do people call you Sir Morel?"

My father made a sound deep in his throat, half-laugh, half-sigh. He spoke slowly, picking his words carefully. "It may be useless to me, but the title is valuable to this *yeshiva* and to the Jews living in Falaise. As long as the Christians in town call me Sir Morel, they consider me noble. They fear that if they don't treat us gently, I might summon some distant patron lord to protect us. Thus, through a half truth I neither promote nor protest, I protect my students and our community. Those boys in town may jeer at you, but as long as they think my title has some weight, they won't hurt you. Christians have harmed and even killed Jews in other towns and cities in Europe."

Of course I knew that Jews living elsewhere in the Diaspora endured more than idle taunts. My friend Sari's father had been killed by a Crusader's sword while on a business trip to the city of York. My father had taken me to her house during the days of her *shiva,* her mourning. I sat with Sari on the floor and listened to her big brothers speak bitterly about how a gang of Crusaders, perhaps drunk with wine or stirred by a priest's sermon to eradicate the unfaithful, burst into Jewish homes, putting all they met there to the sword. Sari's mother, heavy with child, sat and counted her unmarried children on her fingers, over and over again. "How will I provide for them now?" she had cried.

Papa, seeing I was trembling, hugged me tightly for a moment before returning to his letter. As I left the room, I looked back over my shoulder. I would forever remember my father as I saw him then, bent forward, his nose nearly touching the book he was studying, fingers caressing his waiting pen, completely engrossed in his work.

———•———

Soon after we talked about my father's title, my life narrowed to cooking, cleaning, and washing for his students. The endless arguing between my father and Jeanne over her careless handling of the kitchen soured my father's relationship with my nursemaid. She left our service soon after the spoon incident and married a butcher in town.

I cried for days after she left. Jeanne had been my mother, my playmate, and the only person to tell me of life outside the closed world of my home, the synagogue, and the Jewish community. I thought she would miss me, too, the way her tears fell upon her soft cheeks as she bid me good-bye.

I wanted to attend her wedding. But she knit her lips together and would not tell me when it would be.

"But I want to come—I can walk before you with a basket of spring flowers!"

"Up the aisle in the church, Shira?" she asked, eyebrows raised.

"Why not?" I persisted.

Jeanne sighed. "You would upset everyone, Shira—I shudder to think what my husband's family would say, seeing a Jew in front of the Holy Mother and her Blessed Son."

"But"—my eyes welled with tears—"I want to see you get married!"

"Ask your father," was all she would say, turning away from me.

I found my father outside, supervising some boys who were sawing wood for the fire. When he saw my flushed face, he took my elbow and led me away.

"What is it, child?"

"Papa, I want to go to Jeanne's wedding. She said to ask you."

A shadow crossed my father's face, fear and a flash of anger in one dark expression. I pulled back, afraid of a reaction I could only faintly understand. But I was a child and wanted what I wanted.

"Why shouldn't I?" I yelled, not even waiting for him to tell me no.

The boys looked curiously over their shoulders at us. My father clutched my elbow again—painfully this time—and took me inside the house.

The dining room was almost too warm after the cool air in the yard. We stood before a raging fire. "Shira," my father said, keeping his voice soft and reasonable with an effort, "you must never enter a church. You know that."

"I can if I want to!" I said, stomping my foot on the floor.

My father drew back, eyebrows raised. "Your being there would make Jeanne unhappy. Is that what you want?"

"It would not!" I insisted, my open palm smacking the table in front of me. "Why won't you understand?"

My father was not moved by my tantrum. I ran off slamming doors. For days afterward I responded to him in curt, one-word answers. With enormous forbearance, he reacted mildly to my insolence. But I did not attend the wedding.

Papa hired a Jewish girl to take Jeanne's place. Mina's family was delighted that their daughter would serve such a distinguished scholar. But Mina was a superstitious, meek girl who would cower in a corner for a long, shivering hour if she happened upon a bad omen. With fifteen boys living in the house, and twenty more trooping in daily for lessons and meals, such dire portents happened frequently.

I refused to believe the bond between Jeanne and me could change. I visited her at least once a week. Compared to the stone building where I lived, which was large enough to house a schoolroom and many bedrooms, her new home was as cramped as a peasant's or a villein's. The small, thatched building sat in a row of other such hovels at the outskirts

of town, each one cordoned off by a thorn fence and a ditch that over-
flowed whenever all but the gentlest of rains fell. Jeanne's husband built
a large barn in back, where poor doomed animals chewed their cud and
waited for the fell hand of the axe blade. The family used two of the
rooms in the house to store grain and fodder for the beasts, reserving
the third to sleep and eat in. The single family room contained a stone
chimney, with an opening where Jeanne would prepare meals over a
smoky peat flame. She hung her kettle and her one heavy saucepan—
for the stews and soups and pottages that made up most meals—on a
hook over the fire. The room was furnished with a table and three rough
stools, a single cupboard crowded with farm implements and cooking
utensils, and an enormous bed that one day would be occupied not only
by Jeanne and her husband but by all her nurslings as well.

Jeanne spent most of her waking hours helping her husband in the
fly-infested shop in town, selling the hanks and entrails of beef or sheep
or pig. Her husband would enter the shop laden with freshly killed meat
from his slaughterhouse and stop to talk with the housewives or to crow
over the growing pile of deniers earned each day. He rarely spoke to me
beyond a grunt.

As the weeks passed, Jeanne grew noticeably cooler to me. She sighed
when I entered the shop, elbowed me aside when anyone required her
attention. She often cut off my chat about life at home with a curt, "Not
now, Shira." Her rudeness nagged at me, but I thought it was probably
because she worked so hard and had so little. Even I could tell the difference between her life there and the one she had led at my father's
house.

Then one day she asked me to step outside to take our ease. It was a
scorching July day. I was glad to escape the stifling butcher shop, with
its suffocating close quarters, the floor puddled with pools of blood and
sticky, discarded strands of sinew that attracted every possible insect
and rodent.

We went into the yard behind the shop, where Jeanne's husband had
placed a wood bench under a tall elm tree. The kitchen garden needed

weeding and watering, and the few straggling tops of carrots were turning brown in the sun's glare. Jeanne sat on the bench and wiped blood-stained hands on her bespattered apron. She blew the tendrils of hair that had come loose from her kerchief off her forehead.

"You can't come here or to the house any longer, Shira," she said, looking anywhere but at my face. "Father Bartholomew reprimanded my husband about your visits after church last Sunday. Unless you let the priest speak with you about the eternal hellfire you face as an unconverted Jewess, you cannot visit me any longer."

I didn't know what to say. Surely this was not the way she intended to bid me farewell forever. This was too big a moment even for tears. We sat in uncomfortable silence for a long time. Then Jeanne turned to me, her face shining with the earnestness of sincere faith.

"Shira, it would hurt me to think of you burning in hellfire when you could free yourself from your father and his congregation of damned unbelievers. Consider, child. You could marry someone like my Andre and be wed in the church with the priest's blessing. I'd make you a wedding feast. And you would no longer have to wear the *rouelle* or be scorned because you refuse the truth—a truth that would bring you nothing but joy—the eternal glory of Christ Jesus. How can that not sway you?"

While Jeanne had spoken about her religion furtively once or twice during my youth, as our servant she had refrained from attacking my beliefs. I was stunned that she was doing so now. Still not having spoken a word, almost sick with aching for my beloved nursemaid, I blindly rose to my feet and turned to leave.

But I did not escape the butcher's yard. Jeanne's husband, Andre, his apron covered in the blood spilled from a thousand carcasses, stood against the doorjamb of his butcher shop, talking with the other merchants from Falaise's main thoroughfare. All of them had been drinking deeply from a casket of wine they passed from hand to hand, trying to cool themselves on this hot day. The wine made them bold. Andre nudged the man next to him as I edged by.

"That's the girl—the Jewess—that my Jeanne would have me house.

Have you ever heard a new bride ask her husband such a thing? To bring a sinner into our home?"

Jeanne joined the men, her face stony at her failure to persuade me. "Don't fuss, husband. The girl is snared by Satan, her soul damned for eternity. It is a hard thing, I tell you, to raise an ungrateful wretch and watch her cast away salvation."

"Hey, now," Andre grunted, grabbing hold of my elbow. "You should be more grateful to my Jeanne, girl. Without her, you would have starved to death in your Jew house."

It was clear from the scowl on Jeanne's face that she was not in a mood to intervene. Her husband's friends gathered about me in a tight circle. I realized they might torment me to alleviate the boredom of a long, hot afternoon just like the boys from town I had once seen capture and torture a stray dog by putting it down a well. I clenched my teeth and lips tight to hide my fear.

"It's a wonder Jews don't starve to death anyway, turning up their pig noses at good, fresh pork," one of the men grunted, as another reached out and circled, with his finger, the gold brand on my breast. But my child's build and thin chest could not hold his attention for more than a moment.

"Someone *should* feed this one, she's all skin and bones," he muttered, turning away.

"Here, Jeanne, get some of those pig knuckles left over from last night's supper." Andre grinned, pulling me inside the shop. I cried out, begging him to let me go, but he clamped a heavy hand over my mouth and, half picking me up, dragged me inside.

The air inside the shop was so rancid with the smell of meat rotting in the heat of the day that I slipped into a kind of trance. The men forced me to sit on a wooden barrel and Jeanne—who had suckled me at her breast, sung me to sleep, told me fairy tales of beautiful princesses and knights slaying dragons—emerged from the pantry like one of the cackling witches from those stories, holding aloft a trencher of congealed white fat and the gnawed remains of pig bones. But one look at my stricken face moved her. She thrust the pan into her husband's hands and ran off. I listened as her footsteps grew softer and let out one piteous cry of utter desperation.

Someone took up the meatiest of the pigs' feet and brandished it before my face, then touched it to my lips. The rest of the men closed in, eager to watch my humiliation. Struggling and gasping, I wrenched my head to one side. Someone grabbed my hair and forced my face back around. I could tell there would be no escape and felt overwhelmed by the agony of Jeanne's betrayal and of my own defeat.

"Can someone serve me?" quavered a voice from behind the men. An old woman stood by the door, a cane clutched in one gnarled hand. She peered at the men uncertainly. "What is happening here?"

"It is nothing, madame," Andre said, releasing my arm. The huddle of townsmen miraculously broke apart, much like boys being chastised by the town priest. The merchants filed out of the small, confined space. I scrambled away and ran from the shop. I felt as though the legions of the evil eye were snapping at my heels. I ran and ran through the dirt-paved streets into the woods surrounding the town, in time with the chorus in my head: "Tell no one. Tell no one." It wasn't until I was nearly halfway home that I stopped. Wheezing and panting, I leaned over a ditch, retching over the still-sweet taste of the pork that lingered viciously on my lips.

WO

Of an ungrateful guest it is written: Therefore, men fear him:
he has no regard for any who are wise of heart.

—THE TALMUD

PAPA ACCEPTED A NEW STUDENT—a young man named Nicho-
las Donin of La Rochelle. He was a striking figure: narrow body intense
and wiry, piercing blue eyes, and unruly black hair, which he swept back
impatiently.

The day he arrived, I was on my hands and knees scrubbing the stone
walkway. He strolled into our narrow vestibule as though he already belonged, leaving the door open wide behind him and dropping his heavy
chest of belongings on the hard-packed floor with a thud.

"Sir Morel? I am Nicholas Donin of La Rochelle. I come to you for
only a month—when I plan to move on to Rabbi Yechiel of Paris. I hope
you will permit me to study with you until then."

My father, who had emerged from the classroom to greet the newcomer, looked him up and down, the expression on his face unusually
stern. "We are crowded, young man, and we were not expecting you. If you
plan to leave here so soon, why not simply go straight to Rabbi Yechiel?"

"Rabbi Yechiel himself suggested I come here first, for he has no room at all until next month. And were you and he not scholars together in Paris?"

"Yes, we studied together under the great Judah Sir Leon. But—"

"Please, I will be no trouble to you. Don't turn me away!"

I glanced up, alarmed by the young man's vibrant tones. His eyes glittered strangely.

"I will speak frankly, Donin—I have heard of you and that you *do* bring trouble wherever you go. Why should I want you here?"

I looked from the stranger to my father, astonished. I had never before heard him speak so discourteously to a prospective student. My glance moved back to Nicholas Donin, who, rather than looking abashed, seemed almost proud of the accusation.

"My reputation, oh, my reputation! I assure you, Rabbi, I am not the malcontent I have been painted! And does it not behoove you to judge me on my merits, rather than by what is said of me?"

My father looked at me, his lips pursing at my surprised stare. He turned back to Donin. "Rabbi Huna teaches that once a person commits a misdeed for the second time, then it becomes permissible in his mind. It is to be hoped that this is not true in your case."

A tight smile showed on Donin's face. "I sometimes compare myself to Rabbi Elazar ben Durdia, especially in the Talmudic tractate Avodah Zara 17a. Like him, I realize my past behavior is considered sinful by others, but unlike him, I hope to find peace in this world rather than the next."

"Indeed, a strong soap will clean a garment; repentance will clean a soul," Papa quoted. "Shira, please show my new student to the room where Moshe of Amiens and his friends are boarding. Donin, you'll be bedded down with three other boys—I tell you, we are crowded here. And my house will remain a peaceful one!"

With that, he turned sharply on his heel, his quick footsteps toward the classroom echoing in the empty hallway. Donin and I watched him disappear into the room and then turned toward each other.

"This way, Monsieur Donin," I murmured, rising from my knees.

I led the new student up three rickety flights of stairs to the tiny room with its one enormous bed of straw ticking and single window. "You are the servant of the house?" he asked.

Even if he thought I was a servant, he should not have spoken to me. At the age of ten, I was old enough to be treated as a young woman, not as a child. I wondered how old he was. I thought he must be about fifteen or sixteen.

"No," I answered brusquely, staring at the straw-strewn floor. "I am the daughter of the house."

He looked at my dirty, wet skirt and the black curls that I could feel were straggling into my work-flushed face and grinned in apology. "I did not think Sir Morel was so poor that his daughter had to scrub the steps," he said. "My mother in La Rochelle always kept several servants."

"You are fortunate to come from a wealthy family," I said.

"We lived in a large stone house near the quays of the city," he bragged. "My father was a merchant."

"Was?" I knew better than to stay there talking to him. But something about his audacity pleased me.

The smug expression on his face disappeared. "He was lost at sea a few years ago. All our fortune was invested in the ship."

"So you are poor as well," I commented, starting to sidle out of the room. I did not want my father to discover me talking to a young man.

"The rabbis allowed my mother to remarry," he mused. "I don't like her new husband."

He stowed his chest next to the others in the corner, squared his shoulders as if girding himself for battle, and, with an outrageous wink at me, marched down to the study hall.

We ate all our meals in the room behind the classroom, a space that ran the length of the house. It resembled the study with its long tables and benches, which were necessary so that the entire school could eat at a single sitting, but a doorway and several windows looked out upon our garden, making it a pleasant place. The kitchen fireplace had been built with its hearth opening on two sides of the chimney, so its great blaze heated both the kitchen and the hall throughout the year. My father gave himself the home owner's privilege of sitting in front of the fire in the winter and moving away from it in the summer. Wherever he sat, I sat next to him.

So I had a good view of Donin at that first evening meal, watching him surreptitiously as he passionately built an argument about the day's Torah lesson. He interrupted the others as they tried to show him where certain Talmudic passages might contradict his interpretation. He waved his arms vehemently and he called the other students numbskulls and dogs when they offered those passages, challenging their premises as flawed.

"You favor the words of men over the words of *ha-Shem*, of God, and that itself is the worst of all sins," he proclaimed when they tried to show him that the lesson could be understood in more than one way.

The others looked at one another askance, but at one piercing glance from my father they subsided, shrugging.

After dinner I found my father alone in the classroom, pacing up and down. He called to me and I entered.

"Yes, Papa?" I leaned against one of the tables toward the front of the room.

"You thought I was harsh toward Nicholas Donin when he arrived today, didn't you?"

I nodded, even though I hated to agree with him. "I did. And you are always so kind to everyone. I was surprised."

"There's good reason for my unease. Donin has already studied at several other academies in Germany and France. Everywhere he goes, he causes trouble. Rav Solomon ben Abraham of Montpellier wrote to warn many of us rabbis about him."

Papa paused, deep in thought. I was used to his reveries and let him ponder uninterrupted. I know now how unusual it is for a parent to speak about such subjects with a ten-year-old daughter. Reflecting upon it from the distance of so many years, I have to conclude that my father's confiding in me stemmed from loneliness. He could not talk openly to his students and there were no grown-ups in the house with whom he might discuss such topics. His correspondence with other rabbis, as satisfying as it was, was spaced out by weeks or even months and confined to momentous rather than day-to-day concerns.

He continued pacing as he thought aloud, almost as though he had forgotten I was in the room. I couldn't have understood completely, for his ideas were well beyond my grasp. But I was flattered to think I did.

"Of course, one must consider the source. Rav Solomon of Montpellier was censured for inviting Christians to help him suppress Maimonides's followers. He wrote the Franciscan friars and asked them to punish those who abide by the Spanish rabbi's teachings. I saw a copy of his request to the monks: 'You are destroying your heretics, help us to destroy our heretics!'"

I knew my father admired the late Rabbi Moshe ben Maimon, who was known to us as Maimonides. But the Spanish sage's unorthodox writings—and his audacious claim that one could read Torah and the code he had written without having to use the Talmud to help interpret what the Torah said—had created dissent in the Jewish world. Many rabbis were so upset that they banned his work. I had watched not long ago as Papa put Maimonides's books away in a chest, buried beneath some clothing.

"I think," I said slowly, running the tips of my fingers along the edge of the table I leaned against, "we shouldn't listen to what this rabbi from Montpellier writes."

My father was walking six steps up and six steps back, which, with his lengthy stride, took him from one end of the room to the other. He made two circuits before responding, "Oh, if Solomon were the only one who said these things about Donin . . . Yet, the boy was right—I should judge him on his merits and not on scandalous reports spread about him. We shall see, I suppose!"

"He was not polite at dinner, though," I said, turning to examine the other side of the argument, as my early Talmudic training had taught me to do.

Papa stopped short, chuckled briefly, and shrugged. "No, he was not. Well, I will try to temper Donin's enthusiasms before he goes to study with my dear friend Yechiel. At least his passion and fire speak well of his eagerness to learn, do they not?"

I agreed, but neither of us was convinced. And in the middle of the night, our concerns were proven to be well founded. After the lights were extinguished and the house settled down to sleep, a low rumbling emanated from Nicholas Donin's room, a muttering that grew louder and louder, as if a thunderstorm of argument had broken within the house. The room I shared with Mina was directly underneath Donin's room, and I heard shouts about Maimonides and about the Talmud and the Torah—Donin screeching on one hand and the other three boys screaming on the other. To my alarm, I heard the clout of a fist smacking flesh, followed by a series of muffled thumps, as though someone was being dragged from bed across the rushes strewn on the wood floor.

My father slept in the room three doors down from mine. I heard his door opening and closing and his hobnailed boots—probably jammed onto bare feet—thudding up the stairs. With a crash, he flung the door open. I sat up in bed, uncertain whether I should go to help him, and heard him cry out: "What! What is it I see here? Get off him, get off! Moshe, Aberlin, Yitzik! Unhand him! Now!"

There was the sound of scuffling, as if my father had grabbed a couple of the assailants by their shoulders and pried them apart. Other footsteps reverberated in the hallway. I could picture the narrow corridor filling with overexcited young men. Modesty forbade me from stirring from the safety of my room, so I sat listening intently, a blanket clutched at my neck, Mina sniveling in fear beside me.

"Be still!" exploded my father's roar above the agitated hubbub of his students. "Students, *talmidim*—there will be silence here!"

The boys ceased their clamor. The ragged sound of pained breathing penetrated through the ceiling. Mina, grabbing some of the blanket back, cried, "What's going on?"

"Quiet!" I hissed, jabbing her side with my elbow. "Let me listen."

"I want to know what is happening here," my father demanded, his voice carrying through the house as though he were addressing the congregation from the pulpit. "How is it possible that I enter one of my bedrooms to find you three acting like, like . . . why, like thugs? Thrashing your schoolmate, a newcomer to our seminary, someone you are required to treat as a sacred guest! You, Aberlin, you are the oldest. Answer me!"

"We were driven to it, Rav Shmuel!" Aberlin replied stiffly, using the formal title of "Rav" to address my father. "This, this—reprobate refused to be silent and let us sleep. He insisted on telling us dreadful ideas— blasphemies about the Talmud!"

"Yes, and he would not be dissuaded from saying how Maimonides has been vilified by the Jews of Ashkenaz, Rabbi! He finds much to praise in the heretic!"

"Moshe, I did not ask you to speak—but never mind that. Nicholas, you assured me upon entering my home that you were not the malcontent you had been painted as. What say you?"

I leaned forward to catch what was being said. "Shira," Mina sniveled again, "what's going on?"

"Shush! How can I hear when you talk?" I muttered.

Mina turned her back to me and curled into a ball. I threw more of the blanket over her, covering her hair and most of her face.

There was the sound of someone moving forward and being thrust back again. "Stop, Moshe! Do not touch him!" my father cried again. "We will listen to Donin's side of this pathetic tussle!"

"Rabbi," came Donin's voice, rasping in his throat. At the sound of how badly he was hurt, I felt my toes curling up under the blankets. "I thought only to illuminate these students with my ideas—"

"Heretic!" cried Aberlin. "Reprobate!"

"—for are we not enjoined to discuss and debate our ideas with one another?" asked Donin, hoarsely. "But I apologize for waking the house. That was not my intention."

"Hah! Do not listen to him, Rav Shmuel—he is—"

"What he is, Moshe, is new to our *yeshiva* and our ways. You three must—now!—apologize for treating him so harshly, and then you, Donin, must have your wounds tended and sleep in my room for the rest of the night. Tomorrow we can talk this out more thoroughly. And you—all of you standing about uselessly in the hallway there—return to your beds! Now!"

There was some jostling and whispers above in the rooms, but my father stalked up and down the hallways until silence reigned. I waited for Papa to call me to help him, but he obviously decided that Donin's wounds were not severe enough to need a woman's care. Finally, the house settled down for the rest of the night. But peace was not to be long lasting.

———•———

I worked behind the house one windy afternoon, hanging clothes, when Nicholas Donin, his head bent against the steely, hard-driving breeze, stepped around the building. Seeing me, he stopped.

"Are you ready to continue our debate?" he asked, his eyes fixed steadily on my face. I felt familiar warmth rise to my cheeks.

I looked around cautiously but it was the middle of the day. Anyone who might have disapproved of our private conversation was busy elsewhere. Donin should have been learning himself. But his fellow students, tired of his constant arguments that the Talmud was a sinful waste of time and that all time should be given over to study of the Torah and only the Torah, had banished him from their table. When Donin studied at all now, he sat apart from the group, shoulders hunched protectively over his books as though he expected blows to rain down upon him from behind. He ate with the others, but the wall of silence erected by the other students could not have been more isolating if he were incarcerated in the dungeon of William's great keep.

He fought against this outcast state. Just two nights ago at dinner, he had swiveled in his seat to face my father and declared, "It is not fitting that you permit your students to ignore me in this way, Rabbi. They could learn much from me—if they would only heed my words. And their childish behavior hurts me."

My father took a long moment to contemplate the spoonful of pottage he was raising to his lips, then placed it in his mouth and swallowed. The clamor from the other students died down as they elbowed and hissed one another into silence. I too paused, waiting for his reply. Papa's answer almost boomed, reverberating in the unusual hush.

"Yet you do not heed what *they* have to say to *you*, Donin. Debate requires respect on both sides. You are willing only that they should defer to your words—and you show them, quite clearly, that you hold their ideas in no esteem whatsoever."

"That is not true!" Donin shouted, smacking a fist down on the table, making the wooden platters on the long board jump and rattle. "I listen to them, even when—as they always do—they spout utter nonsense!"

"Do you hear yourself?" my father replied as he pulled himself upright in his chair. "Do you hear how you sound, how you disrupt a meal that should be eaten in tranquility? No, Donin, no—until you learn to control your rush to irritation and the wrath you direct at all who oppose you, I will not force my students to engage in debate with you."

Donin pushed back his seat, scraping it on the floor. He rose and rushed outside, stumbling against the students in his path. My father sat with his eyes fixed on his plate. Donin left the door wide open. One of the younger students crept up and shut it so it clicked into place. There was absolute silence as the dozens of boys at the table eyed my father's face. After a moment, Papa let out a pent-up breath and picked up his spoon once more, continuing to eat, his face a serene mask. When the students realized their teacher would not chide them for their part in isolating Donin, they abused the malcontent with loud shouts of laughter.

Now, as I hung the laundry behind the house, Donin sought me out. It was not our first conversation. A day or two after Donin had come to our *yeshiva*, one of my father's students asked a question about womanly modesty and women studying. This led one of the older men to whisper about how I used to take a seat in the classroom before I was banished. For a day or two afterward, students pointed in my direction and cupped their fingers to mutter about me. Donin listened to the snippets of gossip and deduced I knew enough to discuss the subjects that excited him. He needed a more receptive audience than my father and his students. And I? Truthfully, I was grateful when he first approached me.

After all, I had been relegated to a kind of servitude in my own home. On many mornings I deeply, silently, resented the prayer I had been taught to utter in childhood: "Blessed are You for having made me according to Your will." These words resounded in the recesses of my brain, a refrain that followed me through the day. All my days were full, exhaustingly so, and while my father told me every task I performed was given me as a way to worship God through His commandments, the dull ache inside me did not lessen.

My father and his students had a different morning prayer: "Blessed are You for not having made me a woman." Smug expressions flitted across many of the boys' faces when they murmured the familiar words. I would watch thin lipped as they finished their prayers, trooped in to eat the food I prepared, and retired to the classroom for a full day of study. The door would close with a snap behind their retreating backs and I would turn to face the soiled table, the remnants of breakfast piled high, the midday meal scant hours away. So was it any wonder that Donin's conversation tempted and intrigued me?

"Why *do* you scorn the Talmud, Nicholas? Maimonides, your great hero, spent years studying and writing about it. Think of his *Yad Hachazakah*—a book that made the Talmud easier to understand," I exclaimed, watching him lean against the trunk of a tree. As much as I relished our conversations, I hoped to distract Donin from areas of scholarship I knew nothing about. Now shut out from daily learning, I often felt myself floundering during our discussions. Donin was always quick to pounce upon my ignorance.

"Maimonides wrote his Code and made the Talmud unnecessary." He shrugged. "He had the brains to realize that the Torah, given to us directly by God, is all we need to study. We don't need the Talmud to interpret God's word for us. God's word should be enough."

I kept pinning up the sheets, struggling a little with their sodden weight. Donin stood by idly, his back against the tree, arms crossed loosely over his chest. He fixed his eyes on my flushed face. I grew even redder under his intent gaze. Silence built between us. Finally, I asked a question I'd been pondering for many days. It was wonderful to have someone to ask, even if I half feared his answer.

"So all those rabbis, starting from our exile in Babylon to today— scholars who wrote about the meaning of the unwritten Torah, the *Torah she b'al peh*, creating the Talmud—they were wrong?"

He nodded, his expression both scornful and amused. "Studying their arguments in the Talmud means we devote less time to Torah, plain and simple, Shira. Nothing is a more fundamental sin."

I thought his answer was callous and cruel. How many lives did Donin dismiss with his nod?

"According to you and you alone, Nicholas Donin," I exclaimed, dropping a heavy sheet in annoyance and confusion.

I stooped to pick it up. He bent to help me. We rose at the same time, our eyes level, our hands full of damp cloth. I swallowed hard. His brilliant blue eyes shocked me with their intensity. My breath came fast and shallow. What was it about him that excited me so? I hurriedly straightened, taking the sheet from his hands, turning from him to hang it over the line.

He stayed too close to me. His voice dropped to a murmur, but its fervor was unmistakable. "Yes, Shira, according to me. I have long felt it my destiny to be among the great philosophers of our people. I will bring the wayward Jews back to a truer understanding of what is good and pure in our religion. We have muddied the Written Law, our direct inheritance from *ha-shem*, with our own interpretations and codifications. It is not important what man thinks He meant—it is only important what He said!"

I backed away, placing the laundry basket between us. "I know you believe this," I said slowly, relaying the words I had practiced late at night. Lying next to Mina while she slept, I found my thoughts turning to Nicholas Donin. To stop myself from dwelling on his blue eyes, his hair, his narrow frame, I would force myself to think about how to defeat him in argument.

I continued, "You drive people away by insulting them. After the Temple was destroyed, we needed more than Torah could give us. The Talmud is the best of Jewish wisdom. We—that is, my father, his students, Jews all over the world—study it every single day. And you, you come and insist—with no care for the pain you inflict by doing so—that they are wrong and have always been wrong."

"Always the same argument. Can you not think for yourself, Shira?" he exclaimed. He turned away, shaking his head. I felt myself shriveling inside. He walked away, calling over his shoulder, "Every word you utter could be coming directly from your father's mouth!"

His words echoed in my head all afternoon. Where else would my ideas about religion and life come from? When I was with Nicholas Donin, I felt as though I were perched on a dangerous precipice—as though if I were to embrace his way of thinking, I might be propelled blindly, headlong, down a bottomless abyss. It frightened me, in a heart-pounding, pulse-racing, exhilarating way.

———•———

I walked into the kitchen to find Mina crying again.

"Mina? What's wrong now?"

She pointed, silently, to the spiderweb in a corner of the kitchen, illuminated by a dusty sunbeam shining sluggishly through a window. She huddled down to sob against the wooden board of the table. Her tears sprinkled the unwashed dinner dishes.

"Mina? It's a spiderweb. There are dozens of them in the house. Why does this spiderweb make you weep?"

Between sobs and hiccups, she explained that the web, shining as it was, was an omen that someone she cared about would be ensnared by evil forces before the sun set.

I tried, first by gentle words and then with mounting exasperation, to address her superstitions. "Leave foolish thoughts to the Christians, Mina. The Talmud calls such beliefs 'the ways of the Amorites.' Remember, you are protected from such spells by the prayers written out by scribes, both in the *mezzuzot* that hang on every doorpost in the house and in the amulet you've worn since childhood."

But my calm words could not sway her from her horror and fears. When my father called me to take an early evening walk, I was not sorry to leave Mina to her misery.

We walked away from the thatched houses of the town, strolling along the banks of the Ante River, where I could see children playing in the flax fields beyond just as I remembered doing with my own friends. Having turned eleven, I felt much older than the lighthearted, shrieking children. It was early autumn and the air was spiced by the bounty of the harvest. The villeins were busy gathering the last grapes from the vines, their baskets loaded with plump fruit. Within the week, they would begin to press the wine and sow the fields, turning them to prepare for next year's growing season. We Jews had survived another year's Days of Awe, and the world seemed brisk and fresh and new, as it always did after the High Holy Days. The sky was a deep, luminescent blue, the entire world hushed and waiting for the sun to drop beneath the horizon so stars could reclaim the velvety sky.

"Tell me, child, what do you think of my new student?" Papa asked after we had walked silently but companionably together for several minutes. I could feel his narrowed eyes on my face.

"Nicholas Donin? He is very different from the other young men."

Papa shrugged, his mouth twisting in a wry grimace. "Yes, very different. Heed me, child. His ideas are suspect—perhaps even heresy. I listen to the boy politely, even when he is rude and aggressive. After all, he will leave us soon enough. I do my best to correct his misguided thoughts, for, believe me, Shira, that is all they are. But I know how Rabbi Yechiel feels about elevating Torah over Talmud." Papa shrugged again, reaching up to pull back a tree branch blocking our path. I sidled past and he let it snap back into place. "I pity that young man if he continues on insisting upon his controversial notions. He will not find my dear friend Yechiel as patient as I have been."

"Have you told him this?"

"I have. But, with the fervor of youth, Donin refuses to listen."

We walked along silently for a few minutes more. I huddled deep into my wool shawl, feeling suddenly chilled. The early evening air and the pungent aroma of fresh grapes wafting from the fields mixed with a heaviness in my chest. Nicholas Donin would not easily tolerate the disappointment my father predicted he would suffer. Donin was certain he would force the great scholar of Paris to embrace his way of thinking. Then and only then, he had told me, would fools like my father's students credit the absolute truth of what he had to say. But even if Rabbi Yechiel refused to acknowledge his ideas, I knew the young scholar would persist in his arguments, no matter what the consequence might be. There was something immutable about the fires possessing Nicholas Donin, the unstoppable force of a man who felt himself predestined to alter the course of Jewish thinking.

My father took me gently by the elbow and led me to a large, flat rock near the riverbank. We sat. I smiled, happy to have him all to myself this evening. It was a rare day when I could tempt him from his books, and even rarer when he left them of his own accord. But his face did not reflect my enjoyment.

"Nicholas Donin has requested your hand in marriage," he said.

My knees and legs began to quiver. Many of my friends were already plighted to their future husbands. I knew my prospects contained marriage and, hopefully, a large family. Yet until right then, the idea of a match at my age had seemed like something that happened to everyone else. The thought of someday marrying this fiery, combative, wildly fervent young man was not, I must admit, completely disagreeable. But just one glance at Papa's furrowed brow showed how differently he felt.

"What did you say to him, Papa?"

"What would you have had me say to him, Shira?"

I took a long minute to consider, my eyes fixed on the flowing river. My father studied my expression and his own darkened further. "Could you really care for this man?" he asked, his voice dripping distaste. "I would have expected better of you."

"Did I say that?" I retorted. I could feel the telltale blush rising up my neck and into my cheeks, a flush of fury and pent-up feelings that I did not completely understand.

"You haven't said anything yet." To think he could look at me so coldly!

"It's clear what *you* said to him, though! You told him no." My conflicting emotions—my fascination with Nicholas and his new ideas, my love for my father and my duty to him—bubbled together in a massive stew. My head throbbed in confusion.

"I want what is best for you, child." Worry overshadowed the anger on my father's face. He seemed honestly perplexed at my outburst. I noticed he didn't know what to do with his hands, moving them from his lap to his face to behind his back. Their frantic movement touched me, gentling my heart toward him.

I drew a deep breath. I had been brought up to be compliant. No matter what my own feelings might be, I told myself, my father knew better than I whether Nicholas Donin was indeed worthy in thought and deed. I recalled the commandment to honor one's parents.

"I know you want the best for me," I said, every word a separate beat, my eyes lowered. I tried to display a meek and placid countenance despite the heat in my cheeks.

Papa saw my effort and his troubled face cleared. He clasped both my hands.

"My dearest child. Your poor mother of blessed memory would have rejoiced that you have grown into such an obedient daughter. I did not say no," he stated, and my eyes flew to his face, "at least, not at first. I told Donin that I did not want you to leave home yet. You are a child still, I said. When he pressed the point, claiming you could be betrothed and wait until you were older for the marriage rite, I told him I didn't think the two of you were well suited."

My head drooped. Papa put a hand under my chin and raised my face so that he could look directly into my eyes. "You are not happy, Shira? Despite thinking I know what is best for you—and I do—you would wish me to give Donin permission to marry you?"

"Nicholas Donin talks to me about matters I care about, about Torah and Talmud. I cannot tell you how much I miss that, Papa. I am so tired of cleaning and cooking, always more cleaning and cooking. I feel empty inside, as if nothing I do or think is important."

Papa's eyes widened. "Child, child. I had no idea you felt so misused. Your cooking and cleaning *are* important. They make it possible for my students and me to study Torah and Talmud freely and without encumbrance. The Talmud itself tells us there is no duty more indispensable for a Jewish woman."

My chin trembled. "But there is only Mina to talk to during the week and she is always jumping at shadows. I fear if I spend so much time with her, someday I might become as foolish as she. I only get to see my friends in the synagogue these days, the neighbors all treat me as a child, you won't let me study, your students ignore me, and Nicholas Donin is the only one who believes I can think about more than the laundry and the meals!"

The furrows on Papa's brow deepened. "I'm afraid I am a better scholar than I am a father. If your mother were alive . . . Do you miss studying with me so very much?"

"Oh, yes!"

He rose and walked to the riverbank, standing silent for a few long minutes, watching the water flow below us. When he turned back, his face had cleared. He extended his hand and helped me to my feet. "Well, we cannot study together in front of my students—you are no longer a child, even if you are not quite yet a woman. But if you can wake early in the mornings, we can study together before anyone else rises—before you have to work so hard to tend to the house. I will find you another maidservant to help you bear the burden, at least a few times a week— unless . . . do you wish me to dismiss Mina?"

Joy rose within me, making me as giddy as though I had imbibed too much Shabbat wine. To study again with my father! For a moment, I rejoiced. Then I considered Mina.

"No, Papa, please let her stay. It is not her fault she is so superstitious. Perhaps I can help her overcome her fears. As for me, if I can study with you in the mornings and have a little more help in the house, it will be enough."

"So you are no longer tempted at the thought of marrying Nicholas Donin?"

I thought again of those startling blue eyes. Life with Nicholas Donin would be both exhilarating and exhausting. I had to admit that I was captivated by his impassioned claim that, given the chance, he might alter the course of Jewish history. But even I saw how he constantly wore thin the tempers of all who came near him. It was obvious that household peace, *shalom bayit,* would forever elude whatever home he made his own.

"No, Papa. In any case, he leaves us in a week. Now that we're to study together, I would rather stay in Falaise with you."

Papa patted me on the shoulder. "You are a good girl, Shira. I must tell you, I've missed studying with you, too. If only you were a boy . . ."

But I would not let my father's often-voiced longing hurt me, not then.

HREE

... *and the Lord will blot out his name from under heaven.*
—DEUTERONOMY 29:20

NICHOLAS WAS SITTING NEAR THE FIRE in the classroom and looked up as my father and I entered the house. We were walking hand in hand, and I saw how Nicholas's eyes traveled from my downturned face to my father's smile. My father didn't have to say a word. Donin rose, made an exasperated grunt deep in his throat, and pushed past us to retire to his bedroom.

I tossed and turned that night, and Mina complained the next morning that I kept kicking her. I could not stop thinking about Nicholas. He had asked for my hand in marriage, and if I was being truthful, the idea still tempted me. He was so unlike the other scholars! He must really care for me, I thought, and couldn't help the wave of exaltation that washed over me. To banish these feelings—which even I knew were improper now that I had refused his offer—I made myself think about the next morning. I couldn't wait for my first lesson with my father. I worried I might not rise early enough and every time I started to doze off, I found myself waking again with a start.

I left the warmth of the bed when I saw a tinge of color lightening the night sky. Yawning, I draped a warm shawl around my shoulders. Mina muttered and pulled the blankets we shared over her body. I crept downstairs, trying to avoid the loose boards that I knew would creak if I trod on them. I didn't want anyone to wake up.

As I walked toward the kitchen, a hand reached out from the classroom and grabbed hold of my elbow. I gasped.

"Shira," hissed Nicholas. His fingers were ice cold, as though he had been sitting in wait all night. "I need to speak with you."

I stood silent, not knowing what to say. His fingers tightened around my arm.

"Let her go," said my father, who had just come down the stairs himself. "I was going to speak with you today. She does not want to marry you."

"Shira?" Nicholas asked me, jerking me around so his blue eyes could look down into mine. I felt a thrill chase up and down my spine.

"Are you ready, daughter?" Papa asked dryly.

"I am, Papa," I said, looking down at Donin's fingers, which were still curled about my arm.

Nicholas let me go, pushing my arm away as though it might contaminate him. "I will leave your home this morning, Rabbi Shmuel. I will not wait another week. Rabbi Yechiel will have to receive me a week earlier than he expects."

A glint of satisfaction entered my father's eyes. "As you will," he told the boy. "Come, Shira."

I tried to blot out the hurt expression on Nicholas's face by remembering I was going to study with my father, but his disappointment arrested me. I reached over and touched his arm. "Go with God," I murmured. "I hope you find what you're looking for in Paris."

Nicholas's face softened. "And I hope you will not be sorry you refused me," he said.

"She won't be," my father told him, pulling me away.

———•———

It was amazing the difference the early morning study sessions made to my life. Now there was something to look forward to every day. I loved opening the dense pages of text—the passage we intended to study situated in the middle of the page, surrounded on all four sides by paragraphs of commentary. Studying with my father meant I could hear the voices of the sages speaking to one another over the ages, amplified by my wise papa's counsel as he led me through the sometimes convoluted series of ideas that linked one section to the next.

We sat reading from the tractate Berakhoth one memorable morning, spending considerable time on the story of Rabbi Meir and his wife, Bruriah.

"You remind me of her, daughter," Papa said, bestowing a fond kiss on my forehead. "She was another girl who loved to study."

I listened, fascinated by the wife of Rabbi Meir. Bruriah lived during the time of the great Roman Empire. By debating openly with the sages, she became the only woman to be included in the Talmudic commentary, the Gemara.

The passage we read started, "Certain *beryonim*"—which my father translated as "troublers"—"living in the neighborhood of Rabbi Meir annoyed him greatly."

Papa stopped reading and asked, "Tell me, child, how can we be upset by troublers in our midst?"

I felt myself blushing, knowing he was thinking of the now departed Nicholas Donin. And then I thought of the day Jeanne's husband and his friends tried to force me to eat pork.

"They can stop us from considering our duties," I ventured. "They can make themselves more important than what truly is important."

Papa, his eyes on my face, nodded slowly. "The text uses the word '*beryonim*,'" he pointed out.

"I've never heard that word before," I replied.

"Let's look in the commentary," he said, and together we read how the *beryonim* were zealots who armed themselves against the great Roman Empire, with catastrophic results. These rebels were so rabid in the defense of their beliefs that they victimized rich Jews for money to continue their struggle and burned the grain stores, which plunged the city into a winter's famine.

"These *beryonim* did not respect the rights of others," Papa commented. "They set aside common human decency in the pursuit of their own needs."

I knew, again, he was alluding to Nicholas. I pursed my lips and turned back to the text. "'. . . they annoyed him greatly and Rabbi Meir prayed for them to die,'" I read, and stopped, shocked.

"You seem surprised by this," Papa said. "But do we not wish those who trouble us to die?"

"To die?" I asked. "How could a wise man wish for such evil? Was Rabbi Meir not a wise man?"

"He was," Papa told me. "He must have been very disturbed by the hooligans in his neighborhood. You are still young; you don't know yet how it feels to be so upset by someone's wickedness that you wish they would just vanish from the earth. Let's read on."

"'His wife Bruriah said to him: What is your view? Is it because it is written: "Let the sinners . . ."'"

Papa covered the rest of the passage with his hand. "Where is this from, Shira?"

This was a game Papa often played with his scholars. A Talmudic scholar was frequently given just the first few words of a passage and he would need to recall the rest. I knew that my father's memory was prodigious. Mine, unfortunately, was not as good.

"'Let the sinners . . .'" I mused. "Is it from Proverbs?"

Papa shook his head, picking up his hand to reveal the rest of the passage. "Psalm 104:35." He quoted, "'Let the sinners be consumed out of the earth and let the wicked be no more.' Keep reading, Shira."

"'Bruriah asks . . . is it because it is written: "Let the sinners be con-sumed"? Is "sinners" written? "Sin" is written.'"

"What did Bruriah mean? How does the word 'sinners' become 'sin'?" Papa asked me.

I grinned. I loved the wordplay that often changed how a word is pronounced and thereby its meaning. We spent several minutes discuss-ing how the word for "sinner" could be changed by altering certain vow-els. The Torah, of course, is written without vowels, and a reader must know how to pronounce the word from its context. Just by changing the vowels used, a word could be transformed.

"'"Sin" is written,'" I continued. "Moreover, Bruriah says, 'look at the end of the verse: "and let the wicked be no more." Since the sins will cease, the wicked will be no more.'" I looked up. "Bruriah's right, isn't she? If no one committed sins, no one would be wicked."

Could my father tell that I was thinking again about Nicholas, how he might be made good if he refrained from his hurtful conduct and beliefs? If he knew, he gave no sign of it. "Keep reading, Shira," he prompted.

"'Rather pray for them that they may repent, and they will be wicked no more. Rabbi Meir prayed for them and they repented.'" I smiled. "That's wonderful!"

"So you, like Bruriah, believe that we can rid the world of sinners?" Papa shook his head. "If only it were that easy. But in the next passage, you'll see Bruriah herself understood there is some wickedness in the world we cannot leave uncorrected."

A few days later, rather than immediately opening the precious book I clasped on my lap, I turned to my father. "Papa, were there any other women—aside from Bruriah—who studied Talmud? I cannot under-stand why it is forbidden."

"Well, it is said Rashi's daughters studied with him. As you know, Bruriah married Rabbi Meir. Rashi's daughter Yocheved also married a Rabbi Meir—this time, Meir ben Shmuel. When I was young I actually studied with his brilliant son, whom you know as Rabbenu Tam, may his memory be blessed."

I sat back in my chair, smiling widely. If Rashi—France's greatest Talmudic writer, a man whose commentary on the Talmud was now considered indispensible—allowed his daughters to study Talmud, no one could fault Papa for our work together. The idea of other women scholars, including some only a few generations removed from me, gave me hope that someday I too would be able to stop studying in the shadows and in shame.

———◆———

As much as I enjoyed my daily studies, nothing in life was as wonderful as attending synagogue every Shabbat eve. The building itself was not ornate—not like the magnificent buttressed edifices where the Gentiles worshipped their idols. We Jews had to be careful not to call attention to ourselves. The drab, whitewashed synagogue building fit snugly between two houses on the street. Papa explained that in better days our house of worship would have been the tallest building in town, for the Talmud says that any city whose roofs are higher than the synagogue will eventually be destroyed. To avoid this fate, our synagogue builders dug an unusually deep cellar beneath our feet. By doing so, we fulfilled the words of the psalmist: "Out of the depths have I called Thee, O Lord." If our synagogue was measured from cellar to ceiling, it was slightly taller even than the tallest of the town churches.

The building's interior was dark and dank. We had only one small window, built toward the ceiling and kept latched, where outside light struggled to filter in. My father taught me the great prophet Daniel worshipped where "his windows were open in his upper chamber" and we tried to imitate his devotion. But we also feared that if any passerby overheard our prayers, our Christian neighbors might be offended. So we kept our single window barred and shut.

The room was built to surround the *bimah,* the high, circular wooden platform whose steps my father would climb every day. To the east was the *aron hakodesh,* or the ark, a curtained alcove that held our sacred Torah scrolls. Above that burned the *ner tamid,* the eternal light, a bronze brazier kept lit by the bailiff, or *shamash.* Woe would befall a synagogue whose eternal light was allowed to die, for it would quench the flame that had burned since the days of the Temple in Jerusalem, where the first eternal light was lit.

It was in this holy place that I visited my friends for the few brief moments we shared each week. As young girls, we had played together in the fields. Now my friends either worked alongside their mothers or stepmothers, or, like me, tended to households on their own.

"Do you see him?" Miriam giggled, pointing out a boy who stood with his head bowed in prayer. She made sure she stood securely behind the curtained partition, the *mechitzah,* so she would not be scolded for distracting the men. "The matchmaker—the *shadchan*—is talking to Chaim's father about me."

"That one?" sniffed Chava. "He's all right, I suppose. But I've been engaged all this week, girls."

"Already betrothed?" we shouted, only to be hushed by the irritable matrons who rustled their skirts noisily as they shifted on the wood bench and clucked their tongues.

"But have you finished sewing your dowry?" I whispered. "Last week you were worried because you only had five tablecloths completed."

"I was going to ask you all to come and help me this week," Chava confessed, hanging her head so that her blond curls slipped becomingly over her flushed face. "Papa wants me to marry this month."

"Did your father give you the candlesticks yet?" another friend whispered, keeping a careful eye on the older women. Every Jewish bride was entitled to a pair of silver candlesticks as part of her trousseau. Of course, not all parents could afford them.

"He will," Chava said confidently.

Our talk didn't just revolve around boys. We gossiped about our neighbors, poking fun at the women who hissed at us to be silent. My father, as rabbi of the congregation, would sometimes offer a special blessing over a woman who had refrained from gossiping during prayers. Afterward he would say to me, "Someday, Shira, I'll pray the blessing over your name. Seems a long time in coming, Songbird."

When prayers ended, Isaac ben Michelin the *shamash* always announced items of special interest to the community. Sometimes they
were happy—a new betrothal or birth, the successful sale of property,
an impending business trip. Sometimes they were less cheerful, like
the time the congregation was accused of stealing candlesticks from
a local church—an accusation that was withdrawn the next day. One
of the older nuns, cursed with the failing memory of old age, found
them bundled inside her cleaning cloth, half-hidden by the straw ticking of her cell bed. A few times, too, there was a muted announcement
that someone had returned to the fold, having previously converted to
Christianity either voluntarily or at sword-point. My father, like other
rabbis throughout Ashkenaz, always reminded the congregation to welcome the congregant's return to Judaism. This was especially important
if the recent convert had been persecuted by Gentiles, who believed that
by the pouring on of water and muttering of prayers, they possessed a
man's soul for eternity.

And then, there were announcements of an even more dire nature.

———————•———————

I could not believe it.

It started like a normal Shabbat. I was tempted to leave early when
the bailiff came to the *bimah* to make announcements, for a frost the
night before had coated the town's cobblestones in a thin layer of ice.
Walking home would be treacherous. But the thought of the cold wind
keening outside kept me in my seat.

After a few brief pronouncements—Doucette's father would travel
to Portugal to trade for spices, there was a new student arrived from
Mainz—the *shamash* told the congregation that my father had received
a letter from his friend Rabbi Yechiel in Paris.

"I am sorry to inform all of you—particularly the students who
attended *yeshiva* with him just a few months ago—that Rabbi Yechiel
placed Nicholas Donin into *cherem*."

Cherem! I felt dizzy, as if the seat under me were swaying back and forth. I clutched the wood beneath me tightly, feeling I might be pitched onto the floor below. Excommunication . . . the blue-eyed, black-haired young man who had been so ready to argue with everyone, who had sought to marry me, would no longer be allowed to speak with his fellow Jews. We were required to keep a distance of four paces away from him at all times now. If Papa had agreed to our betrothal, I would have been devastated by the news, my life destroyed. As it was, I was horrified and distraught for Nicholas.

After we returned home my father would not allow the students who surrounded him and pelted him with questions to disrupt the tranquility of the Shabbat by discussing such disquieting news. He bade them be quiet and told them he would answer them after Shabbat ended. I sat at the dinner table, stunned. The food tasted like cinders. I felt sick watching the boys gnawing away at the roasted pullet and chiming in joyfully when Papa called for hymns of praise to God.

I spent the next day wandering along the banks of the river Ante in the thin winter sunshine. I barely registered how the peasants who lived on the outskirts of town busied themselves gathering acorns and cords of wood. They called out to one another with greetings of holiday cheer, for it would be Christmastide in a week. I thought how busy Jeanne must be during this season—the time of year when they slaughter pigs and chickens so that every man, woman, and child, rich or poor, in the countryside, the town, and the castle, could eat at least some small portion of meat. I felt unutterably alone, pacing the riverbank in my Sabbath best.

Finally, the sun set. We waited a long hour before performing Havdalah, the beautiful ceremony that bids the Shabbat farewell for another week. We lit the braided candle and passed our beloved silver spice box from hand to hand, breathing in its aroma. Then Papa gathered the young men around him. I sat in the back of the room, pretending to sew.

"I know you're all interested in what happened to Nicholas Donin," Papa began, taking a big breath. "Just as he did when he lived with us, he passionately promoted his heretical beliefs in the *yeshiva* in Paris."

"I studied with Rabbi Yechiel and I'm certain he did not like that," said Aberlin.

"No, he did not," Papa continued. "But despite countless entreaties, Donin would not thrust his ideas aside."

"Did you really expect him to?" Moshe burst out.

I looked up from my sewing, frowning at the student's indignant expression.

"Let us just say that I hoped he would," said Papa, his gentle tones prompting Moshe's head to droop in abashed silence. "But Rabbi Yechiel, after bearing with Donin and with the dissent he wrought in the peaceful enclave of study for a long time, wrote to me that he finally felt compelled to excommunicate him."

"Of course he did," said Moshe, raising his head, his mouth stretched in a grin. My fingers itched to slap him. But Papa, wiser than I, ignored him.

"Yechiel's main reason for excommunicating Donin was to prevent him from polluting other Jews with his sacrilegious notions," Papa continued.

"But, Rav Shmuel?" came a shy voice from the back, using the more formal term for "rabbi" to address Papa. It was Ethan, one of our youngest students. My father smiled at the boy encouragingly. "What happens when you are excommunicated?"

"You know that no Jew can ever speak to him again, that we are required to remain four steps distant from him at all times?" Papa asked.

"I know all that. I mean, what happens in synagogue?"

Papa told the younger boys how Nicholas Donin would have been called into the synagogue a first time and cautioned to redeem himself by disavowing his impious beliefs. Donin clearly had refused to heed the warning. Then Rabbi Yechiel would have summoned him again, to announce, before the entire synagogue, that no one was to speak with him, live under his roof, or read anything that he wrote.

I flinched as I thought of Nicholas Donin standing before the congregation as the candles in the synagogue were extinguished, as someone blew a long, piercing, mournful note on the *shofar*.

For the benefit of his younger students, Papa proclaimed some of the curses that had been heaped upon Donin's head: "Cursed be he by day and cursed be he by night; cursed be he when he lies down and cursed be he when he rises up. Cursed be he when he goes out and cursed be he when he comes in. The Lord will not spare him, but then the anger of the Lord and his jealousy shall smoke against that man, and all the curses that are written in this book shall lie upon him, and the Lord shall blot out his name from under heaven. And the Lord shall separate him unto evil out of all the tribes of Israel, according to all the curses of the covenant that are written in this book of the law."

How Nicholas must have writhed under such disgrace! I could not but wonder . . . isolated and alone . . . how did he feel now?

After my father dismissed the boys, he turned to me.

"So you see, Songbird, Papa does know best for you. Had you been betrothed, or, God forbid, married to Donin, you would either have had to renounce him forever or be excommunicated along with him. And that, my darling, would have broken my heart."

I studied his face, which seemed a strange mixture—compassion for what I must have been feeling and iron satisfaction in having been proved right. I had to know what my father felt in his heart. "Do you feel no pity for him, Papa?"

"I must admit I do. But Yechiel wrote that he beseeched Donin countless times to change his ways. Always, he refused. As he did here, Donin tried to persuade others, including the youngest, most innocent, and most vulnerable of minds, to adopt his heretical doctrines. That being so, Yechiel had no choice. You must see that." His eyes searched my face. "And it will be best, daughter, even if you do not think it now, if we forget that Donin ever existed—almost as if the world swallowed him whole—so that we never hear from him or of him again."

I felt tears threatening to well in my eyes. Excusing myself with a murmured apology, I left the room and found a quiet corner where I could cry unseen. So this man who hoped to change Jewish history was forever banned from his own religion, his own people! And thus, it seemed, my relationship with him was ended as well. Yet despite what Papa said, it seemed impossible that I would never hear of Nicholas Donin again.

OUR

If I make [Eve] of [Adam's] ears, she will be an eavesdropper.

—THE TALMUD

MINA WAS CHOPPING ONIONS for a large pot of soup and I was elbow-deep in bread dough as I punched it down for its second rising when a loud rap on the front door startled us both. It was the middle of the morning, not a time when we generally entertained visitors. At a glance from me, Mina set down her knife, wiped her hands on her apron, and went to see who was there.

She scuttled back an instant later, her eyes wide. "Some men from the congregation are here to see the rabbi. What should I do?"

"To see Papa? Now? But . . ." I picked up the ball of dough, put it in a clean wooden bowl, covered it with a cloth, and placed it on a bench set back from the fire. Wiping my forearms clean, I removed my apron and hung it on its hook near the back buttery. "I'll go see." I was worried. The entire town knew not to interrupt the rabbi and his scholars during lessons.

Stepping into the foyer, where the men milled about impatiently, I grew even more concerned. The town's most powerful Jewish citizens stood there: Durand, the owner of several of Falaise's shops; Haiem à Marseille, whose agents traveled the world finding goods to buy and sell; Acher ha-Levi, Falaise's kosher butcher; and Isaac ben Michelin, the *shamash* of our synagogue. The Jews of Falaise looked to these four men and my father as their leaders. They were the ones who would speak with Baron la Folette, the noble who relayed the king's commands, if the baron demanded an audience with our community.

"Welcome," I greeted them. As an unmarried girl, I cast my eyes down and studied their muddied boots. "My father is in class with his students now. But if you tell me the matter cannot wait—"

"The matter cannot wait," interrupted Acher ha-Levi.

"Then I will fetch him," I murmured. From between my thick lashes, I noticed all four men were scrutinizing me closely. I turned and started toward the study.

"Shira," Isaac ben Michelin called after me, "tell him we will wait in his solar."

Isaac, who visited my father on synagogue business several times a week, knew that the solar, my father's solitary bedroom quarters, was the only room in the house where the rabbi could discuss matters in private. I stopped short. My heart was pounding, but they would not have known that from the calm expression on my face. I nodded and continued on. The sound of the men's heavy boots on the wooden stairway reverberated throughout the house.

———•———

As soon as I heard Papa shut the door of his solar behind him, I grabbed a broom and headed upstairs. Entering the empty room next to his, where five of the students slept, I began sweeping gently. At first I could hear only scraps of conversation. My ears prickled as I picked out my own name and something about Mina. Then, Acher ha-Levi, the butcher whose loud voice always rang across the marketplace, took command of the conversation.

"We'll never get it all out with your muttering. You tell the rabbi if I

leave anything out. Rabbi, Clarice and Bella Tova came to my shop yesterday to ask me to speak with you. But they are only the last in a long
line of cackling gossips who have yammered over the years about how
you are raising Shira. Now"—here the butcher laughed heartily—"I'm
the last man to listen to the chatter of women. Actually, because they all
come to my shop, I'm usually the first man in Falaise to hear—"

"Acher, you stray from the point," muttered Haiem à Marseille.

"I suggested the women talk with you directly, Rabbi, but they were
not willing. So I told them to return that evening and asked Isaac, here,
to join me. We four spent some time—I hope this doesn't offend you—
talking about the scandal."

"Scandal, Acher?" my father said mildly but with a biting under-
tone.

"Rabbi, we know that Sarah's death was hard on you, especially because your first wife died so many years earlier. But you have an obligation to have children, and while you have a daughter, you also need—did
not our blessed sage Hillel . . . ?"

"Yes. A son. While the school of Shammai thought you must have
two sons, Hillel disagreed. He said, as it is written in the first book of
the Torah, in Bereshit, 'Male and female God created them.' To fulfill the
commandment, said Hillel in the Talmud, a man must sire one son and
one daughter. I know it is a failure of mine that I have no son . . ."

My heart ached for Papa. I forgave him for all the times he had yearned
for a boy—times when I felt disappointed that I was not enough for him.
If Hillel himself said the commandment was only complete with the birth
of a boy, I could better understand Papa's discontent through the years.

"Yes, exactly," Isaac said. "But you have not sought out another wife.
If I understand correctly, according to the mitzvah to be fruitful and
multiply—to *pru u'rvu*—you are obligated to do so."

Papa's deep sigh seemed to rise from his tortured soul. "I had
thought . . . after Shira is married . . . I am already so old . . ."

"But, Rabbi, don't you see that it is because there is no mother in the
house that Shira is such a wayward child?" Acher exclaimed.

I gasped loudly, my astonishment rasping in my ears. I was surprised they did not hear it. Was I truly considered wayward?

"A wayward child? My Shira?" my father roared, and I let my breath out slowly, my heart warmed by Papa's offended response.

"Rabbi," Durand said in his usual decisive tones, "we know how much you love the child. Not one of us believes she is deliberately doing wrong. But you are busy, as you should be, with your students. There is no woman to advise Shira, to instruct her how to behave. Mina told her mother and aunt that Shira and Donin spoke together many times and you did nothing to stop it. It was wrong, Rabbi. You know you would scorn such behavior in any other man's daughter."

Silence. I could picture my father hanging his head, not wishing to look at the faces of the men gathered to chastise him. My cheeks felt as though small fires were burning in them; I was furious at Mina's wagging tongue and shamed before my father. I leaned weakly against the rough plaster wall.

"Donin did want to marry the girl," my father finally said, so softly I could hardly hear him.

"And in light of what has occurred, Rav Shmuel—does that make things better or worse?"

"At first," Acher said, taking control of the discussion, "we thought that the best solution was to suggest Shira be married. But now that this story is on everyone's lips, you might not easily find a suitable scholar who is willing to wed her. But if you were to marry a good, dependable woman and she took Shira in hand . . ."

"Do you have one in mind?" Papa asked slowly. Oh, the humiliation in my poor father's voice!

"Two, in fact," Durand said. "Frommet lost her husband last year when he was traveling abroad to Jerusalem and Constantinople. But he was martyred, killed by a Crusader, so she may plan to dedicate her widowhood to his memory. If so, we must honor her intention. But Alyes, who lost both her husband and two sons to the Black Scourge a year ago, would undoubtedly be happy to find herself the wife of such an esteemed rabbi."

"You flatter me," Papa said dryly. "If I am such a matrimonial prize, I am curious why you only present me with widows."

The men's quick laughter was tinged with surprise. "At your advanced age, Rav Shmuel, we thought that is what you would prefer," Isaac replied.

Haiem added, "But if you are interested in a virgin, a *b'tulah*, Rabbi, it would not be difficult to find a suitable young woman—"

"I was joking, Haiem. A little levity to ease my discomfort. I agree, Isaac, at the age of forty-seven, I am too old for a virgin. Your widows would suit me better. Alyes, I think. She has always impressed me as a capable, biddable woman. Do you mean to engage a *shadchan* in this matter?"

"There is a matchmaker in Caen who could be hired. Would you like me to speak with him on your behalf?"

I heard the door opening. Papa led the men out onto the stairway landing and down the stairs. I did not hear his reply. I waited several minutes until I was sure it was safe. It would be better not to be seen by anyone before I had control of my feelings.

But I couldn't stay there for too long. I scurried back downstairs to find my bread had risen too quickly and spilled over the edges of the bowl. I was harsh with Mina for not watching it and made her cry.

Punching the dough back into manageable shape helped calm me—I used the strength of my fury at Mina's tales, at the humiliation brought publicly down on both Papa and me, to batter down the yeast bubbles. I then cleaned the kitchen in a whirlwind of energy, scrubbing until my arms ached.

Papa's face during the midday meal was a study in emotions. I kept my eyes on my plate but I could feel my father staring at me.

As I cleared the dishes after the meal, I let my mind wander. A stepmother! I knew very little of Alyes. She was one of the quiet ones at the synagogue. She and I had never exchanged greetings beyond *"Shabbat shalom"* or *"Hag samech"*—the usual good wishes of the Shabbat or the holidays.

When I was very young, Jeanne had told me Christian stories about stepmothers. One of her favorites was a tale about a daughter whose new mother made her work all day and night with only a crust of bread to eat. Friendless and alone, the girl still managed to meet and marry a princely knight. The hero pulled the daughter on his horse and took her on a magical ride to his castle in the clouds. Enthralled though I'd been by the story, I knew there were no princes in my future, not unless a descendant of King David should find his way to Falaise and marry me. But the wrath of an evil stepmother? That could yet become a part of my life's story.

IVE

Not money but character is the best dowry of a wife.
—THE TALMUD

THE THURSDAY WEDDING BLESSING BETWEEN my father, Rabbi Shmuel ben Solomon, and the widow Alyes took place on one of those exquisite spring days where the deep azure of the cloudless sky could make an observer catch his breath, when the lilting delicacy of the breeze could caress a baby into dreamless sleep.

I had never seen my father appear so resplendent, dressed in a long white embroidered tunic with wide sleeves that he'd brought back from Germany years ago when he studied there. He wore it over brown breeches and hose. As he sat before the boys at breakfast, waving away offers of food, he quizzed them with tales about the sanctity of the wedded state. "Listen to me, boys, what do we read in Kiddushin about marriage? Who can tell me how to treat a wife?"

The first to speak was his best man, none other than Isaac ben Michelin, the *shamash.* Isaac was invited to attend my papa until it was time to lead the groom to the *chuppah.* "Rabbi, does it not say, '*ha-Shem*'s presence dwells in a pure and loving home?'"

"Indeed it does, Isaac, very good. We must be mindful to keep our home a loving one, if we wish *ha-Shem* to remain a presence there. A fine example. Here, one of you young men, what truths have you found in Kiddushin that describe your own marriage or betrothal?"

Caleman, who had been married last year at the age of seventeen and whose wife was living with his parents until he could complete his *yeshiva* studies, blushed deeply and said, "'Marriages are made in heaven.' And, Rabbi, they are!"

There was a genial laugh, and some of the younger boys kicked and nudged one another. Guerchon, betrothed to a young girl in Worms whose father was apparently among the richest men in all Ashkenaz, added, somewhat ironically, "'Who is rich? He whose wife's actions are comely.'"

My father raised his eyebrows. "I might counter that by saying, 'Not money but character is the best dowry of a wife'—and you, dear Guerchon, appear particularly blessed by both!"

Guerchon nodded, obviously trying hard not to appear smug. "Indeed, I believe I am," he said. "But you are rich yourself, Rabbi. Is it not said, 'Who is happy? He whose wife is modest and gentle.'"

"My students, you should all be blessed with such women as my Alyes—a woman who I happily will 'love as myself, and honor more than myself.'"

My head shot up at that. I regarded my father solemnly, but he was not looking at me. He rose, beaming, to a chorus of *"Mazel tov!"* and *"B'ruchim ha'chatan va'kalah!"*

———————

The ceremony was beautiful. The heavens shone upon my father almost as brilliantly as he deserved. I spied him approaching the synagogue, accompanied by Isaac the *shamash*, his students dancing around them, tossing flower petals and singing songs of praise. When I saw how his face shone under the bridegroom's wreath of new roses and myrtle branches as he raptly contemplated married life, I could not help but feel joy for his joy. He strolled to the back of the synagogue through the gate, standing in a clearing fragrant with lilacs and freshly cut grass, waiting for his bride to appear. My father and his bride would sanctify their marriage under open skies, recalling God's promise to Abraham that his seed would be as numerous as the stars above.

As Alyes emerged from the back doors of the synagogue, accompanied by her sisters and mother, who had traveled many miles to attend her, I felt my joy curdle like a cup of new milk left too long in the sun. Seeing how lovely she looked, I grew unsatisfied with my new green dress girded with an already crushed sash of buttercup yellow. I felt like a clumsy child next to the glowing bride. Her gown was a soft shade of peach, the thick veil covering her face and hiding her hair a square of cream-colored lace. The laces of the linen bodice she wore over the dress were untied, in accordance with the custom that no other ties should bind her that day but the marriage bonds. Her mother and her eldest sister took her elbows and ushered her forward. At her approach, four of Papa's students, selected for diligence in study and similarity in height, caught up a prayer shawl at the corners, creating a living *chuppah* of the holy cloth. As the knotted cloth billowed up against the glorious blue of the afternoon sky, I remembered Papa explaining why the wedding ceremony took place beneath a *tallith*, recalling how Abraham and Sarah's open tent flaps always welcomed strangers to their home. Other students came forward and piled the *chuppah* with spring flowers—a gesture that made the congregants murmur in appreciation. It was not a custom we had seen before in Falaise.

Alyes circled her groom and everyone joined in singing *"Adon Olam"*—"Lord of the World." I overheard many comments on the beauty of the bride. I admit Alyes's radiant face and tender smile took me by surprise. I felt a heaviness growing in my chest as I realized once the words of the wedding ceremony were spoken, Papa would honor his bride above all other women—even above me, who had been the daughter of his heart for so many years.

So I winced when I heard my father tell his bride, *"Herei at m'kudeshet*

li im b'taba'at zo k'dat Moshe v'Yisrael"—"With this ring you are consecrated unto me according to the Law of Moses and Israel"—and watched
as he placed the embossed silver band on her right forefinger, the one
closest to her heart. Papa's good friend Rabbi Yechiel, who had come all
the way from Paris to perform the ceremony, faced the east and proclaimed the Seven Benedictions, the same blessings we pray daily in our
Grace after Meals. My father and new stepmother sipped wine from two
glasses. My father smashed his on the low wall surrounding the synagogue garden to recall our exile from the land of Israel even in the midst
of our greatest joys. As the glass shattered, cries of good wishes, *mazel
tov* and *simon tov*, rose in chorus. My father's students led him from the
synagogue into the front room of our house. We women followed the
men, bringing the bride to her groom.

I had worked all the day before with the women of the town to completely rearrange the schoolroom. Study tables were pushed against the
walls, draped in white cloth, and covered with food and flowers. Everyone in Falaise had contributed to the feast. My father and his bride
were ushered to a separate room to partake of a small meal in splendid
isolation. I watched the door of the closed room, feeling more and more
dejected. But I forced a smile on my face as my dear father exited the
chamber, his hand clasping his bride's forearm as he led her forth.

———•———

I knew I could not expect to study with my father for the first three days
following the wedding. He suspended lessons for his jubilant scholars
to free his bride and himself for daily visits to and from friends, relatives, and neighbors. But on the first day possible, I woke early and crept
downstairs to the front room, where Papa and I generally met for our
early morning sessions.

As I quietly padded downstairs, I heard someone moving about the
front room. There was a wide smile on my face as I rounded the corner
to greet Papa and welcome him back to our study sessions. But it wasn't
he who waited.

"Alyes!" I exclaimed. "Why aren't you still sleeping?"

My stepmother, dressed in warm blue wool, a heavy shawl draped over her shoulders and her shorn hair covered modestly with a black snood, held herself stiffly. "And you, daughter? Should you not still be abed? The early dawn is no time for a growing child to be awake."

I shrugged, pinning narrowed eyes on my stepmother's round face. I knew this encounter would forever color our relationship, and I had no intention of letting her abolish my few hard-won privileges. "This is when I spend time with my father. Time we spend *alone.*"

"So my husband told me," Alyes replied, sitting down and folding her hands neatly on her lap. Her soft, slightly throaty voice put no special emphasis on the words "my husband," but they sent a chill down my spine nonetheless. "Knowing that, I thought this would be a good time for us to talk undisturbed."

"About what?" I demanded. "Are you going to stop my father from studying with me in the mornings?"

Alyes gestured to the bench across the table from her, motioning for me to sit. For a tense moment, I tried to decide what would be best: to sit like a biddable child, to continue standing like a petulant one, or to leave the room altogether to find my father. I finally decided the most dignified course of action would be to sit and hear Alyes out. But I fear my flounce into the seat and the black scowl on my face robbed the act of any grace.

Alyes sat across from me, quietly contemplating my stormy face. I was determined not to speak first. The silence built between us until it seemed to take tangible form. Then my stepmother broke it, speaking so softly and hesitantly I had to lean forward to hear her.

"I'm a shy person, you know, Shira. It is difficult for me to speak in public. That's why I almost did not agree to marry the Rav. It took the matchmaker, my own family, and your father many months to convince me."

"Why should your shyness matter?" I asked, confused by the unexpected turn of the conversation.

"There are duties expected of a rabbi's wife. Lead the women in prayer. Tend the sick. Help the poor. I am competent, even capable, in the sickroom, but the other two responsibilities frighten me. And Falaise has clearly felt the lack of a rabbi's wife, a rebbetzin. Your own departed mother, of blessed memory, could not fulfill her obligations when she was always so ill with her pregnancies. But early on, she was a wonderful rabbi's wife. It will be difficult for me—and for you, Shira—to live up to her example."

Alyes could not have chosen a subject that intrigued me more. As she spoke, I realized that the fifteen-year age difference between my father's bride and me meant Alyes had known my mother. It was too painful for Papa when I asked questions about my mother or tried to talk about her. Our neighbors felt awkward speaking about Sarah in front of him. Something lurched inside me now, as though a long-suppressed yearning was roused. I turned to Alyes and breathlessly asked, "What was my mother like?"

Alyes looked down at her clasped hands. "Your own looking glass should tell you how beautiful she was, for you look exactly like her. She had long black hair, which of course we rarely saw after she was married. She had a delicate white face, with brown eyes that glowed like dark gems. Small and lithe, she was at all times neat in appearance. She was always singing and knew the prayers flawlessly. We girls felt as if a dark wood sprite led us in prayer every Shabbat. She knew everyone in Falaise—what they did, what they needed, how she might help them. I cried for three days after she died. My husband didn't understand why. I was a bride myself, a newcomer to Falaise, who had never spoken a single word to her. But her death hurt me."

I peered at Alyes, skeptical at first. But as I looked into her earnestly flushed face, I slowly recognized the sincerity there. Then she drew a small looking glass from a pouch she wore over her belt and pushed it across the table to me.

"If you truly want to know what your mother looked like, look at yourself," she urged.

I took the glass and looked into it. My white face, with high cheekbones, stared back at me in the early morning light. I had my mother's dark eyes. Perhaps it was the candle that stood between us on the table that made them sparkle so. My black hair was thick, springing back from a high forehead in curls that were difficult, sometimes, to contain. The fingers holding the mirror were slight and delicate. I knew I was not as tall as many of my friends, though I wasn't short, either. Did I resemble a wood sprite? My lips parted as I smiled into the mirror, revealing a row of small, even white teeth.

"You look just like her," Alyes repeated. "Beautiful."

At that moment, all my distrust of my new stepmother dissolved. Impulsively, I wanted to confide in her the way I used to confide in Jeanne. I said, "I remember my mother singing to me in such a sweet, low voice, and I think I recall her reciting the prayers. But I was too young to remember anything more. I do miss her, Alyes."

Alyes tentatively extended a hand across the table. I took it. The two of us sat handfast for a long moment. Then I released her, sitting back and trying to think how I might help her become a member of the family.

"Do you want me to help with your new duties? If I were older, I could lead the prayers. We could practice them together. And we could help the poor. I've read a lot about *tzedakah* together with Papa."

"About charity? Have you? Then yes, you could be an enormous help. When my betrothal to your papa was announced, many of the women—and their husbands through them—complained to me that our town has not done enough to help the poor of recent years. I was told, over and over, that they expected me to remedy the situation. But I don't know exactly where to start."

"Well, I think we should consider what Papa has told me about Maimonides, a scholar who was expelled from Spain and settled in Egypt during the last century. Don't tell anyone we're using his ideas, though—Papa says many of his philosophies are suspected of heresy. Maimonides wrote that those who give charity with bad grace are ranked lowest, while those who help the poor sustain themselves truly fulfill the *mitzvah*. Do you want me to find the passage?" I eagerly rose and walked over to the chest where Papa kept his copies of Maimonides's writings hidden. I rooted under the clothes and brought up one of the thick leather-bound books. "It's in this one, I'm certain of it."

Alyes smiled at my obvious enthusiasm. "Yes, go ahead."

I leafed through the book quickly and found the page. "Here it is. There are eight degrees of *tzedakah*. One, the person who gives with bad grace. Two, the person who does not give enough but does so happily. Three, the person who gives only after he is asked to do so." I looked over at Alyes somewhat mischievously. "I guess that includes you and me, right now."

She laughed and I continued. "Four, the person who gives before he is asked, knowing who he gives to. Five, the person who gives to someone unidentified, while the receiver knows the source of the charity. Six, the person who gives secretly to someone he knows, but the recipient never learns where the charity comes from. Seven, the person who gives when neither donor nor receiver know each other's identity. Eight, the person who helps the poor find a job so they can support themselves."

I paused, looking up from the book at Alyes, who had been ticking off the eight degrees on her fingers as I spoke. "Hmm. It's less helpful than I thought. I guess the question is—"

"*How* do we do it? Yes, exactly. But it was helpful, because it shows me my first idea—to set up a table where the poor could come and be served food, as the nuns from La Trinité do—was not as good an idea as I thought it was."

"It's a matter of dignity, my loves," said a deep voice from the doorway, and both Alyes and I turned our heads to see my father standing there, looking at us fondly. "Shira, we have often discussed that every human being deserves the same dignity, and to treat them as anything less than a person is to rob them of life itself. That is why Maimonides was so adamant that people giving and receiving charity should not meet face-to-face. I must admit, however," he said, looking from me to Alyes, "that it is an odd subject for the two of you to be discussing."

"Alyes wishes to help the poor, Papa, as part of her new duties as the rebbetzin. I am trying to help her."

"A virtuous wish, wife," Papa commented. "You are going about your new life precisely as anyone could wish. I know Shira will benefit from your example as her new mother. And now, I hear my students stirring, so I will be off to prepare for the day. You both, I know, will have much to do as well."

I watched as my father and Alyes left the room. I sat for a moment, thinking over the unexpected conversation. I liked Alyes much more than I had thought I would. But with a start, I realized I still needed to resolve the issue of my studying with my father. I was determined not to let our daily sessions slip away from me because he had taken a new wife.

IX

She stretches out her hand to the poor;
Yea, she extends her hands to the needy . . .
She looks well to the ways of her household,
And eats not the bread of idleness.

SO SAYS PROVERBS, as though Solomon the Wise had my stepmother before him as his model. There was not a moment in the day during the first four years of her marriage when Alyes was not engaged in cooking, mending, washing, visiting the sick, or feeding the hungry. All of Falaise came to marvel at this small woman, shy, yes, by her own account, yet braver than a lioness in the face of sickness and poverty.

I was her assistant and the days that had seemed to be so heavily laden with labor were lightened by the addition of even more. As we worked, she asked me to recite the prayers so she could practice them; we sang beautiful hymns as we transformed Papa's academy together into an oasis of order and tranquility. The fathers of potential students had knocked on our door before, but now there was a clamor of candidates who wished to study with us. Papa hired two tutors to work with him and there were plans to build an extension onto the house if town officials allowed it.

As Maimonides recommended, we remained anonymous while providing food for the poor. We constructed a small hut at the farthest corner of the synagogue grounds, well shaded by mulberry trees and accessible from the street as well as the yard. Papa showed the carpenter exactly where to place the hut's two doors. One door was for those who came to give and the other one was for those who came to take. We posted a schedule on both doors, so the givers and receivers would not meet accidentally. Papa had the *shamash* read the times out in synagogue every week for the benefit of those who could not read.

The hut had no windows, but widely spaced pinholes in the rooftop let in light. Alyes and I, with the help of several of our neighbors, arranged the food on three tables—one was for dairy, one for meat, and the third for *pareve,* food that could be eaten at either milk or meat meals. Cast-off clothing and household items were placed on a fourth table. We devised rules, too, for acceptable contributions—clothes were to be neatly darned and clean, food unspoiled.

Because we did not watch the doors, we had no way of knowing if only Jews took our food or if the poor Gentiles of Falaise—and there were many of them—found their way to the charity hut as well. From the volume of food that disappeared each day, enough for ten to twenty people, we suspected that our generosity fed more than just our own community. But that, we told ourselves, was in God's hands.

A scant hour was allotted between our acceptance of donations and the opening of the door for those in need, so that the food would not spoil or attract insects. Even so, at first when Alyes and I cleaned the hut and prepared it for the next day's offerings, we sometimes found food crawling with maggots. We held our noses as we gingerly swept it into a bowl and discarded it in a distant corner of the yard. After that, we declared that food must be covered by cheesecloth or placed inside closed baskets, particularly during the summer.

The hut was just one of the many charities Alyes instituted during her first four years of marriage. When Papa convinced her to allow me to continue my studies, she thought about it and decided I should assist her whenever she left the house to visit the poor and the sick. The more the townsfolk saw me living the commandments, she was wont to say, the less likely they were to carp and complain because of the time I devoted to study. And in time, the murmurs died down.

Yet it was during these pleasant years that I learned how people harbored both generous and malicious impulses. The women who approved our charitable work, who labored alongside us in the charity hut, would eye Alyes's slender frame, nudging each other and whispering that the rabbi's wife had still not become pregnant, all these years after the wedding. Alyes would see them winking in her direction and her shoulders would droop in shame.

"Is it because of the Black Scourge?" I overheard her ask my father once. "It killed my husband, my boys; did it let me survive only to turn me barren?"

Not knowing I was watching, he put his arms around her. "I don't believe so, my darling," he said, kissing her hair. "I believe God will grant our dearest wish. But in the meantime, my life and Shira's are blessed by you. So you must not worry about it."

But Alyes did worry. So when she began to wake up during her fourth year of marriage needing stale bread rounds and barley water to settle her stomach, we all rejoiced. I took on the duty of cleaning out the hut more and more often on my own in the blue twilight of the late summer evenings. For while Alyes woke full of energy, come nightfall she tired easily and sought her bed early, my father's anxious glance following her as she ascended the stairs to their room.

———•———

"Alyes, you must rest."

By late summer, Alyes had grown tremendously, her huge belly pushing out the skirt of her copious dress. It's what happens, she told me, laughing at my fascinated face, when you have already had children—the body remembers how it stretched before and expands more quickly with each additional child. I saw the sadness that she had to blink back as she mentioned her other children. While I wondered sometimes what it must have been like for her to lose an entire family to the Black Scourge, I never felt I could ask her about it.

During one weeklong hot spell, Alyes wilted in the cruel heat. Sleep would not come. Her ankles were swollen, the skin around them cracking and peeling. She wore a leather belt as an amulet, embroidered with red stones and protective verses. When the pregnancy had first been confirmed, my delighted father had indulged her request to clasp one of his belts around her middle. It seemed to both my father and me to be a particularly cruel article of clothing to wear in this heat, but Alyes refused to part with it.

"I am only four months pregnant, child; how can I possibly rest this early in the day?" Alyes asked, nonetheless sinking down onto one of the kitchen benches with a grateful sigh.

"Remember, Mina and I used to do all the work before you came—perhaps not as well, because you have taught me much these last few years. But the cool weather will be coming soon."

"It cannot come too soon for me!" Alyes said, shifting awkwardly on the hard bench, and closed her eyes. "Look, let me rest for a few minutes, then I'll recover my strength. You are a good girl, Shira."

I set a pitcher of water and a wooden cup next to her. "It's fresh water, Alyes. Mina went to the stream for it."

But there was no response. I saw from the rhythmic expanding and lowering of my stepmother's chest and stomach that she had fallen into a fitful sleep.

It was time to bring food to the charity hut. Alyes had baked two extra loaves of bread, and the vines of the kitchen garden were heavy with cucumbers and summer squash. I cut each loaf into four chunks and placed them into a basket. Taking another basket for the vegetables, I went outside to pick the fresh produce.

Stooping under the glittering noonday sun made my head spin. When I stood up, I had to reach out to balance myself. The basket filled with vegetables was heavy and I was grateful the hut was dimly lit, allowing me to escape the persistent glare. As usual, I entered the hut at the end of the hour for donations. Alyes and I always tried to be the last visitors, so we could make sure all was in order before those in need arrived.

The dank shadows of the hut revived me somewhat, but I still felt a buzzing at my temples as I surveyed the small room. Alyes was proud of this particular form of *mitzvah*. Even the Gentiles were taking notice of the Jews' charity hut. The mother superior of La Trinité and a group of priests and nobles from the town had visited. In many of his letters to his fellow rabbis throughout Ashkenaz, Papa used the hut as an example of how true charity can live in the world. He was elated when several of them sent emissaries to Falaise to observe how the hut worked and its effect on the community.

Everything appeared to be in order on this hot day. I was just about to leave when the other door opened and someone stepped inside—a dark figure wrapped in a cloak and hood despite the heat. It happened so quickly. I lowered my head to avoid recognizing the seeker of charity and moved toward the exit. But then the man threw back his hood and spoke my name.

"Shira—don't go."

My dizziness returned at the shock of hearing that particular voice. I tottered, flinging out an arm for balance. Nicholas Donin quickly stepped forward and grabbed my forearm, keeping me from falling.

"Shira—are you all right?"

I could not help myself. I looked into the man's piercing blue eyes

and felt my knees buckling. His warm fingers encased my forearm pos-
sessively. If anyone walked in . . .

"Let go," I demanded, pulling my arm away. "The ban! I can't talk to
you. And even if there were no *cherem* . . . you shouldn't touch me!"

His angular jaw hardened. "Why did I think you'd be different? That
you'd be kind? But I forget," he said slowly, "you only have heard about
my disgrace through your father. You do not know the entire story."

"Nicholas, I trust my father. Completely. I am not interested—"

"Not interested . . ." Donin shook his head and smiled mirthlessly.
"Still just the good little daughter—though you have grown tall over the
last few years . . . tall and beautiful."

I blushed. My cheeks were burning hot, but I felt cold and shaky inside. "Why are you here?" I asked, trying to break the heady spell of his
words and piercing stare.

"All of Ashkenaz has heard of Sir Morel's charity hut. And I—the
pariah, unwelcome in the synagogue, unable even to earn my living
among my own people—I am hungry. Does *cherem* mean I must starve
to death?"

"Of course, if you are hungry, the hut is here for you to take what you
need. But there are times posted—"

"I was waiting, Shira, when I saw you enter the other door. I had to
talk with you. I had to. Should I beg your forgiveness for wanting to
marry you all those years ago? How *wise* you were not to accept me."

I felt my heart shift, heavy, like a stone. "You sound so bitter, Nicholas!"

"'You sound so bitter, Nicholas,'" Donin mimicked with a sneer. "I
am bitter, Shira. Can you imagine what my days and nights are like?
Not to speak with a single soul who believes in the same God I do? Not
to receive the simplest of courtesies—the good-morning greeting, the
gossip of the marketplace, the warmth of another man's hand clasped to
my shoulder? And"—his voice grew husky as his eyes traveled over my
body—"to be forbidden the soft caresses of a beloved wife?" He reached
out a hand again, touching my shoulder, my cheek. I stood still, allowing it, as though enthralled. He continued, more softly now, his words

making me melt inside with pity for him. "I cannot earn money among my own. When I pray in the synagogue, I stand isolated, no man daring to wish me so much as a *'Shabbat shalom.'* Do I sound bitter? Lonely? Mere words cannot express the depths of my despair and solitude!" His hand moved from my cheek to take both of my hands in a tight grasp. I gasped, trying to move away.

"I am sorry—truly, truly sorry—for you. But could you not even now repent of your heretical ways and return to the community?" Tears sprang to my eyes.

His expression softened. "I was aching to speak with someone— anyone—even a foolish girl. But this is just too painful—like ripping bandages from a festering wound. No, Shira. There is no return for me, just a plunging deeper and deeper into the abyss."

"If I spoke with my father . . . ?"

He dropped my hands, moved closer, and put his arms around me, pulling me to him. I stood cradled against his chest, feeling the warmth of his breath on the nape of my neck. He bent and kissed my forehead, lingered with his mouth in my hair. His breathing grew labored. I was terrified he would not let me go. I struggled in his grasp. His arms tightened about me.

"I want—one kiss," he murmured. "I wanted you to be my bride. I want . . ."

Again, fear jangled through my shocked body, giving me strength. I ducked my head, refusing to let his searching lips touch mine. But he was a grown man and I was still only fourteen years old. He reached down and clutched my chin with one hand. He bent and put his lips against mine.

It was as if the world stopped, my entire body transformed into sensation. He devoured my mouth, kissing me until I felt I could not breathe. I could feel his arms pulling me closer, ever closer to him. I pulled and pushed against him, desperate, fighting not only his strength but that part of me that wanted to give in and let him have what he wished. He sensed my struggle and laughed a little, deep in his throat— and unexpectedly let me go.

"Speak of this to no one, Shira. It would not help me and could do you great harm." Donin drew himself back and commanded, "Leave me. I'll wait until you are safely back home before I take some food. I go to Italy, hoping to find a community that will accept me and my ideas. You won't be bothered by me again."

"I wish I could help you . . ." The feeling of hot and cold had returned. I was shaking inside, but my cheeks pounded with heat.

He gave me one last soft look. "I know. But just—just leave." Donin drew his hood over his head, turning away.

I reached out an arm to him, then let it drop. I turned and left, walking quickly back to the house.

I knew I could speak to no one of my meeting with Nicholas. But the thought of his isolation gnawed at me. Two days later, my father gathered some of the younger boys around him in the cool of the summer courtyard for an evening story. He told them how Moses, having brought the Children of Israel to the Promised Land, was not permitted to step foot inside it. I sat a few paces away from them at a stone table, busily sharpening feathers to be used as quills. A full moon was rising, and there was enough light for this task. As my hands moved at the finicky work and my head remained bowed over the pile of feathers, I listened closely and was struck by an unwelcome sense of God's cruelty. I imagined Moses feeling as solitary and abandoned as Nicholas felt now. Perhaps it was a wicked comparison—certainly, hindsight makes it appear so—but I continued to be plagued by thoughts of Nicholas Donin, who was on his way to Italy. And, wrong though it might have been, I could not resist whispering a prayer that he might find what he was seeking.

It was a prayer that would return to haunt me.

EVEN

Male and female God created them.
—Genesis 1:28

I WOULD ALWAYS CONSIDER THE DAY that my half brother was born to be a turning point in my life, the day when I crossed from childhood to womanhood. Although Jewish Ashkenaz considered me marriageable from the age of ten and fully recognized me as a woman when my menses first came upon me, I did not feel any less a child than I'd been when I had played in the flax fields and had been captivated by Jeanne's fairy stories. Even those years when I had been forced to manage household chores on my own had not entirely robbed me of my youth.

But Alyes's birthing was an epiphany to me, teaching me what womanhood really meant: the danger and joy inherent in Eve's legacy, which we both dreaded and desired. As soon as Alyes felt the first contractions, we retreated into the room that had been specially prepared for her confinement, hung with amulets to protect her. I ran to fetch the iron knife that Alyes would keep under her pillow. It was a revelation to me that this knife, with the Hebrew acronym that formed its name,

BARZEL, magically invoked the names of the matriarchs Bilhah, Rachel, Zilpah, and Leah, who would safeguard my stepmother from the dangers of labor. At first there were long hours when Alyes screamed in agony, starting soon after the birth fluid flowed in great force from her. I stood to one side, ready to fetch and carry, console and soothe. The midwife examined her and shook her head.

"It will be a long labor," she said, sitting down on the settle beside Alyes's cot. "Can you go and make us both a cup of broth? We'll need nourishment in the coming hours."

Alyes's contractions stopped in the small hours of the night. The midwife was not alarmed by this and, despite my fears, insisted that we could leave my stepmother and seek our own beds. She sent me to my room, where I threw myself down on the mattress I shared with Mina. I fell into an exhausted slumber almost instantly.

I was rocked out of that deep sleep in the hour before dawn by a persistent pounding on the front door. Mina, predictably, sat up in bed, cowering in fright at the unexpected visitor. Draping a shawl around my shoulders, still groggy from sleep, I staggered downstairs. Mina crept behind me. My father called down to wait, not to open the heavy rope latch of the door. A few of the students milled about, looking bewildered and sleepy.

Papa descended a moment later, a warm mantle thrown over his shoulders. The knocking, which had grown louder, was now so fierce that the entire door frame shuddered.

"Who is it?" Papa called out, yelling to be heard over the noise. "What do you want? You are disturbing a sleeping household and a woman about to give birth. Speak!"

The banging ceased. We all sighed in relief at the sudden silence. "Sir Morel, open the door without delay," a gruff voice commanded. "The baron requires it."

Papa looked around at us, his face a study of indecision. "You should go to your rooms, my *talmidim*, and you, Shira, and you, Mina. I do not—"

The pounding started again, making us all jump. "Sir Morel, open this door this instant or we will bring a battering ram to it!"

"What is it that you want? Who are you?" Papa answered, trying to shoo us out with one hand as he reached for the door latch with the other. Some of the students shrank back, ready to flee; Mina ran to the top of the staircase and stood there, transfixed. But I stood my ground, my heart beating so rapidly that I put a hand to my chest and pressed down to try to slow it.

"I am the commander of Baron la Folette's guard, Sir Morel. Open up, or we will—"

"I am trying to open the lock, give me a moment," Papa cried out. I noticed his hand trembled so that he could barely grasp the thick rope. One of the students, a newcomer to the school, saw this and bravely ran forward, taking the heavy rope cord, slipping it up and over the latch, and unlocking the door.

As soon as the latch was released, the door flew open and a gust of cold January air blew inside, bringing a heavy swirl of snow and ice in with it. The commander stood, arms folded, at the head of a contingent of some fifteen men. These were not the usual ragtag soldiers we sometimes saw loitering in the village, on their way from one of Europe's many battles to another, or even the ardent but inexperienced Crusaders, gathered together by the force of a sermon and the pull of lands to reclaim from the Turks. Instead, these were professional men, their boots polished and their backs ramrod straight. It was ice cold outside, but not one man moved an inch forward into the warmth of the house until the commander, with a slight movement of one hand and the order of "March forward, men!" permitted them to do so.

The commander waited until his soldiers had filed in, then followed them. He was a man with an angular jaw and eyes that, with their steady, piercing gaze, reminded me of the hawks and falcons that the nobles sometimes flew near the castle.

For the rest of my life, whenever anything terrified me, the sensations of that frozen moment reverberated back upon me. Mina hunched on the landing above, sobbing in fear. The boys stood as rigid and breath-less as statues. My father kept himself upright through sheer force of will, one hand gripping his heart. Confined in her room, my stepmother keened shrilly in the agony of labor once again. Rooted to the floor, I felt the cold of the wintry dawn seeping inexorably into my heart despite the fiery heat of my cheeks.

"Welcome to my home, commander," Papa said, one arm flung wide, allowing only a slight tremor to pervade his voice. He moved aside to allow the men to tramp farther within, their heavy boots tracking newly fallen snow in our entranceway.

The commander bowed his head slightly. "Sir Morel, Baron la Fo-lette orders you to come to the keep at Falaise Castle. The abbot, Father Jacques, has learned that a recent convert to the True Faith, one Ferrier Vidal, was seduced back to your heretical religion and was warmly wel-comed in your synagogue. If true, the man will burn for it as a heretic. As for your congregation's perfidy in aiding him, I am sure there will be some new Jew tax assessed upon you all."

A weighty silence followed. Papa looked from one stricken face to the other, as though he were gathering strength from the young men in his charge. A long, drawn-out shriek from the room where my step-mother lay confined shattered his composure. He slumped for a mo-ment against the open door frame. But when he looked back up, his expression was calm and determined.

"Shira, my girl, your stepmother needs you, please do not tarry here," he told me. He turned to the commander. "I'm afraid this summons comes at an inopportune moment. My wife is about to give birth. Could I not report to the keep in a day or two, after she is safely delivered?"

"Impossible," the commander said, not unkindly but decisively.

"Very well. Shira, come here, daughter," Papa said.

I ran into his outstretched arms. He wrapped me in a quick, strong hug, then put his hands onto my head, whispering a benediction over me. I blinked as hard as I could, to keep the tears that were gathering in my eyes from escaping.

"Listen to me carefully, Songbird. You must not tell your stepmother that anything is amiss until after she has delivered the baby. She must be kept calm and happy, even if you are forced to lie to her. Do you understand me?"

I nodded, unable to speak.

"Good. I have faith that you will care for my wife. When I return—in a few hours, I hope and pray—we will celebrate a new life in this house. Go, now . . ." He gave me a little shove, and I started away slowly. But I could not bring myself to mount the steps while he still lingered.

"Meir ben Baruch, come here," my father called. The newcomer who had lifted the latch moved forward. When I'd been introduced to this student several nights before, I had paid scant attention to him, keeping my eyes lowered even as Papa praised the breadth of his knowledge. He was my own age—we were both fifteen—and still young for a scholar. Yet as we sat over our studies the next morning, Papa told me of Meir's seemingly limitless ability to master new ideas. He had, Papa said, a mind seen perhaps only once or twice in a generation.

"Meir, you are new to this *yeshiva* and considerably younger than many of the others, but you are still the most knowledgeable of my *talmidim*. I ask you to take charge of the lessons today. Do not let my absence disrupt our studies. Right, *bachurim*?"

The students murmured agreement and Meir accepted my father's charge with a nod. Just as he had prayed over me, Papa extended a hand over the group of anxious boys and blessed them. Then he turned to the commander.

"I will ask one of my students to fetch my cloak and we can go, sir."

Meir ben Baruch, helped by two of the older students, ushered the boys into the schoolroom. A moment later, one of them emerged with my father's cloak. My father took it from the boy's trembling hands and exchanged it for his mantle. He wrapped the cloak around his shoulders, looking at me all the while with slightly unfocused eyes. Yet another shriek from my stepmother's room reminded me that I had my own duty to perform. With a sob that I could not restrain, I turned and ran up the stairs.

———•———

My brother was born in the fading light of the late winter afternoon. While Alyes had not been told my father had been marched off to the castle keep for questioning, she seemed to intuit that all was not right downstairs. Luckily, our traditions forbid her quitting the room where she was confined, even during those shorter and shorter lulls in her travails. So she had to trust the reassurances that both the midwife and I lavished upon her as we mopped her brow and encouraged her through what seemed to my untutored eye to be unremitting waves of pain.

Downstairs, the boys followed their dawn prayers with additional ones, beseeching the Almighty to safely deliver from danger both my father and the woman I had grown to love as a mother. Meir ben Baruch, rising to the occasion, kept the boys fully occupied with their studies.

I was on the landing, calling to Mina to bring more water, when Mina handed me a note from Meir. She scurried back down for the water. I read quickly. Meir named several boys he planned to send to the town. One boy would be sent to acquaint Isaac ben Michelin with what had occurred; another dispatched to the butcher's stall so that Acher ha-Levi could spread the word; a third to Bella Tova, to ask her to take command of the kitchen for the day, freeing me from that task. I didn't like the idea. I ran downstairs to the classroom. Peering inside, I saw Meir moving among the students, their heads bowed over their books.

"Meir ben Baruch?" I asked. "May I speak with you for a moment?"

I liked the fact that he came out quietly and without fuss. The two of us stood in the hallway outside the classroom, not looking at each other, our voices low and constrained by the awkwardness of our unexpected proximity.

"Should we really alarm the town with what is happening here?" I asked.

Through lowered eyelashes, I glanced at the boy's face and figure.

He was of middling height—though, I reminded myself, boys and girls grow at different rates—and while we were the same age, I was slightly taller. This gave me a better vantage point from which to study him. There were soft brown freckles on his pale cheeks, and his reddish hair was rich and curly. There was an intensity about him—the way he stood, the way he spoke, the sharp glances that he stole in my direction every few minutes—that made me liken him to a Shabbat candle just kindled. Had I said so to the girls at the synagogue, they would probably have considered it an odd object with which to compare him. But there was an inherent spark to Meir ben Baruch that cast a comforting glow over the dull, overcast, nightmarish day.

"I think they must already know," he said. "The soldiers will have led your father through the town. Someone will have seen them."

"But why send Avner, of all students? He is apt to say more than he needs to and will alarm everyone."

"That's why I want to send him. He is fidgeting and whispering and disturbing the others. I want to get him out of the schoolroom for a bit to calm him down. Don't worry, the note he'll carry will reassure the townsfolk."

I looked at the confident expression on his face, nodded, and turned to go. But he reached out as though he would touch my elbow, pulling his hand back before his fingers reached my arm. "Are you all right?" he asked. "I can only imagine how you must be feeling right now."

His words made me want to dissolve into tears. But there was no time for such weakness. "Go ahead and send Avner," I said, hearing my stepmother wail again. I ran quickly upstairs, feeling his eyes fixed on my back as I went.

When it was time for the baby to emerge, the midwife helped Alyes crouch down. She muttered, over and over, "'Quickly the crouching one is freed,'" a verse from Isaiah that purports to hasten a safe birth. An interminable period of pushing followed. Bella Tova and I each clasped one of Alyes's hands in support. I tried to ignore her fingers crushing my knuckles and to blot out the terror I felt at Alyes's head rocking wildly back and forth. Her eyes rolled up into her head, making her seem more animal than human, more primal than my own dear stepmother could ever be. Suddenly, the midwife cried, "I see the head crowning!" In a rush of blood and fluid, the small, wrinkled figure broke loose from Alyes's womb. The midwife's hands moved to clasp him safely. She smacked the bottom of his foot, and the baby let out an indignant bellow that made us all laugh in relief. "A boy!" she crowed, and our joy grew even stronger.

Bella Tova took the baby from the midwife and brought him to a low table where a basin, towels, diapers, and salt were prepared. She washed off the effulgence of birth from his tiny body, counting out that he had, yes, ten fingers, yes, ten toes, ah, all was well with him. In keeping with our traditions, she sprinkled him with salt to ward off demons and swaddled him tightly in a diaper so only his round, red-creased face and deep blue eyes could be seen.

While I would have expected Alyes to move back to her bed, both she and the midwife knew better. Alyes remained in her crouching position, holding on to my exhausted shoulders for support, until she delivered the afterbirth. The midwife caught it in a bowl, covering it and murmuring over it. "I will bury it out back, Shira," she told me, noticing my questioning glance, "so that no animal finds it and eats part of the little man's soul."

The baby, still wailing, was brought to Alyes's breast. Nuzzling like a blind kitten, he found her teat and took hold, almost ferociously. "Ah, this one has a strong *neshamah,* a strong spirit," Bella Tova cooed. "You must be hungry, little mama. I will go and prepare the chicken I know the Rav has been keeping for just this occasion."

"Can you tell the Rav about his son?" whispered Alyes from slack lips. Her eyes were drooping and it looked like both she and her new baby would be asleep in moments.

I looked at Bella Tova and shook my head. She nodded at me, understanding. "Of course I will, Alyes—but you need your sleep now. The Rav will be so pleased that he has a son at last! You go to sleep and dream about what a wonderful scholar this little man will become . . ."

Alyes's eyelashes fluttered on her cheeks and were still. The midwife took the baby from her relaxed fingers and settled him beside her in a small wooden cradle. Then she picked up the bowl holding the after-birth and carried it away.

"Shira," whispered Bella Tova, lingering at the door. "Stay with your stepmama for a minute or two, until I can fetch Mina. She cannot be left alone, you know."

I did know, for of all the birth fears Jewish mothers experienced, the terror of Lilith was the strongest. We all knew about Lilith, the rejected first bride of Adam who devoured babies in revenge for his casting her off. She had been created from the same clay as Adam and, consider-ing herself his equal, refused to lie beneath him when he demanded it. Lilith spoke God's Ineffable Name and through its power grew wings and learned to fly. When she refused to return to Adam, God sent three angels to her, who proclaimed she must kill a hundred newborn chil-dren every day. Only by hanging amulets on the door outside, inscribed with the names of the three angels—Senoy, Sansenoy, and Semangelof—could infants be protected from her fatal breath. The protection of the amulets was not absolute, however, so a watch was kept by the women of the town, day and night, until the boy was circumcised and safe from the threat.

Exhausted, I sat down in a chair beside Alyes's bed and thought about my father for the first time in hours. All the terror I had tamped down into a corner of my soul rushed back as I considered what might even then have been happening to him. Was he being tortured? It was not unheard of—the rack and the thumbscrews were often employed in the dungeons of Falaise Castle. I clamped a hand across my mouth to stop from crying out in fear and horror and—Lilith be damned!—rose to flee the room.

Luckily, Mina was at the door just as I reached it. Shoving her inside, I ran downstairs. Bella Tova was plucking the just-slaughtered chicken at the kitchen table. She called out to me.

"Shira! Shira, come here, child, and let me give you something to eat."

Shaking my head, I grabbed my cloak and headed out the kitchen door. Bella Tova ran to the entranceway. "Shira! It's getting dark! It may snow! Come back inside now."

But I couldn't make myself be that good little girl everyone expected me to be, not when my father was in danger and might die without knowing that he had finally realized his most longed-for ambition. Let me just tell him, I thought, slipping and sliding my way out of the icy yard, they will simply have to let me tell him about his son.

IGHT

*Slay them not, lest my people forget it, but scatter
them abroad with thy power.*
—SAINT AUGUSTINE

I WAS HALFWAY THROUGH TOWN before Meir ben Baruch caught
up with me.

"Shira!" he exclaimed, grabbing my arm and pulling me around.
"Shira, stop!"

I shot a look straight at him. He looked angry, bewildered, and worried, but he held my gaze. Snow began to fall and the rest of the town
sought shelter inside their homes and shops. I couldn't see any faces
staring out from the windows, not that it would have mattered. It felt as
though Meir ben Baruch and I were alone—another Adam and Eve, cast
forth from security into a threatening, mysterious world of deepening
shadows.

"Let me go," I cried, yanking my arm free. "I have to tell my father
about his son. I will never forgive myself if they kill him before he learns
he finally fulfilled Hillel's requirement as a parent . . ."

The intelligence and understanding I had sensed before in Meir's eyes glowed once again, leading me to believe he understood what I needed to do and why. "'Male and female God created them,'" he murmured, showing he too knew the passage. "The girl reads Hillel, yet."

"I will come home as soon as I have told my father," I promised.

We stood for a moment, snowflakes hitting our faces and hair, growing wetter as the snow settled upon us and melted. Meir looked straight into my face as he said, "*Sehr gut.* I mean—that's good. I will go in your stead, Shira. They are men, they will listen to a boy before they listen to a girl."

"No," I cried. "He is *my* father. I must be the one to tell him."

"You are stubborn for a girl," Meir proclaimed, shaking his head. "I've never met one like you. But you know what? It's odd, but I like it."

"I had no thought of pleasing you in mind, Meir ben Baruch—none whatsoever," I said, turning to leave. I was troubled by the thought that my father might be suffering while I dishonored him by my immodest exchange with this young scholar.

"I will go with you, nevertheless," the boy insisted. He fell into step beside me.

We made our way in silence across the slippery cobblestones of the town, turning up the dirt lane that led to the castle. The building's familiar form that perched on the hilltop over my town had always symbolized home to me. But now it had been transfigured into a threat. A glance at Meir made me realize that he sensed the danger that awaited us at the castle.

The path to the keep wound upward and the snow, which had gathered force, made it treacherous. I nearly slipped and was grateful for Meir's quick hand, which grasped my elbow to hold me upright. As we rounded the last curve and saw the gatehouse before us, we involuntarily drew back and looked at each other, reading the dread in each other's eyes. While I would not realize it for many years, that moment bound us together forever.

———————

When Meir and I reached the castle, the clouds that obscured the moon moved aside and the turrets above us shrouded us in deepest shadow. Meir banged as best he could with a half-frozen hand on the heavy guardhouse door. The guard came forward, an irritated scowl darkening his face.

"What do you want on this brutal night, children, rousting me out to face the devil's teeth?" he demanded. His tone, though brusque, was not unkind, and I remember thinking that he could not see our Jew badges, swathed as we were in cloaks and silhouetted in gloom.

"We have a message of some urgency for Sir Morel," Meir said.

"You mean the Jew? He's caused us no end of merriment here today. Some of the guards say he is a disciple of Beelzebub—others that he bathes daily in the urine of a good Gentile baby to get rid of his *foetor Judaicus.* He must do something, for he did not reek any differently than any other terrified man when they brought him past me!"

The guard's cackling laughter and his taunts about my father's body odors made no sense to me. But Meir knew better and was unwilling to let the insult go by uncorrected.

"His *foetor Judaicus*? In Worms, where I was born, we used to hear that old wives' tale, but our Nazarenes—our Christians, begging your pardon, guardsman—realized when they came to know us better that the Latin phrase is nothing more than myth. We Jews smell no different than any man born and we boast no horns, either!"

"No horns? No smell? Hah! That I absolutely refuse to believe. Everyone knows that you Jews are descended from the goat, and that the goat was descended from the devil himself. If you have no horns now, it's because you cut them off when you remove nature's own endowment to your manhood. Perverted creatures!"

The guard ushered us inside, shutting the door behind us. The guardhouse was ice cold, a tiny, thatched shelter only partially closed against the elements. A single stool sat tight against the wall closest to the castle. A thick wool cloak was draped over the stool, half falling to the ground. The guard cast a longing look toward it as he blew on his fingers.

"Guard, may I please see my father?" I asked, wanting to avoid a debate with this witless soul. Glancing at Meir, I noticed a flush of anger in his cheeks at the guard's persistent ignorance.

"Your father, eh? What's so urgent?"

Meir shook his head at me, but I couldn't see the harm in telling the man. "I want to let him know about his son. For he has a son, born this afternoon while your baron kept him imprisoned here against his will."

"A newborn boy, little Jewess? Well, you can't tell me that the infant has no horns! Did you see the babe? He has horns, right? And a tail, all wrapped up in a coil, like the little sow baby that he is?" In his eagerness to hear my response, the guard leaned forward and I smelled the odor of spiced ale and rotting teeth.

I tried to hide my repugnance. "He has no horns, no tail, and he is as perfect as any baby that was ever born," I ground out between gritted teeth. "Please, I want to see my father and tell him—"

"Ho, there, Jacques, what's forward?" a voice called from behind the guard. A man, apparently of higher rank, joined us, stepping into the guardhouse from the castle side.

"These two want to see the Jew."

"What for? Anyway, they are nearly done questioning him. Maybe an hour or so. Go home, children, wait for him there."

I sagged in relief, clutching Meir's sleeve so I would not fall. If they were letting him go this early, it probably meant that he hadn't been subjected to the thumbscrews and the rack. Men who were tortured remained in captivity for days, not mere hours. "Please, may we wait for him and escort him home ourselves?" I pleaded.

"Suit yourselves," he replied indifferently. We were shut outside the guardhouse to wait in the frigid air.

Snow was still falling, but it was coming down more slowly. Above us, the stars broke through the cluster of clouds. We stood on an outcropping of rock, perched over a steep incline, our backs against the mountainside. Below us, I knew, were the houses and buildings of the town, but they had all but disappeared in fog and darkness. We huddled out in the open, wrapping our arms about our bodies to try to warm ourselves. Stamping my feet to bring some feeling back to them, I suddenly thought about how my father might react to finding me alone, there, with a boy. I turned to Meir. "You don't need to stay. I will return with my father when they release him."

"If you think for one moment I intend to leave you alone here, with those men just a door away . . ."

"Truly, Meir ben Baruch, they won't hurt me."

"You are the strangest girl, Shira bat Shmuel. Ignorant and learned, brave and foolish—immodest and—"

"Hush," I chided him, shaking my head as I caught his half-scornful, half-admiring gaze. I worried about how I must look to him, with my dark hair mussed from the long hours of Alyes's confinement, my cheeks red with cold, my eyes shadowed in worry. "You mustn't keep talking!"

So we remained silent, looking everywhere but at each other. But looking anywhere but at him was difficult. I forced myself to think of my stepmother, at home with her babe, or of my father, whom I prayed would be released unscathed soon. But the thought that persisted was that this boy, whom my father praised for his intellect, was named Meir. The Hebrew word for "light" was the same name that had graced the husbands of my much-admired sister scholars, Bruriah and Rashi's daughter, Yocheved.

———◆———

We were startled by a call from the guardhouse.

"Ho, Jews! They want you inside. Come."

We looked at each other, apprehensive. "We do no harm waiting here," said Meir.

"Perhaps not," came the sergeant's voice, "but even so, they want you inside."

The door of the guardhouse swung open. We moved beyond the gates slowly and unwillingly, through the courtyard, and into the main castle.

The keep's corridors were lit with smoking braziers. The air was ripe with the sweat of men and the trapped air of a long winter. The sergeant's heavy boots reverberated on the flagstones as he ushered us through a maze of narrow hallways into a large room on the west side of the castle. The room was wood paneled, with three wall hangings embroidered with mythical beasts. The fourth wall was taken up by a huge hearth, in which an enormous fire roared. Two empty wood chairs, lined with velvet, were pulled up before the fire.

My father stood in the middle of the room, frowning at us both.

"Papa!" I shouted, running toward him. "Papa!"

I grabbed hold of his cloaked arm. He hugged me to him in a swift movement, then thrust me aside. "Shira! Meir! What in the name of all that is holy are you two doing here? Shira, is it Alyes? Has she—"

"Mama Alyes is fine, Papa—and you have a son! A fine, healthy boy!"

The grim expression on my father's face disappeared, replaced by a beatific grin. "A son . . . ," he whispered, casting his eyes toward the heavens as though he was thanking the Almighty.

"Good news, indeed," came a voice from a corner of the room. I turned. A monk stepped out of the alcove of tall mullioned windows, his black habit with a white cowl and scapular swinging as he strode forward to clap my father firmly on the shoulder. "Old friend, this is good news indeed."

"Brother Anton, this is my daughter, Shira. And Meir of Worms here is perhaps the most learned of my students."

"Ah, the genius! I have heard of you, Meir of Worms—the rabbis speak of your mind and heart with admiration."

Meir's eyes lit up at the compliment.

Noting the confusion on my face as I watched the monk and my father exchange knowing looks, Papa smiled slightly. "Brother Anton and I have been friends for many years, since I was a student in Paris. He is of the Gilbertine Order, from a city in England called Lincoln. He and I often discussed the differences between our two religions."

"Your father was relieved to find me here, I believe." Brother Anton nodded, his thin face puckering in amusement. "Better me than the fires and the tongs of the Inquisition, hey, Rabbi?"

"God forbid . . . ," my father whispered.

"When we heard you two were outside, shivering in the cold and probably in fear as well, I had the guards fetch you inside, and—ah! here is some warm food for you both."

A maidservant entered, carrying a heavy tray with two steaming bowls of broth. Meir and I glanced at my father for guidance, for it is forbidden for us to eat food prepared by Gentiles. The aroma of the hot soup made it difficult to resist. My father, seeing the pained expressions on our faces, shook his head regretfully.

But Brother Anton laughed. "It is all right, children—I had it fetched from the rooms of the good Jewess Naomi, the wife of the baron's physician, Liblin Levit à Strasbourg. Because the Jew doctor serves the baron so well, he allowed the couple to set up their own kitchen and pharmacy here in the castle. Rabbi, you know Naomi and Liblin, do you not?"

My father nodded in our direction. That was all the permission either of us needed. The soup was delicious—rich and meaty, with great globules of fat floating on the surface. As I drank it, I could feel my toes becoming prickly and painful. Yet I was glad they were no longer frighteningly numb, for I knew many people who had lost fingers and toes to the perishing cold of our winters.

Meir drank his soup. Then the words burst forth from him: "Rav Shmuel, I did not want to come, but Shira—"

My father put up a hand. "We will talk about this later, Meir."

"He kept the peace in the *yeshiva* beautifully today, Papa," I said.

"Later. Everything is fine at home?"

I nodded.

"Then you must both sit quietly to one side and allow us to finish our disputation. Brother Anton, did you want to call the baron back inside?"

There were two wooden stools near the windowed alcove. Meir sat on one and I on the other. Wide-eyed, I watched as two men entered and took their places on the upholstered chairs by the fire. It was easy to tell which one was Baron la Folette, the king's administrator of Falaise, a fleshy, heavyset man dressed in warm woolen and leather hunting clothes, his boots splashed with mud. Three large dogs followed him, barking and snapping toward us before he brought them to heel with a snap of his fingers. They lay down under his chair, every once in a while looking at us and growling deep in their throats. I would learn the second man was the abbot, Father Jacques. He was even thinner than Brother Anton and his black cassock hung on his spare frame loosely. His fingers were long and white and throbbed with thick blue veins, as did his narrow forehead. Brother Anton wore his hair in a tonsure—a single circular strip of hair surrounding his clean-shaven head. I wondered if the abbot did too, but his black skullcap covered most of his head, making it impossible to know.

"Continue, Brother Anton," said the baron, waving a languid hand.

"Sir Morel, we were discussing why a Jew, once baptized, is a heretic when he returns to your religion, while a Jew not yet saved from eternal damnation is not."

My father laughed. "You were discussing it, Brother Anton. You will forgive me for saying I cannot discuss something I do not believe in."

"Peace, Jew! Let the good monk speak!" snarled the abbot.

"You know what Saint Augustine said of you Jews, do you not, Sir Morel? 'Slay them not, lest my people forget it, but scatter them abroad with thy power.' Your people—unbelievers though you may be—witnessed the birth, the death, and the miracle of the accession of our Lord Jesus Christ. As such, you are privileged witnesses to that miracle. As such, we do you the immense favor of suffering you on our earth, even as you wander, homeless forever, throughout our Christian lands—because you bear witness."

"And this witnessing, you say, makes us superior to heretics?" my father mused.

"Indeed. But once a man sees the light and turns toward it, he cannot turn away without endangering his eternal soul."

"So let me understand you. Does our privileged state as witnesses mean we Jews are not—according to you, my dear friend monk—damned for eternity?"

"Of course you are damned," roared the abbot, and I was shocked at the raw hatred emanating from this bony man. "Tell him, Anton!"

My father looked quizzically at his friend, who nodded slightly.

"Oh, well," my father said with a shrug.

I glanced at Meir, who was trying to hide a smile. My father continued.

"So what difference does it make if he is a Jew returned or not? I must confess, Anton, I'm confused. You tell me that I'm damned, Shira's damned, Meir over there is damned—and Ferrier Vidal was damned before and is damned again. So why must the Church interfere?"

"Because," said the baron, who had watched the discussion through half-opened eyes, stifling yawns, "Ferrier Vidal accepted Christ and was saved for a time. If what I'm hearing is right, you Jews are a special case—don't quite see why, but I accept it if Brother Anton tells me so. But once you're saved, your name is written in Christ's blood, and to renege—"

"To renege is a sin against both man and God!" the abbot shouted.

"If you say so, Father Jacques, I am in no position to dispute you," said my father calmly. "But Ferrier Vidal only stopped to pray in my synagogue briefly, on his way to Milan—and he failed to tell us that he was once an apostate. So while I am sympathetic to your loss of a soul, I cannot see what that has to do with me or my community."

"Do you mean to tell me," Father Jacques intoned angrily, "that you wasted our entire day debating points of the Bible and theology when you could have told us this hours ago?"

"I tried to tell you so when I was first summoned, but no one would listen. And then Brother Anton—a friend whom I have not seen in many years—arrived from Paris specifically to debate me. It isn't often that I have such a worthy opponent. So I was reconciled to the loss of my day."

Brother Anton bowed, a small smile lighting up his thin face. "Thank you, Sir Morel—I, too, enjoyed our discussion. But you must hurry home now, to your wife and newborn son. Your daughter and student have thawed and I believe we have taken our debate as far as we can. If you will permit me to release the rabbi and his two young charges, Baron?"

The baron waved a hand. We were escorted forth, my father and Brother Anton bringing up the rear, talking about various acquaintances from their Paris days.

"Yechiel visits me on occasion and I him—and Moses de Coucy as well. It is easier now than it was in the early days of His Majesty Philippe Auguste. But there are many like Father Jacques, Shmuel, who condemn me for these conversations."

"Do you return to Paris soon? Meir here will be heading off to Paris to study with Yechiel in about two months' time. If any of your students wish to sharpen their debating skills on someone who can serve as a fine whetstone, they should seek him out."

"I have a few who might benefit from it. Oh, don't look so worried, young Meir—they study at the university in Paris with me and are less interested in your soul than in your knowledge of the Torah and Talmud. Although," Anton said with a laugh, "I should be careful saying that out loud. You never know who might be listening."

At the entranceway, I watched, bemused, as my father and the monk clasped each other's forearms fondly. "I hope to see you sometime in Paris, my friend," said the monk.

"Perhaps someday I will visit there. When I do, I will seek you out. May you travel safely, Anton."

"And you, Shmuel, may you stay safe at home as well."

———•———

We brought Papa home and I thanked the loving-kindness of *ha-Shem* for his deliverance. We restored him, a recovered hero of Israel, to the *yeshiva* and to his wife and babe. Only after much rejoicing that evening—jubilation over the safe delivery of both father and child—did he dismiss everyone to sleep. But as we left the room, he called to Meir ben Baruch to attend him. I wondered long into the night what they were saying to each other.

Mama Alyes remained abed, as is our custom, in the room where she lay confined. Her beautiful son—whom we would call Nathan ben Shmuel, named, at Papa's insistence, for her own firstborn son—nestled close at hand. After eight days, the child was circumcised, welcomed into the covenant of our people. Perhaps in these days of our *galut,* our exile, some might regard that as a bittersweet occasion. But it is still the best we have to offer the babe.

Mama Alyes was careful of her child, perhaps more so because she lost two boys to the Black Scourge. Nothing that could be done to defeat Lilith was left undone. Part of me wanted to laugh at all the superstitious trappings—the hanging of amulets, the murmuring of incantations. But after our recent escape from the whims of the Christians, I began to recognize just how thinly spun is the thread that connects us to life.

ART 2

PARIS, 1234–1242

O YOU, WHO BURN IN FIRE, ASK HOW YOUR MOURNERS FARE.
—*Elegy by Meir ben Baruch*

INE

The wealth of the rich is their fortified city.
—Proverbs 18:11

The city of Paris was much larger and more crowded than anywhere else on earth. At least that's what I told my father as the two of us drove past the Benedictine Abbey of Saint-Germain-des-Prés, a fortified church with tall, gray towers built centuries ago. We saw monks directing workmen near the sluggish Seine River, constructing buildings to be used by students of the newly founded University of Paris. We rode through the crenellated stone guard towers at Porte de Buci to enter the city. It was a humid summer's day in 4994—or, as the Christians count the years, 1234. I was nineteen years old. We bumped down the narrow streets on a small donkey cart packed high with the contents of my dowry.

"Paris will be a great city someday, Songbird," Papa said, slipping naturally into his schoolteacher manner, making me sad this was one of the last times he would instruct me. "Think of the immense walled enclosure we just passed through—added by our king's grandfather, Philippe Auguste—or of the Louvre, the great fortress just around the bend to our left. Le Palais Royal is directly ahead. Beyond our line of sight, the towers of Notre-Dame rise on an island in the Seine River. When I was last in Paris, the cathedral walls were still being constructed and now the work is nearly complete. With these grand edifices Paris seems more civilized than when I studied here in my youth. Back then it was more swamp than civilization and more frogs and toads lived here than people.

"But you and your husband will probably travel to many burgeoning cities. He will take you to his home in Worms, and to Italy or the exotic capitals of the East. The blue-tiled domes, fountains, and beautiful stone courtyards of the Mohammedans are more elegant than these hovels of plaster and timber. Paris seems large because you're a little country bird, used to pecking your worms in the quiet shelter of our small town. Hmm?"

My upbringing would not let me contradict my father, but, looking around at the close-packed, half-timbered stone buildings leaning against one another, crowding over the cobbled streets, I could not imagine a city with more buildings or more people. We passed immense stone churches and monasteries where men and even some women shut themselves up to pray their lives away. I could hear the chanting of Latin prayers drifting from arched windows as we drove by. Out on the bustling streets, people were everywhere—lounging in doorways, arguing at the market stalls, drinking companionably at small tables set out under cloth awnings upwind of the stench. When you caught a whiff, the smell rising from the streets was a nauseating mix of dung, fetid sewers, and rotting garbage. Our cart stopped as our donkey shied and brayed, raising its hoofs as if in pain or fear. Looking down, I saw he had stepped into a nest of small rodents. Not intimidated by our donkey's size or girth, they retaliated by biting its legs before fleeing to a more secluded spot.

We crossed the bridge to Ile de la Cité at Petit Point and turned into rue de la Colombe—Dove Street—located near the nearly completed cathedral. I caught my breath as the immense walls of the Cathédrale de Notre-Dame rose in front of me. I had never seen a church as large or as beautiful, with its seemingly delicate stonework tracing exquisite patterns on its outside walls. An army of workmen was busy there, some working on strange stone creatures in a courtyard while a master crafts-man chipped away at a marble stone, creating a stern-faced Madonna who would eventually be brought to form one of the figures in the por-tal of the cloisters. The laborers were busiest around the nave, where they were building a series of small chapels. Still others were working with pieces of colored glass that I would recognize in later years as part of the huge rose stained-glass window.

Papa and I had been invited to be guests at the home of one of his former students, Yitzik ben Ya'acov, until the wedding took place. The houses along rue de la Colombe were all new, rebuilt after the neighbor-hood had been flooded ten years earlier. It was then, Yitzik explained to us on the first evening after our arrival, that the street received its name. Two doves had nested in a windowsill of a house owned by a mason who worked at Notre-Dame. The rising waters caused the house to cave in, trapping one of the doves. But the second remained loyal to its mate, bringing it seeds and water in its beak until the waters receded and the mason could free the bird and restore his home. The street was renamed to commemorate this charming tale of devotion. The mason chiseled stone medallions into delightful dove shapes for each of his neighbors, who mounted them in the walls of their new homes.   •

"Even the *goyim* remember the tale of Noah and the ark, with the dove bringing back an olive branch to show Noah land was nigh," Yitzik ben Ya'acov commented, pointing to this branch in the beaks of many of the stone doves.

"A beautiful story, is it not, Shira? What a moral can be drawn from these two wild creatures—about love and loyalty!" my father ex-claimed.

I smiled. It *was* a lovely tale, especially a few days before my long-awaited wedding to Meir ben Baruch of Worms, after an engagement that had stretched out for many years as my betrothed traveled from one Jewish learning center to another.

We arrived in Paris on a Tuesday at noontide and spent the afternoon resting. Meir was still living in the dormitories that were attached to the Paris *yeshiva,* although he had written me that he had obtained modest lodgings for us nearby. We had exchanged many letters in the four years of our engagement, letters that I often placed under my pillow before I slept. Ours was a courtship of correspondence in which my betrothed's intense intellect was sweetened by professions of the love we two would someday share. I discovered Meir's fluent pen was as ardent as any courtier's.

As I dressed for our evening meal at Rabbi Yechiel's *yeshiva,* my trembling fingers could barely tie the laces of my gown. I studied myself in the small glass I had brought with me from Falaise. Thick black hair curled around my face and down my back. I would be sorry to have my hair shorn right before my wedding, but a wife was required to be modest. I thought I looked pale as the only color in my face rested high on my cheekbones. I stared at my dark eyes for a long moment. Would Meir be pleased with me? And would I be pleased with him? I wondered if I would recognize anything of the red-haired boy who had escorted me to the keep and studied for a few months with my father when I beheld the man whose bed I would share. What was he like now?

The great rabbi of Paris welcomed us, together with his daughter, Deina. She was wife to Judah ben David, a scholar I knew by repute from his correspondence with my father. It would not have been fitting for Meir to greet us, and I did not catch sight of him until we were ushered into the vast dining hall. I looked around the room, trying to locate my betrothed amid the crush of students and teachers. My heart pounded almost painfully when at last I saw him, seated at a table midway down the hall with the students in his charge. I followed Deina to a table off to the side, smiling and nodding as the women seated around me greeted me. As they chattered, asking about my journey and telling me about life as a *yeshiva* wife in Paris, I surreptitiously gazed at Meir from beneath my eyelashes.

No, he was no longer the boy who had studied with my father. He had grown tall during the years, his red hair darkened to a deep auburn, his curls tamed, his still clean-shaven chin jutting forward as he laughed at something one of the students said. I had worried that, as a scholar, he might have grown stooped and frail or be jaundiced or pale. But Meir held himself upright with careless grace, his face sun kissed and smooth. I felt relief that he was so comely. Then other thoughts assailed me unbidden. I pictured lying next to him in our marriage bed, thought of the intimacies that we would share. The trembling that had overwhelmed me in my bedroom returned. I clutched my hands together, hidden in my lap, and tried to regain my composure as I turned back to the women, who were still barraging me with questions and information.

We ate a festive three-course meal, my father enjoying the place of honor beside Rabbi Yechiel on his right-hand side and my father-in-law to be, Rabbi Baruch, seated to his left. Craning my head, I stole some glances at Rabbi Baruch. After all, would not the young man resemble his father later in life? What I saw pleased me. Baruch was a tall and dignified man, his thoughtful gray eyes gleaming with enjoyment as the three men talked animatedly. I wondered at the absence of Bruria, my mother-in-law to be. Perhaps, like my stepmother, she had decided that the trip was too much for her. But that didn't seem likely. Meir had written of his mother's disappointment that the marriage blessing would not be held in Worms, where she might personally arrange the festivities. Something about Meir's letters when he wrote of his mother made me wary. I turned to Deina, but just as I opened my mouth to ask the question, Rabbi Yechiel rose to lead us in the blessings before the meal.

After each guest ritually washed hands and recited the blessings, servants brought out huge tureens of leek soup, with a side dish of smoked herring.

The three rabbis of honor spent much of the meal engaged in a discussion few of the students could fully follow, traversing as they did centuries of scholarship and debating obscure points of law. My Meir, however, listened intently, his face alight with comprehension and delight. Still shaking slightly as I watched him, I found it difficult to tear my eyes away. I was happy to see him sneaking glances in my direction as well.

The women were served last, after the youngest students. I was half-afraid my grumbling stomach would make my impolite hunger known to the women seated around me.

To my right was an empty seat. As we were waiting to be served, Deina, seeing me glance at it, nudged her neighbor, and the two of them laughed.

"She just couldn't stay out of the kitchen, could she?" the woman next to Deina whispered.

"No, there was some delicacy she wanted her beloved son to eat . . . ," Deina replied tiredly, out of one corner of her mouth.

With dismay fluttering in my chest, I guessed the identity of the missing guest. A moment later, a large woman dressed in a dark green overdress tied at the waist with a ribboned belt of twisted cord came striding into the men's section, bearing a large wooden bowl that she placed, with some ceremony, in front of my betrothed.

"Meir, I have made for you *ein Spise von Bonen*—your favorite stew of beans, with the caraway seeds that I brought specially for you from Worms," she declared.

The students around him snickered and my heart sank, thinking of his embarrassment. But if he felt any shame, he masked it well, rising to his feet and taking his mother's hand in his, bringing it sweetly to his lips.

"*Danke, Mütti*," he murmured. "I have not enjoyed bean stew for many years. But you go sit and eat now. You must be tired from your journey."

"Tired? Me? Meir, you should know your mother better!" She threw her head back and laughed.

Still holding her hand, he drew her closer and whispered something into her ear. She patted him on the shoulder and strode briskly in the direction of the empty chair beside me. My breathing constricted and, my heart thudding almost painfully in my chest, I prepared myself to meet my mother-in-law.

"Deina, I must compliment you on the manners of your kitchen staff," Rebbetzin Bruria boomed as she approached. "Your servants were careful not to let me see the faces they made behind my back!"

Deina rose from her seat, a forced smile on her face. "Surely, Bruria, they understood you invaded their kitchen only out of your feelings of motherly love?"

"Well, we wandering mothers must set up camp wherever we can. My new daughter-in-law will discover that to be true before too many years elapse. And speaking of my daughter-in-law, where . . . ?"

I rose hastily, almost upsetting my basin of soup. "I am Shira bat Shmuel," I said, controlling my voice with an effort, making what I hoped was a graceful curtsy. "I am pleased to meet you at last."

"At long last, one might well say," said Bruria, looking me up and down, her glance lingering on my midsection in a manner that made me squirm. Was she actually calculating how many grandchildren I might deliver from between my narrow hips?

Her next words proved that indeed she was. "Your mother had many troubled births, did she not? Here, sit down and finish your soup, although . . ." She seated herself next to me and leaned in, to whisper in a voice that carried down the length of the table, "I saw what went into that soup and can only hope yours is a strong stomach."

Deina dropped her spoon, gasping, and pointedly turned her shoulder to address the woman on her right. I couldn't help the minor reproof that rose to my lips: "It is a delicious soup, especially after such a long journey."

Bruria sniffed, eyeing me balefully, but ignored my slight rebuke, barreling back to the topic that was clearly uppermost in her mind: "I must admit I remain concerned about your mother's history of miscarriages."

"She had a tragic time of it, I'm afraid," I said. Because Alyes had filled the gap so beautifully, it had been many years since I had felt myself yearning for my mother. But at that moment, I would have given almost anything to have her sitting next to me, defending me from this rude woman. Glancing toward Meir, who was watching the two of us out of the corner of his eye as he supervised his young students, I realized with a sinking heart that it was my duty to put aside my chagrin and placate Bruria. "I take after my father's side of the family, physically, I mean. And my aunts all have large families."

"*Gut.* At nineteen, you are old to begin breeding, but a few years of pregnancies will help you catch up. But no miscarriages, mind!"

I smiled and agreed, feeling I was betraying my poor mother. "I hope to have a son this first year, a daughter the next. I see the delight children have brought to my father and my stepmother, and I am eager for that joy."

"Oh, the order in which they come doesn't matter, just so long as they do come and you have at least two of each. That way, even with illness and misadventure, you can guarantee the family name will be safe for another generation. But, here, you're not eating your delicious soup!"

The soup had grown cold and I was now a little suspicious of the small pieces of green floating on top. "I am actually more tired than hungry, I fear," I replied.

"Well, after my own long journey, I suppose you expect me to be weary. But I am never tired. Although only one of us would have had a journey to undertake if you had come to Worms to be married!"

The words slipped out before I could recall them: "Perhaps I should have been married in Falaise—where my stepmother and brothers and sisters could have seen me wed! Then only one of us *would* have had to undertake a journey—and, after all, *you* are never tired."

"Brides should be married from the homes of their husbands," Bruria said, her ruddy color deepening in her jaw and neck. "That is a well-established custom."

Glancing across the room, I saw Meir frowning at us. My father was glaring at me, shaking his head emphatically. My father-in-law-to-be had covered his mouth with a hand. I was afraid he was trying to mask his horror at our argument. But a moment later, he let his hand slip and I saw a grin that he quickly brought under control. As I stared at him, stunned by what his smile revealed, he nodded encouragingly in my direction. I felt the tightness in my chest subside a little and decided to appease Bruria's hurt dignity.

"I agree. That is why I came to Paris, for here is where your son, my betrothed, is living. I look forward to visiting Worms and becoming acquainted with his childhood home, but the trip would have been too far for my father to accompany me. His wife has just had a baby, you know, and he is anxious to return to his family in Falaise. I appreciate your willingness to come to Paris for our wedding—I am delighted that you are here to welcome me into my new family!"

Bruria looked me up and down, sucking in her ample cheeks for a long moment. "It is time Meir consummates the match. Such a lengthy betrothal. He has a brilliant future and needs a helpmate to support him and raise his family. Though, I must admit, there were several merchants' daughters in Worms and the towns nearby who offered dowries far exceeding yours . . . but one should not let old regrets intrude upon new joys, I always say. You are experienced in running a *yeshiva,* so you were a natural choice. And your father is a good scholar, my husband assures me. Your children will continue our family's heritage of learning. So, yes, I suppose I must welcome you."

Bruria's reception of me was as tepid as the soup that they finally removed from the table. The second course was a vast array of meats, including roast lamb, jellied calf's head, and braised chicken, with honeyed carrots and a spiced wheat porridge known as frumenty. Blinking back tears, I picked up a sliver of the braised chicken with my clasp knife and fingers, careful to take only such small pieces as I could convey directly into my mouth. After the servants removed the meat dishes, hippocras was served. I could taste pepper sprinkled into the wine, together with more common spices such as ginger root and cinnamon. The sweet course included chestnuts roasted in wine, a plum tart, and sugared almonds.

The meal was sumptuous for a country girl from Falaise, but I'm afraid it could have been twigs and sand for all the pleasure I took from it.

After dinner, Bruria, Baruch, Meir, my father, and I were ushered into a small antechamber, to complete our arrangements for the wedding feast that would take place in three days. Taking up nearly half a city block, the Paris *yeshiva* was a warren of small rooms and meeting places. This room was furnished with a small table and several carved wood chairs. Small cubbyhole shelves mounted on the walls held numerous books and rolled-up parchments. In time, I would discover that the *yeshiva*'s library was large enough to spill over into most of the rooms. The rabbi employed a young man to categorize the books and papers, so that he could point scholars in the right direction. "Oh, a fight between neighbors over a fence?" he would say. "Try the west room, the one that overlooks the courtyard." The room we sat in, I would learn later, aptly held books and papers written about marriage rites.

Meir and his family sat three abreast on a bench on one side of the table, while my father and I took chairs on the other side. Deina, our hostess, sat at the table's head. She assured us that preparations were under way for the marriage meal. She described the menu she'd planned. But my mother-in-law immediately declared that she wanted to include some German delicacies.

"Rather than fennel in broth, why not some rib-sticking *cholent*? And gingerbread is good for the sweet, but rather than sugared almonds again, why not *einen Krapfen*—a hearty apple tart?"

"Bruria," said Rabbi Baruch wearily, "Deina has taken great pains with the menu."

"I agree, husband, but Meir should have some of his favorite dishes at his wedding. And," she added with a nod in my direction, "Shira should learn what those are."

Meir turned away, biting his lip. I began to regret my decision to hold the wedding in Paris rather than in Worms. But Deina, long accustomed to serving as housekeeper for her widowed father in the most influential *yeshiva* in all of Europe—and perhaps in the world—merely smiled.

"Rabbi Baruch, Rebbetzin Bruria, my kitchen staff is entirely at your disposal. If you will supervise the cooks, Bruria, I promise they will cook a meal worthy of your son's nuptials."

"I would be happy to help," I said. "As my mother-in-law says, I should learn to prepare some of Meir's favorite dishes."

Meir glanced at me, letting me see the warmth shining from his eyes before turning to his mother. "You forget, Mütti, I have eaten in Shira's home. She cooks well enough to suit me."

"Does she make *pashdidot* for the Shabbat? I have traveled abroad myself, my son, and nowhere have I found *pashdidah* like the ones we eat in Worms—not in France, at any rate."

Seeing bewilderment cross my face, my fiancé explained, "*Pashdidot* are small cakes for the Shabbat—a local delicacy in Worms and other German towns. A tale is even told of a small Jewish boy captured by ruffians for the ransom his merchant father would pay. The kidnappers thought they were clever, hiding the boy in a house on his own street until the search for him was exhausted. But the child cried so hard and so loud for his *pashdidah* that he was recovered that very evening."

"I would like to learn to make *pashdidot*, Meir," I said, modestly lowering my eyes. "And also *ein Spise von Bonen* your mama served you specially this evening. Mother-in-law, will you teach me?"

I could not tell if Bruria was pleased by my conciliatory manner, but she said, "We will go to the market and purchase what we need tomorrow. There's little enough time to prepare. Deina, while we are grateful for the use of your kitchen, you can leave the arrangements to me. If the *kinder* had been wed in Worms, as I desired, I would have prepared the wedding feast with my own hands. With your permission, I will do so here."

Deina's smile looked strained, but her answer was gracious. "Certainly, consider my papa's kitchens to be your own for the next few days. I am happy to help . . ."

"We are grateful, child," said Rabbi Baruch.

My father added, "Our womenfolk will not burden your servants any more than can be helped."

Bruria was no longer paying attention, however—she was fishing in a pouch attached to her belt for a heavy purse she had obviously brought all the way from Worms. I looked from her to Meir, who was once again stealing a glance in my direction. "Thank you," he mouthed soundlessly as our eyes met. I looked away, biting my lip to stop myself from smiling. It won't be long, I told myself, and shivered inside.

EN

The enemy boasted, "I will pursue, I will overtake them.
I will divide the spoils; I will gorge myself on them.
I will draw my sword and my hand will destroy them."
—Exodus 15:9

I ARRANGED WITH BRURIA TO MEET HER at Les Halles, the
sprawling enclosed marketplace in the city district called Les Champeaux. Yitzik's wife explained the route to me. She apologized for not
accompanying me, but her youngest child was teething. Having heard
his screams through the wallboards on and off through the night, I understood why she wouldn't take him out in public. I was told to make
my way almost to the gates of the Palais du Ru, then to cross the Seine at
the Pont au Change, where the money changers congregated. Beyond, I
would find the gates that opened daily at nine every morning, as decreed
by city ordinance a scant two years before. I was to meet Bruria at the
gates. She had already told me that she would be armed with her pocket-
book full of coins and several servants to carry the baskets of food.

As I walked to Les Halles, I came upon the breathtaking sight of the
palace where King Louis IX resided when in Paris. I reminded myself

that I had grown up under the shadow of William the Conqueror's stately castle, but as imposing as my beloved keep was, the Parisian palace was a city in itself. Its walls of white stone shone in the early morning sunlight, which glinted off blue and red tiled roofs. The warren of outlying buildings was surrounded by a high wall, flanked by fields and orchards. Peasants, better clothed by regal fiat than most Falaise merchants, bent happily to till the royal soil. I spied a pleasure garden inside the walls, just beyond a grassy expanse, with beautifully shaped miniature trees and hedges trimmed into imaginative shapes. There was also a long, low table in an arbor, spread with a snowy expanse of rich cloth that flapped in the breeze, set with food for any noble who happened to stroll by. A harpist and a lute player sat in an alcove near the arbor, playing a lilting melody that rose above the banter of the peasants and the trilling of the songbirds roosting in the trees. I stood transfixed for a few minutes, feeling as though I had entered one of the courtly romances written a generation ago by Chrétien de Troyes, a writer much revered by the Gentiles.

But I tore myself away after a few minutes of gazing. At Pont au Change, I felt I had entered another world entirely, one of grasping, desperate men—each trying to best the other through cunning and guile. The bridge connecting the two banks of the Seine held not only stalls of money changers, but also moneylenders and pawnshops. I had to pass by a group of students in black, fur-lined robes from the University of Paris, whose bleary expressions, drink-stained gowns, and reddened eyelids made them look as if they had spent more time gambling and drinking than studying. They were gathered around a moneylender's stall, clearly furious with an older man whose wagon-wheel badge marked him as a Jew.

"You Christ-killing bastard, you should be honored to lend money to a Paris university student!" one cried, his clenched fist waving in an unspoken threat.

"Honored, yes, sire, but such honor does not require me to accept less than what I'm owed," the old man replied.

"Look, Jew, I can't repay it all. Not at your rate of interest. A Christian would accept less with good grace; why won't you?" said the debtor, clutching a slender bag of coins to his chest.

"Gerard, don't expect a Jew pig to embrace Christian virtues! He and his kind would rather root through muck for coins that fall into the gutter than look upward for grace and salvation. Don't you remember Father Bartholomew's sermon last week, about the wandering Jew who brings disquiet wherever his foul footsteps land?"

"Aye, and didn't Sebastien tell us how the baron in his village, wearied of the high interest his Jews charged, imprisoned them all and put them to the rack? Hee, there's an idea! Why don't we try that here? Starting right now?"

I had stepped back into a recessed section of a stone wall. I feared the raucous crowd that was now inciting the irate students, but I knew I might get lost if I tried to find a different route to the marketplace. As the student casually proposed torture, I backed even farther against the wall. I wished I could melt into the stones and become invisible.

The squabble grew more contentious. The moneylender refused to accept less money than he was due. He pulled a small paper out of a deep pocket and waved it in front of the students.

"Here, young man, here you wrote the addresses of your university provost and your father. Shall I appeal to them both and tell them that you refuse payment? Shall I?"

"Don't you dare, Jew," the student cried defiantly, but his suddenly pale cheeks betrayed his fear of parent and professor.

Seeing him shrink back, the moneylender triumphantly restored the paper to his pocket and said, "Nor shall I return those books you gave me as security until you repay me. Why should I?"

"But I need them to study for my examinations!" the young man insisted. At his distress, the other students—and some bystanders—shouted even broader insults. One student broke off from the rest, picking up a heavy stick from the ground, and stalked over, waving the cudgel as though he intended to use it. The other Jews who worked in stalls at the bridge gathered to defend their friend. My knees buckling under me as I trembled, I leaned against the stone wall and tried to think of what I should do if a brawl erupted.

Just then, a bevy of Franciscan friars in gray robes appeared around a bend in the road. They were in the midst of a heated argument and did not seem to notice the squabble between the student and the moneylender until they collided with the crowd of onlookers. The men and women the monks had run into cried rough oaths in protest.

"May your barns and bones be cursed if you cannot keep a peaceable tongue in your head!" cried one of the monks, who tried to elbow his way through the crowd and was pushed back.

Another friar added, "And the fruit of your loins as well as the fruit of your lands both be blasted and laid waste!"

Despite my fears, I was fascinated to see how the spectators crossed themselves, some several times, spitting on the ground to ward off evil spirits. A heavyset merchant stammered, "A thousand apologies, good friars. We did not know it was your honors treading upon our feet. We thought it might be more Jew dogs come to defend this miserable usurer."

My heart, which had slowed as I watched the friars, began to beat wildly again.

"What say you—does that Jew moneylender ask too much interest? Let us pass," said a friar, pushing his way through the crowd.

I seized upon the distraction to try to pass unimpeded. I would have to hurry to meet Bruria at the Les Halles gates by nine bells. So I crept gingerly around the edge of the crowd. The press of men and women jostled for position, each eager to watch the Franciscans squash the Jew whom they had judged presumptuous and greedy.

Like most Jews of the age, I knew it was rarely helpful to involve a member of the Christian clergy in a dispute. But when a friar of the Dominican or Franciscan persuasion was drawn in, the situation was exacerbated tenfold. Both orders had been founded during the 1200s, and both took special delight in hounding Jews. Our own Rabbi Solomon ben Abraham had appealed to the Franciscans when he wanted to destroy the influence of Maimonides. As my father had explained to me many years ago, the rabbi had urged these watchdogs of the Christian faith to use their skill in hunting heretics to destroy Maimonides's European followers. The Dominican order, in their attempts to convert nonbelievers, would descend upon a Jewish congregation and force them to listen to sermons about their sins and eventual damnation for hours on end. Both orders employed apostate Jews in their ranks—converts who turned their early Jewish training against us.

It was difficult for me to squeeze past the crowds. I kept my head down and crept along, while overhearing the brewing argument.

"What rate of interest are you charging this poor student, Jew?" demanded one of the friars.

The moneylender stammered that it was nothing—a mere 65 percent.

"Brother Nicholas, what have you to say to this sinner?" the friar asked, turning to a slight young clergyman in the center of the group.

"Jew, tell these poor Christians, is it not true that biblical law forbids taking or giving interest to 'your brother'—in other words, a fellow Jew—whether money or food or 'any item' whatsoever?" he asked.

"Biblical law, your honor?" stammered the moneylender.

"Biblical law, Jew. What you call your Torah. For example, does it not say, in the book of Exodus, 'If you lend money to My people, to the poor among you, you are not to act as a creditor to him; you shall not charge him interest'?"

"You are certainly learned in our Law, master friar. Yes, that is from Exodus. But grant me this, is this Gentile student to be counted among 'my people'—the Jewish people?"

"It was God speaking, fool—so it is *God's* people that we speak of. Do you mean to tell me that Christians are *not* God's people?"

The moneylender's mouth dropped open. He knew better than to admit that we Jews do not consider the Nazarenes to be "God's people."

The way the argument had been phrased made me pause to listen.

Something in the voice caught me. When I had been younger, I knew someone who could pose just so insightful an argument, flawed though it might be. Yet—*Brother* Nicholas? Despite myself, I edged closer to confirm my suspicions. Could it be?

The long black hair had been shaved away, but the crystal blue eyes were the same. There was no mistaking the monk's identity. Nicholas Donin, turned apostate—a Franciscan friar, no less!

My feet were rooted to the street, my eyes fixed on the man who once had asked to marry me. I gasped out, "Nicholas Donin!"

With a falling sensation in my stomach, I saw him turn to look at me.

My cheeks blazing red, I clasped my shawl about my head and shoulders and fled, caring little now whom I shoved as I rushed away. My head buzzed in alarm. Would the man who once wanted me to be his bride allow me to leave unmolested?

Thinking I had stumbled far enough away to be safe, I turned down a narrow alleyway to catch my breath. I felt my confused emotions were etched on my face as blatantly as the wagon-wheel badge on my chest. Was it possible that I still cared for Nicholas? Or was I just shocked by seeing him so unexpectedly and in such a guise?

I leaned against a wall, my head spinning as I tried to catch my breath. A shadow fell over me.

"Is it, in fact, Shira bat Shmuel?" asked a familiar voice. "What are you doing in Paris, Shira?"

"I am not permitted to speak with you," I whispered. "You are . . ."

"Excommunicated? Oh, please. I'm no longer a Jew, so that stricture no longer applies. Even you, my dear innocent, can understand that, can't you?"

I looked up at him, feeling stunned, every nerve in my body ringing. But then I saw his thin lips spread into a gloating smile. Inhaling deeply, I willed myself upright and said with some asperity, "Certainly I see that you are a Franciscan friar now, *Brother* Nicholas. Can you possibly imagine that this makes it acceptable for me to speak to you?"

Donin laughed. "Ah! I remember your spirit when you used to argue with me—and how delighted I was when you did so. You must be, what, eighteen, nineteen now? And grown even more lovely than when I last saw you . . . Whom did your fond father finally bestow your hand upon?"

"I am not yet wed," I stammered. "I am in Paris to be married. To Meir ben Baruch of Worms."

"Meir ben Baruch! Your father *has* done well by you. Some say that Meir ben Baruch will be the most renowned rabbi in all of Ashkenaz someday. Of course, one might assert that achieving a place of ascendancy among a despised people makes the ascendant the most despised of all."

"It is a position I believe you yourself once aspired to," I retorted angrily, stung by the blatant insult. "Not so many years ago, I believe, you claimed you would someday change all of Jewish history."

"Oh, never doubt me, that *will* occur—even if I attain that place in history from outside the fold. And though you may not know it, I have already had a serious effect on the lives of the Jews of Brittany. I don't believe the Jews of Paris—the ones who cast me off—will savor the role I plan to play, a role that you will witness as the wife of Meir ben Baruch. Yes, you'll witness my influence over Jewish history, Shira. I'm glad you will; it makes my revenge even sweeter."

"Revenge? Nicholas, what do you mean to do?"

But he just stood there, oblivious to the stares of curious passersby, a sardonic grin on his thin face. "Did you know I was actually married myself? I found an isolated Jewish community in the Italian countryside where they did not know I had been excommunicated. I managed to live as a Jew again for about half a year. My bride was quite willing to become my wife—at first—for there was a dearth of unattached men in the community. But I had lived as an outcast too long. The neighbors were scandalized by my unwillingness to live by their narrow-minded rules and then even more appalled when they learned of the *cherem*. I often think of my wife and wonder if she misses me. *You* might have been my wife once. Do *you* miss me?"

"Shira!" boomed a voice from behind me. "What in the world ...? Who is this monk—this *man*—you are speaking to?"

With absolute despair in my heart, I whirled around to see my mother-in-law to be, hands on her hips, bristling with indignation, servants from the *yeshiva* peering over her shoulder in astonishment. There was something brutally predictable about Bruria's witnessing my meeting with Donin. Was my life destined to be tainted by my acquaintance with the apostate?

"Well!" said Nicholas, actually laughing at my whitened face. "Had I wanted revenge on you, I could not have planned it better. Farewell, gentle Shira—give my kind regards to your father and to Yechiel, will you? Tell them that if all goes as I hope, I may see them both in a year or so."

———•———

They stood around me in a semicircle as I wept—my father, my betrothed, his father, and Rabbi Yechiel. Bruria, grasping me by my elbow, had walked me back to the *yeshiva* at such a pace that I could barely keep up, particularly in my distraught condition. The servants hurried after us, empty baskets flying out behind them. The onlookers, watching our quick-march parade, pointed and tittered.

Bruria spoke first. "She was standing alone in an alleyway, talking to a Franciscan monk in a highly familiar manner. Baruch, I told you I was not certain of this match. The daughter of our neighbor, the merchant Otto, would surely be better than ... than ..."

For once, my betrothed's mother had no harsh words at her disposal. She allowed her outstretched finger, shaking in rage, to convey her disgust with me.

I stood abashed, my hair snarled in the wool fibers of my shawl, my chin trembling. There was a moment of complete silence before my father asked, "Shira?"

But I could only cry harder, sobs of despair echoing through the *yeshiva's* broad entranceway.

"*Mütti*, what in the world ... ?" Meir asked, but Bruria just shook her head, keeping her forefinger extended accusingly.

"Come, come, bring her in here," Rabbi Yechiel said, noticing the cluster of students and teachers peering out from behind classroom doors. He led us into a small antechamber and pointed, not unkindly, to a stool in the middle of the room, where I collapsed, my hands covering my face and my shoulders shaking.

"I will fetch my daughter," said Rabbi Yechiel, "and you, Shmuel, you talk to Shira alone for a moment. Baruch, you take your son and wife to one side and discover what it was Bruria witnessed. Yes?"

"No ... ," I gasped, raising my head and stretching a hand out in Meir's direction. "She doesn't understand that it was nothing, nothing ... Papa, I will speak, but make them stay here to hear me."

"Of course, Songbird, of course," my father said soothingly, stroking my disheveled hair. "Tell us who you were talking to."

"It was Nicholas Donin, Papa, he—"

"Donin!" said Yechiel. "Here, in Paris?"

"Yes, Rabbi. He has turned apostate—he is a Franciscan monk now."

The three older men looked at one another, their faces grave. Meir's father said, "There have been several allegations about Donin—that it was he who started the rumors of ritual murder in Brittany, for instance, that resulted in the deaths of some twenty Jews of that region. But I did not know of his conversion."

"I heard that he was seen directing the Crusaders who burned down Jewish homes," said my father, his lips compressed. "Telling the knights which men had the most influence in the community so their homes could be burned and pillaged first. But, I must admit, I did not believe the reports."

"Is it not enough to be bedeviled by the Nazarenes—must our own people turn traitor against us?" Yechiel asked plaintively.

"Shira, how did you come to meet Donin again?" Papa asked me.

"He was with a group of monks ... a moneylender at Pont au Change was being heckled by some students from the university . . . the monks stopped to help the Christian students. Donin began quoting Exodus to show that the Jew was wrong in charging interest. I couldn't get around the crowd and I was afraid . . ."

I looked at Meir and was heartened to see his face softening as I mentioned my fear. His mother's expression, however, was as stony and forbidding as ever.

" . . . but I knew I would be late to meet Bruria if I lingered any longer. And it felt like a riot could break out any second. Donin noticed me as I tried to get past the crowd . . . he followed me into an alleyway."

"My child!" my father exclaimed, reaching his hand to my shoulder. Meir, too, took a protective step forward, but his mother sidled between us.

"There was no reason for you to talk to him, however," Bruria proclaimed. "He was excommunicated—a man under *cherem*. It is strictly forbidden for any Jew—especially an unmarried girl—to speak with him."

"Yes, child, you knew of the *cherem*, did you not?" asked Rabbi Yechiel.

"I did, Rabbi—it was proclaimed in our *beit midrash* several years ago. I did not wish to talk to him, but he would not let me go. And"—I blushed as I said this—"I have always felt pity for him. For his solitude and loneliness."

"But what do you know of his loneliness, Shira?" asked my betrothed. I nearly wept at the pained expression lurking in his hazel eyes. "What would make you consider him and his solitude so solicitously?"

If there was ever a moment to confess how Donin had accosted me in the charity hut back home in Falaise, this was the time. But, looking at my distressed fiancé, I could not inflict such a blow upon him. I would carry the secret of that day to my grave, I vowed silently, drawing a deep breath of resolution.

"I suppose I was moved to imagine his sorrow because he spent a month in my father's *yeshiva*," I admitted now. "I apologize for my youthful indiscretion, my husband, but he and I used to discuss some of the controversial subjects that caused you, Rabbi Yechiel"—I nodded in his direction—"to excommunicate him. It was wrong of me to have discussed anything at all with him, I know that now. I am amply punished for my immodesty."

My father's hand moved from my right shoulder to clasp my left hand. "Meir," he said, "when you asked for Shira's hand in marriage, I informed you of her imprudent relationship with Donin. Indeed"—he shrugged apologetically toward my betrothed's parents—"it would have been folly to keep such a matter secret, for the entire town of Falaise knew of it. But Shira's rash friendship and the scandal it caused ended favorably for us both. It was because of Donin that I married my beloved Alyes, so that my new wife might take my errant girl in hand. And Shira refused Donin's suit herself, you know. If someone should be chastised for her error, Bruria and Baruch, I beg that you place that blame firmly on her father's shoulders for not protecting her *tzni'ut*, her womanly modesty, sufficiently. What say you?"

I looked up at my father, blinking away my tears, feeling my cold despair melt away at his warm, protective words.

Meir's father opened his mouth to speak, but his wife forestalled him. "A pretty speech, Rav Shmuel, even a touching one. But you will excuse us if we reserve our answer until we have had time to talk privately. This is a matter of great concern, as you can imagine—not something that we can respond to instantly just because of a poignant fatherly plea."

"Mütti, *bitte*!" Meir cried out, but his father laid a restraining hand on his arm.

"Your mother is only looking out for your well-being. You should be grateful. However, my wife, you will also grant that we should hear everything Shira has to say on her own behalf before we withdraw to discuss the matter as a family. Yes?"

Bruria's nod resembled the motion made by a chicken when it picks at rocky, barren ground—a jerk of the head and shoulders that still, somehow, communicated distaste. My father still clasped my left hand. Taking courage from the warmth of his strong fingers, I spoke.

"There is actually little left for me to say. Bruria came upon us not five minutes after Donin accosted me in the alleyway. He told me of his conversion—also, that he had been married to a Jewess in Italy—" Meir, my father, and Baruch all looked askance at Yechiel, who nodded, his mouth drawn downward in weary disapproval. "But even that community evicted him when they learned of his *cherem*," I continued. "He must have converted not long after that. He spoke of revenge, Rabbi Yechiel, and that he would possibly see you and my father at some point in the future—but I have no idea what he actually meant by that."

"A long five minutes," Bruria scoffed, but her husband interceded once more.

"The span of time is actually not material, wife—it is more the intimacy that disturbs me. And I'm afraid it disturbs me, Shmuel, that the man would reveal so much to your innocent daughter—"

"Nicholas Donin was never afraid of trampling on convention and decency if it suited his own particular purpose," Yechiel mused. "You never met him, did you, Baruch?"

"No, never."

"It may be difficult for you and Bruria to comprehend how unfettered Donin's *yetzer ha'rah*—his evil inclination—truly is. He is possessed by warped ideas and his own conception of their importance to such a degree that he permits nothing to stand in his way. Good manners, respect for his elders, even fear of the Almighty's eventual wrath— none of these sway him from insisting he is right and the rest of us are wrong. He resembles nothing more than a fire in the woods—raging and destroying everything in his path."

"I met him once," said my betrothed, looking at me with a strange, set look on his face, two pinched white marks on either side of his nostrils. "In Mainz, when I was studying with Rabbi Yehuda ben Moshe ha-Kohen. This was before the cherem, of course. I agree with you, Rav Yechiel—he is as dangerous as an unwatched blaze and just as callous."

"This being so," my father chimed in, "you can better understand how Shira might have found it difficult to withstand him—and that he would care nothing about the propriety that would have stopped most men from addressing her, a maiden."

"I did tell him to stop, Papa—I did not seek or welcome his advances. Meir"—I turned to my betrothed, trying to soften the hurt lines on his face—"please understand that I would do nothing—nothing—to willingly threaten our marriage. Perhaps you will think me unwomanly to say this aloud, but I am eager to stand at the *chuppah* with you and receive the blessing upon our union, impatient to start our life together as man and wife."

It was unquestionably an immodest act, but I looked straight into his eyes as I spoke. Something moved between us when I spoke of our union—a current of air charged with some magical power, making my limbs weaken and bringing warmth into his pale face. His lips twitched into a smile, and his shoulders loosened and relaxed.

But Bruria was less easily won over. "We will discuss this as a family and return this evening with our decision about this marriage." She moved between our locked gazes and took her son by the hand, leading him from the room. My heart sank and I felt sick inside. Baruch lingered to whisper into Yechiel's ear and the august rabbi of Paris replied, clapping a hand on Baruch's forearm. As my betrothed's father left the room, seeing my distraught face, my father drew me closer into his arms and kissed my forehead.

"It will be all right, Shira," Rabbi Yechiel told me. "Baruch believes you, as do I. We must allow Bruria to vent her anger and deliberate on the suitability of the marriage, for she would be satisfied with nothing less. But I don't want you to worry, not even for an instant. You and Meir will be wed, I promise you."

Relief flooded through me. "Thank you, Rabbi. I am sorry to have brought all this trouble to your home."

"It was not you but Donin who did that. Come, I will ask Deina to make you a warm drink, to soothe you, and then I want you to repeat everything you've told us about your conversation with Donin. Perhaps if we can discover his purpose, we can forestall him in time."

LEVEN

He has taken me to the banquet hall,
and his banner over me is love.
        —SONG OF SONGS 2:4

IN THE LATE AFTERNOON OF THE DAY before my wedding, I was instructed to come to Deina's home to prepare for immersion in the ritual bath, the *mikveh*. She and her family lived in semiprivacy in several small rooms attached to the main *yeshiva* building. She greeted me as I arrived, asking the servant to take the children outside, to allow us to talk in peace. We sat in a room shaded by long woven draperies at the tall windows, shutters thrown open in the hope of catching a passing breeze. It was a hot, still afternoon, and the only sound was that of a distant dog barking. Deina brought in some honeyed cakes in a straw basket, setting them down on the table before seating herself across from me.

In Falaise, our *mikveh* was in a small, earthen-dug cellar located just off the synagogue, fed by a natural spring and augmented by rainwater that would flow into the pool from several cisterns through a series of ducts. In Paris, where the Jewish community was so much larger, the *mikveh* was located in a separate building, with several attached rooms where the women could undress, pray, even spend time talking companionably without husband or children clamoring for their attention. Men who needed to use the *mikveh* tended to come in the early mornings, women in the late afternoons. A small orphan boy sat outside on the steps throughout the week, earning a pittance and three meals a day by making sure men and women never entered the building at the same time.

Before we set out for the *mikveh*, Deina spoke with me about the rituals I needed to observe before and after the wedding ceremony.

"You have counted, Shira, and have been blood-free for seven full days?" she asked.

I nodded. Before I'd left Falaise, Alyes had described what I would need to do to prove my purity. I was wearing white next to my skin and used a soft white cloth to check twice daily for any spotting or staining. I had brought a special sheet of pure white that Alyes had given to me and had slept on it for the past week, checking it, too, every morning. My stepmother had explained that many brides, excited about the wedding feast to come, disrupted their bodily rhythms and brought on their menstrual flow unseasonably. If that should happen to me, Alyes said, I would not be permitted to stand under the *chuppah* until I had passed through another seven "white days."

"Good," Deina said now. "We will arrive at the *mikveh* an hour before sunset. You will undress completely, Shira, and we will cleanse you from head to toe and comb out your hair so that not one strand touches the other. You will immerse yourself completely in the water and we will pray over you three times. Then you will be pure and able to approach the *chuppah* and sleep in your husband's bed."

The thought of sleeping in the same bed with Meir—finally having relations with him—made me feel a little light-headed. I closed my eyes for a moment, imagining his face close to mine and his fingers exploring my skin. I shivered. When I realized what I was doing, I jerked my eyes open, to see Deina smiling understandingly at me.

"I hope you find your marriage duties are a joy, Shira. When this happens to a bride, there is nothing quite like it," she commented, and then went on: "After you have consummated your marriage, your *dam betulim*—the blood that shows you are a virgin bride—will appear on your sheets. I will check them personally and we will display them to prove you were a *b'tulah* before your wedding."

"What if there is no blood?" I asked, half whispering, for I had heard of cases where there had been none and where suspicion had marred the wedding festivities.

Deina shrugged. "You *are* a virgin, yes?" she asked.

"I am."

"Then just leave it in my hands," she whispered. She leaned forward to make sure no one could overhear. "I assure you that the rabbis will be satisfied with your status—as will your mother-in-law. Yes, she in particular will have no qualms about your virginity."

Surprised, I looked up at Deina's serenely smiling face. She said nothing more, but it was clear from the look in her eyes how much she disliked my mother-in-law—feeling enough hostility to hoodwink her, if need be. The idea of an ally who could actually help me prevail against my mother-in-law was not unattractive. The last few days had not been easy. In private, Bruria continued to rage against our marriage, and in public she bickered in such a way that everyone knew she was opposed to the match.

"You know that you need to separate from your husband after your first intercourse, yes? And that you must act as though you were *niddah*—impure—for seven days, and then purify yourself in the *mikveh* again at the end of that period?"

"I know," I said.

"And then, God willing, you will give birth to your first child some nine months later—although it can take longer with some women. But you are not too young for children, as is often the case with child brides, so we will hope for the best."

We walked through the hot, still streets to the *mikveh* and were greeted at the door by the sound of revelry. The *mikveh* common room was crowded with women gathered in my honor. A table was laid with sweet cakes and wine, and the women were chattering gaily, glad for this joyous respite from their day-to-day duties. My mother-in-law was there, of course, whispering in a corner with some of the older women, her face puckering in distaste as I entered. Deina led me to a room where I could undress and wash my body, making sure the soft cloths she provided reached deep inside every crevice. I had never before realized that the body contained so many folds, nooks, and crannies. My nails were clipped and a pointed knife was used to remove any dirt from underneath them, cutting sharply right down to the skin. Deina and Amyris, another rabbi's wife, used bone combs to untangle my long, black hair from the scalp downward, working slowly and painstakingly through any snarls. When they finally stepped away from my aching head, my hair fell softly down my back, each strand charged and brittle.

Once my body was scoured clean, they pronounced me ready. They wrapped me in a warm mantle and took me out into the common room. I was told to chant a *Shechiyanu,* a blessing thanking God for seeing fit to bring me to this auspicious time in my life.

I was led toward the pool, which glowed with an odd green radiance, as though the untouched waters we had captured possessed the essence of holiness. I expected the water to feel cold against my skin, but there was almost no change in temperature as I walked down the narrow stone steps into the waist-deep pool. I had never in my life experienced anything as soft as that water.

"Stand in the middle of the pool, Shira," Deina said, perched on the edge of the *mikveh.* Most of the women had stayed in the common room, but a few—my mother-in-law among them—had joined us for the sacred part of the ritual.

As instructed, I crouched down, my fingers splayed out, my knees spread far apart, even each individual toe finding separate purchase on the gritty surface of the *mikveh* floor. I felt weightless and buoyant in the water.

"Duck your head and upper body until every inch of you is submerged. You must remain under the water until we tell you to rise. Do not worry—you will be fine," Deina assured me.

I took a big breath of air and lowered my body under the surface of the pool. As the waters closed over my head, I felt as if I were cut off from the world, silence echoing in my ears, my body trying to rise upward against my will. Moments passed and panic began to burn in my throat. Would their prayers take too long? Would they allow me to drown? I wanted, desperately, to burst forth from the water that enveloped me on all sides but forced myself to remain motionless.

"Rise up, Shira." Deina's calm voice cut through the heavy curtain of water. I quickly straightened, dragging air and rainwater into my mouth and nose in my enthusiasm for the fresh air.

"Gently, gently," she counseled, as I sputtered and choked. "Don't touch your mouth or nose or eyes with your hands, or we will need to begin all over again."

My fingers itched to wipe my streaming eyes and nose, but I refrained through sheer force of will.

"Take another deep breath and submerge again," she instructed. But I hesitated, afraid that I couldn't draw enough air into my lungs to survive a second blessing, and I raised a hand to ask for a little more time.

"Relax, Shira, until your breathing slows," Deina said. "We'll wait."

Behind her, I saw my mother-in-law muttering contemptuously to a couple of older women, who were happy to cluck and point with her at this fearful and undeserving bride. The sight of her derision stiffened my resolve. "I'm ready," I gasped, taking a breath and lowering myself again, less forcefully this time.

I don't know if it was because I wanted to prove myself worthy of my Meir or because I had grown used to the water, but this time I kept my panic at bay. Diving down for the third blessing, I felt as though I could have stayed underwater forever. A sense of peace and holiness pervaded me, filling me so that there was no room for anything but wonder. The mikveh, through its purifying, mystical embrace, had transfigured me. As I rose from the water and gingerly made my way up the slippery stone steps, I knew I was ready to become Meir's wife and mother to his children.

———

My wedding took place on a humid, hot August afternoon. Deina and several of the scholars' wives—women who would be my friends in the coming years but who were strangers to me then—gathered around me kindly, attiring me in my bridal finery. In honor of my husband's German heritage, my pale blue gown included fur sewn around the hem, sleeves, and collar. I was first grateful for the heavy ivory lace veil because it so completely covered my flushed face. But as it grew increasingly difficult to breathe, I became impatient for the moment in the ceremony when Meir would draw it aside. I hoped he would not be displeased by the rosy complexion he would unveil.

I had no mother to lead me to the *chuppah* and wished my dear mother Alyes could have been with Papa and me on this of all days. Deina stepped into the breach graciously, moving to my left side while Bruria, looking resigned, accompanied me on my right. The two women led me to my father, who, wearing his Shabbat *tallith* in my honor, took me by the sleeve of my robe and placed me beside my husband.

Meir wore traditional German wedding garb, including the *tallith* I had given him as one of several wedding gifts, and a cowl, a mark of mourning for our exile from Israel in the midst of our joy. The ashes that were strewn over us made us remember our lost Zion as well. If I felt hot and flushed under my veil, my bridegroom seemed equally exasperated by the heat and close quarters. He kept wiping beads of sweat that persisted in sprouting on his broad forehead and lip with the linen handkerchief I had embroidered for him as a keepsake.

Our wedding was officiated by both my father and my father-in-law. Love shone in my father's eyes as he smiled down upon me, and Meir's father gave me a particularly sweet smile as he instructed his son to place the gold band upon the forefinger of my right hand.

These details were among the few that I remember. The entire wedding blessing passed by in a blur of ceremony that did not make my marriage to Meir feel any more authentic than the few looks we had been able to exchange over the years did. The crowd of strangers—strangers to me, though not of course to Meir, who had spent several years studying in Paris—gave a roar of approval when my father proclaimed us well and truly wed. But it did not feel real, not yet.

Our parents led us to a small room. The door snapped shut behind us. For the first time since our walk to William's Keep in Falaise so many years ago, Meir and I were alone together. I found it difficult to raise my head toward my husband. He seemed to be having difficulty clearing his voice. It took him two tries before he could invite me to take a bite of the egg and the chicken that had been prepared for us—foods traditionally set out to encourage the bride and groom's fertility. He brought a morsel of food to my mouth, and his fingers brushed against my cheek.

"It will be all right, Shira, I promise you," he whispered to me, seeing me flinch a little at his proximity. "My bride, I have longed to touch you for so many years now. Allow me?"

He bent down—for he was no longer shorter than I was, having grown quite a bit in the years since we first met—and caressed my forehead with his lips. I was momentarily embarrassed. My forehead, like the rest of me, was slick with perspiration, and I could sense his lips slipping off me. But he moved lower, to linger on the nape of my neck. My eyes closed involuntarily as I quivered under the gentle movements of his mouth.

"Oh, Shira," he breathed softly into my ear. "This evening will seem an eternity until we can be alone together again."

As if on cue, a banging on the door alerted us to move apart, but not before I reached up and touched his face with ice-cold fingers. If the rest of me was burning hot, I felt as if I had no blood at all in my hands and feet. He laughed a little, deep in his throat, before answering the summons.

"Open up, friends!" he called, and the door was flung open.

I felt as though I were in a trance as I was led away from my husband, surrounded by chattering wives and maidens. The women pressed food and wine upon me. Although my hand moved to my mouth automatically, one spoonful, then two, I soon gave up eating and put the spoon down. I remember very little of the evening's festivities—there was singing and some beautiful lute playing, and dancing by some of the men. And, of course, there was the traditional Talmudic discussion—but for once in my life, I chose not to follow along. I sat and smiled and nodded, nearly drowning in sensual thoughts as I anticipated the night ahead.

Finally, the women drew me up from the seat of honor, with giggles and jests that made me blush. My heart thumping in my chest, I looked around the room for Meir and realized that he had already been removed by his groomsmen.

We walked through the quiet city streets to my new home. The sound of our clattering feet on the cobbles mixed with the high-pitched, excited laughter of the women, who urged me on. But, for all of my anticipation earlier in the evening, I found myself strangely reluctant now. Would Meir hurt me in his ardor? Would I be awkward in bed—not please him enough? After so many years of waiting, what if we found we were not truly *b'shert*—meant for each other?

The lodgings that Meir had found for us were just two scant blocks from the *yeshiva*, located off an alleyway. We had let the top floor of a three-story house, with our landlord and his family living downstairs from us. I was eager to see my new home, but my coterie refused to let me look around, leading me inexorably into the bridal chamber.

The small bedroom was dominated by a single piece of furniture— our bed. Set into an alcove next to the bed was a brass candlestick, the single tallow candle in danger of being blown out as Meir's friends gathered around him and teased him in whispers. As the women entered, the men backed away. Reddening under the knowing grins of the women, Meir moved into a corner of the room, looking as though he wished he could disappear through the wall he leaned against.

Deina and Amyris and some of the other women drew me forward to face my husband. Looking over my shoulder, I noticed the women dropped some sweetmeats—candied rose petals and honeyed nuts—onto the sheets. Someone—I suspected Deina, whose kindness I was beginning to treasure—had appointed the room with as much grace as plaster walls and wooden plank floors would permit. The bed was made up with a snowy white sheet, taken from the carved chest that contained my dowry. A goose-feather quilt, which Alyes and I had stuffed during many early winter afternoons spent near the hearth in Falaise, was tucked under two fluffy feather pillows, crisp and new. Amyris drew back the goose-feather quilt, patting the white sheet suggestively before Deina, with a laugh, pulled her arm to drag her away.

The bridal party trooped downstairs, singing songs as they went. Meir and I, standing close enough to touch each other in a darkened corner of our new home, listened as they made their way across the cobbles, the snatches of melody and footfalls growing more and more distant.

We were alone. I felt my insides melting in panic and wished I were anywhere else but there, with my husband. He saw my fear and put aside whatever trepidation and hesitation he was feeling himself. He stepped around me and, taking the candle from the alcove, held it so that it illuminated me as I stood as still as a statue in my bridal dress. He murmured, "'Behold, you are beautiful, my love. Behold, you are beautiful. Your eyes are doves.'"

A thrill coursed through my body as he recited lines from Solomon's Song, that exquisite biblical tribute of a lover to his beloved. Replacing the candle, he reached over and took me by the waist, drawing me to him. I felt myself nearly swooning as his lips sought mine. He held me to him for a long instant. Scarcely breathing, I nestled against him as he whispered more verses into my hair: "'Your lips, my bride, drip like the honeycomb. Honey and milk are under your tongue.'"

He kissed me again, his tongue probing my mouth in a way that made every limb on my body turn fluid and weak. I broke away, gasping a little, but then, so that he would not think I was displeased, I shyly recited in turn, "'O happy that night, When sunk on your breast, Your kisses fast falling, And drunken with love, My troth I did plight.'"

He looked down at me, eyes glowing. "Yehuda ha-Levi? Little love, you never fail to astonish me," he chuckled. "How did you come to know of the Spaniard's love poems?"

I felt like I could lose myself in the depths of his eyes. Light-headed, I replied breathlessly, "We sing them, sometimes, in Falaise—at weddings. Papa owns a volume of his poetry—he most admires the poems of our longing for Zion. But I confess, my husband, I sought out ha-Levi's love poems when I was yearning . . . for you."

"Oh, Shira!" he burst out, as though my words were too much for him. He drew me closer. Through our layers of clothing, I could sense his excitement—his body growing, my own curving about him, both of us moving experimentally against each other.

He broke away, panting. "Shira, my darling, we—we need to slow down. Come, I would see my bride before . . ."

There were two carved wooden cups of spiced wine on the floor near the bed, and Meir, seeing them, picked one up. "Let us drink together," he said, tilting the cup toward me. I gulped the cool liquid. It exploded into flame within me. Meir took a steadying drink and reached for me again.

He kissed me once more. He pushed me back, turned me around, and, with unsure fingers, began to release me from my gown. I was growing more and more excited as his hands slowly and deliberately drew the gown apart and let it drop to the floor. I stepped away and divested myself of my undergarments as quickly as I could.

I stood before him, completely naked. He drew a deep breath and stood back, gazing upon me as though his long-held fantasies had finally been fulfilled. "'Her beauty shames the day-star, And makes the darkness light . . . ,'" he muttered, quoting from the same ha-Levi poem I'd quoted earlier. I began to shiver from the damp air on my body and the anticipation of what was yet to come. Seeing my trembling, he led me to the bed and helped me lie down under the covers.

"Wait just one moment," he said, and moved to one side, quickly stripping off his own clothes, which he laid down in neat folds next to my hastily discarded pile of finery. I could barely bring myself to look at him. The flickering light of our single candle fell upon his broad chest and shoulders. Peering lower, I could make out that part of him that made him a man jutting upward. Warmth flooded my own private parts and, half in longing, half in shame, I closed my eyes. I felt the bed shift with his weight as he lay down on the other side of the bed. He reached for me.

Is there anything like the first night of love? I have heard that some of Israel's brides and grooms are too young, or too unversed in what to do, or just too selfish in seeking their own pleasure, so that one partner rises unsatisfied from the covers and turns sourly against the joys of the marriage bed. But through reading the parts of the Talmud written specifically for bridegrooms, Meir had been carefully instructed in the movements that would bring me pleasure. And my husband was ever the faultless student. He used his fingers, his tongue, and his body in ways that made me gasp beneath him. As Solomon's Song expresses so eloquently, he drowsed among my lilies, found my hiding places.

Finally, just when I felt I would burst if something didn't happen and happen soon, he positioned himself above me, thrusting into me. I felt a slight burning and pulling at his entry into my body, but the discomfort was subsumed by the strength of our passion. Many hours later, I would see the red stain that would tell the world that I was indeed a virgin taken that night. My friend Deina would hang it from our third-floor window for all to see. But right then as we moved together, slick and wet with our own heat and that of the steamy August night, I cried out his name, over and over again, and gloried to hear him moan my own— every part of my being singing in unison with my beloved husband.

When he withdrew from me, I cried out involuntarily, and he held me to him in concern. But I smiled and assured him that the pain was minor, that I was eager to love him again.

"In seven days," he said, moving back and away from me.

Suddenly, I remembered that the spilling of my blood meant that I was *niddah*—forbidden to touch my husband or to hand him anything for the next week. In fact, it behooved me to leave him immediately and find my own bed, for it was there that I would sleep any time my blood flowed.

I removed myself from under the covers, reluctant to leave the hollow of warmth we had created between us. I was rewarded when I saw the relief in Meir's eyes—relief that he did not have to tell me to leave. "I will be counting the days," he whispered to me. "There is a sleeping pallet made up in the next room, Shira, which you can move anywhere you want in the morning."

"Good night, husband," I said, walking away slowly and a little painfully.

WELVE

Be fruitful and multiply.
      —GENESIS 1:28

TWO MONTHS LATER, I WAS DIGGING in the small kitchen garden our landlord had allotted us with our rooms. It was too late in the year to plant anything, but I wanted to prepare the soil for next spring by turning it over and letting it breathe. I worked happily, contemplating the changes in my life since marrying Meir. While I missed my father and Alyes, I loved being mistress of my own household. The proximity of the Paris *yeshiva* and the friendliness of the other wives meant I was never lonely, for there was always someone to talk to and gossip with.

The wives and I walked the streets of the Jewish quarter of Paris together, and they showed me where to shop and where to go when I needed something repaired. We would pass through rue de la Draperie, and Deina would point out the house where her grandparents had lived, before King Philippe Auguste had expelled the Jews and turned the street over to the sheet makers, whose prices for fine linens enriched the king's coffers. Philippe Auguste had also been responsible for the thick, protective walls of the city, against which so many houses were ranged like dominos in a child's game, all slanting at the same angle. Several of the wives even studied together quietly and our husbands were content to let it be so, as long as we remained discreet. I took great joy in the home I created for my husband, whose footfall on the stairs at the end of the day still made my pulse flutter.

I heard footsteps now and I looked up. Brother Anton stood there, a large smile creasing his narrow face.

"Quite at home here, young Shira? Heartiest best wishes on your marriage. I am sorry I wasn't here to greet your father when he came to Paris for your wedding, but I was traveling in the south."

I straightened up, wiping my hands on my apron. Brother Anton had visited us in Falaise several times after I first met him that cold day in William's Keep. He was the Christian with whom I felt most comfortable. During his years in Paris, Meir had also grown attached to the monk. "You are welcome to my home, Brother Anton. Did you come here to visit my husband?"

"Yes, I expected him back from his studies already, for it is nearly sundown."

The sun was indeed flirting with the western horizon. I rose to my feet, Brother Anton reaching out a hand to help me up.

"The time has taken me unawares, Brother Anton, and I must hurry to cook for my husband. Would you join us for the meal?"

"Thank you, Shira, I would be delighted. Would you like me to wait for your husband outside?"

I appreciated the good brother's understanding of our customs. He knew it would be unseemly for him to accompany me into our home unchaperoned, even though I was a married woman and he a monk.

"I will send Jaquet out to you with a drink," I said, motioning for him to take a seat on the stone bench beside the garden. "It is still hot here, even though the High Holy Days begin next week."

"Yes, unseasonably warm. I would welcome something cool. You go ahead, Shira, and don't worry about keeping me company—I have a book with me, as always." He reached into his capacious habit and brought a small, leather-bound book out of a pocket. When I saw the Latin writing on it I shivered at the thought that such matters were being read in my garden.

Jaquet, the Christian maidservant Meir had engaged for me, had the evening meal well in hand. I asked her to pour a cup of wine from the caskets stored in the coolness of our landlord's cellar and to bring it to the monk. Her eyes wide at the thought of a Christian guest in my garden, she scurried off to serve him.

A few minutes later, Meir arrived from the *yeshiva.* I heard him chatting briefly with our landlady before he mounted the stairs to our lodgings. He burst in, all smiles, giving me a quick embrace as I laid out platters on our small table. Then he stopped short, counting them.

"Do we have a guest?" he asked.

"Brother Anton is waiting for you in the garden, husband."

"Brother Anton? Here? How odd." He washed his hands and said the blessing, then descended the back stairs, which led directly to the garden.

As I ladled soup into bowls, the smell of the broth made me remember that cold night in William's Keep, the first day Meir and I realized we were *b'shert,* meant for each other. Today I could smile at the memory, for I had a surprise for my husband I knew would delight him. I straightened up, touched my flat stomach with my fingers for a brief moment, then lit the tallow candles that would illuminate our meal as dusk gathered around us.

Meir and Brother Anton came in and we all sat down for the meal. Brother Anton watched us closely as we said the traditional blessings, as if he were trying to follow the text in his head. Meir broke the bread and passed it, we ate, and we started on the broth.

"Have you by any chance passed by Falaise in your travels, Brother Anton?" I asked, hoping the friar might have a message for me from my father.

"Alas, no, Shira—I have come straight to Paris from the south, from Montpellier."

Meir put down his soup spoon and looked closely at our guest. "From Montpellier? Were you there for . . ."

"The burning of Maimonides's books, yes, I was. That's why I'm here now. I would have gone directly to Yechiel, but my friendly discussions with him have been observed by the Inquisitors and I dare not visit him openly now."

The Inquisition, founded first by Pope Lucius III in 1184 by a papal bull that sought to suppress heresy, had just recently been given new life by Pope Gregory IX, who, in 1231, had empowered the Dominicans to squash the Cathars of Languedoc and the Poor Men of Lyons, followers of the heretical monk Peter Waldo. But my father had explained to me that Jews were generally not the target of the Inquisition, unless they had converted to Christianity and then reneged on their new faith.

"What happened in Montpellier, husband?" I asked, my eyes widening in fear.

Meir sighed. "You know that Maimonides's *Guide for the Perplexed* and other works were placed under ban by our own rabbis, do you not, Shira?" he responded. At my nod, he continued, "Well, the Dominican brothers decided to help us by gathering up Maimonides's works and burning them publicly in the town square."

"But why would they do that?" I asked, turning to Brother Anton.

The monk looked down at his plate, his face flushed. My husband said, "There is an intolerant faction among the Christians gaining ground these days. The three students Brother Anton introduced me to at the University of Paris told me recently we could not continue our conversations. They fear what the Holy Office of the Inquisition might do if they continued their unsanctioned contact with a contaminated Jew."

Brother Anton sighed. "There is definitely an intolerant faction; that's a good way to describe what's happening, Meir. Personally, I do not understand it. Like it or not, your Torah is a part of our heritage, the Old Testament of the Bible. Even if you Jews refuse to accept our Christ as your savior, you are still the living link that connects us to how he himself worshipped as a child."

Meir shook his head, disagreeing. "You must understand that we are truly not the same people we were when the Bible was written and we do not worship in the same way your Yeshu of Nazareth did. When he was alive, there was a Temple in Jerusalem, and we were living in our own land, keeping our Covenant of Zion with our Lord God. Now . . . we are scattered across the earth, our Temple razed to the ground and our religion transformed from one of blood sacrifice performed by a few priests to one of customs and ethics that all partake in."

The friar passed a hand over his furrowed brow and set down his spoon. "This was a delicious soup, Shira."

"You are welcome, Brother Anton," I said, motioning to Jaquet to remove the empty soup basins. Jaquet, who had been hovering in the back of the kitchen, brought out the meat stew and ladled a hefty portion on the monk's plate. She served Meir and then came close to me with the bubbling iron pot.

I took one look at the contents of the stew, seeing the bones and globules of fat and thickly sliced vegetables, and waved her away. Both men looked at me, surprised, as I reached across the table and helped myself to another piece of bread.

"Are you feeling all right, Shira?" my husband asked.

I was actually feeling quite ill, my stomach revolting against the small amount of broth I had swallowed. I had been told I would have these symptoms only in the mornings. Annoyed at my body, I shrugged the question aside, concentrating on eating tiny pieces of the dry bread. I looked up to find both men gazing at me in bewilderment, while Jaquet smiled wisely from her corner of the kitchen.

"I am fine, Meir—perhaps I had too much sun today. Please, Brother Anton, continue what you are saying. I don't want to interrupt."

"If you are sure, Shira . . . ," Brother Anton said. My husband and the friar exchanged puzzled looks but resumed their conversation.

"The fact that Judaism has refashioned itself during the past thousand years or more is precisely the problem, Meir. Would it surprise you to know that some of our clergymen are unaware of that fact?"

Meir laughed, a little bitterly, I thought. "Not even a little bit. It's quite evident that many of you think we're frozen in time—relics from the time of the Roman Empire, or even earlier, from our own biblical age."

"Believe it or not, that impression has saved your race many times. You are given special status as the witnesses of Christ and are considered superior to heretics such as the Cathars or Muslims just so long as you practice the laws of Moses . . . and *only* the laws of Moses."

"We are not eager to disabuse those of you who are ignorant of the true state of affairs, trust me. But you yourself are aware, Brother Anton, there have been centuries of Jewish learning between the time of Jesus of Nazareth and today. Ours is not a religion that has stagnated."

"I do know it, Meir. What I am here to tell you is that other people are discovering it as well. And they are shocked and disturbed by that knowledge." Brother Anton finished his stew and picked up the platter of braised beets Jaquet handed him, helping himself to a large portion.

"Does this have anything to do with the burning of Maimonides's books in Montpellier?" Meir asked, taking the platter from our guest and putting it down beside him.

"It does. Questions were asked by several of the Dominican friars at first, and then more pointedly by Cardinal Romanus, the judge of the heresy court. They wanted to know where these texts came from and why the Jews were interpreting their religious tenets when the Books of Moses are all the Jews need."

My stomach had calmed a little and I dared glance up. I loved watching my husband debate, seeing the completely focused look that transfigured his face and made him resemble one of our prophets of old. The passion that shone in his brown-flecked green eyes at times like these never failed to thrill me. He picked up a hand, sweeping an unruly lock of auburn hair from his face, and replied, "I don't understand how they can possibly think that. We live in a completely different world from the world of the Bible. How could we conceivably live if we did not interpret those Laws—without deviating from them, however—so that they have significance in today's world?"

"Well, perhaps that is so and perhaps it is only reasonable, Meir. But I must tell you that it is dangerous for you and your people to have such questions asked aloud. And the danger is growing because the increasing number of converts to the True Faith are answering such questions candidly. One of the Dominicans suggested that these questions be addressed to a Franciscan friar named Nicholas Donin, who, I believe, studied here in Paris for a while. Did you know Donin, Meir?"

The monk watched as Meir put his spoon down and looked directly at me. Brother Anton turned to me as well.

"Did *you* know Donin, Shira?" he asked in some surprise.

I wanted to weep. Would I ever shed Donin's malicious shadow over my life? I had been so happy about the news I had to share with my husband, only to have the evening ruined by the mention of my old suitor.

"He was a student for a brief time at Rabbi Shmuel's *yeshiva* in Falaise," my husband answered for me, seeing I was struggling with my emotions. "Shira saw him again and talked to him right before our marriage here in Paris."

"He asked to marry me many years ago," I said, my eyes focused on the small balls of bread I had scattered over my plate. "My father thought it would not be a good match, and I agreed with him."

"Your father is a wise man, Shira," said Brother Anton. "Donin is known already as a firebrand among the Franciscans. He is fomenting a good deal of malice against the Jews throughout France."

"We've heard of the Crusader massacres in Brittany," said Meir. "Has he done us more harm?"

"He led Crusaders in forcing conversions in Angoulême. Those who refused to convert were put to the sword. Hundreds of Jews were involved. Now, you must understand, Meir, I am not opposed to conversion—how could I be? But I would rather bring you to the True Faith through mercy and compassion than by the sword."

The thought that Donin was implicated in such treacheries was the last straw. The broth, which had been bubbling up inside me throughout the meal, would not stay down any longer. I cried out, putting a hand to

my mouth, and pushed back my stool and rushed from the table. Jaquet
followed me down the back steps and into the garden. She held my head
as I spewed out the contents of my stomach.

"Shh, shh, mistress. *C'est bon,*" she said to soothe me, brushing back
my hair with a rough but tender hand. "This is only natural."

I could not speak. My stomach was still retching, trying to expel
every particle of food I had swallowed. I sank down to my knees, my
eyes streaming, my nose running. When I finally found the composure
to turn around, I found my husband behind me, with Brother Anton a
few paces back.

What I must look like, I thought bitterly as Meir helped me to my
feet.

"Shira, what is it?" he asked, worried. But Brother Anton, wiser perhaps because he was older, laughed, making my husband reel around
angrily.

Brother Anton raised a hand to ward off his fury. "Easy now, Meir, I
mean no disrespect. It is just that this is such a joyous occasion, isn't it,
Shira?"

"My wife is ill, and you call it joyous, monk?"

I used part of my sleeve to wipe my grimy face. "No, he's right, beloved. I am not ill."

"Not ill?" Meir looked from me to the monk, still bewildered.

It was the Christian who illuminated him. "Is it not said that you
must '*p'ru v'rvu,*' Meir? Be fruitful and multiply?"

Meir turned to me and I nodded, smiling wryly. Meir shouted out,
picked me up, and swung me around, kissing every bit of my tear-stained
face he could reach.

HIRTEEN

Heal me, O Lord, and I will be healed.
                    —JEREMIAH 17:14

DESPITE THE FIRST MONTHS, when my stomach seemed to bob and pitch on a queasy sea, I thrived during each of my pregnancies. Though I was mindful of my stepmother's intense pain during her confinement and my own mother's fruitless suffering, a sense of inner well-being buoyed me with confidence. And while all my children took their time in quitting my body, I passed through every single one of my labors triumphant in the end.

The first of my babies was my darling Chaya. She was the child of my youth and the light of our life in Paris. She emerged from my womb smiling and the sound of her delighted laugh was a song both Meir and I gloried in. I would steal time from my housekeeping to play with my beautiful red-haired daughter, who, with her mottled cheeks and bright hazel eyes, looked exactly like a tiny version of her father.

Despite his studies, his teaching, and finding time to answer the letters that were sent to him from all corners of the globe as his reputation widened, Meir, too, was enamored of our small mite. We would set her out in the garden during the first summer of her life, her small, fat bottom fanning out beneath her as she sat firmly on the flagstone pavement between us. Or we would take her out with us for walks, often ending up at Saints Innocents Cemetery in the Champeaux district on the outskirts of the city. This was a popular place for people to walk and for children to play, and many of the women who lived nearby used the gravestones as a place to hang their laundry. It was separated from Les Halles market by a stone wall. In this green, open space, we would try to talk over her head about Meir's latest work, gossip of the *yeshiva,* or news from abroad. But we constantly interrupted ourselves to coo over the baby, to watch her early steps, sing snatches of songs to her, or just pick her up and hold her when she cried.

My happy Chaya was followed two years later by the more thoughtful Zipura. We called her Little Bird, my miniature dark reflection, and it was enchanting to see my redheaded big girl caring for her little sister.

"Are you sorry this new baby's not a boy?" I asked Meir as we fondly watched the two-year-old Chaya peer into Zipura's cradle.

"I am so grateful for my small harem that there's no room for sorrow of any kind," Meir said, smiling and kissing the top of my forehead. And then, dipping his mouth lower, he whispered in my ear, "Besides, this way, we get to keep on trying for a boy!"

I blushed, counting on my fingers how long it would be before we could share a bed again. Yes, I told myself, you should be grateful for the blessings of your life.

———•———

I was tending my babies one morning when a boy—Schouschan Schemaya, born in Troyes not far from the home of the romance author Chrétien—came running up the stairs and burst into our lodgings.

"There's been an accident!" he panted. "Your husband's hand . . ."

Meir had been watching two of his students wrestle each other during a midmorning break. The match grew unrestrained and Meir decided to intervene just as the stronger boy threw the other to the ground.

In trying to break the boy's fall, three of the fingers of Meir's hand and his wrist were twisted. As we ran toward the *yeshiva*, my children clinging to me and crying, Schouschan panted that my husband was in great pain. ,

By the time we reached the *yeshiva* yard, the physician had already arrived.

"It is nothing to worry about," Vifelin told me after he maneuvered Meir's hand, making my husband scream and writhe in agony. The doctor attached splints to the afflicted hand and bound it in bandages. "It will heal in time. But he is not to use that hand at all for several months."

Meir was not cheered. "It's my right hand, Shira!" he moaned. "I can't write!"

The young boys, huddled together in a sad cluster at the side of the school yard, surged forward. "We can write for you, Rav Meir," one of them volunteered.

Meir smiled wanly at their earnest faces. Another wave of pain made him groan. "I thank you, Nahmias. We will see."

"He should go home and stay there for a few days, until the pain subsides," the doctor instructed me. "He needs to sleep as much as he can, for sleep does wonders for an injured body. I will stop by and deliver some powders that will make him drowsy, otherwise the pain will keep him awake. Dissolve them in wine for him to drink."

Yechiel, who had been standing alongside my husband when I arrived, chimed in, "Do you have an amulet for him also, Vifelin?"

Vifelin nodded. "I keep a store of them that have worked successfully before. For as you know, Rabbi . . ."

"'What is an approved amulet?'" Yechiel quoted from the Talmudic tractate Gittin. "'One that has healed a second and a third time, whether it is an amulet of writing or an amulet of roots . . .'"

Meir groaned once more.

Yechiel, looking concerned, broke off his musings. "Shira, take him home and do not allow him back here until he is free of pain. I need my *melamed* back soon!"

"Do we get a holiday from our studies?" one of the boys was unwise enough to ask, a grin starting to form on his face.

Yechiel frowned at him. "Surely that's not what you're thinking about now, is it?" he asked, eyebrows raised.

"Don't mind him, Rabbi, he's from Waage. They're not very bright there," another *talmid* teased.

A word from Yechiel stopped the tussle that threatened to break out between the boy from Waage and his tormentor. I held Meir by his good arm and led him away.

Meir sat in our garden for two weeks, the corners of his beautiful mouth pinched white indentations as he stoically endured the pain. Nearly all his friends and students from the *yeshiva* stopped by, for they knew that, according to the Talmud, one who visits a sick person removes one-sixtieth of his illness. I did my best to keep these charitable visits brief and sometimes I had to shoo away the younger boys when it looked like they might become rowdy and exhaust my poor husband.

I was worn out with fetching and carrying for him, preventing Chaya—who was delighted to find her father home all day long—from climbing all over him, and tending to my infant. Kele, our landlady, helped now and then, but she had her own household to attend to. Deina and other women from the *yeshiva* also helped, making sure we had dinner on the table every night and taking my small ones for a while so I could rest.

During one of these brief respites, I brought my sewing into the garden, seating myself next to Meir. He had just imbibed one of the physician's doses and was sleepy. His head slumped down on his chest as he dozed.

"Am I disturbing you?" I asked, noting his half-shut eyes.

"No, not at all," he murmured drowsily.

He slept for a while. I set my stitches as neatly as I could, feeling waves of tiredness stealing over me. Finally, I let my sewing drop into my lap and closed my eyes.

"It's the writing that worries me," he said at that exact moment.

I struggled back from near sleep. "How so?" I murmured.

He had pulled himself upright, surveying the bandaged hand in his lap sourly. "I have at least three letters waiting right now. More arrive every week. They should be answered."

It had begun to seem like no one in Ashkenaz could decide issues of Jewish law without consulting my husband. He was inundated with letters seeking to clarify laws and customs by consulting the Talmud. Missives were brought to him by students newly arrived in Paris or by merchants from other cities, who did their local rabbis a favor and delivered letters in return for a blessing. I knew other rabbis received similar letters—after all, I had grown up with them in my father's home. But the number of requests Meir was handed had recently begun to exceed the number my father received.

"Could not your students . . . ?" I asked.

"They are too young, Shira. And everyone else is busy with his own duties. But I sit here and think out the responses in my head and it's worse than the pain not to be able to write them down!"

"How bad is your pain?" I asked, but he shrugged the question off.

"I was wondering . . . ," he started to ask.

I sat there, my sewing on my lap. He looked at me as though seeing me anew.

"You're such a good wife, Shira. The girls are a delight, the house is always peaceful, and you, my dear, are a pearl beyond words. I thank *ha-Shem* daily for the gifts he has given me."

I smiled, pleased at his praise. "I, too, am grateful for our life together."

"You do so much already that I hesitate to ask more of you. But I was wondering if—just perhaps—the reason you always loved studying Talmud was because *ha-Shem* foretold that I would need you now."

I blinked, not quite following. Meir saw my blank look and laughed.

"That sounds terrible when I say it out loud—as though God were so intimately concerned with my struggles that he provided for them years before I would need the help! And yet, should we not see God's invisible hand in everything in this universe?"

"How is it you would like me to help, Meir?" I asked, a little wary.

"Can you write when I dictate, Shira? I've seen your writing, and you have a good hand—a little curlicued, perhaps, but legible and clear nonetheless."

"You want me to write for you?" I was delighted. I had not had much chance to study after the birth of the girls. While I did not lose complete touch—and certainly, Deina and the other wives and I spent many hours discussing laws and rituals, our babies and children in tow—I no longer had a set time to study. It had been many months since I had opened a book even for a brief moment.

"What do you think, Shira? It's a lot to ask a woman, I know."

I sat up straighter in my chair. "I don't think you'll be disappointed in my writing abilities, Meir. I'd be glad to help you."

———◆———

Some letters were dispatched from German towns and provinces or the steppes of the great eastern lands beyond, where Jews were just beginning to settle. Others came from the West, from Normandy, Spain, the Muslim countries, even a few from England. Meir could decipher the various hands with ease, something that would take me many years of close study.

"See here, Shira, this man asks about a ring that a fellow townsman promised to sell on his behalf. Do you notice that no names are used, just letters, aleph, bet, and so on? That's so that the questions can be considered purely on their own merits. For if I perhaps knew Monsieur Aleph, my decision might be biased."

"I am proud so many people seek your advice," I said, delighted. Did not my husband's success reflect well on me, his wife?

"All I can do is interpret the Talmud for them—not being a judge or a king who dispenses justice. Actually, I receive quite a few letters asking me to decide what is right or wrong. I always answer that all I can do is give them the answer they themselves could find, were they to spend the time I've spent in study."

Meir settled back into his chair, the potion having alleviated his pain so that he was comfortable for a short while. We sat at the table in our garden, in two chairs so close to each other they were nearly touching. I prompted, "So. Monsieur Aleph and the ring."

"Yes. Listen to what they write. 'Aleph gave a broker a ring to sell. The broker lost the precious stone of the ring. The rabbis of the town have varied opinions. Some say the broker is responsible for the loss, others think he is not. We ask you to decide the matter, having heard that you are a learned scholar. Our rabbis have agreed that all concerned will stand by your ruling.'"

"They confer upon you a great deal of responsibility, husband."

Meir snorted, his mouth twisted. "If I thought about it that way, I couldn't answer them at all. If I simply tell them what I've studied, it becomes easy. Here, Shira, write this: 'The responsibility of the broker is that of a hired watchman, since he took the ring in anticipation of making a profit. The broker, therefore, must swear that the stone is not in his possession; he must also take an oath as to the value of the stone and must repay that amount to Aleph.'"

I wrote the letter. Meir told me the proper salutations with which to close it.

"Who will carry it so far?" I asked, having addressed it to the rabbis of the town.

"A messenger will call for the letter tomorrow, if you could ask Deina to tell Yechiel it is ready. Could we compose another?"

The girls were still away. I pushed aside my sewing basket with one foot.

"Of course we can," I said.

FOURTEEN

*Shabbat is a queen whose arrival changes the
humblest of homes into a palace.*
—THE TALMUD

EVEN AFTER MEIR'S HAND HEALED and he returned to his
teaching duties, he often asked me to write for him. For the rest of his
life, whenever the weather was damp or cold, he felt pain and stiffness
in his fingers, making it difficult for him to form letters. He often said
that this was the reason *ha-Shem* had imbued me with a desire to learn,
so I could be a helpmate for my husband. I half came to believe it myself. Meir's reputation grew ever greater and more and more letters were
directed to him.

Our lives continued pleasantly for another year or so. Our babies
thrived, and when Zipura was a year old and Chaya three, we began to
hope for the next to announce itself. Meir was given a more advanced
class to teach in the *yeshiva*, young men who were interested in exploring
interpretation and the nuances buried between the lines. Because of his
easy manner and his ability to make sense of the most intricate of Talmudic queries, Meir was a popular teacher. Students from other classes

would come to him with their thorniest questions, lining up outside his classroom door, walking home with him—sometimes even accompanying him through the door and staying for a loud, raucous dinner, where views were exchanged in rapid succession and almost any comment could provoke laughter. To provide for the girls' dowries, we even engaged in a little business, investing a cautious amount of Meir's hard-earned salary with one of his students' fathers, a man who traded in wines and spices in the far reaches of Eastern Europe, traveling to the exotic-sounding cities of Sofia, Třebíč, Riga, Vilnius, Kiev, and many others.

We took active part in the communal society of the Paris *yeshiva*. Every Friday morning I left the girls with Jaquet so I could help Deina buy supplies for the festive meal. She and Amyris and I would meet at the nearby gates of the Grève marketplace, near where the corn arrived on boats and barges up the river Seine. We passed by the mills of the Grand Pont, where the corn was ground into flour. The Grève market opened every morning as the nearby church bells chimed six. While it did not offer the variety of Les Halles, its smaller size made it a friendlier market. The three of us strolled contentedly about, sharing news from our families and the *yeshiva*, bargaining with the shopkeepers, who waved us over with a shout of recognition to offer us the best cuts of meat or the freshest produce.

We brought the heavy baskets back to the *yeshiva*. Leaving the food to be prepared by some of the other wives, we went into the dining hall to adorn the room with flowers or other decorations, such as fruit or bunches of decorative grasses. About five hundred people attended the meal each week. Long tables were laid with white cloths, a mix of wood and metal platters, and communal drinking cups. Everyone brought their own clasp knife and spoon, which hung from their belt in a little pouch.

Jaquet brought the children to me at the *yeshiva* at midmorning and then returned to our house to prepare our lodgings for the Shabbat. This routine suited both my maidservant and me. Jaquet understood how meticulously clean our small surroundings needed to be to satisfy Meir's sense of propriety and that was more easily accomplished without a toddler underfoot. I brought the girls into the long dining hall with me, and while Zipura slept contentedly on my breast, I gave Chaya a weekly lesson on manners as she flitted around the tables, delightedly looking at the preparations for the feast.

"Do we put our fingers in our mouth and then in the food bowl?" I asked her one midwinter morning.

"Nooo . . . ," she intoned, shaking her head gravely, putting her fingers dangerously close to her lips and then letting them fly into the air with a flourish. She laughed.

"Do we sing at the table?"

"Yes!" she cried, brightening.

"Alone?" I asked.

"No. Sing with everybody!" she chirped.

"Where do we wipe our noses?"

She produced a tiny handkerchief that she kept tucked in her sleeve and waved it at me. I inspected the small bit of cloth for grime or soil, because my happy little Chaya was not always the cleanest of creatures. But that day it was spotless. I suspected Jaquet had handed her a clean one before delivering the children to me.

After the lesson in etiquette, Chaya ran off to find friends to play with. Deina's girls were all too old, but Amyris's daughter had just turned five and she was always willing to let my redheaded charmer tag along behind the "big girls." I repaired to the kitchen to help with the final preparations for the meal. The rest of the morning waned in a flurry of mincing, chopping, and braising. By this point, a small army of women occupied the kitchen. Deina tried to prevent the types of arguments that so easily could crop up when so many women gathered together to cook by assigning everyone a distinct task. Even so, there was a tussle this morning over the cutting knives—too few to go around, too many women vying to chop up the fresh white fish at one time. Deina settled the outburst by breaking out in song: "Oh come, let us sing to the Lord; let us make a joyful noise to the Rock of our salvation!" Several other women, including Amyris, Floria, and I, chimed in, singing from the ninety-fifth psalm. "Let us come into

His presence with thanksgiving; let us make a joyful noise to Him with songs of praise!" The incipient argument died like a grape on the vine that did not receive enough rain to drink.

The Friday midday meal was always a small one, a simple repast of bread and cheese that could easily be eaten at each student's seat at the study tables. We gathered the children into a circle in one of the ante-chambers and fed them as well. I retired to Deina's quarters to nurse Zipura. Then it was time to take the children home and prepare them for the Shabbat. But today, as I went to collect Chaya, I was stopped short by a cry of indignation that rose from the main study hall.

"It is a travesty—an abomination before God!"

"He seeks nothing more than our total destruction! I cannot believe even *he* would go so far!" Deina's husband, Judah ben David, roared.

A messenger, his head hanging as if in shame, burst from the room and brushed past me, leaving the door wide open behind him. Alarmed by the fury emanating from the room, shielded from view by the heavy oaken door, I hovered for a minute in the hallway.

"Read it again, Rav Yechiel," I heard my husband say over the babble. "Let us be certain of what is being said here."

"Quiet, everyone. Quiet! Meir is right. We need to approach this crisis calmly and with dispassion. I will read the letter from Jachobe of Rome again. All of you listen carefully so that we can discuss it rationally later."

I listened while the letter was read, hoping Zipura, who was not quite asleep on my shoulder, would not begin fussing and betray our presence.

To the Most Esteemed Rabbi Yechiel of Paris, greetings and salutations from Rome.

I am saddened to write this letter, for it bodes ill for Jews throughout Christian Europe. It seems that one apostate Jew, a Franciscan friar named Nicholas Donin . . .

At the mention of Donin's name, there was an involuntary spate of catcalls and stomped feet. It resembled nothing as much as our attempts to drown out the name of the malevolent Haman—the man who tried but failed to kill the Jews of Persia—during our yearly reading of the Purim Megillah. Hearing it, I felt pain in that corner of my heart where some pity for Donin still nestled. Zipura stirred at the uproar. I rocked her, humming under my breath, for I wanted desperately to hear what evil Nicholas Donin had wrought now.

> *Nicholas Donin begged for an audience with Pope Gregory and, having received it, advised him that there is a book used by the Jews that contains libelous sayings about their hanged God, as well as his mother, whom the Nazarenes revere above all women, living or dead. Donin denounced the Talmud and interpretations such as Rashi's commentaries to the Pope, stating that Jews consider these books to be superior to our Books of Moses, which Christ's followers claim as part of their own heritage.*
>
> *I am informed that Pope Gregory was at first incredulous at these charges, but when Donin reminded him of the burning of Maimonides's books in Montpellier a few years back, he began to listen more carefully . . .*

At this, Judah ben David could not contain his outburst. "I told you all at the time that we would regret permitting the Dominicans to burn these books. I told you!"

His father-in-law hushed him. "Yes, you did, Judah—but there is more. Let me continue . . ."

The baby stirred again against my breast and I moved her from one arm to the other. I had tucked a honeyed biscuit in one of the pouches hanging from my corded leather belt. I fished it out and gave it to her. She smacked her lips over the sweet and gummed it contentedly.

Donin seized the opportunity to inform the Pope that our Talmud and other writings were nothing more than heretical documents and repeated several times that we Jews felt they were equal or even superior in stature to our Hebrew scriptures. Indeed, he told the Pope, it is the value we place in these books that prevents us from conversion to what he calls "the True Faith." If we truly read the Torah and only the Torah, we, like he himself, would understand that the Son of God came to earth to save us from our sins. Because we are an evil and reviled people, he said, who refuse to accept the grace of their crucified Lord, it is no wonder that these later writings are wicked, a mixture of sin and slander . . .

The gasps of outrage could not be contained, but Yechiel continued to read, raising his voice to be heard.

. . . that include ridiculous rules about how to live our lives, combined with hideous and blasphemous stories about the Christians, including specific tales about Jesus and his Virgin Mother . . .

"The only ones telling tales about Jesus's mother are the Christians," Yonah cried. "How can a woman be both mother and virgin? I ask you!"

. . . whom the Jews claim conceived the baby in an adulterous relationship. This horrified the Pope, who demanded that Donin produce his slanders in writing, which he said he would happily do. Rabbi Yechiel, I write to advise you and your congregation of these events, which may stir up even more ill will toward us Jews throughout Europe, who have suffered so much already at the hands of Crusaders. I will write again once Donin publishes his slanders, to let you know exactly what he says.

I heard the rustling of paper being folded. "That's the end of the letter," Yechiel said. "I ask each man to reflect upon these matters in his heart, but do not allow them to transgress upon the sanctity of the Shabbat. One of our ridiculous rules for living, as you know," he said, chuckling softly, "is never to allow bad news to cloud our day of rest. So let us each repair to our lodgings or our rooms to prepare for Shabbat."

I quickly moved past the open door, gathered Chaya up, and hurried out of the *yeshiva* toward home.

———•———

Because I had lingered, Meir came home soon after we did. The children, sensing my disquiet, were cranky and irritable, whining over trifles. Jaquet, who would normally relieve me of the girls so I could array myself for Shabbat, had found mites crawling in several baskets of winter wheat. She was busy in the pantry trying to sift them out—a tedious and weary task. One glance at the tiny, wriggling slugs made me shudder and hustle the children out of the room. Chaya began to wail when she realized Jaquet couldn't tell her the story that she usually entertained the girls with on Friday afternoons.

Meir entered as I was sitting limply in the middle of the floor with the two children, trying to amuse Chaya by telling some stories of my own. He gave me an icy look out of narrowed eyes. "Wife," he demanded, "is everything ready for Shabbat?"

I was nettled by his tone, even though I was certain it stemmed from worry about Donin. I felt guilty for having listened at the door and could see from Meir's expression that he remembered my connection to Donin all too clearly.

"Why would today be any different than any other Friday?" I retorted, flustered.

Zipura, who was sitting in my lap, chose that second to reach up and yank my hair. Chaya, who had given her father an ear-to-ear grin of welcome when he came into the room, froze at his cross expression.

"Pa-pa angry?" she stammered.

"You don't look ready," Meir snapped, ignoring the toddler's question. He spun on his heel and retired into the solar to dress for Shabbat, leaving me with two fretting children.

"Jaquet!" I called out, rising to my feet. But both Chaya and Zipura clung to me with their small, moist, pudgy fingers.

"Mama finish story," Chaya insisted.

Zipura grabbed on to my leg and started to cry.

"Mama!" shrieked Chaya.

Meir poked his head out of the room. "Shira! Can't you control those two girls? It's nearly time for Shabbat."

I would never have expected Meir to help me with the children, but he might at least not have made things worse by yelling. Jaquet, hearing the hubbub, came running into the room, apron strings flying behind her.

"Let me take the children," she said, putting her arms out. "I can finish after you set off for the synagogue. I will be done before sunset, never fret." I surrendered them both to her gratefully. She carried both girls, screaming for me at the top of their lungs, out to the garden.

I had to change into my Shabbat dress. I was furious at Meir but tried to calm myself before facing him. I vowed silently that he wouldn't learn from me that I had listened at the door.

"Jaquet found mites in the winter wheat," I told him quietly as I entered the room. I was glad to hear my voice was steady. "She couldn't take the girls right away. That's why they were unsettled. She has them now."

"It's late," he said. "I expected you to be dressed when I came home. There should be tranquility and peace in the house as Shabbat approaches."

"Of course," I said. "It was just that if we left the mites in the wheat, without attending to them before Shabbat, they could infect the entire basket."

"It's always the mites that spoil the wheat," he muttered. I knew he wasn't talking about our kitchen.

"But Jaquet patiently, quietly, is sifting the contents from the basket and pulling every one of the varmints out. Everything will be restored to its original state, with just a little wheat lost," I said to soothe him.

He looked at me. I knew I looked flushed from dealing with the children and with my suppressed emotions about Donin, to say nothing of my anger that Meir held me accountable every time Donin's name was spoken. The memory of the lonely man wrapped in his cloak, pleading with me in the charity hut back in Falaise, flashed upon me. I wanted to crawl into a corner and cry.

But Meir was right; Shabbat was approaching, and we needed to set aside our apprehension and glory in one of God's greatest gifts to us, the day of rest. So I pressed my cold fingers onto my heated cheeks and said, "There's white fish for dinner tonight, a fresh batch brought in just this morning to Les Halles. So much fish that we had to fight over the knives to chop them up."

Meir said nothing, but his shoulders relaxed a little, and I knew he would not scold or find fault until after the Shabbat was over. By then, my association with Donin would probably be forgotten or at least forgiven. I dressed hurriedly, not to keep him waiting. By the time I was done he was out in the garden, playing clapping games with the girls.

"I'm ready," I said.

He turned to me, scrutinized my dress, and stepped forward to take both ends of my shawl and tie them shut. "Remember, you can wear a shawl on the Shabbat only if you tie the ends together, so the wind cannot blow it off," he teased, for we had written this in response to a query just this week.

"Girls, we need to light the candles and then go to the *yeshiva*," I said, reaching out for Zipura.

My family followed me into the house, where Jaquet had placed candles and candlesticks on our small table. Chaya clambered onto a stool and stood next to me, her head covered with a scarf like mine.

"*Baruch atah Adonai,*" we intoned together, "*elohainu melech ha'olam . . .*"

I looked over her head at my husband and was relieved to see nothing but peace residing on his face and in his eyes.

IFTEEN

"There is a certain people dispersed and scattered among the peoples in all the provinces of your kingdom whose customs are different from those of all other people . . ."
—ESTHER 3:8

A YEAR LATER OUR LIVES—the lives of all the Jews in Paris— changed irrevocably. It was Shabbat and we were in the synagogue. My new baby, Rachel, another redhead who was going to look like her father, was happily sleeping, tucked into my shoulder. It was a windy Saturday, cold for early spring. We were glad to get out of the wind and into the synagogue building. My friends immediately surrounded me, cooing and babbling at the new baby. Chaya and Zipura clung to my skirts until one of Chaya's friends arrived. The three girls found themselves a quiet corner where they could chatter about tomorrow's Purim holiday. I listened with half an ear, amused, as they compared the goodies they would exchange. It was 13 Adar, 5001—March 3, 1241, by the Christian calendar—and we had spent the past week baking and preparing baskets, *mishloach manot,* to give to all of our friends and neighbors. We would receive baskets from them in return and Zipura found a moment to slip back over to me and sing, in nineteen-month-old toddler excitement, "Nuts and sweet cakes and Haman's ears, Mama!"

"Is that what Joie's mama is putting in our basket, lovey?" I asked fondly.

She nodded emphatically. "Nuts and sweet cakes and Haman's ears!" she repeated, jumping up and down in excitement, then racing back to her big sister and giving her a hug.

"You didn't fast on Thursday, did you, Shira?" Deina asked me, referring to the day before Purim, when we commemorate Esther's three days of fasting before appealing to King Ahasuerus on her people's behalf. Deina was visiting her father from Melun, where she and her husband had opened a seminary last year. I was delighted to see my friend again. "I was worried you'd try even though you are nursing and don't have to."

"No," I assured her. "With this little one attached to my breast every two hours, it would be impossible to forget I need nourishment to feed her. I hope yours was an easy fast?"

Deina shrugged. "Easy enough. I like it better when Ta'anit Esther falls on the day before the holiday. Then you have the feast to look forward to. But we certainly could not fast today, on Shabbat, or yesterday, when we needed to prepare for it. Oh, look, the men are filing in now, we should take our places. Shall we?"

My big girls—Chaya was now four years old and Zipura a year and a half—sat next to me, rocking and swaying with the prayers. They were not always this well-behaved, but I had told them both sternly that only good girls received Purim baskets. Chaya was already beginning to lisp the words of the blessings, imitating me. Through the divider, the *mechitzah*, I could see Meir among the men, wrapped in his prayer shawl, his *tallith*. I prayed softly, letting the peace of the Shabbat Queen seep through me.

A door slammed, echoing through the quiet building. The sound of running footsteps reverberated, disturbing our tranquility. We turned to one another, alarm on all our faces. Latecomers to the service knew to sidle in, not to burst in noisily. Someone stood at the entranceway, shouting. We women couldn't make out the words. The men left their places and gathered around the man. Yechiel, who had been praying from the *bimah,* came down. The crowd parted to let him through.

My little ones, sensing something was wrong, clung to my legs as I stood and tried to peer past everyone.

"Shira, what could be happening?" Amyris hissed at me.

"I don't know, but it must be something terrible . . . You don't suppose . . . ?" With my small ones nestled against me, I didn't want to give voice to my fears. Could the Crusaders have come to incinerate us in our synagogue? It was one thing to admire Jewish martyrs who died rather than convert to Christianity, but it was another to make that choice yourself, with three small children to provide for and protect. I remembered how Meir and I had stood outside the castle that snowy night in Falaise, reading the dread in each other's eyes. Fear stole through me and it was as if I could hear my heart beating loudly in my ears over the din. Was it possible I might be slaughtered without ever seeing my husband again? I hugged my girls to me, feeling their bodies shaking against me as they sobbed at the unnamed fear suddenly taking form all around us.

Yechiel broke away from the huddled men. I watched as he made his way back to the *bimah.* He mounted the stairs, his shoulders square, his back ramrod straight. I glanced over at Deina, whose eyes were riveted on her father's face. Her lips were moving and I realized that she was reciting psalms under her breath. As I watched her stare at her father, my thoughts flew for a moment to my own papa. He was safe, I prayed, he and the family in Falaise. Rabbi Yechiel moved toward the pulpit, gripping both sides of the lectern with hands that turned white at the knuckles. Even from a distance, I could see that he was distraught but trying hard to hide it.

"Quiet! Quiet!" he said, his resolute voice projecting over the hubbub. "Everyone must hear this!"

The yelling and shouting ceased immediately. A sickly silence hung like a pall over the worshippers.

"We have been ordered by the prelates of Paris to remain in the synagogue. I have just been handed a note signed by the bishop of Paris, William of Auvergne, that commands us to stay here while Paris authorities enter our homes. They are going to remove every volume of the Talmud they can lay their hands on."

A great cry of protest involuntarily broke loose. Several of the men jumped from their seats. Yechiel threw up a hand to stop them.

"You must all sit down! Everyone must stay here. Guards have been posted outside the synagogue with orders to kill anyone who leaves. I have been assured we are safe so long as we remain within these walls."

"Why are they doing this?" someone called out, and several others chimed in. "Yes, why?" "What do they want with our books?" "What is the meaning of this, Rabbi?"

"Be quiet and I will tell you." The rabbi didn't need to wait more than a moment for silence. "More than a year ago, I received a report from Rome that an old student of mine, Nicholas Donin, an apostate who joined the Franciscan order, was planning vengeance against us of the most calamitous nature. Many of you will remember Donin. The man was a heretic, sowing discontent wherever he went. You will also recall how I was compelled to excommunicate him right from this very *bimah*."

At the mention of Donin's name, Deina's eyes flew involuntarily to my face. I flushed at her glance. I felt ice drip through my breast, a pang of sick anticipation of what would follow.

"Donin first sought revenge against us bodily. Using his authority as a friar, he appealed to the soldiers of the Sixth Crusade, men who were forming ranks in Brittany, Anjou, Poitou, and Aquitaine. He preached to the mobs about how unbelievers—we Jews—lived in their midst. The usual spate of violence followed. It was Nicholas Donin who encouraged the Christians to slaughter our people.

"The pain he and the Crusaders and the mob wreaked on us was horrendous. We have stood bound in the fires of Christian knights for centuries, but these soldiers took torture to a new height. They urged their war horses to ride over the crowds, trampling men, women, and children. More than three thousand of our people perished at the point of the sword, in the flames, or under the galloping horses. And five hundred others succumbed to fear and gave way, converting unwillingly to the faith of the Nazarene God."

All around me was the sound of moans and tears. My girls were weeping uncontrollably into my lap and the baby rooted against my neck, wailing. I sat still, stricken to the heart. Yechiel's descriptions of the death and destruction overwhelmed me. It was almost more than I could bear. In that moment, any lingering attraction to him I had kept buried in a corner of my heart evaporated, like smoke rising from a fire. I felt a painful, diamond-hard hatred taking its place. I hated Nicholas Donin.

Yechiel continued, "Killing and destroying so many lives was not enough for Donin, however. Now he seeks a revenge even greater than our mere lives. Now he wishes to hurt us at our souls, by convincing the Christians to destroy our Talmud and take it from us." Yechiel's voice broke as he spoke and it took him a moment to recover. "He appealed to the Pope in Rome, leveling charges against the Talmud. It is sacrilege to speak of them here, in this holy place, but rest assured he twisted and warped our words in a way that we will never forgive or forget.

"The Pope took more than a year to consider what Donin had said. Some nine months ago, he sent Donin back to Paris, with a letter he wrote to the bishop of Paris. The Pope instructed the bishop to write to the sovereigns of France, England, Aragon, Navarre, Castile, León, and Portugal to seize copies of the Talmud. We had heard rumors that such a threat existed, but again we prayed that it would never materialize. Kings have a long-standing habit of listening to popes only when it is to their advantage. As the months crept past, the leaders of these Jewish communities agreed that the threat must have passed. Obviously, today's events prove us wrong.

"I cannot tell you what will happen next. I will appeal to His Majesty and to the bishop to have our property restored to us. Perhaps there will be a disputation where we can make our case. If so, we may yet prevail.

As many of you know, I am no stranger to refuting the Christians when they accuse us of odd practices."

A chuckle, tinged with relief, rose from many in the synagogue. I turned to Deina, who smiled wanly and leaned over to whisper in my ear, "My father appeared before the king and the bishops many times before. He once managed to convince them that we do not use Christian blood in our rituals, which probably saved all our lives." She sat back to listen as her father continued.

"The Gentiles probably have not considered that they have chosen an auspicious date to seize our holy books—a date that should give us both courage and hope. On 13 Adar, following our first exile from our beloved Zion, while we were living in Persia, our ancestors faced one of the most terrifying dangers ever inflicted upon us. I'm speaking, of course, about Haman's threat to execute every Jew in King Ahasuerus's kingdom.

"On 13 Adar, the sound of hammering was heard throughout the Persian capital as gallows were erected. We faced extinction as a people. But one brave woman, Esther, came forward and explained the truth to the king in a way that forced him to acknowledge we had done no wrong. We prevailed and were delivered from the hangman's noose.

"Could the Gentiles have chosen a more foolish day to harass and threaten us? We will not succumb to fear. We will not succumb to dread. We will return home—and tomorrow, we will celebrate the feast of Purim with joy in all our hearts and remember another man like Donin who tried—and failed—to destroy us."

Someone approached the *bimah*. Yechiel came forward, leaning down so the man could whisper in his ear. Yechiel nodded, straightened up, and returned to the pulpit.

"My friends, the guards have left and the doors of the synagogue are open. You can return to your homes. Remember that this is the Shabbat, a day of rest and prayer and joy. Do not despair. Tomorrow, we will celebrate the holiday of Purim together. And then, on Monday, I will approach His Majesty the king and His Holiness the bishop and discover what lies ahead."

Meir was waiting for us at the exit of the synagogue. I had to stiffen my lip to stop its quivering as I took in my husband's grim expression. He put a hand out, cupping my shoulder briefly before picking up Zipura and holding her to him. I carried Rachel, and we both clasped Chaya's hands. Together we walked home. The familiar streets felt tinged with menace as we passed by homes whose doors were flung open, half the contents of the houses strewn about the streets, bookcases in splinters and books that were not the Talmud heaped carelessly about the yards, many torn or mutilated beyond repair.

Our own lodgings were in a similar state. Jaquet greeted us at the door, tears streaming down her face. Putting my daughters down, I reached over and hugged her.

"I am sorry, madame, but they had swords and there was no way for me to stop them."

"It is not your fault, Jaquet. Every Jewish house in the city was visited by the soldiers. They did not hurt you, did they?"

"No, madame. They insulted me, and seeing the cross I wear, one told me I should not be working here. They laughed when I said I never had a kinder master or mistress."

I gave her another hug, then let her go. Meir had already moved past us into our home. I followed in his wake, stepping over papers and books that littered the floor, along with our silver candlesticks and spice box, some of the children's toys, and clothing.

"They did not steal anything except for books, did they, Jaquet?" I asked, calling over my shoulder.

"They wanted to, madame, but their sergeant would not let them."

I stopped short in front of the doorway to our study alcove. I looked up, searching the bookcase above the table for the volumes of my beloved family Talmud given to me as a wedding gift by my father who knew how much I treasured them. They were gone, along with several other copies that belonged to Meir.

"How did they know to take only the Talmud?" I wondered, looking at the other books scattered about.

"The men had a piece of paper," Jaquet said. "There were Hebrew letters written on it."

I felt ice-cold. Donin or some other Jew must have written the words out. I could imagine him handing out the strips of paper, happily contemplating how the soldiers would compare his words with our books, making very sure they took the exact volumes we cherished.

The bookcase had been half smashed and tipped dangerously, like a drunken sot. The table was swept clean of Meir's writing implements. A vicious knife blade had scarred the tabletop, scratching crosses everywhere.

"I will help you clean up, madame," said Jaquet, her arms full of books. "It will not take us long."

Meir turned. His face was pale with pain, but he strove to speak gently. "Please put those down, Jaquet. Thank you for your kindness, but it is Shabbat and no one belonging to this house will work. Everything will remain where it is until tomorrow evening, after the sun sets."

"Is there any problem with it being Purim tomorrow, Meir? Do we need to leave everything where it is until Sunday at sunset?" I asked.

Meir laughed, a short, bitter laugh. "If I had a tractate Megillah handy, Shira, I would look it up to be absolutely certain. But I am confident that business and even manual labor are allowed on Purim."

"Jaquet?" came a voice behind me, and I turned to see Zipura standing there, her thumb jammed in her mouth. I had been trying to break her of the habit for months but did not have the heart to slap her hand right now. "Did the bad men take our baskets?"

Jaquet, who had stooped to put the books down on the floor, turned to the toddler. "*Non, petite,* they did not. We still have our beautiful baskets for you to carry to all your friends tomorrow—and I'm sure they have theirs to give you, too."

"You restore my faith in mankind, Jaquet," my husband said. "You are a blessing on this house."

"Thank you, Rabbi," Jaquet said, blushing beet red. "I am sorry the soldiers took your books."

"Will they give them back, Papa?" Chaya asked, her eyes wide. One of the joys of her young life was to sit on my lap and turn the illuminated pages of the books in our small library, pointing to the beautiful illustrations while I read to her.

"I don't know, *liebchen*," my husband said, reaching out to stroke her cheek. "I hope so."

"We should have our Shabbat meal." I felt wretched in the face of the mess surrounding us. I had never celebrated Shabbat in a disordered home before. The girls and Jaquet, their faces reflecting my disquiet, turned toward the kitchen.

"Courage, my wife," my husband whispered, putting his left arm around my shoulder. "You and I must show our girls that no one can destroy Shabbat, no matter how hard they try."

With one last agonized glance at our empty bookshelf, I allowed my husband to usher me toward the ruin of the Shabbat meal, which we had left waiting in tranquil glory not three hours before.

That day was a hard one to live through, as my every waking instinct was to restore my home to order. We left the house for late afternoon prayers, to find that the soldiers had visited the *yeshiva* after letting us leave the synagogue. They removed every volume of the Talmud from the classrooms, the synagogue itself, and the rabbi's chambers. The rabbi had stood before the ark, refusing to allow the soldiers to open it and thus profane our Torah scrolls, but it was the only concession he was granted. If our lodgings were in disarray, that was nothing compared to the chaos of the *yeshiva* building.

It was then that I began to understand the deeply rooted affection that my father and husband shared for the esteemed rabbi of Paris. Yechiel stepped up to the *bimah* and led us in prayer as though nothing out of the ordinary had occurred. It struck me that this act, this refusal to allow the desecration of the synagogue and the removal of our books to change our Shabbat celebration, was among the most heroic feats I had ever witnessed. Yechiel's calm demeanor and unfaltering bearing made the rest of us straighten in our seats. Until the sun set, not one person in the community mentioned the tragedy that had just transpired.

After sunset and Havdalah, the ceremony that formally ends Shabbat, we moved quickly to tidy what we could before returning to the synagogue for the reading of the Purim Megillah. Had it not been for Rabbi Joshua ben Levi, one of the sages in Israel two centuries after Jesus's birth, I might have stayed at home and let Meir take the girls with him for the reading. But Rabbi Joshua had proclaimed that women were required to hear the reading of the Megillah, because it had been a woman who had delivered the Persian Jews from Haman's clutches.

Before we left for the synagogue, however, I sat Chaya down at the kitchen table and brought out a small store of stones that we had collected for this celebration. Chaya had written the name "Haman" on about half of these, and my children would use them during the service, banging them together every time the villain's name was mentioned until the name was rubbed off of the stones. I quickly showed Chaya how to form the letters for "Donin" on the rocks that were not yet inscribed and told her to put them on as many as her small fingers could manage.

Meir, curious why the small girl was working so studiously at the table while the rest of us—even my toddler Zipura—were busy tidying up, peered over her shoulder. "Shira!" he called to me when he saw what she was doing.

"Yes, husband?" I asked, poking my head out of the alcove where Jaquet and I were trying to restack the remaining books on the tilting bookshelf.

"Did *you* tell the child to do this?" he asked.

I raised my chin, looking him straight in the eyes. My face felt cold, the hatred I felt for Donin stiffening the bones of my cheeks and jaw. "I thought it right, husband, after hearing what Donin has done to us."

Meir picked up one of the rocks, the straggling child's letters scratched

on it. He studied it for a minute and then raised his head again, returning my unwavering glare.

"Shira, I did not think how this might affect you . . . I should have,"
he said.

I continued looking right at him. The words that felt cold when they
were lodged unspoken in my breast warmed my lips when I finally released them. "The man I once knew and had feelings for died the day
Yechiel excommunicated him, husband. The evil being that resides in
his body is nothing to me. I assure you, it is you and only you who remember my connection to him. I severed it long ago."

Meir said nothing. His eyes—shining, concerned, loving—told me
all I needed to know.

As we left, Jaquet, who promised to finish cleaning up while we were
away, called from the window, "And the desk in the study alcove, Monsieur Rabbi? What shall I do with it?"

Meir looked at me. I had seen him running a pained hand over the
crosses the soldiers had scratched maliciously into the table's surface.
"What do you think, Shira?"

"Will the *talmidim* be burning a straw effigy of Haman tonight,
Meir?"

"I'm certain they will."

"Tell them to collect the desk and use it for firewood."

"A good idea!" my husband said, his hand moving lightly up my
sleeve in a modest caress. "Jaquet!" he called up to her. "Several students
of mine will come for it. Let them have it. We will replace it with another
desk soon."

"Perhaps we should burn more than one effigy," I mused as we
strolled down the street. In the short time since we had extinguished
the Havdalah candle, our neighbors had all cleared their yards of debris.
Our street felt familiar to me once more.

"One of Haman and one of . . . ?" my husband replied, turning to me,
a subtle light in his eyes like a flickering candle flame.

"One of Brother Nicholas, of course, Meir. You would need to make sure they do so secretly, so that the Church authorities do not catch wind of it and punish us. But don't you think the deed might help the students feel better about all this?"

"An inspired idea, my dear," he said, his glowing eyes promising me an unquiet night ahead.

SIXTEEN

Clouds and thick darkness surround Him;
righteousness and justice are the foundation of His throne.

—Psalm 97:2

THE NEXT MONTH WAS UNSETTLED as Yechiel and his son-in-law, Judah of Melun, tried and failed to convince the authorities to restore our volumes of the Talmud. In vain they wrote letters of appeal to the bishop and appeared in the king's court to sue for justice.

Then, three days after our final Passover meal, we received the notification we'd been waiting for. A disputation was convened for June, to take place before the royal pair, His Majesty King Louis IX and his mother, the dowager queen Blanche of Castile.

Louis had been crowned king of France at the tender age of twelve, but we all knew it was his strong-willed mother who actually had ruled the country during his youth. Now that the king was twenty-seven years old and married, he had taken control of the crown. But Blanche still remained an adviser to the young king. There was talk that Louis would soon embark upon his first Crusade, for he had been brought up as an accomplished knight whose heart stirred to be in battle. Less endearing to us Jews was the rumor that he was considering financing his Crusade by evicting all the Jewish moneylenders in the country and confiscating their property.

Nicholas Donin would lead the disputation's prosecution. The list of rabbis summoned before the court clearly bore the mark of Donin's malice: Rabbi Yechiel, Rabbi Moses of Coucy, Rabbi Judah ben David of Melun, and my father, Sir Morel of Falaise. Donin held each of these men responsible for his excommunication, and Papa, I feared, he had summoned for an even more personal reason.

———◆———

The morning of the disputation was a fine June day. My father came to Paris with Alyes a few days before and was staying with us, having left their three sons and daughter back in Falaise to watch over the *yeshiva*. Papa attended a special service with the other rabbis in the morning, where the entire community prayed for the success of our rabbis and the deliverance of our holy books. Every man and woman in the congregation over the age of thirteen fasted to give wings to our prayers to God. The three rabbis who would appear with Yechiel in court sat on the *bimah* with him, each gorgeously attired in his best clothing, spotlessly clean, purified by a dawn visit to the *mikveh*.

We had learned that King Louis would not preside over the trial after all. Yechiel was sorry, for he and Louis had long been known to each other and he had prevailed upon Louis's gracious justice in the past.

"King Louis carries not only a scepter but also a *main de justice,* a staff with an open hand," Yechiel explained, describing the young king's allegiance to integrity. "He has abolished trial by combat and appointed a group of magistrates who administer the law throughout France. I hear these men are forbidden to take fees, drink in taverns, or gamble, thus ensuring that their hearts remain pure."

In his stead, Louis's mother, Queen Blanche of Castile, a courtly lady who loved pageantry and knights in shining armor, jousts of bravery and feats of skill, had appointed herself chief judge. Blanche's affection for courtly love had caused her trouble in the past, and men still coupled her name with that of Theobald I of Navarre. Theobald had been with Blanche's husband during the siege of Avignon and was suspected of trying to poison him. After all, the court whispered, Theobald composed poems to win Blanche's heart and she showed him favor—and possibly even her bed. Even now that Theobald was far away in Navarre, suspicions of secret debauchery clouded the queen's much-vaunted piety. The rabbis despaired that a sacred matter would be decided by such a woman, yet they were determined to proceed as staunch, dignified defenders of our faith.

As we left the synagogue a royal messenger ran up to Yechiel, handing him a note sealed with the imprint of the court. Meir and I lingered with others who saw this. I tried to think what it might mean. Would the day's deliberations be postponed? Had Donin designed a new outrage to confound us at the last minute? Yechiel took the note and retired to his study. The message must have been brief, for a moment later he emerged and called out to my father, "Shmuel! Attend me, please?"

The two men closed the study door behind them. I stood alongside my husband and tried to keep my cold fingers warm by rubbing my hands together.

"It will be all right," my husband whispered to me.

My father poked his head out and, seeing us close by, motioned to Meir. "Son-in-law, may we discuss a matter with you?"

"Go home, Shira, I will return soon," my husband told me, but my father put up a hand.

"She should wait for you, Meir."

Meir and I exchanged perplexed looks. My father impatiently waved him in. "Stay here, Shira," he commanded.

Moments passed. Voices grew louder in Yechiel's antechamber, and I moved close to try to hear what was being said.

"She will not do it! It is his way of hurting her! She is nothing to him now!" I placed a hand against my wildly beating heart. It was my husband who was yelling. What could be in the note that upset my husband so much?

"Nor was she ever, Meir," came my father's measured tones. "She is blameless in this."

"She is my wife and I forbid it!" Meir shouted.

I was not the only one who could hear this. My husband's bellowing was audible to the small crowd of people who waited for some sign of what the note contained. Fingers were pointed at me. I heard whispers that paired my name with Donin's. A flush rose unbidden to my cheeks. I strained to ignore the curious stares and to hear what was being said behind the closed door. But the voices in the study were lowered. I could not make out what Yechiel and my father murmured to Meir or what he replied in return.

My father opened the door again, blinking in surprise at the crowd. "Shira. Daughter, please join us," he said mildly.

I entered, my heart pounding in my chest. My husband stood there, the set look I knew so well on his face—mouth pinched, eyes bright and cold, jaw clenched as though he were refusing to acknowledge a blow. He glared at me. Donin, I thought. Donin has done something terrible.

"Shira. How are you?" Yechiel asked.

"I am well, thank you, Rabbi. Anxious to learn of today's outcome, like everyone in the community."

"Yes. And you will be among the first to know. The note I received from Queen Blanche was an invitation for you to attend her during the disputation."

I found it difficult to breathe. "To . . . what?"

"The queen wishes you to sit among her ladies and watch the disputation, Shira," my father clarified. I glanced wildly in his direction. He was trying hard to remain composed. "You must hurry home and dress."

"I do not want to go!" I cried. My thoughts racing, I pondered the possible consequences of this dreadful summons. If something went wrong, I would be helpless and alone in the Christian court. Donin had proven how wickedly he could act to avenge himself upon us. My brief encounter with him in the Paris marketplace had shown me that I was not exempt from his scorn and taunts. Might he even turn me over to the torturers of the Inquisition?

Even if the queen's invitation was wholly innocent, I was terrified at the thought of sitting, like the rustic, unpolished housewife that I was, among the glittering ladies of the court. Would my lack of manners disgrace my people?

All this was clearly Donin's doing, but I could not understand what he stood to gain by it. Not knowing alarmed me. I looked at my husband, whose stern visage had softened a trifle as he watched uneasiness chase across my face. My voice came out as a whisper. "Meir, why does he torment me so?"

Meir took two steps to me, pulling me to him in a quick embrace. I felt the stiffness in his body and knew I was not yet fully forgiven. It hurt me that my husband would not admit that I was merely a puppet in Donin's vicious performance, my strings pulled in strange, disconcerting directions. But perhaps it was too much to ask that my husband comfort me when he himself felt so helpless in the face of these events.

"There is no need to fear for your safety, child," Yechiel said reassuringly. "The queen mother would lend herself to nothing underhanded or perverse. She promises that you will be under her protection the entire time you are in the palace."

I looked at the rabbi over Meir's protective shoulder. I felt dizzy. In a moment, they would laugh and tell me it was all make-believe and I would go home and tend my children.

My father reached over to touch my arm. "Shira, it is nearly time for us to present ourselves. We will not be able to wait for you. You must hurry home and dress in your best clothing. Meir, will you take my songbird to the gates of Place de Grève? The note says that someone will be waiting there to escort her to the queen's chambers." My father directed a searching glance at my husband, who said nothing and then nodded. I stepped out of Meir's embrace and we turned to go.

"There is one more thing, Shira," Rabbi Yechiel said, calling us back. "I know Donin as well as you and your father—perhaps even better.

He will seek to confound us. He may isolate us from one another. Your father and husband have spoken to me with pride of your study and writing. Rather than approaching your appearance at court as a calamity—natural though it is to feel that way—consider it your duty to act as a woman of valor, an *eshet cha'il*. Like Esther, you have a unique opportunity to help your people. If the queen asks your opinion, give it, clearly and honestly. If you are not asked, memorize the events unfolding before you. Sit down after the day is over and transcribe them, so that our people in centuries to come will remember what happened, no matter what the outcome."

"But no one would believe the account of a mere woman, Rabbi," my husband protested.

I turned around to stare at him.

"Do you believe what your wife tells you, Meir ben Baruch?" Yechiel asked.

I looked at my husband, eyebrows raised, waiting for his response, a flash of indignation crowding out almost every other emotion in my breast.

"Well, yes, mostly," my husband admitted. "Shira is an unusual woman."

"Esther was equally unusual, as was Yael, who brought the nail down on Sisera's head, and Hannah, who watched as her children were killed, one by one, by the Greeks, down to the youngest of them. Our annals are filled with unusual women, Meir."

"Of course, Rabbi," Meir said. But despite his immediate, respectful response, I felt my husband did not fully agree. "I will bring her to the palace."

"And then come inside yourself, if it is permitted," my father said. "I would like you to bear me company throughout the day."

My husband gave a small half bow. "I would be honored, Rabbi Shmuel."

We left the room, saying nothing to the crowd gathered outside the door. Rabbi Yechiel would decide what to tell them. We walked halfway home in silence. I was exasperated at Meir and was determined that my husband would be the first to speak.

Finally, the tension between us was too much for him. "What are you thinking about?" he asked.

There was so much I could have said to him. I could have told him that I was upset he did not trust me wholly, that he did not understand that this situation was not of my making, and that if anyone was suffering, it was me and me alone. I could also have said that his immediate dismissal of any good I, as a woman, could do in this situation hurt me deeply. But from his frown, I could tell that saying any of this would serve no purpose.

"I'm trying to figure out what to wear," I said instead, to lighten the mood. But he thought I was serious.

"Women!" he scoffed, laughing slightly.

After a thoughtful pause, he added, "Your blue Shabbat dress with the lace kirtle, I think. And the large pearl hung from the gold chain I gave you after Jonathan's father paid us our earnings from his trip to Poland."

"A fine idea, husband," I said, reaching for his hand.

EVENTEEN

. . . he told him to urge her to go into the king's presence
to beg for mercy and plead with him for her people.
—ESTHER 4:8

A BORED-LOOKING BOY, his purple livery crusty with lace, lolled at
the gates of the palace, waiting for me.

"Deina has said she will look in on the children, and of course Jaquet
is there as well," I said to my husband as we parted. I was worried about
the baby, for I was still nursing her. At the thought of her going hungry,
my breasts filled with milk. I could have cried from annoyance as I saw a
wet patch form on my lace-trimmed kirtle, the flowing, short dark blue
tunic I wore draped over my lighter blue dress. I took the heavy figured
silk shawl I had hurriedly borrowed from Amyris and draped it over the
offending spot, carefully pulling out the gold chain so that my one piece
of jewelry was not lost in all the layers.

I looked up to see Meir staring at me, a strange look in his eyes.

"What's wrong?" I whispered.

"I can't bear to let you go to Donin, looking so beautiful," my husband said softly into my ear.

I wanted to kiss him, to reassure him. But the boy standing before us, eyeing us as though we were some kind of rare creatures, discouraged me. I reached up and adjusted my headdress, a linen coif of pure white, to make sure it covered all of my hair.

"It will be all right," I whispered in response.

Meir smiled. I could see the effort it took him. "I will see you at a distance if they allow me to attend your father."

"They won't. No Jews allowed in except those expressly bidden," said the page. "Come on, dame Jewess, you are expected."

I tried to keep pace with his long strides. He knew the palace well and I soon lost track of the pathway we walked through the twisting corridors and immense antechambers. I caught glimpses of beautiful wall hangings, tapestries, gold-wrought mirrors, and enormous portraits hung in intricate frames. The walls and floor were polished marble. I skittered on the smooth surface until I grew used to taking quicker, smaller steps. As we walked on and on, my legs began to ache.

Finally, the page opened the door to a small antechamber. I caught a glimpse of a room decorated in soothing shades of green and blue. "The friar will take you to the queen when he's done with you," he said, a disturbing leer on his young face.

My heart plummeted. There could only be one friar.

Nicholas Donin, in a well-brushed gray habit, wearing his black hair in a tonsure, turned from the window and smiled at me. His intense blue eyes sparkled as though he had imbibed some kind of intoxicating draught.

"Shira bat Shmuel! Welcome!" he said, extending his arms in greeting.

"I am Shira eshet Meir, Brother Nicholas," I said icily, drawing Amyris's silk shawl tightly around me. "And you have no right to accost me without my husband present."

If anything, his smile grew even wider. "You need not fear for your virtue, Shira. I am a monk; I have taken a vow of chastity."

"You will forgive me for saying I put as little credence in your chastity as I do in your interpretation of Christian charity, Brother Nicholas. The dead Jews of Anjou, Poitou, and Aquitaine cried out for your mercy and you were deaf to their pleas."

"You put their deaths at my door, but it is their own stubbornness that killed them."

"You give yourself too little credit." I turned away, unable to stop the shaking in my limbs but unwilling to give him, of all people, the satisfaction of seeing it.

"No, Shira. I have never been guilty of giving myself too little credit." He laughed. I turned back and glared at him incredulously.

"You can have no reason for wanting to see me in private," I said. "The queen mother is waiting for me."

"The dowager queen is probably still abed. It is whispered throughout the court that she is ill, possibly in the last weeks of a difficult pregnancy, though no one dares say so aloud. But she rests often. And she has a long day ahead of her."

"I would rather wait for her alone, then," I said stiffly. "Please tell the page who brought me here to take me somewhere else."

Donin came closer. I shrank away. "You fear me?" he asked, as if amazed.

"You are reviled and disgusting to me," I said. "But I do not fear you. One cannot fear an insect."

"An insect! I assure you, Shira bat Shmuel eshet Meir, I will not be trodden underfoot. Do you remember when I told you I would shape the course of Jewish destiny?"

"I have wiped out every memory of you, because remembering you after what you have done soils me," I responded hotly.

His eyes widened, and he reached out and grabbed hold of both my shoulders. I could feel his fingers digging into my flesh. "Take care, Shira, take great care. We are alone and there is no father or husband to protect you here."

"I thought your vow of chastity was to be enough," I flared back. "Let me go!"

He released me, giving me a little push that made me stagger backward. He pointed to a gilt chair. "Sit down," he commanded.

I sat. I averted my face, looking around. The room was small and windowless. Wax candles burned on a small table between us and on the mantelpiece. I fixed my eyes on an immense portrait of a beautiful woman sitting in a garden, her child in her lap, surrounded by angels. The entire room appeared to have been decorated to provide a setting for this painting. My eyes widened as I realized this must be a picture of Mary and her child, the boy they claimed was Son of God. Her face is so composed, I thought. How could the painter, knowing how the baby would grow up only to die, have painted her looking so serene?

Donin pulled another chair close to mine. If he had reached out, he could have touched me. "Shira," he murmured. "I have thought about you so often."

I said nothing, studying the jewel-like blue of the mother's robe. Rays of light flowed from her white face and a crown of rays hovered over the naked baby's head. The angels attending them, bent as though in worship, were almost unbalanced by their enormous wings.

"Do you know what you are looking at?" Donin asked, turning his head to follow the direction of my glance. "That is the Holy Mother and her Babe."

Looking more closely, I saw she wasn't actually sitting in a garden—there was a thicket of roses and ivy decorating the borders of the painting, with smaller angels and other mythic creatures populating the greenery. Mary was hovering, as if she were standing in air, in a field of brilliant azure.

"'Thou shalt have no other gods before me,'" Donin whispered, edging his chair even closer. "Shira, listen to me. Listen. I can see you are moved by that portrait. That is the Holy Mother and her beautiful Babe, the Messiah—Christ—who died on the cross to absolve us all of sin. Let me fetch a priest to baptize you. Let the Holy Church embrace you. Let me save you."

I pushed my chair back, away from him, casting my eyes to the marble floor beneath my feet, flustered and confused. Was my gazing at such a picture forbidden? Donin's pleas sickened me. "You killed hundreds who refused to convert. Did you implore them so sweetly as well?" I asked.

Donin shook his head. "Once more, you heed only one side of the story. Do you recall the day I asked you to listen to me, and you told me you trusted your father? If you knew the torment I endured at the hands of men like your father, and Moses of Coucy, and Yechiel . . ."

"So I was right—you summoned them here for revenge! You don't really care if I convert, Brother Nicholas. My soul is nothing to you. It's revenge you want, revenge on my father, revenge on me for refusing your hand in marriage."

Donin leaned back in his chair, smiling maliciously. "The disputation will begin in two hours. Suppose we put you on the stand instead of Yechiel and the others? Wouldn't that surprise the court? A beautiful Jewess defending her people so passionately?"

The idea robbed me of speech and I sat there, gaping at him. "Can you see yourself as another Esther, Shira?" he continued. "Pleading with royalty to save your people from destruction?"

I said nothing, thinking of Yechiel's words earlier that morning.

"Yet I will be the one who saves your people—*our* people. What did I always say, Shira? That I would have a hand in Judaism's future. I will cleanse the Jewish people of their mistakes, and you will all thank me and beg my forgiveness on bended knee."

I studied him closely. His youthful intensity had hardened into an obsessive zeal that could not be stripped away by reason. He reached out and pulled me up, his fingers curved around my elbows, keeping me at arm's length.

"I want you to be there to watch me triumph over Yechiel, over Moses, over your father," he whispered, looking directly into my eyes with the mesmerizing stare I remembered so well. "The queen will keep you safe from the fury of the crowd. I am certain that, after today, after you learn exactly how you have been lied to all these years, you will yearn to become one of the blessed. You of all people will not need to be converted by force, for your pure heart has always been filled with the desire to do what is right."

"You delude yourself," I said coldly. "I am a daughter of faith—a rabbi's daughter, a rabbi's wife. I have no room in my heart for you or your false god."

"Today will decide the matter for you, Shira. I made sure you would be in the audience for this purpose. It is *your* soul that will be on trial today."

———◆———

Queen Blanche was sitting among her ladies-in-waiting. One of them was fanning her, for it was hot this morning, while another strummed on a lute and sang romantic ballads. The room was like a bower—the walls painted with ivy murals, the wall hangings depicting gardens and gracious ladies and courtiers. Real flowers floated in crystal bowls or were dried into potpourri, which gave the room its unusually sweet scent. Blanche looked up as the page stationed near the door announced us: "Brother Nicholas and Shira of Falaise, wife to Rabbi Meir, Your Majesty."

"Ah, Brother Nicholas. So your long-awaited day has finally dawned," she said, allowing him to bend over and kiss an extended hand. She scrutinized me closely, curiosity and distrust warring in her eyes. Trying to curtsy gracefully, I controlled my trembling legs and dipped down. My cheeks flared red as I heard the tittering of the queen's ladies-in-waiting behind us.

I had never thought I'd stand so close to royalty. From beneath down-turned lashes, I studied her. She was bloated and older than I would have thought, in her fifties. I wondered at the rumors of her pregnancy, for surely she was past childbearing age. Her nose was her most striking feature, protruding over puffy lips. She was dressed in a loose seafoam-green gown, with a heavy gold-link chain on her breast. A large, intricately wrought cross sparkled with rubies and diamonds and hung from a dark velvet ribbon. Her black hair, sprinkled with gray, was covered with a simple lace mantilla. A small jewel-encrusted crown sat on a low table by her side.

Her dark, deep-set eyes regarded me. The singing had stopped and her ladies gawked at me as though I were some species of wild animal caged for their amusement. "Shira of Falaise. Welcome to my court."

"Your Majesty," I murmured, curtsying again, more adeptly this time.

"Go, Brother Nicholas," she told him with a wave of her hand. "You must prepare. I will have a care for your little Jewess."

"Thank you, Your Majesty," Donin said. He bowed, cast one last searing glance in my direction, and then left the chamber.

The queen rose, slowly and painfully, motioning to her ladies to remain where they were. "Shira of Falaise, let us sit apart and chat privately," she said. She walked over to an alcove of the room. I sat on a carved wooden chair while she lay down on a cushioned daybed, arranging herself into a prone position with a bit of struggle.

"So," she said, out of breath, "Brother Nicholas has told me much of your romance." Her French was perfect, colored only a little by the sound of her Spanish upbringing.

"Hardly a romance, Your Majesty," I replied. I remembered what my father and Rabbi Yechiel had said of this woman. She was enamored of the idea of courtly love, of tales of knights and forbidden romances. It would have been easy for Donin to beguile her into thinking our relationship was one of thwarted passion. Perhaps, I thought, if I can convince her that he lied about that, she will question his statements about religion more stringently during the disputation.

"Brother Nicholas says that you were the only one who believed in him when he studied at your father's home, and that your father refused to allow the two of you to be married. You would not call this a romance?"

I had to be careful. I did not want her to consider me callous to the nature of true love. "Your Majesty, it is true that Donin lived in my father's house and studied with us. He sought to engage my feelings by discussing faith with me. But he imposed on my youth and my inexperience in a calculating way. Even so, when my father asked me if I wanted to marry him, it was *I* who refused him. Since then," I hastened to add, noticing how she reared back in surprise, "I have found what we call in Hebrew my *b'shert*—my soul mate, the one who makes me whole. We believe that every man and woman has only one true *b'shert*. That is why I cannot call Donin's attempts to entice me a romance."

"*B'shert...*," mused the queen. "So you are one of the lucky few who has found true love . . . tell me of him."

I thought of Meir. Much as I loved my husband, the mundane details of our life together—his scholarship and teaching, our small home, our daughters—would hardly entertain the queen. "Before we were wed," I said haltingly, "my father was taken prisoner by Baron la Folette."

"The baron serves my son well in Falaise," the queen said with a nod.

"I was young and foolhardy and thought to force my way into the castle," I said, looking for ways to make our simple story into more of a courtship tale. "Meir of Worms—my *b'shert*—saw me leave my home. He followed me. It was winter and snow fell all around us. The way was treacherous and he helped me climb the mountain. Once I might have fallen had he not caught me in time. When we arrived, it was he who demanded to see my father. For a long time, we were left standing alone in a kind of vigil outside the keep."

"He was chivalrous to you?" Blanche asked. "He did nothing unseemly?"

"On the contrary, Your Majesty. Unlike my experience with Nicholas Donin, who strove to compel me to act immodestly, Meir treated me with proper respect and attention."

"You say that Brother Nicholas was unchivalrous?"

"Oh yes, Your Majesty."

She frowned. "So go on about your romance with—what did you say his name was?"

"Meir. There isn't much more to speak of. Except . . ."

"Yes?" She leaned forward eagerly.

"There was a moment—the moment before we approached the castle. I was so frightened. He, too, must have been apprehensive, but he
controlled it, as every good champion does. We drew closer. And Meir
looked into my eyes and I into his . . ." I stopped for a moment, embarrassed. How could I make her understand?

But it appeared that I didn't need to, for she breathed out, her hand
resting lightly on her heart. "And you were one?" she asked, smiling
happily.

"We were *b'shert* and both knew it, Your Majesty."

IGHTEEN

Rav Yehuda says, there are twelve hours in a day.
The first three hours God sits and learns the Torah.

—THE TALMUD

I SAT WITH THE QUEEN'S LADIES-IN-WAITING toward the back of the immense hall. The room was filled with gilt chairs and small, low tables, hung with mirrors and sconces where candles burned brightly. The long windows flanking the sides of the room stood open to pleasure grounds beyond, and filmy curtains swept in and out gently with the June breeze. As we waited, the women pelted me with impudent questions. Why was my dress cut so high and my hair completely covered? Why did we Jews refuse to eat pork? Was it true that Jews drank Christian blood and ground Christian bones into their bread? What was it like to make love with a man—here the maiden blushed fiery red—whose manhood was clipped?

I wondered if my quiet answers made any impression at all on the silly girls, who giggled and searched for something even more bizarre to ask.

The queen entered. The small crown I had seen on the table in her rooms now sat atop her lace mantilla. She walked slowly through the room, everyone curtsying or bowing deeply as she moved past them. She stopped to greet individual courtiers, smiling upon most but frowning terribly at one or two. "That's Léon, the third son of the Count de Gracy, the one who seduced Amalie," one of the ladies-in-waiting whispered to another as the queen stopped to speak to the young man, his head bowed as if in shame. "She's been waiting for a chance to reprimand him in public."

The queen finally made her way up to a dais, seating herself upon her throne, a massive, carved wood chair cushioned with velvet. One of the ladies-in-waiting ran forward to fan her flushed face and another brought her a drink. She sat back for a moment, eyes shut, as though the mere procession through the room had exhausted her. Whether she was pregnant or not, I felt sympathy for the burden of her heavy body.

Side doors opened and a page stepped forward. "Your Majesty, Brother Nicholas of the Franciscan Order craves your permission to enter, with his assistants—Thibault of Sézanne, Father Thomas of Chantimpré, Wilhelm of Burgos, and three recent converts to the one True Faith: Thomas, Bernard, and Baldwin."

With a gracious nod, the queen assented. Donin entered, followed closely by the other men. Donin was dressed in his monk's robe. One of his companions was attired in the dark gown of a professor at the University of Paris, a crushed-velvet cap with a long gold tassel on his head. Another wore the somber black cassock of a priest. But the last four had arrayed themselves richly in long embroidered tunics belted at the waist, their sleeves flared wide. The men bowed to the queen as a group, then turned to seat themselves at a long wooden table on which several heavy tomes were piled. My heart stood still as I recognized volumes of my own Babylonian Talmud among them, the distinctive figured gold ornamentation on their bindings catching my eye.

A second side door opened and a second page stepped forward. "The Jewish leaders of Paris, Melun, Falaise, and Coucy," he announced. "Rabbis Yechiel, Moses, Judah ben David, and Sir Morel."

My heart hammered wildly, half in pride and half in fear, as the rabbis walked forward, their heads held high and their bearing regal. Of course I watched my father most closely. His chiseled face was impassive, any apprehension he might have been feeling well concealed. I must remember to tell Alyes how well he bore himself and how proud she and my brothers and sisters should be of him, I thought.

The rabbis, too, bowed before Her Majesty and were escorted to stools on a low dais, set directly to the left of the throne.

"Your Majesty," said the first page, "several dignitaries of the Church would like to witness these procedures. May Walter, Archbishop of Sens; William of Auvergne, Bishop of Paris; and Adam, Bishop of Senlis, seat themselves in the audience?"

"I would be honored to include these gentlemen as witnesses of the proceedings," said Queen Blanche. "Please also ask my son's chaplain, Geoffrey of Belleville, and the chancellor of the University of Paris, Odo of Châteauroux, to join them."

These requests had obviously been rehearsed ahead of time, for all of these men, arrayed in clerical garb, were waiting outside the grand hall to be ushered in.

There was a slight pause as Her Majesty was brought a small repast. I looked over the heads of the chattering ladies at my father. He was searching the crowd. When he saw me, he relaxed a little, and I realized how nervous he had been on my behalf. I thought then of Meir, who had been refused entrance; of Alyes, who had accompanied Papa all the way from Falaise; and of Deina, waiting for word of both her husband and father. How anxious they must have been for us all!

A servant removed the small table that had held the queen's meal. At a signal from her attendant, Nicholas Donin rose.

"Your Majesty, lords and ladies, members of the clergy. We come here today to investigate a matter that has long been fomenting scorn and disdain in the hearts of the heretic Jewish population we suffer to live among us. That matter is the book they call the Talmud."

Donin picked up a volume of the Talmud from the table—not mine,

I was glad to see—and brought it over to the queen. He opened it and showed her several of the pages. He then allowed court clerks to take some of the other copies and display them throughout the room. The crowd, taking a first look at these beautiful volumes, was captivated by their brilliant illuminations, by the careful calligraphy our scribes employed to form each letter perfectly, by the blocks of text surrounded by generations of commentary. There were appreciative murmurs for the beauty of the work.

"Can you read it?" one of the ladies-in-waiting asked me when a volume of the Talmud made its way to us. I nodded. "What does that say?"

She had pointed to Baba Batra 21a. I translated: "'If you strike a child, strike him only with a shoelace.'"

"Only with a shoelace?" she giggled. "What good is that?"

I smiled. "Were you beaten as a child?" I asked.

"Of course! Weren't you?"

"My father wanted to beat me once. I lied to him, saying I had completed a task when I actually hadn't. He remembered this passage in the Talmud, took the lace from his boot, and hit me with it. I remember thinking that he loved me enough to treat me gently despite his great anger and I never lied to him again."

"Huh!" said the lady-in-waiting. "My father used a heavy birch stick."

The books were collected and the clerks carried all but three of them out. I saw my father watch them disappear with a look of longing. Would they ever be returned to us?

"They are exquisite, aren't they?" Donin said. "But their exotic beauty is misleading. They are full of lies and slanders. And they are the reason why these Jews refuse to accept our beloved Christ as their Savior. If the Jews living within Christian borders have any rights at all, if we are to tolerate them among us, then they must live according to the laws of Moses and only the laws of Moses. There are truths buried within the Old Testament pointing to the Coming of our Lord Jesus. Christians who were born Jews—as I was myself—can be brought to salvation if their only books were composed before Jesus's birth. We cannot permit the Jews to write or to study subsequent works, especially not those that contain insults to God and His Son."

Yechiel opened his mouth as though to speak, but Donin held up a hand. "Guards!" he called.

Several of the queen's guards presented themselves, lances resting on the ground before them.

"Remove all of the rabbis but Rabbi Yechiel," Donin ordered. "Let each of them be incarcerated remotely from one another, so they cannot collude in their statements. We will question them one at a time. By doing so, you will see that they cannot defend this blasphemous book they hold so dear."

I half rose in my seat as the guards marched the three rabbis off the low dais and down through the long hall. My father, alert to my trepidation, motioned with his hand that I should remain seated and silent. I tried not to burst into tears as I watched him and the others being escorted out of the room.

Yechiel rose and faced Donin. "You have unlawfully seized my people's property and summoned me here to answer your questions before this august assemblage. I would hear your grounds for doing so."

"I merely ask you about an ancient book," answered Donin. He cast a quick glance in my direction, smiling upon seeing me seated among the ladies of the court. "I don't deny that the Talmud is some four hundred years old, of course—"

"Four hundred years!" Yechiel cried in outrage. "You dare suggest . . . When you know well it is a sacred book, portions of which the Lord Himself dictated to Moses upon Mount Sinai—fifteen hundred years ago!" Yechiel turned then to address the queen. "Please, my lady! I beg you, do not make me answer this impudent friar, for he has ever been ignorant and stubborn about matters of our faith. The Talmud he speaks of so scornfully was entrusted to us by the Lord God. It is an honored book of great antiquity.

"Many of your learned scholars, even your Saint Jerome, studied it.

None has ever taken issue with it before today, none thought it required investigation by a court such as this. Your learned doctors of scripture and philosophy—most more knowledgeable than Brother Nicholas—have learned from our writings and were content to do so. They recognized that it was only fitting we should use the Talmud to comment and consider the Scriptures—"

"No one has taken issue with the Talmud?" Thibault of Sézanne burst out, rising from his seat in indignation. "What about Agobart of Lyon? The sainted convert Petrus Alphonsi from the last century? Or the revered abbot of Cluny Petrus Venerabilis, who investigated the Talmud with the assistance of Jewish converts like Brother Nicholas and the men who help him?"

Yechiel listened politely. When Thibault ended his tirade, he said, with a bow toward him, "I would know the name of my learned accuser."

"This is Thibault of Sézanne, Rabbi," said Queen Blanche. "We are remiss in not introducing you to the members of the prosecution. Gentlemen, please rise."

They did so.

"Rabbi, Thibault of Sézanne is particularly knowledgeable about your Talmud, having written and published the book *Extractiones de Talmud*. Father Thomas of Chantimpré is a renowned professor of philosophy and theology, a man of great learning who has been active in converting heretics throughout Europe. Next to him is Wilhelm of Burgos—"

"I know of Wilhelm of Burgos's reputation and of his book. *Bellum Domini contra iudaeos et contra iudeaeorum haereticos,* is it not?" Yechiel asked. "I did not read it myself, but my dear friend Rabbi Moses of Coucy did, and he was extremely upset at the contents of your manuscript and your accusations against us as heretics, sir."

"As he is a Jew, I would not expect him to be anything but," said Wilhelm dryly. I squirmed in my seat as mocking laughter rose from everyone around me.

The queen continued, "I cannot tell you a great deal about the converts, Thomas, Bernard, and Baldwin, except that they, like Brother Nicholas, were brought up in your faith and found the grace of God in time to save their eternal souls." The queen crossed herself. Everyone in the hall, except for Yechiel and me, followed suit. I was riveted and repelled at the sight of Donin fervently crossing himself not once, but four times, apparently once for each of the other three apostates and once for himself.

"As for Brother Nicholas, I believe you know him well, do you not, Rabbi?"

"All too well, Your Majesty. The last time I saw your Brother Nicholas, he was my student. For fifteen years, he rebelled against the pronouncements of our wise men, choosing to believe only what was written in the Torah of Moses and despising our Talmud with a fervor that contaminated many of the young men studying with him. Since the time we excommunicated him he has sought to strike at the heart of my people, using distortions and lies.

"The Talmud he accuses must be understood as an ancient and revered document that enfolds the historical spirit of my people—a people older than yours, my lady, a people who have suffered greatly through their exile from their homeland for generations. I know many Christians think of the Talmud as a book of spells or a catalog of our dealings with Satan. Nothing could be further from the truth. The Talmud is a collection of our interpretations and discussions about the Torah and the Law, debates that have taken place over centuries as rabbis and scholars tried to understand God's word better. From the days of the prophet Ezra's Great Assembly to the writings of Rashi, the greatest of all commentators, just two centuries ago, we have striven to perform the Almighty's will through these discussions. Nothing in the Talmud should be carelessly—or, as Donin would have you do, intentionally—misinterpreted or read without full understanding of why each passage was written. The scholars of our community spend lifetimes trying to master the multitude of interpretations of our Torah contained by this book. Nicholas Donin would ask you to rip pieces from their pages and place meanings on them that were never intended."

The court sat hushed, impressed by Yechiel's sincere peroration. I wanted to cheer. He gauged correctly that his audience was moved and turned to the court, saying, "You must also realize that we are prepared to die for the Talmud, if we must. Each one of us, from the oldest, most feeble of our elders to the youngest of our children, would willingly step into the fires to prevent you from destroying this great book."

One of the queen's clerks interrupted. "Yechiel, no one thinks of harming your people."

I closed my eyes at the hypocrisy, thinking of the horses' hoofs riding over the panicked and helpless Jews elsewhere in France. Yechiel must have thought the same thing, for he scoffed gently and said, "I'm afraid it becomes difficult to contain the rabble when someone like Brother Nicholas spurs on soldiers and peasants to cleanse their neighborhoods of their Jews."

Queen Blanche leaned forward. "Rabbi, I hope you will accept my word as queen and mother of His Royal Highness King Louis that I will personally defend your people and their possessions. It shall be considered a crime against the realm if anyone lifts a hand against you."

Yechiel bowed low. "I would expect no less from you, gracious lady, and I accept your assurances with gratitude."

Nicholas Donin, who had been shifting about impatiently as this exchange took place, opened his mouth to speak. But Yechiel, perhaps hoping to end the matter while the court still felt sympathetic toward him, added, "May I also request, Your Majesty, that an appeal be sent to His Holiness the Pope, to hold this hearing before the papal tribunal in Rome? Otherwise this matter will be tried not only in France, but throughout Europe in individual courts. The Papal See would be best equipped to hear the matter and pass judgment on it in a manner that could be accepted by all of Christian Europe."

The queen sat thoughtfully considering this appeal, but Donin gestured to his cohorts, who rose indignantly from their seats.

"Your Majesty, this is a most insulting request," cried Wilhelm. "We have spent months preparing our prosecution. Does this man imply that you are not qualified to hear this matter?"

"I urge Your Majesty to instruct this Jew to answer any questions Brother Nicholas might pose. Surely the rabbi only wishes to move the matter to Rome to postpone the inevitable and because he fears to look foolish before your court!" Baldwin chimed in.

All around me murmurs and whispers of indignation clearly showed that the court would resent any attempt to dismiss the case. The small hope Yechiel's plea had kindled in me was extinguished.

The queen nodded. "We will listen to this matter."

Donin stood and took up one of the three volumes of the Talmud the guards had left on the table. He turned to a page he had marked with a slip of paper. "I will translate a passage that illustrates the foolishness this book contains," he said. "I warn you that this concerns the idea of human sacrifice—something we, as enlightened people, no longer believe in. Do not be alarmed."

"Human sacrifice," one of the ladies near me whispered in fascinated horror. "I told you the Jews drink blood!"

"'The man who sacrifices part of his seed to Moloch will be punished, but the man who sacrifices all of his children will not,'" read Donin. "Can you imagine anything more absurd?"

I looked around, my heart sinking as I heard the scorn in the crowd's laughter.

But Yechiel was equal to the challenge. "Brother Nicholas reads this passage aloud to prove our words make no sense. And yes, it makes no sense to hear them without understanding their deeper meaning. This passage speaks of human sacrifice as a venal and terrible act, and not, as Brother Nicholas implies, as a ritual that Jews practice. Indeed, the reason why a man who sacrifices all of his children goes unpunished is because the crime is so base that human justice could not remotely begin to remedy it. Instead, it is said, such a man can only be punished by divine judgment, by our Lord God."

This quieted the crowd, but Donin stepped up again. "The Talmud further preaches that Jews have a right to degrade all those who are not Jewish. They call them Gentiles, and they write complacently of killing and cheating them. This includes Christians, Your Majesty. The Talmud encourages Jews to kill and cheat Christians."

"Only if you do not understand that the Talmud represents the opinions of many scholars over several centuries can you accept such a statement as true," Yechiel corrected. "In fact—and here I must quote from memory, for I do not have a volume of the Talmud to consult—in Chullin 94a, it states: 'As Shmuel said: "It is forbidden to deceive anyone, even an idolatrous Gentile."' The rabbis taught in Gittin 61a: 'We support poor Gentiles with the poor people of Israel, and we visit sick Gentiles as well as the sick of Israel and we bury the dead of the Gentiles as well as the dead of Israel, because of the ways of peace.'

"And, further, you cannot confuse Gentiles and Christians, as Brother Nicholas would have you do," continued Yechiel. "Nicholas Donin is citing passages that describe our historical dealings with ancient enemies. If you read them closely, you will see references to the idol-worshipping Canaanites and Cutheans, rather than Christians. You must further understand that many of these passages derive from our people's bitterness and frustration when confronted by these pagan adversaries.

"In fact, the Talmud is clear that righteous Christians can attain salvation and should be treated by Jews with friendship and acceptance. I speak for all Jewish scholars in Christian Europe when I say we do not group Christians together with pagans—and it is pagans we mean when we speak of Gentiles."

At this the convert Bernard rose from his chair. Donin motioned for him to speak. "Your Majesty, this is yet another example of how Jews twist the truth. When I was a student at various Jewish seminaries, we spoke of Gentiles insultingly and maliciously—and we meant Christians when we did so."

Blanche was clearly displeased. "Well, Rabbi?" she asked. "If the Jews—who are nothing more than guests in this land, as in many others—speak slightingly of their Christian hosts, I promise you I will not consider that a small matter."

I understood why Yechiel would want to distinguish between Gentiles and Christians, for doing so would considerably lessen the impact of Donin's charges against the Talmud. But was what Bernard said correct? Was it not common for someone in the community to say "Gentile" and mean "Christian"? Did we not mock them for their beliefs and their ignorance of our own?

I thought back to Nicholas Donin telling me that this disputation was a fight for my soul and I closed my eyes, suddenly weary. I would talk about this with Meir after I returned home, I promised myself.

Donin began to speak of several of our Talmudic fables, one in which God argued with the sages and lost, another in which He sat in Heaven, studying Torah and Talmud, just as we do here on earth. Donin drew shocked titters as he asked the crowd what they thought God decided to wear that morning and if He combed His hair before sitting down with the sages. "Can you imagine another so-called holy book that makes a mockery of the Lord God?" he asked. "These presumptuous passages show how far from the truth and from salvation these Jews have come."

Yechiel shook his head. "Speaking of God in this way is not limited to the Talmud, Brother Nicholas, as you well know. It is present, also, in the books Jews and Christians share, in the Torah—or what you Christians call the Old Testament. Is it not written, in Genesis, that we are created in God's image? Is it not said in Deuteronomy that the tablets of the Covenant were 'written with the finger of God'? Further, when you talk about arguing with God, do you not remember the story of Abraham, who demanded that God appear before him and argued with him over the lives of the people in Sodom and Gomorrah? Or that God spoke to Moses face-to-face?"

With a pang, I remembered how Meir had once told me that most Christians did not study their own Gospels. Instead, their priests told them the stories from our Bible and their own during their church services. From the murmurs and whispers throughout the room, I could feel how Yechiel's examples shocked the assembled courtiers.

The rabbi continued, "Once again you try to mislead this court into thinking we depict the Lord—who is our Lord as well as your Lord—as something small and meaningless. The truth, instead, is that we give the Lord so much respect that we try to find ways to grow closer to Him. We do so through our stories, allegories, and fables, which we do not take literally. No one who understands our deep reverence for God would ever suggest otherwise."

Yechiel had been on his feet for several hours now. I knew he had not eaten all day, for all of us in the community were fasting. The queen saw that he was growing exhausted. In her genteel way, she turned to Donin. "How much more of this matter is there, Brother Nicholas? The hour advances, and I become weary. Shall we adjourn until tomorrow?"

"There is a great deal more to discuss, Your Majesty. Tomorrow, if it please you, I would like to devote the day to speaking about the vicious way the Talmud talks specifically about our Lord Christ and His Virgin Mother."

"Very well. Let Yechiel be confined so that no one can speak with him until tomorrow. Make sure all of our rabbinical guests are comfortably housed and fed."

The guards led Yechiel out. I remained in my seat, not knowing what I should do, hoping against hope to be allowed to go home. But just as I was rising to try to find my way out, a guard approached me.

"Shira of Falaise? You are to sleep in the palace tonight, so that you do not communicate the happenings of this day to your Jewish friends. I will lead you to your quarters."

"Is there any way I can at least let my husband and children know I am safe?"

"There is to be no communication. Come with me."

I rose. I was exhausted, dizzy with having fasted all day. My knees buckled under me.

"Come!" The guard's strident tone cut through my light-headedness.

INETEEN

Not every Louis born in France is the king of France.
—RABBI YECHIEL

THEY LOCKED ME IN A SMALL ROOM with one small barred window in the high reaches of the castle. The room was sparsely furnished with a pallet of straw and a thin blanket, a wood stool, and a table, on which a pitcher of water stood. I drank thirstily and lay down.

I was nearly dozing when a sharp rap on the door startled me. The door burst open, and a guard entered, carrying a platter of food.

I had not eaten all day and it smelled delicious. But the moment I looked at it—the piles of smoking meat nestled together with a slab of runny cheese and a huge, crusty loaf of bread that touched both—I knew I could not eat it. The very sight made me sick to my stomach.

A small bunch of grapes lay to one side, put there as a kind of garnish. I took that and retreated back to my cot.

"Can you take the rest away?" I asked, my voice thin and weak.

"What? This came direct from the queen's kitchen, I'll have you know. Every man in the guard would be pleased to eat it!"

"I invite you to partake, then," I said, closing my eyes and putting a grape in my mouth. The fruit filled my mouth with glorious flavor. I would have to eat these slowly, I told myself, but could not stop from reaching immediately for a second grape. And then a third.

"But . . . you're hungry, madame, I can see that you're hungry. Why won't you eat?"

"I appreciate Her Majesty sending me the food, but I am not allowed it. I wish I could eat it, for I fasted all day, and you're right, I'm starving. Please, you enjoy it."

"Pigheaded Jews," the guard muttered under his breath. He seated himself at my table and proceeded to eat the meat and the cheese. I put another grape in my mouth.

"You want me to bring you more grapes?" he asked between bites.

"I would welcome any uncooked fruit or vegetables. And if you could arrange to bring some to the rabbis, wherever they are imprisoned? I hope they are as comfortably housed as I am?"

The guard grunted, ripping a large hunk from the bread. "As far as I know, they are. I'll get them some fruit as well. Not vegetables. I wouldn't feed my dog raw vegetables. You Jews are queer folk."

"I don't usually eat raw vegetables either," I said, smiling faintly, my eyes lowered. "But I can't eat anything prepared in your kitchens."

The guard finished eating and picked up the empty tray, heading toward the door. "They'll think you're one hungry matron," he said with a laugh.

I suddenly had a thought. "One moment!" I said, calling him back.

"Yes?"

"Is someone standing guard outside my door?"

"I will be—after I return from fetching you fruit. I'll lock you in while I'm away, so don't consider trying to escape."

"Can you refuse entrance to someone I don't want to see?"

"That depends. I wouldn't refuse the queen or any of her ladies."

"Brother Nicholas?"

"Well, that would be tricky. He's an important man, especially during this trial of yours."

An evil man, I thought to myself. "What if I gave you this?" I said, reaching around and taking off my gold chain with its suspended pearl. I dangled it before him.

"Why do you want to refuse him, anyway?"

"Because I fear for my virtue. I'm here now because he commanded it. I am a good and loyal wife and I don't want him anywhere near me."

"Is that a real pearl?" the guard asked, eyeing it covetously.

"A real pearl and very expensive."

"Hand it over, then."

With a pang, I gave it to him. What would I tell Meir? But it would be worth his anger to keep Nicholas Donin from my door that night.

———•———

I slept intermittently, my dreams filled with Donin leering at me, setting books on fire before me, tearing pages out of the Talmud and holding them up to ridicule as the crowd that surrounded us laughed and laughed. Morning finally came, and I rose, my head aching and my limbs stiff. I prayed and used some of the water still in the pitcher to wash my hands and face.

I had to wait hours before anyone came to fetch me. The palace clearly moved at a different pace than the world of ordinary people outside its gates. As I did not have any paper to write with, I sat quietly on my stool and tried to fix the previous day's debate firmly in my mind. Memorize the day, Yechiel had said to me. By midmorning, I was confident that I could write out a clear and comprehensive account as soon as I had the chance.

The guard took me to my place in the hall. "You were right, madame," he said as we walked down the marble hallways together. "The monk came to your door last night. He was not pleased to be refused entrance."

"What did you say to him?" I asked, curious.

"I told him queen's orders. That put a stop to his demands."

"I am grateful to you."

"Here." The guard reached into a pouch and pulled out my necklace.

"But that was payment!" I exclaimed.

"I have a wife of my own. I only hope she'd do the same thing as you, madame."

Tears prickled in my eyes. "Thank you. I did not know what I was going to tell my husband when I returned home without it."

We walked the rest of the way in silence. The guard marched me to my seat in the hall, and I sat down, grateful for the comfortable chair. The ladies-in-waiting looked scornfully at my rumpled clothing.

"Did you sleep in a barn last night?" one of them asked with a sniff.

"In a prison cell," I answered.

———•———

I had hoped at least to catch a glimpse of my father and reassure myself of his health after his daylong imprisonment. But only Yechiel was led into the room that morning.

Donin stood at the long table, checking his notes and rifling through the one volume of the Talmud still left in the room. He looked up at one point and surveyed the area of the hall where the ladies-in-waiting were seated. When he found me, his eyes narrowed in anger. I felt a tremor of fear and lowered my gaze to my lap. When I dared glance up, Donin was studying the book again.

The queen was the last to enter. Unlike yesterday, there was little ceremony. She simply walked through a side door and went straight to her throne.

"She had a bad night," one of the ladies-in-waiting said to another, stifling a yawn. "She tossed and turned and got up every few minutes to make her water. She's in a hellish mood."

"Your Majesty," Donin began, clearing his throat, "I would like my learned colleague, Thomas of Chantimpré, to address the court and explain why today is a vital day in this disputation."

"I will hear the father professor, but he must promise not to pontificate endlessly," the queen said, a sour look on her face.

Brother Nicholas sat down, and the priest rose. "I will be brief, Your Majesty. The Fourth Lateran Council, in its infinite wisdom and care for the citizens of the Christian realms, resolved in its sixty-eighth canon that secular rulers—such as your august self—have the power, the responsibility, and, yes, even the obligation to guard against blasphemy in all its forms, but particularly blasphemy against the Lord Jesus and His Holy Mother the Virgin Mary. In the spirit of this resolution we appeal to Your Majesty to deal harshly with those Jews who insulted Jesus in their books, passing heinous lies down from generation to generation so that the children of Zion are never given a chance to save their immortal souls."

"I accept the resolution with my entire heart now, as I have always done," the queen said, her ill temper lifting as she acknowledged the spiritual appeal. "Truly, there can be no more imperative duty for a Christian ruler."

"Then I need speak no more, my lady. It is Brother Nicholas's sad duty to show where the Talmud defames Jesus and His blessed Mother. Hearing this, and accepting the letter and the spirit of the Lateran Council, you will have no choice but to wholly banish this book through sacred fire and prohibit the Jews from ever setting down their sacrilegious slanders again."

Father Thomas sat back down. Brother Nicholas rose. "Your Majesty, I would like to apologize in advance if what I say shocks or upsets anyone in this court, for the language used in the Talmud is nothing less than appalling."

Donin went on to speak not only of "*Toldot Yeshu*," the story of Jesus, but of other places in the Talmud where Jesus's birth and background are discussed. The comments were damning. The crowd gasped and hissed as Jesus was named the bastard son of a whore, a sorcerer and a thief, and, perhaps worst of all, one who never ascended to heaven but whose body was dragged before Queen Helene, his remains confounding the claims of his followers.

As he spoke, Donin punctuated the foul statements with taunts to the audience. "They call our sweet Lord a bastard. Why do you let them do so? They call His mother a whore—one taken in uncontrollable lust even while she bled from her monthly courses. The Jews consider that this conception makes our Lord an object of shame. Here the Jews claim Mary lied to cover up the fact that she lay outside of the marriage bed and hoodwinked Joseph and the elders into thinking she was a virgin. They say here that Jesus was nothing more than a common criminal. A false prophet who is to be ridiculed through the generations. Why should the Jews be allowed to remain in your cities and towns and villages? What does such a people deserve?"

Seeing Donin like this, I could well imagine how he spurred the crowds elsewhere in France to murder and mayhem. I sat, stunned and frightened, as I watched evil unfold before me. They will burn our Talmud, I thought with despair. They will kill us or exile us to other lands. No matter how kind some of them may be—my Jaquet, for instance, or Brother Anton, the kindly guard, even the queen herself—they will turn against us and revile us and cast us out after this.

Indeed, the truth of my fear showed itself in the dainty lady-in-waiting sitting directly in front of me, who, beside herself with indignation and loathing, swiveled around in her seat. Grasping my shawl, she pulled me into her face. "Is that truly how you Jews talk of our Lord?" she said angrily. "We will show you what becomes of infidels who scorn and murder our God." She shoved me sideways, so that I sprawled into the laps of other ladies, who pushed me away, disgusted.

I straightened back up in my seat, keeping the sobs that rose within me trapped in my tightly closed mouth. Looking at Nicholas Donin, I could see a satisfied smirk on his face. He rode the emotion of the crowd and the fear in my face like a skiff on an unsettled sea. His eyes gleamed maliciously, and I could almost hear him whisper in my ear: *See, Shira? See what happens when you deny me and my truth?*

But Yechiel faced the crowd, calm and resolute. "Your Majesty, yesterday you said those who came to jeer were to be rebuked and that the duty of this court was to listen to both sides with equal forbearance. Have Nicholas Donin's accusations today changed that just declaration?"

"They have not, Rabbi. We will heed your defense."

"Very well. My lady, Donin quotes many tales of a man named Yeshu, and I cannot deny these tales exist. But sometimes he is called Yeshu Gedara, the bastard son of Sotada, a soldier, and Panthera, a whore. Other times he is called Yeshu son of Joseph Pandera, who lived in Bethlehem. If you read these accounts carefully—something Brother Nicholas would not like you to do—you discover that Yeshu Gedara was born and lived in Lydia, which is not near Nazareth or even Bethlehem, and that he was not crucified but stoned. Nor was the site of his execution Jerusalem, but that same Lydia—a beautiful city close to the sea, where date palms and orange trees grow in great profusion.

"Jesus Gedara was a false prophet, yes, who deserved the painful death that he suffered. But he was not Jesus of Nazareth. Nor was Yeshu the son of Joseph Pandera the same Jesus you worship.

"Nicholas Donin knows that. He knows you cannot discover these facts for yourself, and he seeks to dupe you into hatred of us. We tell stories of many men in our Talmud. There are several named Samuel, for instance, and a few called Elazar, and quite a number with the name of Moses. These men did not live at the same time or in the same place. And Brother Nicholas knows this, too.

"I beg you to remember that I excommunicated Nicholas Donin. Since then, he has wanted to revenge himself upon us, and he seeks to use you, Your Majesty, and the members of your court, as tools for his retribution. I implore that you not allow him to mold your minds to his nefarious purposes."

I sat clasping my hands together in sheer admiration. Truly, no one could equal Yechiel of Paris. He stood there, unperturbed, and through his quiet words swayed the mood of the crowd.

Donin, sensing this as well, stood to strike a counterblow. "Yes,

Rabbi? Then perhaps you will tell me where I am twisting the text when I read of Jesus condemned to an eternity of hell, immersed in boiling excrement?"

The room gasped as one. The queen half rose from her seat, but Yechiel, shaking his head, said, "Your Majesty, it is still as I have said. This is another Jesus we speak of. After all," he said, pausing dramatically, "not every Louis born in France is the king of France."

That, too, drew a shocked gasp from the audience, but there were titters interspersed as well. The queen, however, looked less amused.

Donin opened his mouth to speak again, but the queen forestalled him. "Why do you harm your own cause—spoiling your good odor, as my ladies-in-waiting might say?" she asked him. "The Jew, out of respect for you, has succeeded in proving that his ancestors did not insult your God. But you, you persist in trying to make him confess such blasphemies that would torture the mouth of any true Christian. Are you not ashamed?"

Donin stood, obviously stunned by the queen's admonition, but Thibault of Sézanne rose and spoke up. "Your Majesty? It seems to me appropriate to ask the Jew his opinion of what his Talmud *does* say about our Lord Jesus Christ."

"Yes, that would be fitting," said the queen. "Rabbi Yechiel, I would ask you to tell us what the Talmud says."

Yechiel sighed. "Very well, Your Majesty. The Talmud is not always kind to Christ, but I believe that is more the fault of the men writing at the time than it is the fault of Jews living in Christian Europe today. You must remember that Jesus and his followers did all they could to undermine the Law, the very foundation of Judaism. For this reason, we reject his teachings and deny his divinity. You will not like my saying this, but you have exhorted me to truth, so truth you shall have: Jesus deceived and beguiled Israel, purported to be God, and denied the essence of our faith."

My heart sank as the crowd gasped in shock. I looked at the queen, whose face was frozen in disapproval.

"I believe we can dismiss Rabbi Yechiel and summon Judah of Melun to testify tomorrow," said Thibault, well satisfied.

———•———

I lay down in my prison cell that night better fed, for my guard—who told me his name was Gillet—fetched food from the gates of the palace, where the Jewish community had established a vigil.

"They sit there with candles, ashes on their head, praying and moaning," he told me. "Your husband is among them, for when I asked, someone pointed him out. He says to tell you that your children are fine and well tended to but they miss their mother. And this rabbi who has talked for two days straight, his daughter is there as well. It is she who had food packed in baskets for you and for all the rabbis, and bid you break your fast and gather your strength. And here, someone gave me fresh clothing for you, which I'm sure you'll be glad of."

"Thank you, Gillet! I will dress in the morning and be better fit to appear in court."

Deina had sent a simple pottage of beans in a clay bowl, which was cold but delicious, with some bread and cheese. I ate every morsel. Assured that Gillet would not allow Brother Nicholas into my cell, I closed my eyes and fell into the first deep slumber I had enjoyed since I was imprisoned.

But I awoke suddenly in the early hours of the morning, shaken to realize I was not at home. I sat up, clasping the thin, ratty blanket to my chest, despair flooding me as I recalled where I was. Memorize the day, Yechiel had said. I feared that yesterday was one day I would never forget.

It is *your* soul that will be on trial, Nicholas Donin had told me. As I shivered in my bed, I wrestled with my soul. The hatred I had felt all around me for us Jews had been a palpable thing, a hideous monster with razor-sharp teeth. I realized that I was helpless in the face of it: I could not protect my children, and nothing I did—neither prayer nor reason—could prevent the mob, so roused, from trampling me and mine and thinking it a thing well done.

Why would anyone remain Jewish in the face of this? I asked myself. Why do it?

For a few minutes, I contemplated what it would mean to turn Christian. Meir would never acquiesce. Chaya was probably too old to accept it. But Zipura and the baby and I—my aching, hot breasts leaked a little as I thought of my youngest girl—the three of us could find a quiet village somewhere, perhaps a port town where newcomers were not eyed with the same suspicion as in farming villages. How to live? How could I provide for the girls? What would it feel like—and here I broke down and wept—to know that my husband, my father, my stepmother, would say prayers for the dead after we left, that my friends would mourn me and never speak to me again?

This was what *he* felt, I realized once again. This was why Nicholas Donin was so possessed.

It is an accident of birth that I am Jewish and not Christian, I thought. Had I been born to it, I probably would have made a fine Christian. I would have enjoyed going to the enormous churches that I passed in the city and praying in their vaulted halls, the sun pouring in, colored by huge plates of stained glass. I would have crossed myself and prayed to the Virgin Mother to intercede for me when I wanted a favor, the way I sometimes saw Jaquet do. I might have married a scholar from the University of Paris, or a sailor or soldier, a craftsman or . . .

The thought of marrying anyone but Meir made me weep even harder. I could not picture not having my impassioned, brilliant, stubborn, intense husband as the center of my life. Our love is *b'shert*, I said, recalling what I had told the queen. Had I been Christian and he Jewish, and had we somehow found each other . . .

But these are idle fairy tales, I scolded myself. It is the rest of your life you need to consider. Could you give up your faith to save your life and the lives of your daughters?

I was flooded with dozens of memories. Zipura jumping up and down excitedly over the Purim baskets. Chaya placing a small kerchief on her ruddy hair to light the Shabbat candles with me. My husband

and I poring over the Talmud together, finding the reasons why we worshipped as we did. Going to the *mikveh* and sharing love with my adoring husband. My father holding me in his lap, telling me stories. All the moments that gave my life shape and meaning.

I could not do it, I realized. Even if it meant death, I could not be other than what I am.

The darkness of the early morning hours gave way as dawn peeked into the room through the thin slit of the window. I rose, washed my face and hands, and prayed.

"Blessed are You, oh Lord, Master of the Universe, for having made me according to Your will."

WENTY

Before a man is born it is declared in heaven whom he will marry.

—THE TALMUD

"SHIRA!" I HEARD ALYES CALL. "SHIRA! OVER HERE!"

I stood, feeling slightly befuddled, outside the gates of the palace. All around me the Jews of our community were cheering our rabbis, now safely delivered from the hands of our inquisitors. My stepmother hugged me. My two older girls grabbed me around the knees and clung to me. My father, looking tired and worn, smiled at the picture we made, the four of us laughing and talking in unison.

I broke away, looking around. "Where is Meir?"

The last day of the disputation had been unexpectedly short. When Judah ben David was called in, it took less than half the morning to realize that his answers were not going to differ from Yechiel's despite all the traps set for him by the prosecution. But where Yechiel had been fervent and compelling, Judah was calm and methodical. The queen grew restive as his long-winded explanations droned on and on. Her clerks suggested that the disputation reconvene as a Church tribunal and she agreed, charging Geoffrey of Belleville, the king's chaplain, to relay the tribunal's decision to her son.

"Where is Meir?" I asked again now, looking around. I could not believe he would not be there to greet me.

"I am here, my wife," his deep voice sounded behind me. I saw, with some confusion, my husband emerging from the same gates I had just exited.

"What did she say, Meir?" Alyes asked. And Chaya chimed in, "Yes, Papa, what did the queen say?"

"The queen spoke with you?" I asked, amazed. Why would the queen summon my husband for an audience?

Meir took my arm. He stooped slightly to stare into my face, his eyes glowing as he grinned at me boyishly. I knew that look. Whatever had happened in the queen's presence was his secret for now. His fingers trembled as they grazed my sleeve. "We will speak of this later," he told the girls firmly, never taking his eyes from my face. "Come, let us bring your mother and your *grand-père* home, girls, to that festive meal you and *Grand-mère* prepared over the last three days."

"That sounds wonderful," I said, brushing Meir's hand with the lightest of touches. I longed to kiss him, to fall into his arms. But I would have to wait until we reached the privacy of our own home.

I spent the afternoon and evening nursing my little Rachel off and on. Deprived of her mother, Rachel had given my family a difficult time and now was reluctant to let me go, whimpering whenever I tried to put her down. I was content to keep her on my lap or to lie down with her on the bed. As she slept fitfully against me, I wrote out an account of the last few days, wanting to commit everything to paper before I forgot.

"And so," I concluded, "Judah ben David of Melun stood against his accusers, his bearing one of poise and dignity, like his teacher before him able to defend the Talmud with adroit debate." Rachel stirred against my breast, and I added, "Thus was the insect Nicholas Donin, may he remain ever childless, utterly defeated."

I titled the document "*Vikuach*"—"Disputation"—and set it aside. I would deliver it to Yechiel tomorrow.

Night had fallen. The girls were snuggled in our bed, having given up theirs to their grandparents. Rachel finally let me put her into her cradle. My father and his wife slept soundly in the next room, my father snoring. I looked around for my husband. He was not in the house. Wrapping a light shawl around my shoulders, I crept downstairs and outside. Meir sat on one of the benches under the grape arbor.

"There you are, husband," I said.

He rose and took three steps, covering the space between us more quickly than I could have imagined. He swept me into his arms, bringing his dear face down upon mine, raining kisses on my cheeks, my lips, my throat, his lips lingering in the sweet hollow between my breasts.

"Come with me," he whispered, drawing me into the secluded privacy of the arbor. "Our house is too full of people, and I must have you, tonight of all nights."

There was a soft mound of new grass in a corner of the arbor, a place where the girls often played. We lay down on it. Meir reached over, his hands tracing my body, taking possession of my breasts, my hips, that inner core where blood beat a demanding pulse deep inside me. When I reached for him, he moaned. "Let me," I whispered, releasing him from his trousers. I was aflame, as though this were another wedding night. I felt half-shy of making love outdoors, but his smell upon me—that heavy, musky scent of man—made me frantic for him.

He entered me, calling my name softly. I felt him move within me and my passion built, higher, then higher still. He kissed me deeply, exploring my mouth, before moving his lips back to my breasts. I felt myself floating, feeling nothing but pure sensation and love. This, I thought, in the throes of ecstasy, this is what I could never leave. It was more than passionate fulfillment. I felt this night's lovemaking symbolized our married life, complete with its rich rewards of prayer, learning, family, and abiding love.

Spent, we lay together, panting heavily. Meir kissed me again, more tenderly. Tears fell onto my cheeks, and he kissed them away.

"*B'shert* . . . ," he whispered. "You told the queen we were *b'shert.*"

"And are we not, husband?"

"Oh, yes, my darling. We are." He caressed my cheek.

"You told the girls the queen wanted to ask you some questions about the family. What did she really want?"

Meir laughed. "To tell me that Nicholas Donin never touched you. That you gave up your pearl to protect your virtue. That the guard, who impressed her by giving you back your pearl, invoked her name in denying Donin entrance to your cell."

"Queen Blanche was pleased with Gillet?" I was glad to hear it, for the guard's good deed came at a most welcome time.

"Apparently, Donin complained to the queen that she put you under lock and key. She said that he told her he wanted to argue with you again, feeling he was close to possessing your soul for Christ. She refused, saying that you had called him unchivalrous. She called the guard in for questioning and she was moved to learn you would sacrifice your prized possession, telling me that it showed a pronounced romantic spirit. I quoted the passage from Proverbs about the woman of valor, especially the verse 'Far beyond pearls is her value,' and we agreed that you are just such a wife."

TWENTY-ONE

*I saw how they gathered you up, / plundering your volumes
like booty from a pagan city / burning you in the city square*
                                        —Rabbi Meir ben Baruch

ANY EUPHORIA WE JEWS OF PARIS might have felt at our success
in the queen's court was soon dispelled by the more stringent examina-
tion by the Inquisition. There was no ceremony and no delicate ma-
neuvering. Our rabbis were not even present to plead our case. Where
Queen Blanche might have been persuaded by Yechiel's poignant pleas
for justice, the men Louis gathered to pass judgment on the Talmud had
no heart and no understanding. As they turned the pages of our sacred
volumes, they saw only sin.

In a letter to King Louis, the chancellor of the University of Paris,
Odo, wrote:

> *We found these books to be full of innumerable errors, abuses,
> blasphemies, and wickedness, arousing shame in those who speak
> of them and horrifying those who listen. These books should not be
> tolerated in the name of God without injury to the Christian faith.*

We therefore refuse to restore them to the Jewish masters and
decisively condemn them.

At dawn on the day of the burning, I lay beside Meir in bed. Neither one of us had slept all night. I felt empty of tears, empty of emotion, having wept and sighed and, with my despairing husband, tried to find some way to view this calamity in any but the most catastrophic of lights.

We dressed in the early morning light and went outside together. It was a warm June day, but neither of us could draw any comfort from the simple pleasures of birdsong or the roses scenting the yard. Meir stood to one side and prayed. I watched him, my heart aching as I realized that there was nothing I could do to help him through the day.

The girls woke and I fed them. I didn't think I could swallow a bite. Meir had told me that he would fast this day. My father and Alyes, unwilling to stay to watch the burning, had already returned home to Falaise. Papa bid us stay away from the market square on the day of the burning.

"It will not be safe, Shira," he told me. "Crowds and burning create riots; riots mean dead Jews. You must do what you can to keep your family safe."

"We won't go," I had told Meir last night. "We'll stay home."

"You won't go, obviously," my husband replied. "It's your job to watch the children. I think I must witness what they do, however."

I did my best to try to persuade him otherwise. I had worn him down sufficiently by morning and I thought I had won. So when the hour of ten bells approached and my husband came to kiss the girls good-bye, I was surprised, dismayed, and furious.

"You don't mean to leave us!" I protested. "You told me last night you would stay to protect us."

"I cannot have this tragedy occur so close by and not witness it, Shira," he told me, looking away from my flushed face. "Something compels me to the market square."

"Then I will go with you," I cried.

"No," he said. "I forbid it. You must stay and keep the girls safe."

"How exactly?" I asked bitterly.

"Hide them and yourself. Whatever you do, do not take them to the *yeshiva* or synagogue. That would be the worst place to go, the first place the mobs will attack."

"Monsieur Rabbi," Jaquet said from the doorway of the pantry. "I can take the girls and madame to my mother's home. It is a small hovel on the edge of Paris and will not be comfortable for them. But no one would look for Jews there."

Meir looked at the plain Christian serving maid with strong affection. "Jaquet, this family is grateful to you, as always."

"Jaquet will take the girls, Meir, and I will go with you."

He kissed the girls, who clung to him, crying. He kissed me, looking straight into my eyes. "You go with Jaquet," he said. "We will all return home this evening. Shira, you understand me?"

"I understand, husband—but I cannot promise to obey."

He turned from the door. His eyes flashed in anger and his jaw stiffened. "Do you want to kill me? How can I do what I must if I don't know that you are safe?"

"Then let me go with you. Jaquet can take the girls. I could not bear the day otherwise."

"This is foolish, wife. Do my desires, my commands, mean nothing to you?"

"I will see that the girls are safe and I will come find you."

He shook his head. "I will not order you to stay with them, for I could not bear to be angry with you today of all days. But I want you to stay safe with them, and I hope that you will, for love of me." He left.

I sat at the table feeling completely depleted, my head in my hands.

"We should go, madame," Jaquet said. "It is a long walk."

———•———

Jaquet's mother was not pleased.

"You bring Jews here to me today, when all the talk in the market is of the burning of their evil books?" she hissed at her daughter. The girls, exhausted by the distance and frightened by their miserable surroundings, held on to my hands, speechless. The baby slept, peacefully, inside a cloth sling I had placed next to my body.

"Madame, we are grateful for your kindness and cannot praise your daughter highly enough. Jaquet has come to be one of the family," I ventured, to placate her.

The old woman snorted and spit on the floor. "Pshaw. One of a Jew family. Better we should have drowned her at birth, like her father wanted."

I looked at Jaquet, who smiled sheepishly. "She's always said so, madame, but I never knew my father. He left when I was a baby. My mother has always been a little . . ." She touched her forehead. "But you needn't worry about her." She unwrapped a bottle from a bundle of rags she had been carrying. I saw that it was a cheap bottle of spirits. "Mama? Madame Shira has brought you a present."

The woman's eyes lit up when she saw the bottle. "Well. That's better. Get me a cup, you," she said, pointing to Chaya. "Make yourself useful."

"Mama?" Chaya asked, clinging to my hand with both of hers.

"Let me, madame," I said, pulling the girls off me and sitting them down on a hard wooden bench. Better the splintered wood than the bed or the floor, I thought, both of which must be infested with mites and possibly worse. I found a stained wooden drinking cup in a cupboard, jumbled together with tools and rags, and brought it to her.

"Ah!" she said, grasping the bottle by the neck and filling the cup up to the brim. "Nice." She downed the liquid in a few quick gulps and poured herself another cupful. The girls watched wide-eyed.

Jaquet went outside and returned with a broom. "I'll clean up what I can, madame," she told me. "My mother will drink herself into a stupor and she'll sleep the day away. We'll be back at home by evening. I'll make sure the girls bathe before I bring them into the house. You go, now."

"Are you sure?" I asked.

"Your husband needs you more today than your daughters do," she said, blushing.

I studied her. I had known for some time now that Jaquet adored my Meir. Looking around at the filthy hovel where she had been raised, I could see why. It wasn't passion or desire she felt for him but appreciation, because he gave her something no one else had ever given her before—the feeling of belonging to an orderly, dependable home. But I had not realized that my serving maid cared so much for Meir that she, too, sensed the force of the blow my scholarly husband was about to endure.

I had to trust her. I took her outside, so that the girls would not know I was leaving them until it was too late. "If something happens to both Meir and me . . . ?"

"I know how to reach your father," she assured me. "I will get the girls to him, safely. I swear it on . . . well, on this." She touched the cross that never left her chest. I eyed it warily. "It's the most sacred thing I own, madame," she said, seeing the fear that washed over my face.

I touched her arm. "The most sacred thing you own is your loyal heart, Jaquet. Take care of my girls today. I will see you in the evening."

She reached out as I scooped the sleeping baby off my body. Rachel stirred fretfully in her sleep. I dropped a quick kiss on her soft red hair and walked back to Paris, my eyes burning with unshed tears.

—◆—

By the time I reached the streets near the market square, I was fighting the crowds. The news that the priests were creating the greatest bonfire ever seen and consigning the condemned books of the Jews to the flames swept Paris into a holiday mood. Shops were doing a bustling trade in fans and straw dolls. The fans, of course, would be used by the faithful to help strengthen the blaze; the dolls were small effigies of Jews to throw on the fire.

I took a moment to hide my *rouelle* under my light summer shawl. As

I elbowed my way through the crowd, I began to question my decision to come. Would staying with the girls not have been the better course, preferable to planting myself squarely inside this mass of humanity as they anticipated the spectacle of their faith's triumph?

But my husband needs me, I reminded myself, and shuffled forward a few more inches.

The throng was held back by guards and horses, stopped several streets away from the market square. I was hemmed in on all sides, the smells of the sewer and the sweat of the mob almost overpowering me. The guards forced us back against the stone walls of the shops that lined the street, clearing a pathway. The far-off rattle of carts could be heard in the distance.

"Madame Shira!" came a cry. I turned my head. Two of my husband's former students, Nahmias and Schouschan, were standing beside me. They were a few years older than when I had seen them last, the day Meir broke his hand, but they were not yet men, and the infectious excitement of the crowd shone disturbingly in their eyes. "You should not be here," Nahmias said, yelling into my ear over the shouts of the crowd. "Where are your daughters?"

"Safe," I answered. "I'm looking for Rav Meir. Have you seen him?"

"We know where he is," Schouschan said importantly. "We can take you to him after the carts pass. The guards won't let us move now."

It was true. The crowds stopped jostling and waited expectantly. The sound of heavy cart wheels on the cobbles drew nearer.

"Do not be alarmed. We are going to grab a couple of books off the wagons when they pass by," Schouschan whispered in my ear.

"Not alarmed? They'll kill you!" I whispered back, looking around to see if anyone had overheard.

"Not us, Rebbetzin. We are quick, nimble. If we lose you in the crowd, you have only to follow the carts. Rav Meir and the other rabbis from the *yeshiva* are in a group near the pyre. They are being held at sword-point there, but they say on the street that Queen Blanche issued orders no Jews are to be killed today. So don't worry."

Don't worry, I repeated to myself. The refrain reverberated through my aching head. Don't worry. Don't worry.

I wrenched my thoughts away from my darling Meir, whom I could not help at this moment, back to the boys, whom I could. "No matter how quick you think you are, you mustn't try to rescue any of the books," I pleaded with them. "Even if Queen Blanche said no Jews are to be killed, the guards here would ride after you and punish you. You can't outrun a horse."

"But we can find a place to hide until they give up!" retorted Nahmias. "Here they come!"

Everyone around us pushed forward. We were swept to the edge of the street, teetering perilously over the refuse and night soil piled high in the sewer. The guards pushed us back, and for a moment, I thought I would be crushed between the soldiers before me and the crowds behind me. But then the first cart came around the corner and everyone settled back to watch.

"We're going to wait until the last carts have nearly passed," Schouschan whispered. "There are twenty-four of them."

Twenty-four open carts, each one piled high with volumes of blessed books, monuments to centuries of learning and faith. The books slid against one another with each bump in the road. Their dark leather covers looked faded in the bright sunlight. We had heard rumors that our sacred books had been stored in a warehouse open to the elements, and looking now at the enormous mound of books, I believed it. But their frayed covers made them no less dear. I stood there, mouthing psalms, thinking of my father, and his father, back all the way to Babylon, where scholars had gathered as much knowledge as they could find and once more embarked upon the conversation with God that He had initiated with Moses that holy day on Mount Sinai.

Our finest philosophies have flourished in exile, I suddenly realized. Moses led an enslaved people out of Egypt to the Promised Land, and, on our way, God favored us with laws that shaped us into the people we have been for millennia. By the rivers of Babylon, I thought, we sat and brought the writings of God and the writings of the people together into the Torah, and the great teachers contemplated them in a magnificent debate that has lasted until today, a day when our Christian overlords would extinguish those ideas until nothing more than ash and memory remained. I remembered the 137th psalm and, watching the carts roll by with their burden of our history, I murmured lines from it under my breath:

By the rivers of Babylon, there we sat, sat and wept,
as we thought of Zion.
There on the willows we hung up our lyres,
For our captors asked us there for songs, our
tormentors for amusement,
"Sing us one of the songs of Zion."
How can we sing a song of the Lord on alien soil?
If I forget you, O Jerusalem, let my right hand wither;
Let my tongue stick to my palate if I cease to think of you,
If I do not keep Jerusalem in memory even at
my happiest hour.
Remember, O Lord, against the Edomites the day of
Jerusalem's fall;
How they cried, "Strip her, strip her to her very
foundations!"

"Strip her, strip her to her very foundations!" was a sentiment living and breathing here, in Paris, centuries later, I thought. We, too, could do nothing but sit, sit and weep. The wheels grinding slowly on the gravel underfoot seemed to crush the breath from my breast. I found my cheeks wet with tears I did not know I had shed.

"Someone's looking at us," Nahmias whispered. "Wipe your face."

I dabbed at my cheeks with the back of my hand. The boys were counting now, under their breath, "Fifteen. Sixteen."

The line of carts seemed interminable. How many volumes of the

Talmud did they contain? How many households had they denuded? It seemed to me that if every Jewish home in Paris gave up a volume or two of the Talmud, it would still be impossible to fill up this many carts. There were thousands upon thousands of volumes there. But then I recalled the library of the *yeshiva*. I remembered how so many scholars, like my Meir, each had treasured libraries of their own. And perhaps the officials had reached outside of Paris, as well. Perhaps this was every volume of the Talmud in all of France. Certainly they had taken every one my father possessed, as well as every one from the students in his *yeshiva*.

"Nineteen," the boys counted. "Twenty."

"The Jews must be the devils themselves, to possess so many books of black arts to try to defeat Christ and his angels," I overheard one merchant mutter to another. There was fear and fury in the whispered exchange. I thought of Meir being held at sword-point. Would Queen Blanche's assurances that no Jews would be harmed this day be enough to restrain the ill will of the mob?

"Twenty-two," the boys shouted. I reached out a restraining hand too late. Of one mind they left my side, squirmed past the guard, and, racing over the cobbles, each filched a volume of the Talmud and began to run down the street with them.

"Catch them! Catch them and burn them!" people in the crowd shouted as they waved their arms and pointed to the runaways.

The boys tried to zigzag left, then right, but the crowds refused to let them through. One of the horsemen rode after them, wheeling his horse before them to cut off their escape. Another hemmed them in from behind. The two boys stood, huddled together, the heavy leather volumes clasped to their chests. With wide, terrified eyes, they looked up at the guards who were towering on horseback above them. The first guard pulled his rapier out of his sword hilt, waving it threateningly.

Without thinking, my heart pounding in my ears, I wrestled my way through the crowd, through the muck, and ran the distance of half a street, where the boys had been captured. "Stop! Don't touch them!" I heard myself yelling.

"Burn the Jews! Burn them with their devil books!" came the chant from the crowd lining the street. "Kill them, cut off their hands, slash the flesh from their bones!"

"They are under the protection of Her Majesty, Queen Blanche," I panted, throwing my arms up to shield the boys. "Don't hurt them!"

I wrested the books from their arms and threw them down on the street. I recalled what Yechiel had said during the first day of the disputation—that every one of us Jews would walk into the fire to save these works—and I felt ashamed. When they heard of this, would my husband, my father, and Rabbi Yechiel condemn me as a coward, as a traitor to my people? But these are just boys, I thought. I couldn't stand by and watch them get killed.

"They didn't mean it. They just got carried away by all the excitement," I gasped, looking up appealingly at the soldier. "Leave them be. I'll take them home with me now. Please. Please."

The guard lowered his rapier, unmoved by my begging. "As if we didn't know half a dozen of these wretched heretics are out on the streets, trying to steal back these works for their depraved and accursed masters," he snarled at me. "But the queen's too tenderhearted a woman and she said to spare your lives today. So we will spare your"—in an instant, his rapier flashed out and sliced deep into Nahmias's arm; Nahmias grabbed it, howling in pain—"worthless lives," said the guard.

The horde cheered. A second later, the sword nicked Schouschan's forehead and cheek. Blood gushed from both wounds. The mob roared its approval.

"Now the Jewess!" someone called out, and another shouted: "Stab the Jewess!"

I stood frozen, feeling the pain of cold steel before it was visited upon me. But the carts were rumbling down the street and the other soldiers were marching after them. The horseman resheathed his rapier and rode away, leaving me untouched.

In their haste, they had left the books behind them in the road. The crowd was dispersing, following the carts. Quickly, despite their wounds, the boys pounced upon the two books and hid them under their shirts.

"We need to bandage your wounds," I said, looking around to see if we still attracted attention.

"No need," muttered Schouschan, stooping down to scoop up some mud from the side of the road. "I hear good mud stops bleeding." He dabbed it on his forehead and cheek, and on Nahmias's cut arm.

"No, that's . . . no!" I protested, cringing at the thought of the filth they were applying to their bodies. But the boys would not let me touch them.

"We're going to hide these in a safe place, Rebbetzin. If you want to find Rav Meir, follow the crowds and the carts," Nahmias whispered.

"And, madame," Schouschan said, "thank you. You probably saved our lives."

"Come on, Schouschan!" his friend called, and the two of them darted off before I could stop them.

———•———

I reached the market square with difficulty. It was crammed with people, every inch taken up with good Christian citizens eager to watch the burning. Peddlers sold hot cakes and pies. Bottles of wine were passed from hand to hand. Priests moved through the crowd, exhorting the faithful to be grateful for the blessings of this special day, many selling indulgences to the receptive throng.

Inch by inch, I slowly moved up to the pyre. The guards were still unloading the carts, piling the books in one enormous mound, cursing as the mountain grew higher and as books tossed on the top tumbled off and had to be restacked.

Looking around, I saw the boys were right. Guards surrounded our rabbis, who stood to one side, my Meir among them. Every once in a while a guard pushed or shoved one of them, spit on them, or cursed them, but for the most part, the guards allowed them to stand near the pyre, wrapped in their prayer shawls, mute witnesses to the impending carnage.

On the opposite side, an immense platform had been erected, for the Church dignitaries who sat on specially built benches under a linen awning. The queen was not there—court gossip said her birth pangs were expected daily—but many of the men who had appeared in her court sat in comfort, complacently watching the mob. And in their midst, of course, was Nicholas Donin.

Brother Nicholas, in his gray habit, was not a courtly figure, but he drew attention with the sheer delight he exuded. He was reveling in this day, in his revenge—a revenge so vast even he must have had difficulty comprehending it. He could not keep still. One moment he was at the edge of the platform, calling out to the guards, bidding them to add more books to this corner or that, and then the next, he was talking to the king's chaplain or the bishop of Paris. I watched as Donin walked over to the other side of the platform and stared at the Jews huddled before him, gloating, heckling them, asking if they, now, finally realized how wrong they had been to excommunicate him those many years ago.

I felt nothing for him but hatred. In his elation at our sorrow, in his prodding to cause even greater pain, he became the despicable insect I had labeled him. Having contemplated him for a long, stomach-churning moment, I faded back, unwilling to let him catch my eye. God only knew what he would do if he realized I was witnessing his day of triumph.

All of the books were finally discharged from the carts onto a massive pile surrounding a stake. The grand executioner, wearing a fearsome full-face black mask through which his eyes glinted, rose from his seat at the side of the dignitaries' platform. After he was handed an immense stick with oil-dipped rags tied at the end, he turned and bowed to the bishop of Paris.

The bishop stood. "Let us pray," he said, his voice rising above the clamor.

The crowd quieted. The bishop spoke of the glorious deed they were about to witness, invoking the name of the Father, the Son, and the Holy

Ghost, as well as the angels and the souls of the faithful departed, all of whom, he said, looked down on the good, God-fearing, pious Christians gathered in the square in Paris that day.

"We shall kindle this mountain of sin, take holy fire and burn the accursed words that have been concealed from us for generations—words that encourage the Jew to defraud you, to kill you with impunity, to insult our Lord Jesus Christ and His Blessed Mother Mary. We will burn them to ash and bury them in the unhallowed ground of the charnel yard. And we will strive to bring the Jew to redemption and salvation here in Paris as we do elsewhere, especially in that holiest of lands we fight for, seeking to wrest our most sacred soil from the hands of the infidel followers of Islam!"

A roar of approval burst from the mob, and, standing alone and unprotected in their midst, my Jew badge hidden by a single layer of cloth, I trembled in terror. The grand executioner moved forward. One of the guards kindled his immense torch, and the mob roared in delight. He strode with the flaming stave toward the thousands of volumes and lit them on fire.

At a signal from the bishop, a group of choirboys stepped forward and began to sing. Their voices rose to heaven like the small angels they resembled, in their white gowns and purple banded cinctures. In the yard, children and grown-ups alike set straw dolls on fire and threw them onto the blaze. Others stepped forward to fan the flames or to catch the fire from an area that was burning well and touch it to another section that had not yet kindled.

It took a moment or two until the entire heap caught fire, but then every book on the pyre was alight and burning. The smell of the burning pages was undeniably pleasant—reminiscent of autumn leaves being kindled or a heavy log burning in the cold of a wintry house. It would be years before I could fully enjoy the warmth of a fire in the hearth again. The volumes that had first caught fire were already shriveling and curling under the blaze, leather covers charring and crumbling, the jewel colors of illuminated pages glowing in flame-lit brilliance until their edges grew smaller and smaller. The mound crackled and shifted, red ashes peeking through.

I could not bear to watch any longer. I turned toward my husband. As I feared, the sight undid all his defenses. Meir was standing as close as he was allowed to the pyre, his *tallith* draped over his head, his eyes full of sorrow. Tears were streaming down his cheeks unimpeded, his mouth contorted in pain.

I broke through the crowd and ran to him, not caring what he or the other rabbis would think. The guards pushed me back and away, but I squirmed through. "Meir!" I cried.

He looked at me out of dark, haunted eyes. He collapsed against me, sobbing with dry, racking gasps, his entire body sagging under the weight of his heartache and helplessness. In that moment, I knew I was right to come, no matter how he or anyone might chastise me for it afterward.

I stood there, motionless, propping him up while he cried, watching the tower of books shrink into an ever-smaller pile. Those that had been buried at the bottom now caught flame. I did not glance at the platform again, for I did not care to know if Nicholas Donin saw me. I comforted my distraught husband with the same murmurs that I used for my children when they were sick or in pain.

Long hours passed as we witnessed the destruction. The crowd waned. Guards who had been corralling us became our protectors, escorting us home. My husband was still reeling as though someone had struck him a physical blow. I helped him upstairs and into bed. Then I went and sat alone in my garden until the girls and Jaquet came home.

WENTY-TWO

I cannot find my way back to you.
Your ways, the path of righteousness, are mourning.
—RABBI MEIR BEN BARUCH

"MEIR. YOU MUST EAT."

I came into the garden, holding out his bowl, which was still full of pottage. He had drifted away from the family meal and was sitting outside on a stone bench, his head bowed. He looked up briefly and turned from me. I stared at him for a long moment, then brought the bowl back into the kitchen. I waved away my daughters' questions. Clearly, today would not be different.

The entire congregation had mourned a full seven days, and then an additional week upon learning that Nahmias had died because his wound had become infected. He was a martyr to our faith. Schouschan had been ill for several days, but the physician had been able to lance and clean his wounds. While he would forever bear the scars of the guard's rapier upon his forehead and cheek, he survived. I could not help but feel that Nahmias's death was my fault. If only I had prevented him from putting filth on his wound to stop the bleeding. But Deina and Amyris

scolded me when I said so, claiming instead that I was a heroine for having saved both boys from the guard's sword.

The two volumes the young men had rescued were hidden away in
someone's cellar, and scribes were copying them out, working night and
day. Rabbi Yechiel had dispatched several other scribes to Falaise, where
my dear father was doing his best to remember as much of the Talmud
as he could, dictating pages to five scribes at a time. Yechiel was writing
letters of appeal to the Pope, the bishop of Paris, and the king, to lift the
Church's directive against our studying the Talmud.

Slowly, the community recovered from the blow. Classes were not yet
being held, but we tried to return to a semblance of normal life, despite
the echoes of violence we could still hear on the streets of Paris. Some of
the *yeshiva* students were summoned home by concerned parents; some
of the congregation sought more hospitable lives elsewhere in Europe
and beyond. But those of us who remained tried to see past our anguish
and fear. "We won't let this defeat us," said Yechiel from the *bimah* one
Shabbat. "We cannot let this defeat us."

But my Meir was not present at the synagogue to hear Yechiel. He
was deep in a crisis of faith all his own. He barely moved, did not eat,
and looked so pale and weak that I feared for his life.

The doctor visited him and left shaking his head, saying there was
nothing he could do to cure a broken heart. Yechiel came and exhorted
him for an hour. I allowed the girls to go to him, but he sat wanly as they
tried to cheer him. They emerged from the room confused and upset.
And nothing I did—no subject I brought up, no joke I made, and no
memory I invoked—could clear the storm clouds from his face.

Jaquet and I prepared every food imaginable to help him through his
bereavement. Round foods, symbolizing the circle of life—boiled eggs
and lentils and round loaves of bread—sat on his plate untouched. After
our mourning was complete, I tried to encourage him to go off to the
yeshiva or to take a walk with me. He haunted our house like a ghost,
moving from the bedroom to the kitchen to the garden, where he sat in
the brightening summer sun and grew thin.

Finally, in desperation, I read poetry and psalms to him. The 137th psalm, which had touched my heart as I watched the Talmud-laden carts drive by, made tears flow in an unending stream down his cheeks. And then I read him the beautiful poem of longing by Yehuda ha-Levi, the Spanish poet whose poems of exile spoke to us so vividly, despite having been written nearly two centuries ago. This was a poem we both loved:

My heart is in the East, and I am at the ends of the West;
How can I taste what I eat and how could it
be pleasing to me?
How shall I render my vows and my bonds, while yet
Zion lies beneath the fetter of Edom, and
I am in the chains of Arabia?
It would be easy for me to leave all
the bounty of Spain—
As it is precious for me to behold the dust of
the desolate sanctuary.

Meir put his head down on my lap and wept, and I wept with him.

The next morning, I woke from a restless sleep to find that Meir was not in bed. In his anguish, he had taken to roaming about the house at night. I rose to search for him, my heart heavy with the fear that we would not ever be able to rouse him from his pitiful state.

I saw him outside and approached him tentatively. I stopped short, shocked at what I saw.

He was sitting in the garden, his hair wet as though he had been to the *mikveh*, neatly dressed, slowly eating a crust of bread that he dunked in new milk. Next to him were several pieces of paper. I could see his beautiful handwriting scrawled in lines down the page.

His face brightened as he saw me. "My darling, that was a wonderful idea of yours to read to me yesterday. It made me remember that we are not the only ones who have suffered under a catastrophe like this. And as poetry soothed the spirits of those other writers, making it possible for them to struggle onward with their lives in Babylon and in Spain, so, too, has it remedied the pain in my heart. I have been up most of the night, writing in the moonlight, and when the sun rose this morning, I felt the pain lift from my heart for the first time since the burning in the square."

I tiptoed toward him, feeling as though any noise might destroy his newfound calm. "May I read it, Meir?" I asked.

"Of course, beloved," he said, pushing it toward me.

I moved away to a corner of the arbor, not wanting him to watch me. I had no doubt that it was a beautiful poem, for it was not the first one he had written. But his poem described something so deeply personal that I wanted to read it by myself. It began:

O you, who burn in fire, ask how your mourners fare,
they who lodge in your home's courtyard,
who gasp in the dust, pained and stunned
as they watch your parchment burning.

They walk in darkness, light denied,
still hoping daylight will shine on them, on you.

Ask how your people fare:
sighing, weeping, brokenhearted,
lamenting your birth pangs.
They mourn like jackals, like ostriches.

The tears flowed down my cheeks as I read the next few stanzas. Having struggled to feed him, I was particularly moved by these lines:

How could food ever taste sweet to me
after I saw how they gathered you up,

plundering your volumes like booty from a pagan city
burning you in the city square?

I cannot find my way back to you.
Your ways, the path of righteousness, are mourning.

My tears nearly blinded me as I read on, the anguish that touched his heart so clearly expressed. And then, finally, after one last cry of mourning, my husband found his peace:

I don sackcloth to watch the conflagration
kindled to divide you from the Lord,
lit to decimate your hilltops!

The Rock will yet console you,
compensate you for suffering,
restore you from captivity,
raise you up from degradation.

Once again you will wear a crimson ornament
take your timbrel to go forth in dance,
reeling for joy.

My heavy heart will lift
when the Rock sheds His light upon you,
bringing radiance into darkness,
illuminating your shadows.

I read it all again and, with tears in my eyes, walked over to my husband and kissed him.

"The Rock—the Lord—shall indeed shed light upon our Talmud again, Meir, I am certain of it. It is a beautiful poem. Will you send it to Papa and show it to Yechiel? They will both take great comfort from it."

Meir held me to him, and my heart rejoiced as he picked up his head to listen to birdsong once more. He kissed my forehead. "My dear one, I have been like one wandering in a dark abyss. Only your tenderness and caring helped me rise forth from it. You, my darling Shira, have ever been my light of day."

The girls found us wrapped in each other's arms and climbed between us. The baby whined, and Meir cheered her by picking her up and throwing her in the air, making her shriek and laugh. Meir's elegy had poured a kind of balm on all our hearts. At my urging, the girls and I ran around wildly, pretending we were Miriam's daughters, playing the red tambourine as Moses's blessed sister had once done, celebrating our safe deliverance from our enemies.

PART 3

ROTHENBERG OB DER TAUBER, 1244–1245

ETERNAL GOD, OPEN MY LIPS, THAT MY MOUTH
MAY DECLARE YOUR GLORY.
> —*Psalms 51:15*

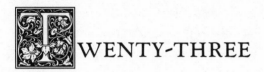WENTY-THREE

The beams of our house are cedars; our rafters are firs.
—SONG OF SONGS 1:17

CHAYA AND ZIPURA RAN THROUGH the four stories of our new house counting and arguing. To stop them from squabbling, Meir took them by the hand, putting little Rachel on his shoulders. He counted aloud with them. I heard their voices echoing through the empty hallways. "Nineteen. Twenty. And here—the last room of all—twenty-one!"

In the entranceway, I sat down on top of a pile of our belongings, feeling as though my legs, which were cramped from the long days of travel, could not support my heavy body. How had we ever come to live in twenty-one rooms in this foreign land of Germany? I thought. I shut my eyes and thought with a pang of homesickness of the lodgings in Paris we had left forever. Even my childhood home in Falaise seemed more like a home than this empty barn of a house. While my father's home in Falaise was not small, it was always crammed with people, so it felt crowded and never big enough. For a moment I sat and longed for my old familiar life. Meir, who had rejoiced when the community of Rothenberg had invited him to come be their rabbi and run their *yeshiva,* could not understand why I wanted to remain in Paris. His own feelings about the city had changed irrevocably the day the Talmud was torched, two years ago.

"Aside from being exactly the type of position I have hoped for, we can finally leave this accursed city behind us," he had urged, gleefully waving the letter that contained the community's offer. "You knew we could not stay at the *yeshiva* forever. I told you that someday I would attain a congregation of my own. I'm delighted it's in Germany, near my childhood home."

"But it takes me from my country, my home," I had protested.

"It will become yours," he had promised me, kissing me on the forehead, the letter joyfully crushed between his long fingers.

Throwing off my melancholy now, I made myself rise to take my own walk through our new home. I wanted to stretch out my arms to embrace the spaciousness of the empty rooms, with their tall, bottle-glass-green windows, smooth flagstone floors, and whitewashed walls. Of course, I reminded myself, this house would soon fill up with students. I thought of my father's home bursting at the seams and smiled. We expected the first boys to arrive next week.

Meir met me, having left the girls to explore the top floor. I heard Rachel calling to Zipura, "Look out that window. What's that sparkling there in the sunlight?"

"That's the river, Rachel. Chaya, do you remember the name of the river?"

"Papa told us, Zipura—the Tauber. That means 'pigeon.' A river named for a bird. Look how high we are! Take Rachel's hand, would you?"

I smiled at that. My beautiful, kind Chaya, then nine years old, always looked out for the two younger girls. I took a moment to reflect on how different my daughters were from one another. At seven, Zipura was the pensive one, always dreaming, creating little worlds from sticks and stones in the garden. Rachel was more active and friendly—a five-year-old busybody who stuck her little turned-up nose into everyone's affairs. But Chaya was the one I relied on.

Seeing me smile, Meir put his arms around me. But his arms could not quite reach all the way around my waist. I was pregnant again. Much as I hoped for a boy this time, this pregnancy wearied me more than the others had. Organizing the move and traveling had been taxing. Lucky for me, the two older girls could help me with the work.

"Well, *geliebt*? What do you think of our new home?" Meir asked.

"That means—'beloved,' does it not? I think you need to stop using German words I don't understand."

"Nonsense. You are fluent in French, Hebrew, Aramaic, Latin, even a little Italian and Arabic. You will pick up German quickly enough."

I looked around. We were standing in an enormous hall that we would convert into one of the main classrooms. The tall windows looked out onto a beautiful garden and courtyard. My kitchen was in its own wing, with an enormous fireplace and multiple pantries and cellars. The long line of privies was at the back of the yard. They were secluded by a strategically placed row of bushes that would keep the stench from fouling the house. I sat down in the window seat, leaning out to breathe the fresh spring air. I could see exactly where I would plant my kitchen garden. The synagogue was right next door.

"It is a wonderful house, Meir, but our few odds and ends will barely fill our own rooms. Does the community not plan to furnish the rest of the rooms?"

"I need to check with the *shamash*. They promised me in the letter that we would not need to worry about any of that. You saw it."

"I know, but it is one thing to read a letter and another to be faced with—what did the girls say?—twenty-one empty rooms."

Meir laughed, kissing my forehead. "You're going to miss Jaquet, aren't you? One of the first things we need to do is find another maid-servant. Maybe more than one."

I smiled ruefully. Jaquet was married now to a young craftsman who chiseled statues for Notre-Dame. If Meir had had his way, she would have come with us. The night she told us her intention to marry, blushing in bashful delight, my husband stood off to one side as my daughters and I clustered around her, hugging and kissing her. But when she looked over my daughters' heads at him, he quickly congratulated her with the rest of us.

Later, in the privacy of our solar, he had argued with me over the match, pacing from one narrow window to the next, stopping every so often to peer out at the slanted, uneven line of Parisian rooftops.

"He makes idols, Shira. We're allowing this young woman who has lived with us for more than ten years to marry someone who chisels idols, as if we were living back in the ancient time when Abraham was born in Ur. How can we?"

"It's not our choice. She is Christian, not Jewish, and not a daughter of the house, no matter how fond we both are of her. Her betrothed makes a good living and she tells me there's enough work at the cathedral to last two lifetimes. Besides, he sculpts gargoyles, not idols. And she's so happy to be getting married, especially now that we're leaving."

Meir frowned. "I don't know the difference between an idol and a gargoyle. I'm not even sure I know what a gargoyle is."

"I didn't either, but she explained it to the girls. They are mythic beasts who carry water in their mouths. The word comes from *'gargouiller'*— 'to gurgle.' The stone creatures are used as drainpipes to clear rainwater off the cathedral's steeples."

"Christians and their graven images! Why not just use a drainpipe?"

"Notre-Dame must be beautiful, Meir. I have often wished to go inside. I never will, of course, but I have been tempted."

"Paris . . . ," Meir said bitterly, looking out of the window again. "The temptations of Paris."

His sour voice had caused a pang in my heart. How different he was from the young, eager scholar I had wed! The memory of his bright face in the midst of his students, laughing openly at a joke one of them made in the *yeshiva* yard, flashed through my mind as I noted how his perpetual frown pulled down the corners of his mouth.

I reached over and squeezed his hand. "These have not been easy years for you, my darling."

It was true. Meir had recovered outwardly from the burning of the Talmud two years ago, but the event still haunted him. As he walked the streets of Paris, raw memories flooded through him. He would return home morose after passing through the market square. He valiantly tried to set the incident aside, but something always brought him back to that wretched day. Much as I loved our home in Paris, his constant pain wore me down, reconciling me to our move to Germany.

I looked over at him now, to try to judge if my sacrifice had been worth it. There was a new calm about his face and a quickness to his step that suggested it had.

"We should walk through town," Meir suggested. "Learn where everything is."

Upon hearing we were going out, the girls quickly came running downstairs, excited by the adventure of their new home. We lived just two streets from the Marktplatz, a broad avenue crowded with merchants and housewives. The children broke away from us when they saw a beautiful circular fountain brimming with green water in the middle of the gray-cobbled street. Water flowed from odd carved heads with enormous protruding tongues. The girls clambered onto the fountain's wide ledge, delightedly paddling their hands in the cold water. Across the square was a clock tower with a blue cupola. The church, a gray stone building with turreted windows and a sloping red roof, towered over everything. The houses, made mostly of brick or plaster, had round red and black tiles unlike any I had ever seen. Many of the houses were half-timbered in dark brown wood, their wattle faces painted bright colors—yellow, orange, even one a pale melon green. Others were fashioned from the same gray stone that paved the streets. The houses nestled so close together that any additions had to be stacked on the top floors. Our four-story building was more common than I'd first thought.

We walked through the bustling little town and out to the ramparts. An enormous red-roofed tower of gray stone rose to command the protective walls.

"Look, Rachel. That's where they stopped us and asked what business we had in Rothenberg," Zipura said, pointing to the guard tower.

Meir put an arm around her, who was standing still, staring at the tall structure rising into the brilliant blue sky. "What are you thinking, Little Bird?" he asked her.

"They keep a close watch on this town, Papa. Do you think that's good?"

Meir shrugged. "They guard us from other knights, other armies. That can't be bad."

Zipura put the tip of her finger in her mouth. Seeing my eyes upon her, she removed it. "Yes. That can't be bad," she murmured, sounding unconvinced.

"We should stop at the bakery to buy some food for dinner," I said. "Then we must go home and finish settling in while there is still light."

The kosher bakery, like most of the other shops we would frequent, was just off the Marktplatz. Stores had been located much farther away from our home in Paris. I looked forward to being able to send the girls out on errands to the shops. We entered to the sound of jingling. Rachel laughed, pointing to the small bell tied above the door. The warm smell of baked goods made us all remember how long it had been since breakfast.

"Welcome to Rothenberg," cried a stout man in a long white apron, his face lighting up as we walked in. "You must be Rav Meir!"

Meir smiled. "And you must be Lublinus. The *yeshiva* is everything you claimed it would be in your letter. This is my wife, Shira, and my three daughters, Chaya, Zipura, and Rachel."

"Welcome, welcome. Here, girls, would you like to try a Rothenberg specialty? These are *Schneeballen,* snowballs!"

He handed each of the girls a round ball of dough that was fried and sugared. They ate them greedily. Lublinus laughed and handed one to Meir and me.

I took a bite. The dough, fried hard on the outside, was soft and flaky inside. "Delicious!" I said in my faltering German. "Snowballs in the springtime!"

"We like our snowballs all year round here," Lublinus laughed. With his girth, he reminded me a little of Acher, the butcher of Falaise. "I am glad you like them, Rebbetzin. Now, how can I serve you?"

"We're here to buy our dinner. We must keep our meals simple until we are settled in our new home," I said, switching to the Hebrew that Jews throughout Ashkenaz could speak to one another. "Would you sell me some crusty rolls and new milk?"

"Yes, of course. Would you enjoy cheese with the rolls? Godliep, just two doors down, is our cheese seller."

"That sounds delicious, thank you," I said, reaching over the counter to take the rolls and the pail of milk. Meir handed Lublinus the coins as I was still struggling with German pfennigs and hohlpfennigs.

"I will be over tomorrow with the others to bring you your furniture, Rav Meir," said the baker, leaning over the counter to wave good-bye to little Rachel as we left his shop.

Two doors down, Godliep's cheese store was housed in a yellow-painted building that looked like a large slice of soft cheese. A crowd of vivacious women was gossiping as they placed their purchases into the straw baskets they carried over their arms. They looked up at us as we entered the store and I realized with a start that I did not know if they were Jewish or not.

As we had crossed the border from France into Germany, Meir had had me unpick the stitches that attached the *rouelle* to our clothes. Having grown up with the gold wagon wheel displayed on my chest, I found it difficult to venture outside without it at first. But here in Rothenberg, as in many other German towns, we were not required to distinguish ourselves as Jews. It was both exhilarating and disconcerting.

"You are Godliep? I am Meir ben Baruch and this is my family," Meir said to the moon-faced man smiling behind the counter.

"Ah! Welcome, Rabbi, welcome! Ladies, our rabbi and his family have arrived!"

The women greeted us with a chorus of salutations and a stocky woman, whose name I would learn was Frommet, pushed forward.

"Rabbi! Rebbetzin! Delighted you are here at long last," she exclaimed. "You will have dinner with my family this week. Plan on it, *ja?*" She clapped a heavy hand on my shoulder. I smiled, not quite sure how to respond. She reminded me of my mother-in-law. The resemblance grew stronger as she stepped back to survey my body. "You carry low; it is a boy this time. Finally, you probably are saying to yourself! Yes, definitely a boy."

"I hope you are right," I replied. "We are praying for a boy."

"God is good," she said, casting her eyes up to heaven. Then, looking at me with a twinkle in her eye that dispelled any resemblance to Bruria, she added, "And if He were not, we would need to pretend He is, to survive this life, *ja?*"

I laughed. The girls clamored to understand the joke, and Frommet smiled widely. "Your mama and I are just telling old wives' tales. Nothing to worry your pretty heads about! Such sweet *Mädchen*, Rebbetzin! Have you made a *shiduch*, a match, for the big one there yet?"

"Not yet," I said, wanting to laugh at the thought. After all, Chaya was only nine years old. But when I glanced at Meir to share the joke, I was disconcerted to see him studying Chaya with an intent look on his face.

The bell over the cheese maker's door tinkled, and several other women pushed inside. "Ladies!" Godliep cried out. "Look who is here! Our long-awaited rabbi, Meir ben Baruch of . . . of Paris, Rabbi? Of Worms?"

"Of Rothenberg," my husband replied firmly.

———

The girls and I took our seats in the women's section of the synagogue for our first Shabbat. While the synagogue in Rothenberg was not nearly as large as the one we attended in Paris, the building was well constructed and spacious. The housewives of the community worked hard to maintain its glossy wood pews and ark in pristine condition.

I was nervous for Meir as he mounted the *bimah*. Just the day before, he had learned that the community's cantor had taken a position in another town, so Meir would need to sing this evening as well as pray. I knew Meir had a wonderful voice. But it is one thing to sing songs of praise with your fellow students or in the warm embrace of your family and quite another to lead an entire congregation.

I need not have worried. Meir's tenor soared out, as though the angels themselves had gilded his throat. I read satisfaction in his contented face, his upright stance. In Paris, he had first been the student, then the *melamed.* Here he was the rabbi and, it appeared—judging from the smiles flowering around me, the quiet side conversations whenever he opened his mouth to sing—the cantor as well.

After Shabbat ended, the *shamash* asked Meir if he would be willing to serve as Rothenberg's *chazan* and combine the roles of cantor and rabbi into one. If I did not mind, Meir said, the wide grin on his face making my heart rejoice, he would ask the congregation to donate the extra income to charity.

"We do not need it, Shira, not with this enormous house and the fees I will earn as head of the academy. And our investments in trade are prospering."

"But would it not be better for you to have a *chazan* to rely on, husband? It will be tiring, singing and praying throughout every service."

"Perhaps. But I felt as though I were soaring up there on the *bimah,* singing praises to *ha-Shem*. I would at least like to try doing both for a while."

Looking at his bright face and the glow in his eyes, which I had thought was forever lost, how could I do anything but agree?

WENTY-FOUR

This is My covenant with you and your descendants after you, the covenant you are to keep: Every male among you shall be circumcised.
—GENESIS 17:10

THE THREE-DAY DONKEY CART JOURNEY from Worms to Rothenberg took just enough time for Meir's mother, Bruria, to miss the birth of our son. Six hours after I finished my labor, she swept in to find me confined to my solar, tucked between the birth sheets. Frommet and several other women attended to my needs, taking turns guarding the baby from Lilith and fetching food and drink for me. And of course my helpful little Chaya, my most dependable child, was at my side.

In her typical fashion, my mother-in-law proceeded to stir the pot.

"Well! A grandson from you at last," she said, setting down her bundle of belongings with a thud on the floor. I craned my neck to look at the size of the bundle and relaxed. She couldn't be planning that long a stay.

But a knock at the door dispelled that happy thought. "*Mütti?* Where should I put your other bundles?" my husband called, sounding more like an obedient child than the rabbi of Rothenberg and the ecstatic father of a newborn son.

"You did prepare a room for Baruch and me, didn't you, Shira? Surely in this enormous house there must be some corner where the grandparents can rest their weary heads."

Frommet took one look at my drained face and my mother-in-law's belligerent one and stepped in before I could answer. "Shira, let me take Rebbetzin Bruria to her room so she can rest after her journey."

I let my eyelids droop in anticipation of my mother-in-law's protest. Sure enough, Bruria put her hands on her hips. She looked up and down my neighbor's ample frame and said, "Rest? I am never tired. Thank you for looking after my daughter-in-law, but surely you must have work to do in your own home. I will take charge of my son's family, especially my darling little Suesskind."

My eyes opened wide. "Suesskind? Sweet child? That's a German endearment, yes? Because the baby's name is going to be Dafyid."

Bruria shook her head, fixing a baleful gaze on my startled face. "No. Suesskind. I prayed earnestly to God to let you have a boy this time. I swore to Him that if He did, the infant would be called Suesskind."

I plucked irritably at the sheets, which felt suddenly heavy. Swearing an oath to God was a serious matter. But I could not call my child by that dreadful name.

"And speaking of the sweet child—where is he?" Bruria asked. "Where do they have you hidden, my angel?"

I had just fed him and he was sleeping peacefully, tucked up warmly in his cradle. That didn't matter to Bruria, who swooped him up, pulling at his swaddling clothes to check if he was dirty. When he started to cry at being roused, she swiveled on me accusingly.

"Seems like this little man's hungry, Shira! You must not have fed him properly."

Before I could say a word, Frommet, who had watched Bruria upset all our orderly arrangements from a corner of the room, calmly plucked the baby from her arms and rocked him with a practiced motion. He instantly fell back to sleep and Frommet laid him down in his cradle.

"I will take your mother-in-law to visit with her son and granddaughters now, Shira, and we will let both you and the baby sleep," she said, each word spoken with quiet emphasis. "Bessel will watch over your rest so that Lilith does not destroy your peace."

Flaxen-haired, shy Bessel, who was staring wide-eyed at Bruria, moved her chair close to the cradle. She folded her hands in her lap, limpid blue eyes gazing on the baby.

"This way, Rebbetzin Bruria," Frommet said. "Mother and child need rest."

Bruria looked at the determined faces in the room and left grumbling. I called down silent blessings on my new neighbors and shut my eyes to sleep.

———•———

Never before had I regretted the Jewish tradition of secluding the mother after childbirth. Removed from other household duties, it gave me the leisure to get acquainted with my newborn and to rest between feedings. But confined to the room where I gave birth for three weeks after this delivery, I began to feel isolated from what was happening in my household. And Bruria, I knew, was taking full advantage.

Even though I could not leave the room, my husband would be permitted to visit me after the naming ceremony and circumcision, which would take place on the baby's seventh and eighth day of life. But, worried over Bruria's choice of name, I could not wait until then. I asked Frommet to relay a message to Meir about the baby's name. I impressed upon my neighbor just how important the name Dafyid was to me. I had my heart set on calling my firstborn son by my maternal grandfather's name. Unlike other rabbis, who argued against the custom, Meir favored naming children for relatives who had passed on.

Frommet bustled off on this mission, squaring her wide shoulders. She looked like a ship nosing out of a port. I had grown to depend on Frommet during the short time we lived in Rothenberg. More active than any three women in town combined, she hid a kind heart beneath her ample chest and brusque manner. There was not an act of charity in Rothenberg that she did not have a finger in, and many of them bore evidence of her entire fist.

I sat waiting impatiently. But when she returned, she looked disappointed. She handed me a note from Meir. It was kinder, perhaps, than the letters he wrote in response to ticklish questions about Jewish ritual and practice, but it was no less definite:

> *My dearest, Frommet tells me you are upset about naming our glorious little boy Suesskind. I am sorry to hear it. However, my mother swore an oath before God that this would be his name were He to grace us with a son. Perhaps she should not have done so, but if we disregard her wishes, she will be forsworn. This must be avoided at all costs. I know you agree. Besides, Suesskind is a sweet name and apt for this boy we have both longed for. I have no objections to it. As for the name Dafyid, we will simply have to have another son. I promise you, we will call him Dafyid. I am anxious for these long days to pass so I can see your face and kiss your dear lips again. I am so proud of my Shira, who has given me a boy at last! Your loving Meir.*

I crumpled the paper in my hand and flicked away a tear. The baby woke and fussed. Bessel ran to fetch him to me. I held him up and looked coldly in his eyes as he wailed. He sensed my disquiet and screamed louder. It took a minute or two, but his consternation finally pierced my heart. I brought him to my breast.

"I will name you Suesskind, since your papa would have it so. But I will call you Dodi—'beloved'—for you are, despite your dreadful, dreadful name."

The baby, drinking greedily, gave no sign of having heard me.

———•———

In one of her frequent visits to me, Chaya reported that Bruria had taken charge of the preparations for *Shavuah ha-Ben*—the festive meal that celebrates the first week of a boy's life. Chaya told me how her grand-mother spent her days preparing the wafers and little cakes that we served on such joyful occasions, turning the house upside down as she cleaned it to her satisfaction. I chafed at the thought of her rearranging my house, but as long as it kept her from me, except for short visits when she would cuddle the baby fiercely to her ample breast, I found I could bear the nuisance.

In many communities, the naming celebration occurs after the cir-cumcision, but in Rothenberg it takes place the evening before. "Lilith's threats are overcome on the evening of *Leili Brit Milah*," Bessel explained gently as she set out food for my midday meal in her slow, deliberate manner. Chaya sat and rocked the baby so I could eat in peace, listening wide-eyed as Bessel explained about Lilith. Bruria had sent up a dairy meal to help my milk flow—a cup of curded pot cheese and warm bread spread thickly with rich butter. I ate both with relish while Bessel con-tinued, "We wives keep vigil against her with you all week, but the men and children join the watch by feasting at your home the evening before the *brit*. Once we give this little one his name, Lilith is often fooled into thinking the eighth day has already elapsed and moves on to less pro-tected babies."

"And then we won't have to worry about her stealing the baby's breath anymore?" Chaya asked, dropping a kiss onto the baby's soft head. I smiled, watching her cuddle the infant. She was so gentle with him!

"That's right," Bessel said quietly. "God grant that it comes to pass."

Three days before my baby was to be circumcised, the *shamash* walked up and down the street prior to afternoon prayers, inviting the women of the town to come and join me so together we could bathe the baby for the first time. Led in by a beaming Bruria, the women took the screaming baby from my arms and gently lowered him into a luke-warm bath, throwing coins into the water to help pay my maidservant for all the extra work my confinement created for her.

Meir and I had hired three servants to cook and clean. The one re-tained to care for the baby was an eleven-year-old girl named Judda.

Not much older than my Chaya but much less capable, Judda had never worked before. I found I had to teach her how to do practically everything. But she came from a poor Jewish family who lived on the outskirts of Rothenberg and Meir considered it a *mitzvah* to hire her.

Judda reached in for her coins as soon as the women lifted the baby, wet and howling, out of the water. Frommet, seeing her, slapped her hand.

"Gently, girl, no one is going to take those from you."

I pointed to the pile of soft towels Bessel had left, and Judda, with an ugly look at Frommet, picked one up and wrapped it around the dripping child. I sighed as she carelessly covered the infant's mouth with the cloth. Bruria reached over and took him. She uncovered him, sending the girl, with a sharp poke, off to the kitchen to fetch refreshments. Bruria wiped him dry and handed him to Frommet, who restored him to me.

Judda returned with a platter of cakes. She tripped over the door frame as she entered, nearly spilling the contents of the platter. I saw Bruria shaking her head, whispering to one of the older women. She gestured toward the maidservant and then to me. Once again it was easy to see I was not the wife she would have chosen for her son. I sank back into my rumpled bedsheets, closing my eyes.

———————

The afternoon before the *Brit Milah,* I heard raised voices downstairs. Chaya was sitting with me, embroidering a tablecloth for her dowry. The baby, for once, was sleeping soundly and did not wake at the loud voices. Chaya and I looked at each other, startled.

"Do you want me to find out what is going on, Mama?" Chaya asked.

But before she could leave, little Rachel rushed in, her face alight with the importance of her news. "*Großmutter* and Papa are fighting," she informed us.

"Nonsense!" I scolded. "Your father wouldn't raise his voice to your grandmother. Don't tell tales, Rachel."

"No, they are, Mama, truly!" My little girl glared at me. "It's something about tomorrow."

Oh, how I chafed against the restriction of staying in my room after this particular birth! "Chaya, please go quietly and see what is happening," I asked.

I hated asking her to spy on her father, but I could not just sit there and wait to hear some sanitized version of the story. My eldest daughter, uncomfortable at the task I gave her but obedient nonetheless, crept out. I pointed to the chair she had just vacated, and Rachel, still annoyed that I doubted her, flounced into it.

"Did you hear any of their conversation?" I asked.

"Something about *Großmutter* wanting to be the *ba'alat brit* tomorrow and Papa won't let her," the little one said sulkily. "But you don't believe me, anyway!"

When a boy was circumcised, it was traditional to ask a couple to act as the baby's godparents. Grandparents and relatives were often honored in this way, and seeing as this was our first son, I could understand why Bruria assumed she would be the *ba'alat brit*. While Meir and I had not discussed it, the moment I learned my parents-in-law planned to attend this birth I knew they would be the *ba'aleh brit*. I could not imagine Meir going against his mother's wishes. I sat, straining to hear what was being said, waiting for Chaya to return.

Finally, there was quiet in the house. Chaya slipped back into the room. "Well?" I demanded.

Her face was flushed and her pretty mouth twisted in a grimace. "*Großmutter* saw me standing on the stairs and scolded me," she muttered. "Papa says he will punish me."

My heart sank. Meir, adoring parent that he was, could be stern when he thought the girls were misbehaving. I knew I should not have dispatched my poor daughter. I cast about, considering how to deliver Chaya from a punishment she did not deserve.

"Did you tell Papa I asked you to find out what was going on?" I probed.

She shook her head. "*Großmutter* was so angry she wouldn't let him listen to anything I tried to say."

"I'll find a way to explain to Papa," I said. "Don't worry, you won't be punished. What was the matter, anyway?"

"They were yelling about *Großmutter* appearing before the congregation," Chaya said. "I'm not sure why."

"*I* could tell you more, Mama," little Rachel chimed in. She was squirming in her chair, impatient. I looked over at her, eyebrows raised. "*Großmutter* was showing Papa and *Großvater* the dress she was going to wear tomorrow and a lot of new jewelry Papa hadn't seen before. She told them she would feel so proud, sitting in front of the congregation with Suesskind in her lap! And Papa told her, in his rabbi voice, that he didn't think a woman should ever enter the men's side of the synagogue, but especially not if she is wearing jewels, which would distract the men from sacred thoughts."

I sat up in bed, startled. It was not unusual for a woman to be allowed in the men's section for this particular occasion, for there was no other way for the *ba'alat brit* to hold the baby in her lap while the *mohel* circumcised him. I realized I had been strangely comforted at the thought of Bruria's capable hands holding my small son as they cut away his foreskin. Who would hold him now?

I didn't want the girls to venture back and possibly make things worse, so I forced myself to be patient. Guests began to arrive for the festive meal. I could hear people entering, greetings ringing out, the sound of singing and lute playing. The clear voice of Meir's dear friend Alexander ben Salomon Wimpfen rose above the hubbub, regaling our guests with one of our Jewish legends. Meir would lead the men in Torah study soon. At that point, the women would troop upstairs to visit me, bringing me a portion of the special meal, helping me keep vigil over the baby on this last night. Finally, the *ba'alat brit* would fetch the baby, taking him downstairs to be named.

Frommet led the women upstairs, holding a generously filled plate of waffles aloft. A few of the women hadn't seen the baby yet and they huddled around the cradle, oohing and aahing at the little man, who was dressed in a beautiful white gown. His little red wrinkled face looked up sternly at his audience. He glared at everyone out of bright blue eyes, delighting the women who tried to tickle a smile out of him.

Waiting for a moment when everyone's attention was elsewhere, I gestured to Frommet to come over to my bedside. I asked her if she would do me a favor.

"Anything, Rebbetzin Shira! What do you need?" she said, her voice booming.

Lowering my own voice, I explained how concerned I was that a woman would not be holding my son in her lap tomorrow. We shook our heads together over the idea of a man being gentle enough to soothe a hurt infant. Then I pulled out a note I had written to Meir.

"Would you take this to him? He may not be willing to touch it, and if so, please ask him if you could read it to him."

"I can't read well enough, Rebbetzin," Frommet said, crestfallen. "My father thought it was a sin to teach girls to read and write."

I stared at her, annoyed that I had not considered this possibility. Living in Paris in the midst of all those rabbis' wives had made me forget most women could not read or write beyond the small amount they'd need for the marketplace or the household accounts. I was sorry to have embarrassed Frommet. She noticed the chagrin on my face and laughed, shrugging.

"I don't regret it, Rebbetzin, I promise you! There isn't enough time to struggle with learning in addition to all the things I do in a day. What if I were to hold the note for Rabbi Meir while he read it? Wouldn't that be just as good?"

I brightened. "It would! Thank you, Frommet."

The Torah study was soon over. Bruria came and took the baby for his naming ceremony. The women trooped downstairs to witness it. Bessel stayed with me, sitting placidly by my side, her hands folded in her lap. I waited impatiently. I heard the murmurs of the ceremony, the loud cheers of congratulation. The lute player started again and the noise level rose, the way it does sometimes right before a party breaks up. I threw back my soiled sheets and walked restlessly over to the window, making sure I couldn't be seen from the street below. I wasn't allowed outside, but I thought a breath of fresh air would help me feel less confined. Below me was the sound of life—people leaving our party, others just walking up and down the street. The street torches were being lit by my neighbors, their children running off to buy something for the family's dinner, rounding the corner to the Marktplatz. How many times had I seen my girls off on similar errands, watching as they dashed away with a coin tucked into a palm or a sleeve? I felt stifled at having been cooped up for so long. And I wouldn't be able to leave the room for another two weeks.

Frommet returned. "Rebbetzin," she gasped. "You should be in bed. Bessel, what are you thinking of?"

"Oh . . . just give me a minute by the window, Frommet. I'm so tired of just lying there."

"No, no, it's bad for you. Come on, now."

I let myself be led back, and the bedclothes were piled in a suffocating heap on top of me. I wondered who had invented this custom of not changing the sheets on a newly delivered mother's bed for three weeks after the birth, thinking petulantly that it could only have been a man. Bessel, whose cheeks were spotted with shame at having let me leave my bed, hurried over with a drink. I waved it away, feeling irritable. She sat back down, her face troubled.

"Bessel," I said, striving to keep my voice calm so as not to upset the gentle soul any further, "I loved those waffles but didn't get any of the little cakes my girls told me their *großmutter* made. Could you fetch me a few? Frommet will stay with me while you do."

Anxious to be of service, the woman scurried off. I turned to Frommet. "Well?"

She handed me another note. "Here. I have no idea what he wrote, but I can tell you he was not happy while writing it."

My heart sank. I opened it and read:

*Shira. What an odd time to write to me! I am astonished and a
little bit upset with you, but I realize your moods are not steadfast right now and will indulge you. Yes, I know that you sent
Chaya to find out what was going on and I will not punish her
for something that was not her fault. That was not a wise thing
for you to do, but I see from your note that you realize it and
regret it. So we will say no more of the matter.*

*As for my mother, she will not come dressed in fine clothing
and jewels to distract the attention of praying men in any synagogue that is in my care. No woman shall, for it might cause the
men's attention to wander, which, as you know, is a sin. In addition, my learned darling, you should remember that this mitzvah
of the* Brit Milah *is and has ever been the father's obligation.
Abraham took his tribe and, by his own hand, circumcised them.
There were no women in attendance that day and women should
not attempt to snatch the commandment from us now.*

*I see that your gentle woman's heart is torn by the thought of
our baby's pain and that you want a woman to hold our son on
her lap while he is brought into the covenant. I understand and
honor that, but no baby boy yet has died of the pain, nor—I can
assure you—even remembers it once grown. It is just womanly
foolishness on your part to wish for this. This is* my *son and I will
have a care for him. As the* ba'al brit, *his grandfather will hold
him, and I assure you that his hands and lap will be as gentle as
any woman's. So put your cares aside.*

*Calm yourself, wife. I am eager for you to reemerge from your
confinement. The house is not as tranquil without your presence
and we all miss you, especially your adoring Meir.*

I put the note aside and closed my eyes. Frommet watched me, concerned. Bessel returned, holding a plate piled high with little cakes. I
took one and ate it, feeling every bite would choke me.

Downstairs, the baby started to cry. Rachel brought him back up to me and I took him and nursed him.

"We named him, Mama! We named him!" The little girl danced around my bed. "He is our own Suesskind, now and forever, *Großmutter* says, and she has fulfilled her promise to the Lord! Isn't that wonderful?"

The small mouth circling my breast tugged hard, sucking life greedily. My girls had been gentler. I made myself smile at Rachel as she whirled in dizzy circles, knocking against the bed in her enthusiasm. "Wonderful," I said. "Yes, of course it's wonderful."

———◆———

With the naming ceremony completed, the women did not feel they had to stay in the room with me any longer. So I should have enjoyed my most restful night since giving birth. But instead, what little sleep I did snatch was troubled by dreams.

I dreamt of Lilith, her filmy white dress spread wide like wings as she hovered over Suesskind's cradle. "This should not have been the boy's name," she hissed into my ear as she leaned down to kiss his baby lips and suck the breath out of his lungs, "so it won't protect him from my wrath. You should not have allowed him to be given the wrong name."

I woke then, sitting up in bed with a gasp. The moon was full and there was a bright patch of clear light in the room. I looked over at my peaceful infant. Shaking my head to clear the cobwebs of evil dreams, I laid myself back down on my rumpled sheets and tried to find a cool spot. Exhausted, I had just begun to doze when the baby woke, wailing to be fed.

I brought him back into bed with me and drowsed off while nursing him. While he tugged at my breast, I dreamt again. This time Nicholas Donin, in his friar's garb, came into my room and took my baby. Laughing at me, Donin laid the baby at the very top of the huge mountain of books. I stood alone in the empty Paris square and watched helplessly as the executioner lit the flame.

I jerked myself awake, knocking my infant from my nipple. Indignant, he screamed, his small face creased in angry wrinkles. In a cold sweat, I hushed him and moved him to the other breast. My fear must have soured my milk, for Suesskind nursed fitfully now. Finally, I propped him on my shoulder and burped him. A huge puddle of baby vomit flowed from his mouth onto my bedclothes.

It took all of my patience to wipe the baby clean, change his clothes, and put him down. Disgusted, I looked at my bed. I knew I was not supposed to change the bedclothes for another two weeks, but the idea of lying on these sheets repelled me. I got a soft cloth and cleaned out what I could, and then I flipped the sheets over and remade the bed. There, I thought—it's the same sheets, but now at least I can sleep on them.

Putting my head down on my pillow, I fell instantly into a deep sleep and dreamt the final, most terrifying nightmare of all. There was a hammering on the door in my dream, and Meir and the men appeared outside my room. My mother-in-law, dripping with jewels, came and took the child from his cradle and handed him over to them. In my mind's eye, I followed the baby down the long hallway, down the stairs, out the door, and into the synagogue. There were no women allowed, only men. They crowded around him. My father-in-law took the baby and put him on his lap. The *mohel* was paid in silver coin. He took a knife, which flashed in the light of the eternal flame. The knife was large, long and curved like an Arabian scimitar, and it grew until it was bigger than the baby. The men sang and laughed while the *mohel* bent over the baby and cut. There was blood everywhere. The baby cried and cried and no one comforted him.

I woke to the sound of the baby crying. God, I thought. Oh, God. I rose and brought the baby to my breast. I sat beside his cradle on the floor and let him nurse. "Hush, Suesskind," I said, using his name for the first time. "Hush. You won't remember the pain, my baby. Your papa says you won't and I believe him, for he is a good man, the best man I know. Hush, now, sweet boy. Hush. Mama's here. Mama's here. Mama loves you."

TWENTY-FIVE

Arranging marriages properly is as difficult as parting the Red Sea.

—THE TALMUD

"SHIRA!" MEIR CALLED. "SHIRA!"

More than a year had passed, and my baby was sitting up and eating pottage now. Dodi was a fat, curly-haired blond boy with a deep-throated laugh that the girls often provoked from him. I was grateful for the girls, especially Chaya, for it would have been difficult to run the *yeshiva* and tend to the newborn without them. Judda was more of an encumbrance than a helper and I hoped to convince Meir to find her other employment as soon as I had weaned the baby. Now, when my husband was calling for me, was she anywhere to be found?

"Here," I said, thrusting the spoon in Chaya's hands, "feed your brother."

I walked out of the kitchen and into the main house, where Meir was standing in the entry hall with a slight young man.

"There you are, Shira! This is Jacob ben Moshe—may he join us for dinner this evening?"

"Yes, of course," I said. "We always have enough for all your students."

"I'm not a student, Rebbetzin," Jacob said, hanging his head. Straw-colored hair straggled into his eyes and he reached up nervously to push it away. "My father is a rabbi, but I have never been gifted in study. I live with my parents and work for a local shopkeeper."

Meir clasped a warm hand on the boy's shoulder. "We cannot all be scholars, Jacob. And besides, soon you will be the husband of a rich girl and work with her father to help him in his many business enterprises."

"Not if Rav Judah has anything to say about it," Jacob muttered, talking to the floor. There was an awkward pause.

"You're welcome to our home and I'm delighted you'll be joining us for dinner," I told him.

"Thank you, Shira," Meir said, indicating with a glinting smile that I could go.

Jacob partook of a meager meal crowded among the raucous students, leaning over his plate as though he feared someone might steal it from him, even while he seemed indifferent to the food itself. Only later that night did I discover why this strange guest had joined us. As was his custom, Meir came to bed after seeing all of the boys were asleep. I was sitting up, rocking the baby. Having napped in the middle of the afternoon, the little one waited for his father to put him to bed. It was the happiest moment in both their days. I handed Suesskind to Meir, who spent a few minutes telling his son a nonsense story of the animals in Noah's ark and how they each brought a special sound along with them.

"What sound did the lions make?" he prompted, and Suesskind, clapping his hands, roared along with him.

Finally, Suesskind's head drooped and his father put him in his cradle. The sweet child curled on his side and put the tip of his thumb into his mouth. I looked down at him in the candlelight and smiled. "I'm still having trouble breaking Zipura of that habit. But I don't know how to tell a toddler to stop doing it," I said with a sigh.

"Do you want me to talk to Zipura about it?" Meir asked, climbing under the covers beside me. He stretched, groaning in sheer exhaustion. "Oh, that feels good," he said, finding the warm hollow of the bed next to me, kissing me on the forehead. "Blow out the candle, would you?"

I did, then lay next to him in the soft darkness. "Jacob ben Moshe seems like a nice boy," I murmured. "Quiet, though."

"He's having a difficult time. His father affianced him several years ago to the daughter of Rabbi Judah of Düren, who is both influential and rich. The fathers agreed that Jacob would live with his bride in her father's home. Rabbi Judah thought his daughter should stay in the comfort of her wealthy home and Jacob's father agreed. But when Jacob arrived to live with the family, it appears that the girl—I believe her name is Doula—took one look at our little Jacob and went crying to her father."

"But they were already betrothed, you say?" I asked. For us, a betrothal was as binding as the wedding itself.

"Five years ago, when Jacob was even smaller than he is today. He has a timid nature and the only way he will become wealthy is by marrying Doula. But I spent part of the afternoon with him and I can tell you that underneath all that hurt and humiliation and the diffidence that stems from it—having been willfully ignored by his bride and her family—he's a good soul who would make the girl a fine husband."

I shifted in bed, moving the quilt more securely over my shoulders. "It doesn't seem fair he should be treated so poorly."

"No," Meir mused, tugging some of the covers back. "I'm going to write the rabbis in Düren to see if I can help the boy. I've written Rabbi Judah directly and the letter I got—let's just say it was not particularly kind or polite."

I snuggled into Meir's warm shoulder. "I know you'll take care of it."

"I'll try, anyway," Meir said, spacing his words out as sleep threatened to overtake him. "Good night, beloved."

In an instant, he was asleep. As I felt the warmth of his body next to mine, the delicious softness of the feather quilt above me, tiredness crept through my body. It's good, I thought, to be in our own home, warm and safe, with our loved ones all around us.

———•———

Matches were made in Rothenberg by Nachshon the *shadchan*. This plump, harassed little man was a constant visitor at the *yeshiva*, as the young men studying with my husband were particularly attractive to families looking for a good marriage connection. In our community, scholarship was most esteemed among the boys, wealth and family among the girls.

I was always amused by the way the *talmidim* would act around Nachshon. Some of them would preen and strut before him, thrusting out their small chests, carrying more books back and forth to class than they actually needed. These boys, I would tell an amused Meir, were our peacocks. Others skulked by Nachshon, avoiding looking directly into his eyes, either too shy or too ashamed of their appearance or not yet ready for a match. Once in a while I would point one or another of them out to Meir, who would call the boy aside and explain to him that every man in the Jewish community must be wed. It was their duty to embrace this obligation not with trepidation but with modest delight.

So I felt no unease when Nachshon knocked on our door early one spring evening. The boys were out in the courtyard, enjoying the longer leisure hours before dark. My daughters sat to one side, sewing in the soft twilight and watching their brother toddle about. Meir was in his study cogitating on the arrangement of prayers in our synagogue. He wanted to impose some order on how we said our daily devotions. It had been an all-consuming occupation of his since he assumed the role of both rabbi and cantor for our congregation.

Usually, I would take Nachshon directly to Meir, for marriage was a man's business. But I didn't want to disturb my husband, knowing how rare and precious his hours of solitude were. "Let me show you where the *talmidim* are," I said, leading Nachshon through the long hallway to the side wing of the house, where we could step outside into the flag-stoned courtyard.

"Thank you, Rebbetzin. But I'm actually here to see Rav Meir—and you."

Cold fear suddenly clutched at my heart. I swallowed, looking at the smiling face of the man who made hundreds of matches a year throughout our part of Ashkenaz.

"Rav Meir expects me," Nachshon added in his gentle way.

"She's only ten years old," I replied. "It's too early."

"Your husband asked me to make inquiries, Rebbetzin. I've done so. You'll be pleased to know that there are many, many fine young men who would be delighted to become betrothed to your Chaya."

"This way," I said between clenched teeth.

We found my husband surrounded by several volumes of the Talmud, both the Babylonian and Jerusalem versions. One of the greatest attractions for us in settling in Germany was that the ban against the Talmud was not as strictly enforced there, although we followed, anxiously, through letters and messengers, the progress of Yechiel's fight to restore the Talmud to worshippers in France. The Pope, Innocent IV, was in the midst of his own struggles. Fearing an attack by our emperor, Frederick II, who wished to rule over a good deal of Italian territory, Innocent had fled to Lyon. Yechiel and others traveled there, petitioning the Pope that his destruction of our sacred books was wreaking havoc with our day-to-day lives.

Usually, the sight of my husband sitting contentedly among his books warmed my heart. Not this evening, however.

"Meir, Nachshon the *shadchan* here tells me that you commissioned him to find a match for Chaya," I said without preamble. "He's here to talk with us. Unless you feel I don't need to be here for the conversation," I added, letting the words drop from my lips with bitter emphasis.

Meir's head jerked up at my tone; he looked surprised and annoyed. His gaze shifted from my pursed lips to the matchmaker's embarrassed face.

"Nachshon, give us a minute, won't you? The garden is very pleasant this evening. I will send someone to fetch you when I've had a chance to discuss this matter with my wife."

"I know the way, Rabbi," Nachshon said suavely, bowing himself out.

"Sit down, Shira," Meir said to me.

"I don't want to sit down," I said, walking up and down the room, unable to keep my limbs still. "How could you do this without talking to me about it? Without consulting with me? She's my daughter too, you know!"

"Shira, you're upset about nothing. Nachshon and I were talking one afternoon and he suggested that it was time. I agreed with him. Chaya is ten years old, and that is old enough to be betrothed, even married. Just because you and I were wed so late—"

"That has nothing to do with it!" I lashed out. "I'm angry because you didn't tell me!"

"I should have," my husband agreed, trying to sound soothing. "I'm sorry."

I looked at him, eyes narrowed. Sitting there surrounded by his volumes, he had the air of the wise scholar. I felt he was patronizing me. Of course, looking back, in all fairness, no attitude he could have struck right then would have satisfied me. Striving to keep my voice calm and even, I said, "I would have told you she was too young. And you knew that. So you decided not to talk to me about it at all. Don't think I don't know the way your mind works, Meir. I've seen you deal with other people this way. I just never thought you would treat *me* like this!"

"I'm the girl's father, Shira. This is my responsibility, not yours. You've done your job—done it beautifully—but now it's up to me to provide for her."

"That's it, then? You'll betroth her to some scholar—and Nachshon says that the daughter of Meir of Rothenberg can have her pick!—and she'll move into his parents' home until she is old enough to consummate the match? And I'll never see my daughter again, except at her wedding and perhaps once or twice after she's delivered a child? I'll never see her again. My Chaya!" I collapsed into a chair and burst into tears.

Meir rose and came to stand behind me. "Shira, calm down. Calm down. We don't know whom Nachshon has found for her. If it's that important to you, we can find her a match nearby—so you can see her more often. I never thought you'd be this upset. *Why* are you this upset?"

Why was I this upset? Meir was right, this was his duty. I should not have been surprised he took it seriously. And my beautiful, kind, capable daughter—her illustrious heritage aside—was a catch for any young scholar. But the thought of my little girl leaving us choked me. I should have been prepared, I thought, as I struggled to stop weeping. If Meir had confided in me, I might have been prepared. *He* should have known what I would have felt.

"I'll send Nachshon away and ask him to come another evening," Meir said. He put a hand out and touched my back lightly. "Shira, I will find her a good husband. How can you think I wouldn't be as worried about my little girl as you are? I will find her a good home, a good man—"

"I wanted her to find her *b'shert*!" I cried out, raising my tear-stained face.

"*I* will find her soul mate for her," my husband said, his voice shaken as he looked down at me. "I promise you."

———•———

As we were mulling over the list of candidates for Chaya's hand and I struggled with the notion that soon I would lose my daughter, my husband found that his personal support of Jacob of Rothenberg's marriage to Doula of Düren was not adequate. One evening, Jacob presented himself at our home, waving a letter. Curious, I escorted him to my husband's study.

"Look, Rabbi," he burst out as he entered the room where Meir was working with one of his advanced students, "this came for me yesterday."

I went to the window seat and sat where I wouldn't be underfoot but could still see and hear everything. The student graciously shut his book

and left the room, nodding at the unspoken apology my husband offered him with a quick, rueful smile. After the door closed and the three
of us were alone, Meir took the letter and read it aloud.

To Jacob ben Moshe, greetings.

    You have solicited letters from rabbis in Düren and else-
where to demand that you be allowed to marry my most beloved
daughter, Doula, and force her to leave her father's home to go
to Rothenberg. I am bewildered why you think that this long-
awaited wedding is questioned by us. Rather, my daughter is
the one to be pitied, for you abandoned her after your betrothal,
rather than marrying her. She was mortified when you left.
    Now you demand that she be sent to Rothenberg to be wed.
My Doula is a gentle child, brought up in great wealth. You ask
her to disgrace herself by living in such poor quarters.
    You are treating her as a deserted wife—an agunah. *There-*
fore, Jacob, either reconcile yourself to living with us here in
Düren or agree to a divorce, allowing my daughter to choose
another.
    I told the rabbis how you grew sick in my home, after I had
hired teachers for you and supported you for a year. They agreed
I was right in sending you back to your parents, lest your illness
spread. Now that you are well, I welcome you back to finally
make my daughter a happy bride.
    Too much time has already elapsed. I demand your response
within two months' time. I have been assured by the rabbis that
this demand can and should be enforced by whipping or by plac-
ing you and your family under ban from the Jewish community
until you agree.

                                              Signed, Judah of Düren

Jacob sat while Meir read the letter, looking more and more dour. I watched the young man, puzzled by his expression. Didn't the letter give him everything he wanted? Maybe he didn't like the tone his father-in-law used, but I reminded myself that the man was a wealthy merchant. Perhaps he was used to issuing commands to his underlings. But Jacob looked as though something unsaid between the lines of this letter upset him.

Meir put the letter down on the table. "So?" he asked, noticing the boy's demeanor. "What am I missing?"

"You go straight to the heart of the matter, as always," Jacob said. "The messenger who delivered this letter to me waited in the alley beside my house. When I left my house a few minutes after I read the letter, intending to come here to show it to you, the servant grabbed me by the collar, pulled me back into the alley, and beat me. Look!"

Jacob lifted his tunic, wincing with pain. Purple and black pummeling marks stood out on his white skin. I pulled back, horrified at the sight. Meir rose from his seat, walking over to take a closer look. He bent over, peered at the boy, and stood back up, shaking his head. "That makes no sense."

"There's more, on my arms and legs. The servant beat me on my body where the marks could not be seen. As he struck me, over and over again, too many times to count, as I cowered on the ground, the very breath pounded out of my lungs, he told me to stay far from Düren's borders lest he and Judah's other servants beat me again. He said Rabbi Judah had no intention of ever letting me marry his daughter. If I persevered, he said, the servants were instructed to make a widow of Doula before she could ever consummate the match." Jacob pulled down his tunic. "I begged him to stop. But he said he would receive a gold coin for every punch he delivered to my stomach, arms, or legs, up to forty gold coins. And he was going to make sure he received payment in full. After a while, I could only lie there and writhe as he decided where else to strike me."

"But this is villainy!" Meir cried out, his face red with fury. "How dare Judah do this?"

"He is a rich man and I am a poor one, Rabbi. That is how."

"No," cried my indignant husband. "The law in the Talmud is the same for the rich as for the poor, and even the weak have their rights! This is a crime!"

"Well, what should I do? You can see I don't dare go to Düren. And in his letter, Judah's ultimatum gives me a scant two months to travel there and marry Doula."

Meir paced up and down his study. Jacob slumped in the chair my husband had vacated. Finally, Meir paused, drawing in a deep breath. "You cannot go to Düren. It would mean your life if you were to set foot in that town. Are you still resolved to marry her? You need not, you know."

Jacob thought a moment. "I am not a handsome or a rich man, Rav Meir, but a promise was made to me and to my family. If I give in to Rav Judah's threats, people will think the worst of me. But if I marry Doula and make her happy . . . her father will be reconciled in time."

Meir looked closely at the young man. Was he, like me, trying to decide if Jacob's stubbornness stemmed from greed? But my husband must have been satisfied with what he saw, for he concluded, "Your bride must come here and marry you then. I will write about it again. All will be well, boy. You must go home and heal."

———◆———

Meir was slowly making greater sense out of the prayer service and our daily customs. He spoke to me about it more than once, for it consumed every waking moment that was not taken up with writing responses, teaching his students, or being a loving father to his children and an ardent, caring husband to me. One night, as we lay together after making love, he told me he hoped this work would help shape Jewish life for centuries to come.

I had heard such words spoken before—by Nicholas Donin—and they sent a shiver through me. Then I chided myself for equating the two men. Where Nicholas Donin had had nothing but destruction in mind—and was continuing to do harm to Jews throughout Europe, according to the letters my husband received—my Meir wanted to shape Jewish destiny to keep it whole. It would be his act, he said, to prepare the world for the Messiah to come.

"You and I both witnessed the conflagration," he said, holding me to him. "We saw the Christians' malicious faces as they burned our Word, our Law. Yechiel writes he is making progress with the Pope in Lyon, but I fear that his efforts will bear little fruit. We must find a way to make our daily and weekly prayers—the core of our faith—something every man can perform, regardless of whether he is learned or not. I believe that we need to put order into our daily lives so that the same prayers are said in the same way here in Rothenberg, in Paris, in Bohemia, and in Poland. We need to find a way to stamp them onto our hearts, to emblazon them as a burning brand into our very soul, our *neshamah*. Then, Shira, they cannot wrest our centuries of learning from us unless they kill us all."

I nestled beside him. "Is this not what Maimonides tried to do, through his *Mishnah Torah*? To make our customs simple enough for the common man to embrace?"

Meir sat up, half pulling the covers off me in his excitement. "Yes! Oh, Shira, my darling, you still manage to astound me. You are right. I need to read Maimonides again. That will help me."

"But the ban . . . ?" I asked, bewildered, as I pulled the quilt back into place over us both.

My husband laughed. "The burning in Paris changed the minds of many of those who were opposed to Maimonides. You do not hear the ban spoken of any longer."

"I'm glad," I said, feeling sleep beginning to steal over me. Meir saw my flickering eyelids, laughed, and kissed them. He turned over, either to lapse into sleep himself or to spend the rest of the night in tranquil reflection. He is so happy here, was my last waking thought.

During the next Shabbat, Meir stood at the *bimah* and sang, for the first time, a verse from a psalm that he wished to add to the service from that point forward. It had a transcendent quality to it, a simplicity that touched the hearts of all who heard it.

"*Adonai sifatai tiftach u'fi yagid techilatecha*—Eternal God, open my lips, that my mouth may declare your glory."

The congregation rose as one as he sang. There was something about the phrase and the melody that urged people from their seats and prepared them for the holiness of the words that followed. It was an entreaty to us to give voice, in much the same way the watchword of our faith, the Shema, was an eternal call to listen and to heed that God is One.

We all then launched into the Amidah, the familiar prayers that are always said standing. "Blessed is our God, God of Abraham, God of Isaac, God of Ya'akov . . ." The congregation spoke the words aloud, but quietly and each to the beat of his own rhythm, each man wrapped in the benedictions we pray three times a day.

Afterward, during our Shabbat meal at the *yeshiva,* Meir's students asked him about the new prayer.

"Where did it come from, Rabbi?" asked Ephraim ben Jacob, a student from Westphalia.

"You tell me, Ephraim," my husband said, smiling at the sea of expectant faces. Every time I watched his joyful exchange with his students, it warmed my heart. The bitterness of Paris seemed more and more distant. "Does anyone know?"

Moses Parnes, one of our local students from Rothenberg, spoke up. "Is it not part of the fifty-first psalm?"

"Well done, Moses! And what is happening in this psalm?"

"Penitence. David repents his sin of lying with Batsheva, another man's wife."

"Yes. David tries to connect with God once again. But is David completely focused on speaking with God in this psalm?"

After a pause another student spoke up, "Rashi says that David wished God to make an example of him, to forgive him so that other sinners would repent and return to God."

"Yes, Baruch. But my question is something different. Does David approach God with a genuine *kavvanah*—a purity of heart and single-ness of focus, with a true sense that he stands before God?"

The boys were silent, considering the entire psalm. Despite my many cares in making sure all were fed, I did likewise. My husband waited a moment before saying, "In the beginning of the psalm, David searches for ways to address the Lord. As he makes one excuse after another for his sin, he prepares himself to appeal to God. Consider, now. How do we prepare ourselves for the Amidah?"

The boys were quicker to answer this question.

"We sing verses from the Torah and psalms."

"Exactly. And can someone tell me what the sages of old said about preparing for prayer?"

"In Pirkei Avot 2:18, it is said: 'Do not make your prayers perfunc-tory, rather, they should be true entreaties before the Holy One, blessed be God,'" said Moses Parnes.

The sudden glow of satisfaction in Meir's eyes put a smile on Moses's face. "Yes! That is the passage that made me consider adding David's entreaty to the Lord to help him pray before the Amidah. Anyone else?"

"Does it not say that the sages used to wait an hour and then pray—so that they could better focus their hearts on God?" Baruch asked.

"It does. And can anyone recall what Rabbi Hisda said on this sub-ject?"

"That a man should always enter two doors into the synagogue and then pray, for it is written in Proverbs 8:34, 'Waiting at the posts of My doors.'"

"But what does that mean, entering two doors into the synagogue?"

The boys leaned forward to hear the core of Meir's intention. "Think back to the psalm of David. He is anxious to make his peace with God, but he has to ease himself into it—like walking the distance of two doors before the tranquility of prayer can transport you. And then he entreats the Lord to open his lips—not to give any more excuses, but to sing of God's glory. I have noticed that it is like that with many of us—that we must first prepare our souls and our lips before we can face, with all seriousness, the Amidah. For the Amidah must be prayed with full conviction and not merely said quickly, out of rote. It is as Rabbi Shimon used to say: 'When you pray, make not your prayer a fixed form, but make it an entreaty and supplication of love before the Almighty.'"

"So you added the verse from David to . . . ?" Baruch asked, still not quite following.

I held my breath, waiting for Meir's answer. His students sat, rapt, as if knowing that his answer would shape something new for them and for coming generations.

Meir smiled. "To help us all take the last two steps in that distance of two doors. When David spoke those words, he was truly ready to set all outside concerns aside and to appeal directly to God. This should be our way to mark that we are ready to stand and open our lips and declare, as in the flow of a river, the true glory of God, with full focus of heart and soul."

Meir laughed, dispelling the awed hush in the room. "At least, so I would hope."

Chaya's reaction to her impending engagement shocked me. I expected tears and clinging. Instead, while she was not joyous, she placidly accepted the idea. She did not even appear to regret leaving us. As far as I could tell, she wasn't thinking as much about a husband as about the adventure of living in a new place. Until her eyes lit up at the notion of leaving Rothenberg, I had not understood how little she liked her new home.

"Could you find me a husband from France, Papa?" she asked. Although it was summer, we were sitting in the room where the girls worked during the winter. On those dark, cold days, their chairs drawn up to the fire, they darned socks or sharpened quills, patched pots or concocted possets, all under my watchful eye. Now we were sitting by the open windows, hoping for a cooling breeze. The courtyard, where we would ordinarily sit, was full of scholars and honeybees, both buzzing about. We had discovered that students did not always respect family limits. For Meir to receive any respite from questions and incipient thoughts, he had to seek refuge far from his beloved *talmidim*.

"From France, little one? That would take you farther from us than your mama wants, I think."

"Yes, but . . . ," she said with a shrug. "Closer to France? I loved living in Paris."

I studied Chaya's broadly smiling face, feeling betrayed by her excitement, and said, "The boy—your betrothed—will probably be studying somewhere in Europe. Tradition says you will live with his parents until he is ready to provide you with a home. I would prefer it to be somewhere nearby so we could visit you. You would be lonely for us after a while even if you don't think so now."

Meir patted my hand for a few seconds too long. I pulled it away. He ignored me, saying, "We are located in a fortunate area, Chaya. There are several young men whose families live in Würzburg, for example, which is a bigger city than Rothenberg. There are some whose families live in Heilbronn. Or, if you want a smaller town, Fürth," he said.

Chaya giggled. "You make it sound like you'd like to find me a husband who lives just beyond our gates," she said.

"Not all of the candidates are so close by," Meir said dryly. "We have had inquiries from the fathers of young men who live farther away. One in Lincoln, for example. I'd be interested in pursuing that connection, for the young man bids fair to become known throughout all of Europe for his brilliance." I threw him a fulminating glance. "But your mother . . ."

"Lincoln!" breathed Chaya. "England! Oh, Mama, just like the stories of William the Conqueror you told us when we were little. I have always wanted to visit the English isles because you came from Falaise. Oh, yes, Papa, let's talk to that one."

I looked down at the floor, feeling the tears threatening to overcome me. If Chaya moved to England the chances of my ever seeing her again were poor. I pressed my lips together tightly, holding back the protests that struggled to burst forth.

Meir was telling her more about the student. "His name is Avram ben Menashe. He is, by all reports, truly gifted. He is studying in Worms with my father. You could meet him there. Perhaps you might even live with your grandparents for a short time while you are betrothed to him. You would get to know him, the way I got to know your mama when we were betrothed and I was studying with your *grand-père.*"

I looked up, my face contorted in bitterness. "So this is your mother's idea, Meir?" I asked.

He looked at me sheepishly. "My father wrote to me about Avram. I can't claim my mother had nothing to do with it. But the boy won't be staying with my father long. He is going to Paris soon."

"To Paris!" Chaya said. "Oh, Papa, I want to meet him."

"And these other scholars?" Meir said. "They would keep you closer to home, and there are one or two I wouldn't scorn calling son-in-law."

"No, no, I want to meet Avram. Oh, Papa, I love you so much!" Chaya gave her father a quick hug and danced off.

Meir couldn't look at me. I sat down at one of the girls' little tables and leaned my elbows on its surface, cupping my chin in my palms, saying nothing.

"I should have . . . ," he said tentatively.

I couldn't bear it. I scraped the chair back and stood, leaving the room quickly. I walked aimlessly around the rooms downstairs for a while before taking refuge from prying eyes in the buttery off the kitchen. I ducked down in its cool interior, hidden behind a stack of shelves, and sat and cried.

————◆————

A week later, Meir found me supervising one of the maids who was cleaning the students' bedrooms. He was clutching several letters, one of which I could see was in my father's hand.

"You've heard from Papa!" I cried joyfully. "How are he and Alyes and the children?"

"I don't know," Meir snapped, putting the letters down on the counterpane before me. "He didn't say."

I glanced up at him and saw that white, pinched look that overtook his face in times of great distress. "Is something wrong in Falaise?" I asked, waving the maidservant out of the room.

"It was a letter about young Jacob's marriage woes, not a personal letter," he replied. "All of them are letters about Jacob. I want you to read them and tell me what you think. I am now . . . unsure."

"Papa wrote about Jacob?" I said, picking up his letter and looking at the one beneath it. "And this one is from Rabbi Yechiel?"

My husband turned to the door. "I'll be out in the courtyard. The tone of these letters . . . read them now please and come talk to me when you're done."

I turned to them nervously, the one from my father still clutched in my hand. My eyes widened as I read:

> It is my opinion that the youth be forced either to marry his bride
> on her terms or divorce her. The overlord of Rothenberg, acting on
> the mere rumor that Rav Judah's daughter would settle in Roth-
> enberg, is already seeking ways to secure his daughter as a hostage,
> so, beyond the deprivation and poverty awaiting her, it would be
> dangerous for her to set foot in the town. The youth ought to be
> forced by flagellation or the use of the ban to either marry his bride
> in Düren or to divorce her. None is excluded from our ban, except-
> ing, of course, our honored teacher Rabbi Meir.

Rabbi Yechiel's letter was more calmly stated but just as precise. He, too, recommended issuing a ban unless Doula was freed from her be-trothal or Jacob was sent to Düren for the wedding. All of the letters, in fact, said the same thing—that while my husband was excused from censure, Jacob and his father should be whipped or banned from the community until the matter was settled to the satisfaction of Doula and her wealthy father.

Out in the courtyard, Meir paced up and down on the flagstone walk, his hands twitching behind his back. His students stood in small hushed groups, whispering among themselves and gesturing nervously at their teacher's fierce glare and the grim set of his jaw. "Send the boys back to their studies—they are upset by your dark frowns," I whispered to Meir.

His head rose and he looked around, suddenly aware of the uncertain expressions on his students' faces. "*Bachurim*! Why do you linger here when there is studying to be done?" he asked them, attempting a smile. "Go on, now. Off with you all!"

The boys went back to their desks.

"These rabbis are missing an important piece of information—that Jacob would be threatened by Rabbi Judah's servants if he set foot in Düren," I said.

"No, I was clear about that when I last wrote. They know it," Meir said, kicking a bit of gravel beneath his feet. "They think I wish to bring Doula's wealth into Rothenberg. Perhaps they even think Jacob has offered me a bribe if I can help him win a rich bride."

"Meir . . . Papa would never! And you lived and worked with Rabbi Yechiel for years. Neither of them would suspect you of such a thing."

"How can they not . . . when I suspect them of the same? Rabbi Judah has money to spare—enough to build academies, to hire scribes. What if he offered to pay them if they censured Jacob and prevented him from marrying Doula? Who would not be seduced by such thoughts? Me? Can I honestly tell you that I was not?" He stooped and picked up a smooth stone, hefting it in his hand, throwing and catching it.

"Were you?" I asked, a half smile on my face.

"That's what has me out here in the middle of the morning, disrupting my students' studies and my own. My beloved teachers fall just short of pronouncing the ban against me. I will tell you this, Shira, Jacob's case is lost for two reasons—because Doula's wealth has assured her of a more favorable judgment and because I was not persuasive enough in defending the poor and the weak."

"Is the case irretrievably lost, then?" I asked, reaching out a hand to take the stone from him. But he moved back a pace and kept it, tossing it nervously from palm to palm.

"I will not counsel Jacob to run the risk of suffering a whipping or being banned from the Jewish community. I've failed him."

I wanted to put my arms about him and pull his head to my shoulder. But the eyes peering at us from the study windows stopped me. "Papa did not mean to upset you," I said instead, my words slow and faltering.

"Shira, don't be foolish," he snapped. He chucked the stone away, watching as it clattered across the flagstones. "I don't know what he intended but I certainly won't be writing to him any time soon."

"He excluded you from the ban and called you 'honored teacher.' His judgment was against the case, not against you."

"It doesn't feel that way to me. I have always held your father in the greatest of esteem and for him to write to me in such a manner . . . you will do as you please, but I don't intend to request his opinions or write to him again."

"And Rabbi Yechiel? His letter was more temperate."

"Yes, I agree. Cutting off relations with the great rabbi of Paris would be foolish; I will simply be more careful in the future."

"But cutting off relations with the unimportant rabbi of the little town of Falaise is fine, then?" I asked, indignant at the insult.

He turned away. "You do as you please. I would not tell you to do otherwise than to honor your father. Just don't include me in your greetings to him."

He started back into the school building, letting the door slam behind him. I looked up again at the windows and the students withdrew their heads as though they were turtles retreating into their shells. I stood in the courtyard alone, feeling bereft. Did Meir blame me for my father's letter? I stared at the closed door, my feelings in turmoil. Instead of following him, I repaired to the kitchen and spent the next hour banging together the half dozen loaves of bread we needed each night—bread that the boys complained later was lumpy and doughy.

———•———

It was a bad week for letters. Three days later, my husband sought me out yet again, another missive in his hand. Whereas the other letters had upset him, this one had put an exultant look on his face.

"It's from the *shadchan* in London," he said. "The match has been made with Avram ben Menashe and we should arrange to send Chaya to my parents to meet her groom and be handfast."

I was standing in the sanctuary where Meir held daily prayers, my hands full of the oily cloth that I used to polish the oak wood of the lectern. I dropped the cloth and, trembling, took up the letter. Tears gathered in my eyes and I found it difficult to read the words. Stricken, I looked up at my husband's face.

"Shira, you have to stop this," he said with displeasure. "She is ten years old. Old enough to be betrothed. Her in-laws will care for her and when she is old enough, her husband will join her. My father writes that he is a brilliant young man with a good heart. And she wants to live in England . . . because of the stories you told her. So instead of weeping, I advise you to take joy in this." He took the letter out of my hand.

"She is too young to leave me," I whispered. "It is breaking my heart."

"I would not have her spoiled and pampered the way—" Meir broke off, shaking his head.

"The way Papa spoiled and pampered me?" I shot back. "Go ahead, say it!"

He stood silently for a moment, deciding whether to speak out or to stifle the words trembling on his lips. Had he been less disappointed in my reaction, perhaps he might have swallowed his words. But he looked at my smarting eyes and out-thrust chin and did not hold back.

"I love you, Shira, you know I do, but your upbringing was . . . un-conventional at best. And while it brought you some joy, it also made you unsettled and immodest. Don't think I haven't seen how you consider yourself better than the many fine women here in Rothenberg, just because you can read Torah and Talmud and think you can interpret."

I clutched the lectern with both hands, my knuckles reddening as I crushed the wood against my palms.

"*Think* I can interpret? So *this* is what you think of me, husband— foolish in loving to study, foolish in trying to understand? I'm shocked you married me, then."

"We should not be talking so to each other," Meir said, a look of dismay on his flushed face. "You need to compose yourself."

"I am perfectly calm!" I shouted. "I am not the one who brought up the subject of being pampered and spoiled! Pampered and spoiled! When I spend my days cooking and cleaning so that you can bury your nose in your beloved books . . . and you say *I'm* spoiled and pampered!"

"It is the woman's role in life, Shira—your way of observing the commandments. Think of the proverb we recite every Shabbat, praising the woman of valor, who watches over the ways of her household, does not eat the bread of idleness, and is honored by the fruit of her hands. To wish for something more flouts God's purpose when he fashioned you from Adam's rib."

I gasped. "You were not above asking for my help when you couldn't write, back in Paris. You were happy to have me working alongside you then. It is only now, when you have students you can employ as scribes, that you want to put me back into the place God fashioned me for. And to rip my woman's heart out by tearing away that piece of it that is my darling daughter. How dare you!"

"Shira! Be quiet! Someone will hear you!" he responded, taking two rapid steps forward and smacking a hand down on the oily lectern.

Sobbing, I pushed past him and ran from the room. To my utter dismay, I found Chaya standing outside the door, looking upset. She must have heard every word. I wanted to say something to reassure her but could only give her a quick pat on the shoulder as I slid by, seeking refuge in our room upstairs.

WENTY-SIX

Great is peace between husband and wife.
—THE TALMUD

PERHAPS BECAUSE I WAS SO UPSET, my womanly courses came upon me nearly a week early. I was helping Chaya pack the heavy wooden chests that contained her belongings and dowry when I felt the familiar cramping. Using the examining cloth in the privacy of the latrine, I found the first thin traces of blood.

I didn't bother to tell Meir. We were still barely speaking to each other, and when we had to do so, we used formality more appropriate for chance-met strangers than husband and wife. When he asked me for the salt during the evening meal, I picked it up and set it down with a snap on the table before him. Jewish law forbid me from handing objects to him until I had finished bleeding and visited a *mikveh* to purify myself.

He looked up at me, surprised. Meir was very conscious of my body's cycles and knew this was early. The set look on my face made him shake his head, resigning himself to a solitary bed for the next twelve days. A student asked him a question and he turned to answer it.

It was a particularly painful week. Not only was I bent over with racking spasms, but Chaya and I had to finish preparing her to leave us. I wept constantly, until I felt empty of tears. Chaya clung to me, distressed by my sadness, aware that this leave-taking meant an entirely new life for her.

I watched her on our last Shabbat eve together. I tried to set aside my misery, but all I could see was my darling flitting through the room, setting the table, arranging the flowers, singing psalms in breathy snatches as she helped me. Chaya had grown tall in the past year, and her red hair, which she wore braided down her back, escaped in little curls on her high white forehead.

Little Rachel, my other red-haired daughter, still stocky and rosy cheeked, crept up from behind. My eyes were fixed on my eldest girl, so soon to be torn from me. Rachel shocked me by saying, "You will love us too a little after she leaves, Mama?"

I gathered the girl into my lap, kissing her round, freckled face. "I love you now, Rachel, you know I do."

She squirmed uncomfortably. I set her down. "No, Mama, you love Chaya," she said calmly. "You love her so much you don't care that you make Papa and Zipura and Suesskind and me unhappy because she's leaving."

I gaped at her. "Is that what you think, little one?" I whispered, feeling my womb twist inside me.

She shrugged. I picked her up again and held her tight against me, whispering into her soft curls. "I'm sorry, Rachel. I love you very, very much. I'm sorry if you thought even for a moment that I didn't."

She snuggled against me, reassured by my touch and my words. My head whirling, I chastised myself for my selfishness. How could I have neglected my other children? For Rachel was right—I had done nothing during these past few days but concentrate on Chaya and my unhappiness in losing her.

After I set the child down again and rose to finish Shabbat preparations, I sought out both Zipura and my little Dodi, clasping them both to me wordlessly. Their eager arms made tears spring to my eyes and I had to blink them back. I could not touch Meir, of course. In my confusion, I wasn't sure if I wanted to.

Chaya left early that week. Meir took her to Worms and returned a few days later, reporting that she was happy in her grandparents' home. She and Avram had been properly introduced and seemed to like each other. The betrothal ceremony had taken place the evening before Meir returned to Rothenberg. Chaya was learning English so that she would be ready for her life with her in-laws once Avram left Worms to head to Paris. He would return to his home in England when she was ready to bear children. The actual marriage ceremony would take place then. Perhaps, Meir said, looking at me out of the corner of his eye, I could make the trip over the channel to see the wedding. Or perhaps I would wait until my daughter gave birth to her first child.

I said nothing, just nodded and left the room.

At our midday meal, Meir asked me for the salt. I placed it with a snap before him. He looked up at me, eyebrows raised, and I shrugged. He could not pose the question he so plainly wanted to ask with the mass of students around us, so he turned away to launch into a long discussion about one of Rashi's interpretations.

He sought me out after the meal was over. I was sorting the vegetables in one of our cellars, moving those sprouting new growth or softening in spots into the straw basket to bring up to the kitchen so we could use them in the coming week's meals. "Shira? Are you still bleeding? Do you need to see a midwife? A doctor?"

In fact, my bleeding had stopped more than a week before but I had simply not bothered to go to the *mikveh*. All of the restrictions about touching my husband still needed to be observed.

I had never lied to Meir before and I didn't do so now. Not exactly. I picked up an onion and held it up to the light provided by the thin slit of window, turning it over and over. It still felt firm and had no sprouts, so I returned it to the storage bin. "I'm fine, husband. I simply have been busy and haven't had time to visit the *mikveh*. Perhaps later today or tomorrow."

"Make it today, Shira. I have missed you . . . ," he whispered.

But I didn't find time that day. There were candles to be made and several students were sick and needed tending. I didn't find time the next day, either.

My bitterness over Chaya forced me to realize that I had never really been happy about leaving Paris. While I enjoyed the companionship of the warmhearted women of Rothenberg, I was faced with blank stares every time I spoke of a passage of the Talmud. I missed the other rabbis' wives who would respond to me with wit and understanding. In some ways, my life now reminded me of the hard days when I was struggling as the young housewife of my father's *yeshiva*—and there were even more boys to care for now, as well as three young children of my own. It was easy to blame Meir. So for nearly a week, I played this strange game. Excuses were plentiful in a home that doubled as a school. Every evening, Meir would ask me for the salt. Every evening, I would set it down before him rather than putting it directly into his hands. I could see he was growing more and more angry with me. But I was so clouded by my own resentment that I didn't care.

Then, one late afternoon, I sat sewing by the light of a branch of candles. Zipura and Rachel were doing some whitework beside me. Little Suesskind was on the floor before us, crowing happily as he toddled from one sister to the next, who made faces at him and tickled him.

"You all look quite snug," Meir said, standing at the doorway.

"Papa!" Rachel cried out happily. I did not look up from my sewing, but the girls put theirs aside and clambered up to hug their father. My Dodi followed them, his fat little arms stretched out, singing, "Pa. Pa. Pa!"

I glanced up from my sewing, admiring the sweet tableau the children made with their father, their black, red, and blond heads tight against his waist as he put his arms around them and bounced them in a little impromptu dance. For a fleeting moment, I regretted I had not gone to the *mikveh* and could not join them. Meir looked over their heads at me and I shook my own. His expression hardened.

"Girls, take your brother out so I can talk with your mother, please," he said, trying with obvious effort to speak lightly.

"I want to show you my neat stitches, Papa," Rachel protested. But Zipura, who in her quiet way was more attuned to the unspoken words of her elders than any of my other children, took the younger ones by the hand and led them out.

I bent my head back over my sewing. Meir came and sat next to me and put a hand out. I flinched away.

"This is not going to work, Shira," he said. "It is not healthy for you to cling to your irritation like this. To punish me because you are angry at losing your oldest daughter."

"That's not it at all," I murmured. "I'm just—very busy, Meir. There is so much to do every day."

"I see," he said, leaning back. "Let's examine that statement, shall we?"

I glanced up at him from under lowered eyelids. His own eyes were twinkling, as though he had already figured out how to reason me out of my bad temper. I felt myself flush with annoyance. I was not a child to be treated so!

"No, let's not," I retorted. "Let's allow me to simply get on with this immense pile of sewing, as a dutiful wife should."

The moment I said the words, I realized the phrase "dutiful wife" was ill-chosen. He would latch on to the description to show me that I was wrong. Inwardly cursing myself for a fool, I stammered, "I was in the middle of giving the girls a lesson in sewing, Meir. I wish you'd send them back to me."

He ignored that. "A dutiful wife," he said pouncing. "Is that what you are?"

Tears of frustration prickled my eyelids. Stupid, stupid, I chastised myself. You're married to the sharpest legal mind in all of Jewish Europe . . . how can you be this stupid?

"From daybreak to sunset and into the night, I cook and clean and tend your children and your students, cater to everyone's needs . . . ," I said, ticking each point off on my fingers, drawn into the argument despite my instinct to flee.

"Do you cater to mine—to your husband's?" he asked. The sly smile on his face made me see red.

"Are you fed? Clothed? Do I not bring honor upon this house by the way I conduct myself in the marketplace? Do I not raise your children so that they will be a blessing upon you? What is it exactly that you lack, husband?" I spat out hotly, now past caring what I said.

"Do you want me to tell you—exactly—what I lack, wife?" he said, amused.

"Yes," I cried. "Tell me. Exactly!"

He sat back, templing his fingers together on the table, looking more like a teacher or a parent than a husband. He infuriated me. My impending defeat tasted like cinders in my dry mouth.

Then suddenly he leaned forward, abandoning the learned pose. "You have denied me the infinite pleasure of sleeping with you next to me. Of . . . even deeper pleasures while you are in my bed," he whispered, the sounds tickling my ears.

I looked up into his eyes and was caught by the passion lurking deep inside them. I felt myself grow light-headed under the embrace of his words, which sent a shiver of desire through my body. Had he said nothing more, I would have willingly gone to the *mikveh* a moment later.

But then he sat back and added, "You also present yourself in musty clothing, looking like a slattern. You excite comment among my students, who whisper to one another as they see you set down the salt before me, night after night, that Rabbi Meir has a rebellious wife—an *esha moredet.* This cannot be allowed to continue."

I felt myself stiffen. I set the sewing down in the basket beside my stool and deliberately turned to face him. "An *esha moredet!* And how does the famous Rabbi Meir wish to deal with his undutiful wife?"

"Rabbi Meir wants her to stop acting like a fool," Meir said grimly. "He wants her to conduct herself as the loving wife she has always been."

"And if she will not?"

Meir stood up, pushing the chair back sharply. "You have such depths of learning, my wife—it is the accomplishment you are proudest of. Why don't you tell me what a rebellious wife merits?"

I shook my head, staring up at him defiantly. "I'm unclean and cannot talk of holy things. Nor am I allowed to touch a sacred book to find exact commentary on the subject."

"Very well, I will tell you. I am entitled to deduct one dinar from your *ketubah*—your dowry—every day you continue to be stubborn in this way, for a year. And then, if you still refuse, I can divorce you."

Now it was my turn to act amused, to feign satisfaction. "Maimonides, you know, said that a wife who finds her husband repugnant is entitled to an immediate divorce."

Meir glared at me, the hurt clearly written on his face. "So you find me repugnant? Very well. Realize, however, that if I were to grant you a divorce for that reason, it would strip you of your dowry completely. For Maimonides also said that if the wife's intention is to cause her husband anguish, she loses her *ketubah* entirely."

I shrugged. Caught by the allure of the legal ramifications, he added, "Besides, Rabbenu Tam said that the ordinance of the *moredet* used in this manner is improper, for a husband should not be coerced to give his wife a divorce instantly. And I agree with this. After all . . ."

Suddenly I realized that with this discussion of divorce, we were digging a pit that grew deeper and deeper with every word we uttered. I could not bear it. Where would this lead? How had my resentment and Meir's inflexibility brought us here?

The pallor on my face spoke volumes. My husband, glancing down at me as he pontificated, broke off his statement. He hovered as close as he could without touching me.

"Shira, this is not what either of us want," he said, his tone very different from the one he had been using up until then.

"No," I agreed. "No."

I stood, leaning over the table to blow all but one of the candles out. "Can you ask Judda to have an eye to the children, Meir? I will return in an hour."

———•———

Our lovemaking that night was not unalloyed delight, for we had grown stiff and unfamiliar with each other. It would take time to break down the defenses each of us had erected. As we sought each other's warmth after he withdrew from me, I cried a little into his shoulder. He put his arms around me and clasped me to him.

"I am sorry, Shira, for upsetting you so," he murmured. "For . . . everything."

"Chaya *is* happy?" I asked. "She is content?"

"She is delighted with her betrothed and he is pleased with her. And my parents are treating her most gently—yes, even my mother the pot stirrer!"

I laughed a little, blinking my tears away. "That won't last long, but Chaya is not like me; she won't see the poison in your mother's comments. Can you imagine what would happen if we sent Rachel to her?"

Meir chuckled. "The house would fairly sizzle with the heat of the two of them fighting. You know, I never thought of it before, but Rachel is a good deal like my mother."

I drew back, aghast. "Don't say that."

He pulled me back to him. "Oh, yes. And Chaya, my happy little sprite, is a lot like your own mother, I believe, from what you have said Alyes told you about her. And Zipura—"

"Zipura is your child," I said. "Dreamy and thoughtful."

"And our boy?" he asked.

"Our boy? I don't know, really. He is a good boy . . . stubborn, though, when he wants something. He loves when we read together or I point

out the letters to him. But when it's time for me to stop the lesson, he wails and cries."

"Your child?" Meir said. I looked up at him. In the moonlight, I could see the tender smile on his lips and I nestled closer.

"Perhaps," I agreed. "Good thing he is a boy, then."

ART 4

LINCOLN, 1255

O YONGE HUGH OF LYNCOLN, SLAYN ALSO
WITH CURSED JEWES, AS IT IS NOTABLE . . .
    —*Geoffrey Chaucer, "The Prioress's Tale"*

WENTY-SEVEN

Like a bird that strays from its nest is a man
who strays from his home.
　　　　—PROVERBS 27:8

BOWING MY HEAD UNDER THE EAVES of the slanted roof, standing on the uneven floorboards scattered with straw that would be swept
out every other day, I held Chaya's second-born baby in my arms and
prayed that this one, unlike her first, would survive his first few days
of life. As I nestled the small, warm body close to me, I looked out the
window onto the unfamiliar streets of Lincoln. My daughter and her
husband had rented four cramped rooms in a brick-and-wattle house
that seemed about to tip dangerously over into the steep street that led
to the gray towers of Lincoln Cathedral. Accustomed, now, to the luxury
of my large home in Rothenberg, I'd found it difficult at first to have to
twist up the winding stairway to their small attic solar. But the love that
filled their home warmed my heart.

　　Ten years had passed since Meir and I had reconciled and in the
spring of the year 5015—1255 by Christian counting—my small world
had changed inexorably. Now a forty-year-old woman, I saw encroach-

ing age in my thickening wrists and the protruding red knuckles on my hands, in the softening skin about my neck. But there was scant time during the busy years to contemplate such changes, nor did my still-ardent husband seem to perceive them. If he was saddened that our passion had not produced another child, he never said so. Chaya and Zipura were both wed—Chaya to her beloved Avram ben Menashe, and Zipura to a Spanish disciple of Moses Nahmanides in Spain, a worthy scholar named Yuceph de Lebanza. Even my little Rachel was handfast. My sixteen-year-old daughter, however, still lived in our home in Rothenberg; her betrothed, Binyamin ben Zuiskind, was a destitute orphan who studied with Meir. Binyamin's extraordinary mind had prompted my generous husband to waive his usual fees. The couple would have difficulty supporting themselves before young Binyamin was old enough to establish a school of his own, which could be many years off. But it was clear that the two were meant to be together. Meir planned to hire the student as a *melamed* in a couple of months and we would let the young couple marry and live with us.

A year ago, my Suesskind, a bright young scholar of nine, had been living and studying with his grandfather in Falaise when news came to us of my father's death. I mourned him for weeks. It had become difficult to correspond with him as he grew older and feebler. Alyes had never learned to write or read and my father's other children were too preoccupied with their own affairs to worry about a half sister they barely remembered. After the funeral, Suesskind returned home and was studying with his father for at least a little while. It was a delight to have two of my children living under my roof.

The past ten years had passed relatively quietly outside our small world of Rothenberg. We had taken heart from Pope Innocent IV's investigation into the increasing number of charges of Jewish ritual murder with their resulting atrocities, for previously the Pope had judged such charges to be lies. Our friends in Paris were still trying to have the Talmud restored to them, but when an appeal to the Pope caused him to ask the king of France to reinvestigate the matter, the Talmud was condemned a second time. My Chaya wrote how the English king Henry III had demanded that Jewish worship take place in a whisper, so as not to offend the pious ears of Christian passsersby, and had prohibited any Christian from working in a Jewish household. But we were too inured to such restrictions to pay them much mind.

Meir's opinion was increasingly sought after by both rabbis and community leaders throughout Ashkenaz, particularly after he had successfully negotiated a financial squabble between the Jewish communities of Bohemia and Moravia back in 1249. Wenceslaus, king of Bohemia, had appointed his son Ottokar margrave of Moravia, granting him the income from the Jews of that territory. Where previously the two communities had paid their shares collectively, now Moravia considered they no longer needed to contribute to the king's taxes. Through several deft feats of negotiation, Meir managed the impossible—to satisfy both parties.

The letters that flooded Meir's study had less to do with ritual law than my scholar husband would have liked. He often spoke wistfully of how Rashi, two centuries earlier, had been solicited to satisfy questions of faith and practice, but now that so many books about ritual were available throughout Europe, most of the queries addressed to Meir concerned civil matters. "Look at these," he shouted at me one particularly aggravating day, waving a stack of letters in my face. "These ask me about business, marriage contracts, inheritance, taxes! This one," he said, extracting it, "is about two men squabbling over a horse sale! And they sent me the same matter to adjudicate three times, Shira! Three times!"

I laid my hand softly on his shoulder to soothe him. "It is because your opinions are so highly valued, my dear."

"If my opinions are well regarded, they should have listened to me the first time," Meir said, sitting at his desk and laying a fresh sheet of paper in front of him. "I will write and tell them so."

I could not help smiling a little at the fury with which my husband began scribbling his answer. But by the time Meir turned to the legal

ramifications of the matter at hand, his tone would have cooled to one
of sound judgment.

His students were thriving under his care. Several of them devoted
themselves to watching his every step—for their saintly teacher, they
said, was so precise in his observance of Jewish ritual that his example
was well worth emulating. It made Meir uncomfortable to have his habits so slavishly emulated, but it flattered him as well. I noted he would
often clarify why and how he chose to act in a certain way to young
Samson ben Zadok, who would scurry off to make a note in the small
bound book of blank pages he always carried.

Knowing how capable Rachel was, I left the *yeshiva* for several
months in my daughter's care without a qualm. I was setting out for
Lincoln. Chaya's letter pleaded with me to help her through her second
labor, an event she anticipated with all of the dread and eagerness of a
mother who had previously lost a child.

I had never been on a journey on my own, and I was fortunate that
my father-in-law knew a wealthy merchant who was traveling to England
to trade with the descendants of Aaron of Lincoln. As the merchant owed
my father-in-law a favor, he agreed to leave a month earlier than he originally intended. Moyses Rothermaker of Worms was used to such ardu-
ous journeys and was rich enough to surround himself with comfort.
Our traveling alone together might have raised concerns for my virtue,
despite Moyses's advanced age and my own unassailable reputation as a
wife and mother. So I would share my bed with Leah, a shy young Jewish
girl whom we would collect during the first leg of our journey from her
home in Mainz, conveying her to her bridegroom's family in Stamford,
which we would reach about two days before arriving at Lincoln.

Meir waved good-bye to us, his arm around Rachel's waist, trying to
smile despite the worry for my safety that glimmered deep in his eyes
as I bid my family farewell. Moyses Rothermaker's well-sprung carriage,
drawn by four swift horses, conveyed us to the ship that would carry us
across the channel. The trip across Germany and into France took us
eleven days, the merchant's skilled coachman driving us at a rapid pace

of about thirty miles a day. I soon grew weary of the journey and of the inns we arrived at after dark, which we left in the thin light of the early dawn. The names of the towns and the hostelries blurred together after a bit, and after a few days, I could not have told you whether I was in Köln, Aachen, or Ghent. Finally, we arrived in Calais, setting sail within two hours to catch the tide. Our trip across the channel was a peaceful journey and I was glad to be spared the horrors of seasickness. We were greeted at the docks by yet another expensively furnished coach, hired in advance, and started on our way to Lincoln.

The weather changed upon our arrival in England, and with all the rain the roads were mired in mud, which slowed us down. We were not able to make our way into London, which I very much wanted to see. Our route bypassed the great city and I suspected I would die without ever seeing it.

A fortnight after crossing the channel we finally arrived in Lincoln. I had not seen Chaya for many years, and as the carriage drove through Stonebow, the gate to the southern entrance of the city located directly under the castle keep, I was almost beside myself with excitement. My merchant companion spoke knowledgeably about the city's history: it was established during Roman times and used as an important stronghold for William the Conqueror, who erected both the cathedral and the castle on the highest peak. The castle's forbidding facade reminded me of the keep in Falaise.

Chaya and Avram lived in the Jewish-populated Steep Hill quarter, a stone's throw from the castle and near the sumptuous house of Aaron, where my companion was headed. As the carriage made its way up the incline that gave the quarter its name, Moyses continued to explain that Lincoln was one of twenty-one cities in England that were considered Jewish centers by the royal crown. Lincoln's Jewish population was second only to London's. Like London, Lincoln possessed an *archa*, an official chest, safeguarded by its three locks and seals, containing a copy of all deeds and contracts involving the Jews in the towns and villages surrounding Lincoln.

I listened politely to Moyses, but my heart was hammering in my chest. It took all my composure not to stick my head out of the carriage window and shout for my daughter. I had seen her only twice after she had left our home, and I wondered what changes the years had wrought. The carriage pulled to a halt in front of her small quarter-timbered house, which was nestled tightly between two others. I smiled at Moyses, barely able to contain myself a second longer.

"I am so grateful . . . ," I began.

"Pooh!" he said, waving away my thanks. "I know. Don't mind me, now, head out to your girl."

As quickly as I could, I descended from the carriage. A rumpled young man stood in the doorway, his face smiling tiredly.

"You must have angel's wings, Mother Shira," he told me. "She's safely delivered of a little boy—just yesterday."

I gave my son-in-law a shy hug. We didn't know each other well, after all, even though Chaya wrote at length about her much-loved husband in her letters. But the two times I had seen Chaya before her trip across the channel, I had been pleased to meet Avram, whose sweet disposition had delighted me.

"May I go up to her?" I asked as the merchant's servant brought in my trunk.

"You want nothing to eat or drink first?" my son-in-law asked. I shook my head and he nodded. "Later, then. She's anxious to see you. She's in the room at the top of the stairs. There's no mistaking it—she hung dozens upon dozens of amulets on the door to keep Lilith away this time."

I mounted the stairs quickly, stumbling a little over their uneven surface. The door jangled a little from the metal and stone amulets as I yanked it open. "Chaya?" I whispered into the gloom of the shrouded room.

"Here, Mama! Oh, Mama!" said my dear girl, sitting up in bed, her arms reaching out to me.

I fell into them, and we laughed and cried together, tears mingling on our cheeks. She had not changed. Oh, she was a woman now, not the child she had been when she left my house. She had grown tall and her slender body had developed curves. Her beautiful red hair was shorn, her face had lengthened with the years, and her cheeks were pale with exhaustion. But she still had the same beautiful smile.

Finally, I let her go. She fell back, exhausted, against the bedclothes. "Amelie, show my mother my son," she said, her English falling so precisely from her pretty lips that it was easy to hear that it wasn't her mother tongue.

A young servant girl, round red face beaming, pointed to the sleeping infant in his cradle. I smiled at her and shook my head, to tell her without words that she should not disturb the sleeping mite. My English still came halting and slow to my lips. I peered into the cradle and saw him, tucked warmly under a blue blanket, his little head covered with a warm wool cap.

"He's beautiful," I said. "Oh, Chaya, you must be so happy."

But Chaya shook her head despondently. "No, I won't say I'm happy, not yet, Mama. Not for another seven days. I was so thrilled by my first boy, I was careless. I was always in the room with him, of course, and the neighbors came and stayed. But there must have been a moment when our attention wandered, when I slept . . . I haven't slept since this baby came. I don't dare."

I looked at my daughter's worn face and believed her. "Well, now you can," I said, coming over to smooth out the bedclothes and push her farther down into their warmth. "Mama's here. You need not worry about a thing."

"You won't—you won't move?" she murmured, her tired voice the thinnest of threads. I could see her fighting against the waves of exhaustion trying to claim her.

"I won't stir, I won't sleep, and your beautiful boy will be absolutely safe with me," I said soothingly, brushing back her thick red hair from her forehead.

In an instant her eyes stopped fluttering and she slept. I walked over to the chair beside the crib and sat in it. Despite the luxury of the merchant's hired carriage, my bones ached from having been jostled through this foreign land. But I ignored my own tiredness, because I was overjoyed to be with Chaya and to see my grandson. Feeling needed, I kept one eye on the infant and the other on my sleeping girl.

———•———

The seven days that Chaya had dreaded flew by and her small boy thrived. He kept us awake with his lusty wailing. I told Chaya that if Lilith tried to steal this one's breath, despite all our incantations to the angels Senoy, Sansenoy, and Semangelof inscribed on amulets and whispered over the infant's head, she'd have a struggle on her hands. This boy was a fighter, showing his strong spirit by the way he kneaded Chaya's breasts with both hands as he nursed, wrestling against the swaddling cloths we wrapped him in.

I was so pleased when Avram told me they wanted to name the little boy Dafyid because Chaya had told her husband that I was disappointed I couldn't name my only son after his great-grandfather. Honoring my husband's expressed wishes in the matter, I refused to hold the baby in my lap when he was circumcised, despite being invited to do so as his godmother. When I explained why I wouldn't, Avram said it bespoke a modesty he wished more women evinced. I laughed inwardly as he complimented me. After all these years, was I actually being praised for remarkable modesty?

Moyses Rothermaker planned to return to Worms after the Jewish High Holy Days, which would allow him several months to travel to the towns and villages throughout Lincolnshire and purchase both pure wool and woolen broadcloth textiles, employing agents to ship them across the channel to markets throughout Europe. Both Lincoln and nearby Stamford were particularly well regarded for the quality of their wool cloth—known as scarlet cloth in Lincoln and haberget in Stamford. I was pledged to travel home with him. This gave me a full four months to visit my daughter, her husband, and their infant. Recalling how Bruria upset me whenever she interfered in my household affairs, I tried to help without being intrusive, which was sometimes hard to do in such a small household. But mutual goodwill carried us through as well as anyone could hope.

I was delighted by the affection Chaya and Avram shared with each other, an affection they showed by the innumerable small touches that passed between them each day. I remembered how Meir had claimed that he would find our daughter's *b'shert,* and I thanked God privately for His part in helping my husband keep his promise.

I was further pleased by the friends that Chaya had made from among the young wives of scholars who taught at the Peitevin *yeshiva,* the great academy of Lincoln. As I listened to these young women talk knowledgeably about their husbands' studies, I realized anew how much I missed Deina and my friends in Paris. Frommet and the others were all good, well-intentioned housewives, but it had been many years since I had heard discussions such as these.

As Meir's wife, I was honored by a visit from Berechiah de Nicole, the chief rabbi of Lincoln. Avram and Chaya were flustered by this great man's visit to their home, but I had lived long enough with a much-honored man to take it in stride. We sat for a few minutes and discussed the differences between the *yeshiva* I helped run in Rothenberg and the Peitevin *yeshiva,* and he asked me some of Meir's opinions about eating food prepared by Gentiles—a matter of grave concern to him, he told me.

The days were long and happy. The sun struggled to peek out from behind the thick, puffy clouds that seemed to perpetually dot the English skies. Wildflowers blossomed in thick patches in every green corner. Even the rain fell in a gentle sheet of moisture that bathed the earth and left no furrows in the roadways. It seemed as though nothing could mar the pleasure of my stay in Lincoln.

WENTY-EIGHT

This poore widwe awaiteth all that night / After hir litel child,
but he came nought.

—GEOFFREY CHAUCER, "THE PRIORESS'S TALE"

ONE LATE SUMMER DAY, after I'd been in England for two months,
we strolled to the pleasant vineyards of the Bishop's Hostel on Drury Lane.
As we huffed our way to the crest of Steep Hill Road, Chaya was stopped by
Hanna de Nicole, whose husband Leo was in trade. He took private instruc-
tion in Talmud from Avram once a week. Hanna was sitting on the single
step outside her house on Michaelsgate Road and waved us over.

"We have to be polite," Chaya told me under her breath as we approached.

"Why would we ever be anything else?" I asked, pinching her elbow
playfully.

Chaya rolled her eyes in a way that made me think of the little girl
learning manners from me at the Shabbat table. "Chaya!" I laughed despite myself.

"Good evening, Mistress Hanna!" my daughter called out. "Isn't it a
lovely evening?"

"It is for some," Hanna de Nicole said sourly.

"This is my mother, Shira of Rothenberg, come to help me with the baby—come all the way from her home in Germany." My daughter turned to me. "Mama, this is Hanna de Nicole. You've met her husband Leo already. The children are all healthy, Hanna?"

"Mine are well—and yours, too, I see," said Hanna, peering into the little bundle where Dafyid was wrapped in several soft blankets to keep the evening air from invading and poisoning his delicate small body. "But maybe not little Hugh."

"Little Hugh?" I asked.

"He's the bastard boy of a serving girl named Beatrice. He's disappeared, and the Gentiles are in an uproar about it. A lot of them met over there"—she nodded toward the small church of St. Michael's, which stood in the shadow of the great Lincoln Cathedral—"just an hour ago, to talk about it. One of them, Giff, who buys cloth and spices for his master from us, stopped to tell me about it. Giff's a good fellow, if a little simple."

"How old is the missing boy?" I asked, my heart going out to the lost child and his mother.

"Eight years. Maybe nine. Some would say that's old enough to fend for yourself, but in this cold world . . ."

I shuddered, thinking of what I would have felt if any of my children had gone missing at the age of eight or nine.

"Perhaps he ran away?" Chaya ventured. "Was his mother kind to him? He was, after all . . ." She blushed, still young enough to feel shame at the word "bastard."

"Born on the wrong side of the sheets?" her less squeamish neighbor laughed. "According to Giff, that wasn't held against him. The girl was engaged to wed a lancer who went off on one of these skirmishes over in France and was killed."

"It's a terrible shame," Chaya said. "I hope they find him. We must be going. I promised my mother a walk to the Bishop's Hostel. We've been cooped up all day, working in the house. And it's such a beautiful night."

We walked on.

———•———

We were sitting inside the house a day later, taking turns rocking the baby, when someone knocked loudly at the front door.

Amelie went to open it. She came scurrying back to us, looking alarmed.

"It's soldiers from the castle, mistress," she said to Chaya. "They want to search the house for little Hugh."

"Let them in," Chaya said calmly, handing me the baby so she could cover her exposed breast.

"Yes, but—" We all looked up as a tall, flaxen-haired guardsman stepped into the room. "They came in without being let," Amelie finished.

"Good afternoon," Chaya said, striving to look unflustered as she smoothed the cloth she had hastily pulled over her chest. "You're welcome to my home, guardsman."

"Sorry to bother you. We're searching the houses up and down the street for young Hugh. It's said he was last seen playing with some Jewish children just a couple of doors down. So we're looking at the houses on Steep Hill first."

"I hope you find him," Chaya said.

For soldiers, these were an orderly lot. Comparing them to the ones who had stolen the volumes of Talmud from us in Paris, maliciously scattering and destroying our belongings, I admired the quiet way these men looked into everything, returning most things to their proper places.

"Do you know young Ernaut and Gamaliel?" the guardsman asked just before they left.

"The sons of Jornet the tailor?" Chaya said. "They live just two houses down. They're good boys."

"They're the ones young Hugh was playing with. Since you know them, can you tell me the names of other boys they would usually play with?"

Chaya turned white, with good reason. Such a slip of the tongue might mean that innocent boys would be delivered to the dungeons of the castle to be tortured until they confessed. My tenderhearted daughter would rather have cut her tongue out than been the unwitting instrument of such agony. But now she had trapped herself.

"I . . ."

"Take your time, mistress," the guardsman said, leaning his back against the whitewashed wall. "I'll wait."

God forgive me for what I did then. Prising a needle out of a pouch hung over my belt, I surreptitiously poked the baby a couple of times in the fleshy part of his bottom. Little Dafyid screamed in indignation, his face turning red with choler.

"I can't keep him content, Chaya. You need to nurse him again," I said, thrusting the baby at her. "I'll take the guardsman out so you can tend to your baby in peace."

Smiling at the young soldier, I led him away from the screams of our darling boy. The guardsman's small troop of three men were waiting for him at the kitchen door, drinking all the new milk they could lay their hands on.

"Wait!" said the guardsman, putting up a hand to stop me when I would have left him. "I didn't get an answer from the Jewess. Who usually plays with Ernaut and Gamaliel?"

"Oh, I'm sorry," I said, hanging my head. "I'm a stranger in town myself, come from my home in Rothenberg to help my daughter through her first months as a new mother. I don't know the boys in town."

The soldier muttered, "We don't have time to wait now—but tell the Jewess that if we don't get the answer elsewhere, we'll be back. Let's go, men."

———

One morning as I was waiting for our loaves of bread to brown in the baker's oven, I was startled to see Brother Anton standing there looking at me with a quizzical grin on his face. Although I knew his order was based in Lincoln, I was still surprised to see him as I associated him with Paris and Falaise.

"I'll never get used to the way you Jews roam from country to country," he said to me after we greeted each other with a cry of delight. Many of the customers in the bakery—nearly all Jews wearing the yellow badge in the shape of the stone tablets required in England—stared at us in confusion and alarm. "We Christians tend to stay in the villages where we were born, but you Jews wander the face of the earth as though there were no devouring monsters at every corner."

I didn't wish to cloud our reunion by voicing my sudden thought that one could find monsters in quiet villages as well as in their outer reaches. "Didn't I read somewhere that Christ condemned the Jews to a life of wandering as penance for not recognizing him on the cross?" I asked, making Brother Anton's slender, patrician-nosed companion stare at me in disbelief.

Anton laughed, holding his stomach. He had gained weight over the years and his girth stretched his black habit and white scapular uncomfortably. "I had forgotten about your learning, Shira. You shock my friend the priest here, who is not used to well-read women. Let me introduce John of Lexington, my host in Lincoln."

I curtsyed, feeling the stares of everyone in the shop burning the back of my neck. "Father John. I'm pleased to meet any friend of Brother Anton's."

The priest looked at Brother Anton for guidance, clearly uncomfortable. Brother Anton laughed at his distress.

"Shira's father is Sir Morel of Falaise, Father," he said. "A learned man, someone I knew many, many years ago, back in Paris when we were all students."

"A long time," I said, my smile drooping. "You haven't heard of my father's death then, Brother Anton."

"Oh, Shira, I'm so sorry. I hope it wasn't . . ."

"He died the way most of us would wish to go—peaceably, in his own bed, surrounded by his loved ones. We should all be so blessed."

"He was a wise man—and a good friend," Brother Anton said. "The world is poorer without him living in it." He shook his head back and forth, absorbed in his memories.

"Do you live here in Lincoln, Shira of Falaise?" Father John asked me.

"No, in Rothenberg. Germany. My daughter lives here, with her husband and newborn son. I made the journey to help her for a few months."

"Shira—that makes you a grandmother," said Brother Anton, delighted and appalled. "It is hard to believe that the little girl who so bravely forced her way into William's Keep is a grandmother now. Time moves too swiftly, Father John."

"Every tick of the clock brings us all one step closer to God's grace in heaven, Brother Anton," pronounced the priest, crossing himself. Then he seemed to remember that I was a Jew and damned. "Well, not all of us, perhaps," he amended mildly.

"Why are you here, Brother Anton?" I asked, looking around at the people jostling by us, edging past to reach the counter or head out the door, their arms filled with warm bundles of bread. "For all we Jews wander, you yourself travel to the oddest places—Falaise, Paris, Montpellier—and now here, to Lincoln."

"My order—the Gilbertine Brothers—was first established in Lincolnshire, Shira, so in a sense I'm actually at home here. I am visiting the Hospital of the Holy Sepulcher—founded here in Lincoln to aid the poor and the sick. During the last few years, I have made a study of medicine as I travel through Europe and the Holy Land. It is my mission to share what I know—and to keep learning."

"Brother Anton serves as an example to us all," said Father John, his eyes darting around the bakery.

My loaves were waiting and I had taken enough of their time. "It is good seeing you again, Brother Anton—and to meet you, Father John."

"Give my good wishes to your husband—is he here with you?"

I shook my head. "Back at home with his school and two of our other children. We have four."

"Four! Well, I would bless you all, child, but your daughter's good neighbors might be offended by my Christian benedictions."

I laughed. "They just might. Farewell."

———•———

As August waned, I began to think about the journey home. Chaya had settled into a routine with Dafyid and the High Holy Days would be upon us before we knew it. I was starting to miss Meir and the other children. I wished Chaya might live closer to us. But it was clear that she was happy precisely where she was, and that, I told myself firmly, would have to content me.

Amelie and I were hanging the laundry in the tiny alleyway behind Chaya's house one afternoon. We were laughing companionably over my poor attempts at English when a series of shrieks coming from a home several doors down stopped us, making us look at each other in shock and dismay. We dropped the laundry into the basket and hurriedly crossed the back lots to reach the home of Jopin, a trader in Lincoln's renowned woolen cloth.

As we reached the house, we saw a strange tableau. Jopin's young wife—a girl perhaps fifteen years old—was leaning against the family's well, spewing forth the contents of her stomach on the ground nearby. Jopin was pacing next to the well, wringing his hands before him. His servants were running up and down the length of the yard. Several other neighbors who had hurried over at the sound of the screams were looking at one another, confused and alarmed.

"What's happened?" Amelie asked one of the servants.

"Mistress came out to fetch some water," the woman said. "The bucket hit something soft. We thought it was a dead animal—you know how they sometimes get trapped in a well? But when master came out to help her, they found—"

"Someone has to go for the guards!" came the cry from one of the neighbors who had been bold enough to peer into the well.

"Go for the guards? Are you mad? What will they do to Jopin here? What will they do to all of us?"

Fear gripped my heart. I grabbed the servant's arm. "Found what?" I demanded.

She pulled away. "A boy. There's a dead boy down there."

I went over to the young wife, who was still retching despite having emptied her stomach. The smell rising from the well made me cover my nose with my hand. "You should come inside, out of the sun," I urged. "Come on, away from here."

She shook her head. "No, I won't leave," she gasped, barely able to get the words out as dry heaves overpowered her. "The soldiers will be here soon."

Someone tapped my arm. I looked up. Father John of Lexington hovered over us. The look of the man in his priestly robes made several of the neighbors draw back in alarm. A few terrified souls chose this moment to hurry away. Out of the corner of one eye, I saw Amelie moving quietly out of the yard, heading back to Chaya's home.

"Shira of Falaise, is it not?" Father John asked. "Brother Anton's friend?"

"Yes, Father. There has been a terrible discovery here."

The look that crossed the man's face appalled me—a look of incredulity and accusation. "I'm not at all sure this was a discovery," he said carefully. "I think—perhaps—something more."

"There's a boy down the well, Father John! What are you thinking? That these poor people . . . ?" I could not complete the thought.

But he could. Crossing himself, he went over to Jopin and took hold of him. "We will wait here for the soldiers," Father John said. "They're on their way."

"We are lost," Jopin moaned. "Lost."

"If it is what I suspect, then you are not merely lost and not merely damned," Father John said, shaking his head sorrowfully. "There is a special pit in hell for those who murder innocent children."

The thought of the missing Gentile boy had not occurred to me before now. Blinding realization forced my protests to the back of my throat. I hoped against hope that this was a different boy who had, through some misadventure, perished in the well. For if it was the Christian child—the one they had been searching for—little Hugh . . .

The guards pushed into Jopin's yard. I recognized the same guardsman who had visited Chaya's house. His eyes moved over the assembled group and I saw the light of recognition in them as he saw me. Jopin and his family were placed under guard in one corner on a bench by an elm tree. The wife lay limply in her husband's arms as their sons wailed, inconsolable. The soldier forced the boys to sit beside their parents, his rapier at the ready should any one of them attempt to flee.

Working together, the other soldiers pulled the poor small body up out of the well, having to maneuver his limbs where they had wedged in the rocks and vines below. The broken, waterlogged body was laid on the grass. There were bruises up and down the tiny limbs and a huge gash on the forehead. The child's ragged clothing fell open, the garments looking as if they had been sliced by a sharp knife.

A woman's shriek rent the air. A serf with a black kerchief covering her sandy hair came running forward. She threw herself down in the grass next to the ruined body and hugged the stinking, bloodied corpse to her. "Hugh," she cried, "oh, my baby, my little boy, what did they do to you? What did they do? Oh, Hugh . . ."

She desperately kissed the child's face, forehead, and cheeks. Father John gently moved her away. "Hush, now, Beatrice. Hush. He is safe and in the arms of his Father up in heaven. Shh."

Beatrice would not be quieted. My heart went out to her as she tore herself from the priest's grasp and flung herself back over the child. "Oh, my boy . . . ," she wailed over and over. "My only baby . . ."

Father John pulled the dead child out of her arms. "Guards, the Jews here must accompany us as we take the boy to the cathedral," he said. "Take them all."

I was glad now that Amelie had gone back home. My Chaya would be desperate when she learned her mother had been taken prisoner. A look of fear and despair passed among the neighbors. Our only crime was a desire to help. Our selfless deed might well result in our torture and death. I thought about Meir and how he would fare without me if I perished in this distant land. At least, I thought, as I walked in the cluster of Jews forced to follow the small cavalcade taking the body to church, my children are grown and don't need me any longer. At least that.

The great cathedral towered at the summit of Steep Hill Road, its tall spires glinting in the sun. We crossed through the smaller churchyard of St. Michael's and up through the Minster Yard, approaching the church from the south. Terrified though I was, I looked around curiously as the guards forced us inside. Living as I had for so many years under the shadow of the great Notre-Dame of Paris, I had never before visited a cathedral, never set foot inside a holy Christian edifice.

I was awed by the spaciousness of the cathedral's vaulted interior. I compared it to the synagogues where we huddled to pray as softly as we could, so that Gentiles passing by would not be offended by our devotions. In our synagogues, the eternal light struggled against the gloom of our shuttered sanctuary, whereas here there were pointed arches filled with glass and huge circular windows that poured colored sunlight onto the floors. But to my surprise I saw that part of the interior was ruined, heaped in a pile of rubble. I would later learn that a monk, Hugh of Avalon, had built the cathedral. His central tower had collapsed some twenty years ago and was just now being reconstructed.

We Jews were told to sit in an area where laborers were lifting heavy stones. The guards made us perch uncomfortably on a mound of rocks, where they could keep an eye on us and still witness the service. The workmen broke off, coming over curiously to help the priest lay the small, ruined body in the nave of the church with pomp and ceremony.

News spread rapidly. The townspeople came pouring in, glaring at us as they passed by to pay their respects to the dead boy and his mother, Beatrice, who was distraught with grief and barely acknowledged their greetings. Again, almost despite myself, I found myself pitying her. But I couldn't stop wondering what would become of us.

When the service was finally over, we were marched down a brief incline from the church to cross the roadway and ascend Castle Hill. We walked by the stately mansion where Moyses Rothermaker was living with the grandchildren of Aaron the Jew. Moyses, I knew, was off on one of his journeys. I wondered if he would leave for Worms without me now.

As we were led up the verdant Castle Hill, Jopin's wife began to cry. Her voice rose to a hysterical pitch that grated on our already frayed nerves. I tried to calm her, but she would not be comforted.

"They will put us all on the rack—me first, for I found him first. They will tie me down and turn the wheel until . . . oh, the pain! I feel it already in my bones. I feel it! The agony! Stop it! Stop . . ."

Jopin had been walking ahead, his head ducked toward the ground, a desperate look etched on his face. He stopped short and let us draw close. As we neared, he reached over and slapped his wailing wife. The force of the blow cut off her tears with an abrupt shriek and she began to whimper quietly instead.

"Be still, Elfrid," he growled. "It's bad enough what they'll do to us, without you chilling all our blood with your caterwauling!"

While I couldn't help but agree with his sentiment, I was appalled to see how quickly he resorted to violence. I decided he could not do worse to me than what might be done in the castle's torture chamber and asked the question that was uppermost on my mind. "Did you kill that boy?"

"Did I . . . ? God, no, woman!" he gasped, staring at me in dislike and distrust. "Who are you, anyway? How did you come to be in my yard? I don't know you."

"I am Shira of Rothenberg, come to help my daughter, Chaya eshet

Avram, through the birth of my grandson. I was hanging laundry when I heard the screams and . . . came to help."

"You'll have cause to regret that before the day is over, I think," he muttered.

"I already regret it," I said. "But if no one here killed the boy, surely they will . . . realize that?"

Jopin gave a short bark of a laugh. "Have you ever been tortured, Mistress Shira?" he asked. At my quick shake of the head, he grimaced, kicking up dirt and stones as we walked. "No. I have not, either, but I've heard enough stories of what men do and say when they are in that much pain. I won't wait."

"What do you mean, you won't wait?" I asked, bewildered and alarmed.

"You'll see," he said, turning away from me, his next words chilling my blood. "It won't matter what they do afterward. Nothing matters anymore. We're dead right now, Mistress Shira. We're already dead."

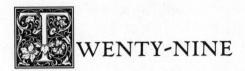WENTY-NINE

Most falsely do these Christians claim that the Jews have secretly
and furtively carried away these children and killed them, and that
the Jews offer sacrifice from the heart and blood of these children.

—POPE GREGORY X

NINE OF US WERE LED DOWN into the bowels of the castle. The
stairway grew narrower and more precarious the farther we descended.
Stones skittered under our feet and I stumbled more than once, grabbing the jagged walls to steady myself. Despite the heat of the August
day, it was cold and dank there. The air smelled of a century of frightened men's sweat and blood. We were directed into a large room that
contained a single bench, a heap of straw, and a soil bucket.

No more than an hour passed before the heavy door was flung open.
Father John stood looking at us, an expression of sorrow and grief on
his face.

"Remove Jopin the Jew to the next room," he instructed the guards.

Jopin, who had been leaning against the wall, found it difficult to
stand without support. His knees buckled under him and he nearly fell
to the floor. The guards had to seize him by his elbows and lead him out,

half dragging him. Elfrid began to sob. Jopin's sons clung to his legs. I
got up and fetched them back. Their small bodies pressed into mine as
they wept in terror.

"Father John! Can the boys not be released? My daughter can care
for them. I don't ask for the rest of us, but these are mere babes. What
point is there in keeping them here?"

He looked over at the small children. "'The sins of the father afflict
unto the sons for several generations . . . ,'" he said.

"'Fathers shall not be put to death for their children, nor children
put to death for their fathers; each is to die for his own sins,'" I retorted,
quoting Deuteronomy 24:16.

Father John shook his head. "Brother Anton warned me about you.
I am not fond of learned women, Shira. Women should know their
place."

I bit my lip, pushing back further protests. I pulled the boys before
me, letting Father John get a clear view of their tear-stained faces, hoping pity might accomplish what my arguments could not.

"We will see what happens after their father is questioned," Father
John said firmly, turning away.

The door shut behind him and there was the sound of the heavy oak
bolt being pushed into place. I took the boys over to the farthest corner
and, putting them on my lap as I sat on the filthy floor, sang them a lull-
aby. Worn out by their fears and the long hours of waiting, both little
heads nodded and they fell into a deep sleep.

We others could not rest, for Jopin's cries were clearly heard through
the solid stone walls. His agony chilled us all. I lay next to the sleeping
boys, cradling them in my arms on the stone floor, hoping that their
father's screams of pain would not rouse them. They stirred restlessly as
his shrieks rent the night, but exhaustion kept them asleep.

Finally, the door opened again. The guards thrust a limping Jopin inside. He was nursing one arm that looked as if it were badly hurt, maybe
even broken. A thin line of blood trickled from his swollen lips, and his

left eye was puffy and bruised. He collapsed in a heap in the corner. We gathered around him, the children waking with a start.

"Da!" cried the eldest one.

"Where are my boys?" Jopin cried. He winced as their bodies collided against his, but his unhurt arm reached out and he hugged them to him, tears rolling down his face.

The rest of us withdrew to a corner, allowing the family as much privacy as we could.

"That was altogether too short a time," one of the men, Mileon, whispered. "He should have been in there another four or five hours, at least. He told them something."

"What could he possibly have said?" Calamond said. "They just realized that he had nothing to confess and let him go."

"You're a fool, Calamond," said Mileon. "Innocent men are carried out of the torture chamber, not allowed to walk out on their own two feet. Something's not right here."

———•———

Caught in our own dark, shadowy nightmare, it seemed as if we had stepped out of time altogether. Finally, the door was flung open again and three guards stood in the opening. We all tensed, not knowing who would be taken away to be tortured next. Elfrid started to whimper.

"Clear them all out of here," said one of the guards to the other two. "You. Jews. You're free to leave."

Free! We couldn't believe it. We rose, warily looking at one another, our bewilderment showing in our uncertain movements. Jopin, however, did not seem surprised. Mileon noticed it at once.

"What did you tell them?" he demanded. "What did you say?"

Jopin ignored him.

We hastened toward the door, Jopin leaning heavily against Elfrid. We moved up, up, until we reached the castle gates. Avram was standing just outside the castle grounds with a group of men who sought entrance to appeal for our release. They gaped at us as we exited.

"Mother Shira!" Avram cried. "Oh, praise the Lord!"

I fell into his arms and hugged him tightly, clinging to his strong young body so I wouldn't collapse. "Chaya?" I asked.

"Let us hurry right home to her," my son-in-law said gleefully. "I cannot believe they let you go."

We had started away when a scream stopped us in our tracks. We swerved back to look. Mileon had seized Jopin's wounded arm in a relentless grasp and was twisting it. Jopin was screaming and writhing in pain.

"What did you tell them?" Mileon demanded. "Why did they let us go?"

Elfrid stood stock-still, weeping helplessly, crying out for aid. Desperate, Jopin shrieked, "Guards! Help me! Help!"

A guard strolled over, moving slowly and deliberately. He stood, his hand on his sword, and looked calmly at the two men. Mileon dropped Jopin's arm and turned away. Jopin collapsed against his wife, who could barely support his weight.

"Let us go home," I said, turning away. I did not want to cloud my children's joy at my return, but instinct told me Mileon was right. Jopin had confessed to something under torture that did not bode well for any of us Jews.

———◆———

The next day Amelie told me a man in Christian garments was at the door. "He says he knows you. A Brother Anton."

"Brother Anton?" I cried, surprised but delighted. "Tell him I'll be with him in a moment."

"He looks angry," Amelie warned me.

I dipped my hands into the washbasin and patted water onto my face to freshen up, running a comb through my thick black hair. I covered my head, hurriedly placed my light summer shawl over my shoulders, and went out to him.

"Welcome to my daughter's home, Brother Anton," I said, entering to see him sitting somberly at the edge of a settle. "I don't know where Chaya is, but I'd dearly like for you to meet her. Last time you saw her, she was in here," I touched my stomach somewhat coyly and looked up, expecting a twinkle or laugh in return.

But Brother Anton's eyes were dark and troubled. "Some other time, perhaps, Shira," he said. "I'm here because I need to discover—for the sake of my own soul's ease—if what Jopin told Father John was true."

A frisson of alarm moved up and down my limbs. I sat down on a bench across from Brother Anton, pulling my shawl tighter about my shoulders. "I don't know what he said," I replied. "He would not tell us. He was badly hurt, however—I think his arm was broken . . ."

Brother Anton looked away from me. "I have ever been a friend of the Jews; you know that, Shira. But learning of this . . . abomination . . . has unsettled me greatly. And the rumors of it are spreading like wildfire from house to house. I'm not sure you—any of you—are safe."

"What did he tell you?" I whispered. I wished he would look at me.

But he kept his head turned away. "He said that the Jews of Lincoln kidnapped the child and kept him secreted in a remote room in town. That every year the Jews try to take a child, to sacrifice him as Christ himself was sacrificed. That when you had little Hugh secured, the elders of the city sent for Jews throughout England, and they convened in a secret room, draping themselves in their best prayer shawls for the occasion. That there was much singing and dancing in joy at possessing a boy to torture—"

"You cannot believe any of this!" I cried, aghast.

"Let me finish. According to Jopin, the men gathered around the boy and set him on a stool in their midst. One of them took the part of Pilate—"

"I don't know who that is," I said, squirming uncomfortably on my seat.

"Pilate was the Roman governor who condemned Christ at the request of the Jews," Brother Anton replied, finally glancing at my face. "And just as Pilate condemned our sweet Lord to the cross and then called for water to wash his hands, so, too, did this elder Jew, after condemning the poor child to death after torture."

I felt sick and dizzy. Reaching up, I felt my damp forehead. Brother Anton was now studying my face closely. I prayed that my expression did not show him anything but the truth—that this story was nothing but the fabrication of a man under torture who had already determined this lie was the best way to escape from pain.

"After they condemned the child to death," Brother Anton continued in a wooden tone, "they surrounded Hugh and beat him mercilessly, until his blood flowed. They took basins and filled it with his blood, putting their fingers into it to taste it and declaring that they would put it aside for the next time they needed to bake unleavened bread—"

"Stop it!" I cried. "You cannot give any of this . . . incredible story credence. No one who truly knows us could suspect us of this. You knew my father, Brother Anton—you know my husband. You and Rabbi Yechiel studied together. Could any one of them do this? Could they?"

"Until yesterday, I would have said no, Shira," Brother Anton said sorrowfully. Once more he refused to meet my gaze. "But I have heard what Father John said to Beatrice, the boy's mother. And he was present in the prison when Jopin confessed to all of this—confessed long before the pain would actually make him lie just for relief. The Church's torturers are skilled, you see. They know the difference between a man telling the truth and a man grasping at deceits just to escape the pain. Jopin was still lucid. He was not lying."

"He told me," I said, suddenly remembering, eager to correct the misapprehension, "that he would not wait. As we were being led away, he said he was afraid of the pain and that he would not wait. I didn't understand what he meant at the time. But is it inconceivable that a man who is not in pain might concoct a plan to avoid the agony of torture before it overwhelms him? What did they promise Jopin if he spoke out?"

Brother Anton looked up, considering this as a possibility. "He was to be freed—his family to remain untouched. But others are to be examined—every Jew in Lincoln. You need to go home, Shira, back to Rothenberg. Take your daughter and her family with you."

HIRTY

Have you seen the gates of the shadow of death?
—JOB 38:17

I TRIED TO CONVINCE THE CHILDREN TO LEAVE, but they refused to believe that they were in danger. When the Jews of Lincoln learned how Jopin had pointed the finger at the rest of the community to save himself and his family, the city's rabbis called Jopin before them and questioned him closely. Avram told us how Jopin finally broke down after hours of prodding and confessed that he conjured his tale of horror so his torturers would be sure he was telling them the truth. For who could make up such a tale? After much heated discussion, fearing what deeds the frightened Jewish community might be driven to as a result of his fraud, the rabbis pronounced *niddui* against Jopin and his family—a lesser form of excommunication. Usually *niddui* was dispensed in seven-day spans, but Jopin's crime of testifying against his Jewish neighbors was so enormous and dreadful that the rabbis set a three-month sentence.

Now armed with the facts, the rabbis sent one delegation to the town officials and another to the king, explaining the true state of affairs.

When the outrage of both the Jews and the Christians of Lincoln died down, the rabbis congratulated themselves that they had prevailed. Life went on as usual. I tried my best to believe that we had been delivered from harm.

Right after the High Holy Days, a few days before I was set to depart, Lincoln grew crowded. People were arriving from all over England for an important wedding—that of Bellaset, daughter of Rabbi Berechiah de Nicole. A steady stream of Jewish merchants and scholars entered the town, the boardinghouses were filled to capacity, and several of the townspeople—Chaya included—boarded wedding guests who had nowhere else to stay. We housed a young family from London. The husband had been a student at the *yeshiva* before his father had died of plague. The boy had to give up his studies to take over the father's business. He was a constant visitor to Lincoln. But this was the first time his wife and two boys had come to the smaller city and they found it all an adventure.

We were sitting down to the evening meal just two days before the wedding when sounds of excitement reached us. The visiting boys rose from the table, ran to the door, and came tearing back again.

"It's the king, Mama, King Henry is coming!"

We all clambered up at that, buzzing in excitement. We went out to the street, where people were standing in surprised delight to watch King Henry III's cavalcade. I had never seen such beautiful, strong horses. The knights who rode by on them carried gonfalons—long, narrow pennants—declaring their allegiance to one or another of the noble Norman houses. Ladies were conveyed in curtained carriages that clogged our roadway. A few of the curtains were not closed all the way, and we could look into the carriages and glimpse visions of silk and lace, sparkling jewels and painted faces. The slow parade ascended to Steep Hill, making its way to the castle.

Finally all that was left of the parade was the dust they stirred up. We returned to our meal. "Did anyone know King Henry was coming to Lincoln?" Chaya asked her husband.

"We in the *yeshiva* knew nothing, but why would they tell us?" Avram replied. "It means nothing to us, after all. Perhaps the king is on his way to a hunt or to make war somewhere. But it is too bad Dafyid isn't old enough to remember that he once saw the king ride by in all his glory!"

———•———

The two families—Chaya's and that of our houseguest—were walking to the synagogue when horsemen in royal livery rode by us three abreast, forcing us to huddle against the gray stone buildings in the street. They clattered up to Jopin's house, which we were just about to pass, and stopped. A page ran forward and grabbed the reins.

The horsemen kicked the door in. There were screams inside the house.

"We should go home," Chaya said, gripping the shrieking baby to her breast. But Avram ignored her, standing transfixed.

Jopin, a sling lying useless against his chest, was dragged outside, the riders ruthlessly pulling on both his healthy and broken arms. He was wailing in pain and crying out, "No! I have a pardon from Father John of Lexington. You cannot take me! I'll fetch the pardon! Elfrid!"

Elfrid ran out, waving a piece of paper in the air. "Guards! Guards! See here! His pardon!" she cried.

"A plague take your pardon," one of the horsemen cried. "His Majesty, Henry the third, has revoked your pardon this day. You, Master Jopin, are to be made an example of!"

"No," the man screamed. "No!"

They hustled him onto a horse. A guard climbed up behind him, wrapping his long arms around Jopin's trembling frame. The others mounted their own steeds. They wheeled about, pushing us against the stone wall of Jopin's house, and rode off.

Elfrid stood at the doorway, looking stunned. Remembering how her husband had endangered the entire Jewish community to save his own skin, remembering the *niddui,* I turned from her.

"We should go right home," I urged, "and leave Lincoln."

"Is that what you and Rav Meir would do in Rothenberg? Leave your neighbors to face trouble on their own?" Avram retorted. I hung my head, knowing full well we would not. "We must go to the synagogue," Avram added, "and warn everyone."

———

We arrived at the synagogue to find our warnings were unnecessary. The king's guard was at the door, and they hustled us inside to imprison us with the other members of the congregation. Chaya and I, who had been trapped in a synagogue years ago in Paris when soldiers ransacked our homes and stole our copies of the Talmud, clung to each other. Avram, aghast, left us to seek out the other men.

"I'll be back in a moment," he said to his wife, kissing the palm of her hand.

"What will happen now, Mama?" Chaya whispered.

"It's in the hands of *ha-Shem,* child," I said, reaching out to soothe my daughter—and myself—by stroking her red hair. Now that the crisis was upon us, I felt calm. "We will face whatever comes as bravely as God allows."

We waited and prayed with the other women for a long hour. Finally, an emissary from the king arrived and mounted the *bimah.* "This day, we have taken Jopin de Nicole prisoner, he who confessed on your behalf to the criminal and ungodly torture of a poor Christian child. He had obtained, by dint of his confession, a pardon by a local clergyman. His Majesty, hearing of the perfidious misdeeds of this miscreant, has seen fit, in obvious wisdom, to revoke that pardon."

Soldiers entered the doors, their swords drawn and pointed at us. Screams of fright rang out. People stumbled to their feet and tried to find an exit, but the soldiers had planned too carefully and all doors were manned. The hubbub was deafening, and the sweaty odor of fear—a stench you never forget, once you have smelled it—pervaded the room. I was proud to see my daughter concentrating fiercely on comforting her child.

"You will all step outside the synagogue now. No one will be harmed if you do what we say," the emissary commanded.

Fearful that we were walking to our death, we moved outside. The soldiers pushed and shoved the recalcitrant ones. Men and women were kept separate. There was a large open courtyard in front of the synagogue building, and we stood there in two clusters, threatened by the soldiers' weapons and the jeers of the Christians.

"Here they come," someone cried out, and two horses rounded the corner. A knight rode on one and led the other at a brisk trot. I gasped at seeing Jopin being dragged on the ground behind it. He was secured to a horse's tail by a chain bound tightly around his wrists, the length of the bonds just long enough to force him to follow a few paces behind the horse. Jopin had probably managed to run behind the horses for a few miles before stumbling and falling to the ground. He had been dragged painfully ever since.

Jopin's body was a mass of blood and dirt. I found my lips moving, sending an entreaty to God to let this all end soon, to end his agony and our own.

The soldiers forced us to follow in a mass behind the horse and man, climbing up the steep city streets. I gave my arm and my strength to my daughter, who stumbled more than once.

At sunset, we arrived at the castle grounds. A gallows had been erected outside in one of the pleasure gardens, and the king and his court were waiting for us.

There was a sound of trumpets. The king stood up from his wooden throne, standing over our heads on the platform built directly across from the gallows.

"Let the Jew be hanged," he proclaimed, "and let it be a warning to these other Jews that we will investigate this matter until we are satisfied that we have learned the truth. If Jopin has, as the elders of the Jews of Lincoln claim, told a lie to escape torture, he has done his people immense harm and we will punish him for it now. If, however"—and here the king glowered down upon us—"it becomes evident that his tales of horror are accurate, then every Jew in Lincoln will pay the price for their crime." The king waved a hand at his commander and reseated himself on his throne.

The commander gestured toward his soldiers. Jopin was lying on the ground, as if unconscious. Was he dead already? I wondered. Two soldiers took him by the elbows and dragged him up the gallows steps. Seeing the noose hanging before him, he cried out. I looked around the courtyard for Elfrid and the boys and found myself grateful I could not locate them. I remembered how the boys' sturdy bodies had thudded against their father as they ran to him in the dungeon. I wondered what would become of them now.

The noose was put around his neck; a hood covered his face. I turned away, to avoid watching these last few desperate moments in a man's life. I murmured a psalm under my breath, my eyes fixed firmly on the ground beneath me. There was a shout and the sound of a heavy rope creaking, of Jopin struggling for breath. And then, everything was still.

We can go home now, I remember thinking.

The king rose and left, followed by his court. The king's emissary, the man who had rounded us up in the synagogue, stepped onto the vacant platform.

"Listen, Jews. You are to be taken from this place and carted off to London to await trial. The carts are pulling up outside even now."

The deathly silence with which the congregation of Lincoln heard this was broken by a woman's scream. The floodgates of emotion poured open. The castle garden echoed with shouts of protest, with wails, with the cries of young children. Small Dafyid woke at the sound and began to cry. Chaya took him from me and clutched him to her breast, tears falling down her cheeks. She stared at me, looking for solace from her mother. What consolation could I possibly give her? I felt as though something had broken inside me and I had nothing left to give anyone. But I roused myself with a start. My child and grandchild needed me. I forced my drooping head up and looked back at my darling girl with as much love as I could muster.

"The king's inquisitors will hear testimony from each of you," the king's emissary continued, "and you will live or die based on their decision."

We were hustled into the carts, packed in tightly so that they could carry off as many of us as they could. I sat with Chaya and the baby. Avram was in another cart with other men. Once in a while I saw Chaya touch her lips to her palm, her eyes shut, and I knew she was trying to feel the last kiss her husband had bestowed upon her.

The journey to London took several days—days that felt like years. They fed us scraps of bread and water. The carts were open to the elements and we were pelted with heavy autumn rains. Our sodden clothes clung against our wet bodies. The stench of so many unwashed and terrified people huddled together was overwhelming. It was a miracle no one died on this agonizing journey, but several of the older women and younger children hovered perilously close to the brink of death. Those of us who had strength gave our bread to the weak. I had to stop my nursing daughter several times from contributing hers.

Finally, the towers of London came into view, the mystical, fog-bound city I had often conjured as a child as I imagined William the Conqueror's triumphal entrance. I had never pictured myself arriving there in such ignominy, however. The city folk stood in the doorways of their homes or huddled together in the twisting, narrow streets, pointing excitedly at the carts carrying the Jews, some pelting us with stones and rotten vegetables. Clearly, the story of little Hugh had made its way to London.

We were to be incarcerated in the great Clink gaol. Our carts clattered across London Bridge—the only bridge that spanned the River Thames. Underneath, dozens of wherries chopped across the river's swell. As we pulled up to the jail gates, sobbing broke out among the women and children. I half rose from my seat to note that each man was wrapped in his prayer shawl, fervently beseeching the Almighty for mercy. I raised my arms, as I often had seen my father and husband do, and called out that we women should pray for relief. The women brokenly murmured to the Lord, saying the prayers with me.

We drove inside a courtyard in front of a forbidding stone building. The thought of being sealed up inside the high walls terrified me. But the women looked to me for guidance now. Through gritted teeth, I called out psalms for us to recite together. The carts halted, but the guards motioned for us to stay in our seats.

There was some confusion at the doors of the prison. The jailers and the soldiers who brought us began arguing with one another. A man emerged from the thick entrance doors, a heavy chain worn as a mark of his rank on his out-thrust chest. He stood before us, standing on the top step of the prison, and looked us over distastefully.

There were more than a hundred of us, mostly men, of course, but the women and children who had been present at the hanging had been brought along as well. Apparently, no provision had been made for women and children, and the jailer refused to take us.

"I count ninety-two men," said one of the jail guards, having been dispatched to tap each of us on the head as he called out a number, "thirty women, and assorted children."

"Free the women and children," said the man with the chain. "I have no room for them."

At that, a great wailing broke out, for as much as we feared prison, we feared separation from our men more. But the guards were adamant. Not even allowing us so much as a farewell, they wheeled the cart with the women and children around and drove it out of the gate. Chaya thrust Dafyid into my arms and hurried to the rear of the cart so that she could gaze at her husband one more time. She stole one last brief glimpse of him.

"What will we do, Mama?" she asked as the cart pulled up outside the prison walls and stopped. We were ordered to remove ourselves.

The young mother who had been our houseguest and who had made the weary journey back to London with us spoke up. "You will come home with me," she said, to my infinite relief.

The other women were as quickly taken up and housed by fellow Jews. Our hostess, Margarede, lived in Milk Street. Jews in London either lived there or in Gresham or Wood streets, or in the longer-established neighborhood of Ironmonger Lane, where the *yeshiva* was housed. A few still lived near the synagogue, in the area known as the old Jewry, but most had been crowded out when the Londoners built the Monastery of St. Thomas of Acon and the Church of St. Mary Colechurch. Margarede's house was not large but she made us feel welcome, although we were worried for Avram; for Simeon, Margarede's husband; and for the rest of the Jews who'd been taken.

The first thing our hostess did was set out a meal, food that we ate guiltily, thinking of our men, whose stomachs were undoubtedly still empty. Yet we were ravenous after our ordeal of bread and water. My hand trembled as I lifted the first morsel to my mouth and I could barely contain myself from gulping down all the food set before me and then asking for more.

As she fed us, Margarede told us how a little more than ten years past, London's Jews had survived their own accusation of ritual murder.

"A child was found, dead, with gashes on its body. According to an apostate Jew, these were said to be Hebrew letters, although my father, who saw the corpse, said they were not. The body was brought to St. Paul's Cathedral, where the priests burned it to excise the Jewish devil they said was residing within. We were much frightened, but in the end, it came down to enriching the king's coffers by sixty thousand marks." Margarede smiled tightly at our shocked faces. "Oh, it was an enormous amount, I know, but we found it, as we always do. And you'll see, Chaya, this will be the same type of affair. King Henry is probably just feeling his purse pinch him and, having heard the story of Hugh and the well, decided to take advantage of Lincoln's Jews to find some ready cash."

Most of the women were at the prison gates in the morning and on all the mornings following, appealing to the guards with sweet words and ready bribes, trying to convince them to let us visit our menfolk.

We were never allowed in. As the days passed, we grew more and more dejected.

I realized that my merchant friend must have left for Worms without me, and part of me wondered, idly, how I would ever make my way back home. I dispatched a letter to Meir through a Londoner who was heading to Paris, confident that somehow Yechiel would find a way to send it to my husband. In my letter, I explained that I could not leave Chaya until her husband was restored to her. The pain of missing my husband, Rachel, and Suesskind seared my heart and the letter grew damp with tears as I wrote and sealed it.

Finally, there came word. Eighteen of our men were to be executed the next day for refusing to plead their innocence or guilt. Desperately, we sought to find out whether Avram or Simeon were among the eighteen. But the rumors of exactly who was to be hung conflicted, and, sitting at Margarede's table after arriving home from the jail gates, we realized we had no choice. We would actually have to attend the hanging to discover who was to die.

———◆———

Dressed simply, our yellow tablet badges put aside for the day, we made our way to Smithfield, the site of public executions. We had to travel outside the walls of the city, where the smaller houses of the outskirts gave way to plowed fields and open pastures. I felt some of my heaviness of spirit lift from me as the noise and filth of London's crowded streets grew distant. Margarede told us of the great St. Bartholomew's Fair that took place there every year. The gallows were erected at the edge of the horse market.

Under other circumstances it was a day that I might have considered beautiful, with a touch of cold in the air warning us of the harsh winter to come. The sky was filled with high, puffy clouds and the sun shone brightly down on us all. We were not cheered by it. The crowd around us, which had made the trip in the middle of the day for the thrill of the execution, was in a jovial mood. It was the same type of frantic hilarity I remembered from the Paris burning. Watching the people file into the fairgrounds, shouting and calling out to their neighbors, I wondered what would be sold there as a token of the day. I did not have to wait long to find out. Peddlers were doing a brisk business in small bits of stained cloth, said to have been cut from little Hugh's bloodied clothing as he lay in state in Lincoln Cathedral.

"These be saint's relics before too many days," the hawker who thrust them into our faces declared. "There be signs and miracles happening in Lincoln already. The boy was a martyr in Jesus's name."

Shards of wood, said to have been used to pierce Hugh's flesh by the vicious Jews, were also sold, as well as the ubiquitous straw figures, this time decorated with small tails and horns. I shuddered to see parents tell their children that these dolls were Jews and then watch the young ones amuse themselves as they waited for the hanging to begin by playing at "Little Hugh and the Jews."

The men were brought to the market in an open cart, fenced about with a thistle mesh whose sharp thorns kept the prisoners in and the indignant crowd from doing more than pelting them with stones and rotten fruit. A cry rose from my poor daughter's lips as she saw her husband being driven into the yard and ushered from the cart onto the gallows platform, his hands tied behind him with heavy rope bonds. Margarede—obviously relieved her husband was not numbered among the condemned—helped me hold back my darling girl as she struggled against our restraining arms. I finally handed the baby to our friend and wrestled my agonized daughter into a tight embrace.

"Chaya!" I whispered, vehemently but softly so I could not be overheard. "You must stop. You cannot go to him. The crowd will kill you if they discover who you are. Think of Dafyid. Avram would want you to live for Dafyid."

"I must get closer at least, Mama," the girl moaned, her eyes filled with suffering. I saw a shadow of her father's grim expression when I looked into her tortured face. I wanted nothing more than to allow her to break down against me and to join her in weeping. But we were in public, in danger, and it could not be.

"We should leave," Margarede murmured in my ear. But Chaya, hearing her, shook her head vehemently.

"No, I must stay. It is all I have left to do for him," she muttered. "Mama, help me!"

"We will stay if you feel you must," I agreed. "But you will need to control your feelings. Later, sweetheart, we can mourn together. Oh, Chaya!" I clenched my lips tightly together, finding my own control perilously close to shattering. I wished, oh, how I wished, that Meir was there to help me shepherd our daughter safely through this misery.

I motioned to Margarede to hand the baby back to my daughter. I knew the feel of the infant next to her would force her to think of him, not of her own feelings or even her husband's agony of body and mind. I grabbed hold of her sleeve and kept her close to me for the same reason. I would watch over my girl and let no harm come to her, I told myself, and she would do the same for her child.

We crept closer to the gallows. Eighteen men stood in a line. Some, like Avram, held themselves erect through sheer force of will. Others appeared so fearful, their trembling limbs were barely strong enough to keep their bodies upright. I did not know the Jews of Lincoln as Chaya did, but even I recognized many of these men, some of the richest and most influential in the town. I thought again of what Margarede had said about the king enriching his coffers through this tragedy. Noting just who had been selected to die, it seemed possible that her accusation might be true. Their belongings would default to the crown, including everything my Chaya owned in this world. I felt sick thinking these men would die and their families would suffer just to fill the king's treasure chests.

A man stepped forward, clothed in priest's robes, wearing the hood of an inquisitor. He quieted the crowd by stretching out his arms and recounted the horrific murder of little Hugh.

Knowing what I knew about my people, knowing every word the man said was a fabrication and a lie, I still found myself moved by it. Looking around at the tear-stained faces in the crowd, particularly the faces of the mothers, each one clutching her own small children to her protectively, I began to understand the hatred the Christians felt for us. We held ourselves apart from them and they knew nothing of our actual lives. Instead, they were fed these bizarre stories about us—tales of horns and curly tails, of drinking Christian blood, of worshipping in Satanic ways. The hatred I had felt for Gentiles since the burning in Paris—always excluding individuals like Brother Anton and Jaquet— melted away just a little in the light of understanding.

But I realized my sudden enlightenment would not help Chaya get through the day. My daughter strained against my hands and tried to move closer to her husband. As she neared the gallows, we could both see that Avram was standing with a hood over his face. Chaya's own face crumpled as she realized she would never look into her beloved's eyes again. Despite my cautioning her to keep silent, she cried out. "Avram! Avram! Can you hear me?"

It seemed to both of us that Avram stiffened at the sound of her voice. At that moment, Dafyid woke. Hungry, sensing his mother's torment, the infant began to wail. Avram heard the cry of his child and straightened up to stand even taller. Somehow, I knew my son-in-law would go to his death comforted by the fact that he had, in this limited but poignant way, been able to hear his loved ones bid him farewell.

The inquisitor's speech finally wound up to its frenzied conclusion, and he led the eighteen men to stand on wooden crates beneath the gallows. Heavy nooses were dropped around their necks. I put my arms around my agonized daughter and pulled her close to me. Voices praying filtered up around us. I felt Chaya's trembling and my own body began to shake. I felt cold and disoriented, and took several shallow breaths to keep myself from fainting.

The executioner kicked away the crate holding the first prisoner, then the next, and the next. Each man kicked the air, struggling against the suffocating rope. Avram was sixth in line. As the executioner drew closer, Chaya huddled against me. Margarede gently stepped up so that she stood close by, not wanting to interfere with our grief, but ready to help if the need arose. The executioner kicked away the fourth crate. The first men had already stopped moving and were hanging still, dead. The fifth crate. Now it was Avram's turn.

Chaya turned to me with a cry, her head hidden against my shoulder momentarily, then turned back to watch. In the second she averted her face, the executioner kicked her husband's support away. Like the others, Avram tried to find purchase in the air. His entire body quivered as he fought against the darkness overtaking him. Pallid and suffering, Chaya watched him while the baby against her breast screamed. Tears rolled down my cheeks. The crowds cheered as Avram twitched and struggled for air. And then he too was still.

My girl collapsed against me. Margarede took the baby. We hustled my nearly fainting daughter away from the crowds as quickly and unobtrusively as we could.

"Too much for her, eh?" a kindly man at the edge of the fairgrounds said as we moved past him. "Give her some strong meat and ale. That's what she needs to stiffen up and watch such good hangings!"

ART 5

ENSISHEIM, 1256–1293

. . . IT IS PRECIOUS FOR ME TO BEHOLD
THE DUST OF DESOLATE SANCTUARY.
                    —*Yehuda ha-Levi*

HIRTY-ONE

The Lord's curse is on the house of the wicked,
but he blesses the home of the righteous.

PROVERBS 3:33

IT TOOK NEARLY TWO MONTHS FOR CHAYA, the baby, and me
to travel to Rothenberg. Unlike my trip to Lincoln, which was accomplished in luxury and speed, we had to find our way using public conveyances. Chaya was morose, her mourning a heavy pall she put on every dawn. I could do little for her but move her from cart to boat to carriage, make sure she fed the baby when he cried to be nursed, and play with the infant when she would have wrapped lifeless arms about him.

A light snow was falling when we stepped out of the farmer's cart that had brought us the last few miles to the Marktplatz in Rothenberg. Home at last! The fountain with its sneering faces seemed to light up in welcoming grins as we hoisted our few belongings past it. A cry rose from one of the nearby shops, and our good neighbors surrounded us, taking up our baggage and gently helping us the last few blocks home.

Meir ran out of the classroom as soon as he heard the bustle of our arrival and Rachel flew from the kitchen, apron strings flying out behind her. I saw at a glance that my youngest daughter had gained both inches and maturity while I was away. We embraced one another, passing the baby from hand to hand, our joy only tempered by the sadness of what we had endured.

Meir clasped Chaya in his strong arms and she clung to him. He reached out a trembling hand to touch my face. His eyes hungrily followed the sound of his grandson's laughter as the baby chortled at the students who were tickling him. With a start, I realized this was the first time Meir had seen his grandson. The heavy burden of the journey lifted from my heart and I looked with comfort on the people and the surroundings that I loved.

"But where is Suesskind?" I asked.

Rachel laughed. "He is in Barcelona, Mama, with Zipura. He was invited to study with Rabbi Moses ben Nachman. Papa thought it was a wonderful opportunity for him."

I looked at my husband, who nodded. "He has a good mind, our son. I traveled through Europe at his age, moving from school to school. I never went so far south as Barcelona, but I did not have a sister who lived there, either. He will flourish there."

I put aside the pang I felt at Suesskind's absence to notice the well-ordered household. Rachel had managed beautifully in my absence. "Did you marry Rachel off to Binyamin ben Zuiskind while I was away, Meir?" I asked, only half joking.

"No, Mama, Papa said we should wait for your return. But you are back now and we can get married. Oh, Mama, I am so glad you are back." Rachel hugged me.

Chaya had begun to droop in her father's arms, the pain that was never far from her heart overtaking her. I gave Rachel a squeeze and turned her toward my elder daughter. "Rachel, take Chaya and the baby upstairs to the solar so she can rest and nurse her son," I suggested.

Rachel led her older sister away, the students who had milled about faded back to their studies, and I stepped into my husband's sheltering arms. "Oh, Meir," I murmured, wanting to cry but holding back the tears so I would not distress him. "How I missed you."

"And I you," he said, whispering the words into my hair. "When I heard how you were taken prisoner, I . . . I cannot tell you how I survived the waiting. It was weeks before we heard you were released. I could not eat, could not sleep. The news of you all being taken to London nearly undid me. And then to hear of Avram's execution and to know that you and our poor girl witnessed the hanging . . . and here I was, unable to help you, unable to do more than pray. It was . . ." He shuddered.

I nestled against him. "I longed for you," I told him. "The thought of you helped me through the worst of it. Whenever there was danger, it was you I thought of. What would you do, how would you act? It helped."

Rachel came down the stairs, smiling to see us wrapped in each other's arms. "I'll just step by and go to the kitchen." She laughed.

I reached out and took Rachel's strong, brown hand in mine. "It seems to me that you are more than ready to be married yourself, darling," I told her. "Tomorrow let's plan a beautiful wedding for you."

———————◆———————

The day of my youngest daughter's wedding blessing was clear and cold. Snow lay in heavy drifts outside, and Meir organized several of the students to remove it from our walkways.

I rose early, for there was still much to do. We had decked the *yeshiva* hall where Rachel would celebrate after being wed with greenery and pinecones, covering the tables that we moved against the walls with snowy white cloths. Chaya, whose efforts to put aside her mourning made me want to cry for her pain, was already in the kitchen, kneading the dough for a long apple pastry. There would be salt fish and meat pies and a simmering *cholent* stew for the feast. Before we guided our guests to the synagogue for the ceremony, we would pour wine and cider into kettles to warm, adding some precious spices to tantalize the tongue.

Seeing that Chaya had the kitchen staff well in hand, I went upstairs to my Rachel. She was sitting up in the bed she had shared with her sister and the baby, playing with him. "He is so sweet," she said, tickling his stomach. "Isn't Dafyid the sweetest baby, Mama?"

"He is a dear baby," I said, kissing my girl on the forehead as I took the infant. "As were you."

Rachel moved back under the covers, pulling her knees to her chin. "I'm so glad Papa will be the one to marry us today."

I nodded. Meir and I had not been able to attend either of our other daughters' weddings. Both Lincoln and Barcelona had been too far to travel to. Because he would officiate, Meir was even more excited than I was.

As we dressed later, I told my husband, "I feel like this is our moment of joy, not just Rachel's and Binyamin's. All day long I've been reminded of our own wedding. And of my papa's, so long ago in Falaise."

Meir, grandly attired in a long blue wool tunic, his leggings a rich burgundy red, picked up his Shabbat prayer shawl. "You look as beautiful as you did on the day we married," he said.

I shrugged, turning from him. "Nonsense. I'm a grandmother now, I'll have you know."

He laughed, dropping a kiss on the top of my head, and left the room. I peeped into my looking glass. No, the flush of youth had left me forever, but I stood tall and straight before the mirror. My gown of deep green velvet, with its tight sleeves and high neck, set off the warm glow of my cheeks. I wore a heavy gold necklace with rubies that sparkled in the candlelight. My hair, modestly tucked under an embroidered wimple, was still rich, dark, and full.

Our guests were arriving. People had come from far away to be with us during this hour of celebration. I stood at the entrance of the *yeshiva* to welcome our friends, rabbis from neighboring communities, and students who had left us to study elsewhere, some now rabbis with congregations of their own, others judges or community leaders. Meir was surrounded by them. I could hear him laughing, enjoying their stories. His grandson had been handed to him and he held the boy proudly in his arms. The little one peered over his grandfather's shoulder, eyes wide at the number of people who thronged to greet the great rabbi of Rothenberg.

———◆———

After my daughter Rachel's wedding to her beloved Binyamin ben Zuiskind, I picked up the threads of normal life again. Fifteen years passed as if in a blur. Much of them were spent quietly at home, but the world's great affairs—at least as they pertained to the Jews—had a way of infringing upon our simple happiness.

Chaya kept in touch with the Lincoln community through Bellaset, the daughter of Rabbi Berechiah de Nicole, whose wedding joy was ruined by the accusations, imprisonment, and hangings. Bellaset wrote to tell Chaya how seventy-nine more men were convicted of torturing and killing little Hugh. All were hung at the fairgrounds of Smithfield. Of the men imprisoned, only three were released. One was Bellaset's father, the chief rabbi of Lincoln, who received a royal pardon. After she received that letter, Chaya's mourning deepened and it was hard to rouse her from her sorrow. She spent much of her time alone with her infant, eating only because he fussed at her empty breast. To this day, I believe only Dafyid's particular brand of toddler mischief—for rarely have I seen a baby find more trouble through innate curiosity and pluck—kept Chaya from dying of grief.

Chaya remarried three years after our return from England. I made sure Meir chose a scholar from Rothenberg, for I had no intention of letting my darling leave me again. Her new husband, Moses Parnes, was a good man and she made him a good wife. The all-consuming love Chaya had felt for Avram was set aside, and the couple gave us four more grandchildren—another boy and three delightful little girls. Moses was a plodding type of fellow who served Meir as a *melamed*. He was probably best known in our little world for the story he would recount to the students about my husband.

"I don't know how it happened in a household with such notable housewives," he would say, "but Rabbi Meir once forgot to perform the ceremony of Eruv Tavshilin—to allow one to prepare a Shabbat meal on the eve of a holiday that fell on a Friday. And, as you know, you are not permitted by law to cook or prepare food for the Shabbat on a holiday."

"So what happened?" one of the little boys would prompt him as Moses sat back and waited for the boys to try to puzzle out this conundrum.

"What happened? Well, our beloved Rabbi Meir is a learned man who knows the Talmud like no other man before or since. So where other men would go hungry, he hunted through the volumes of Talmud to find the appropriate passages. And find them he did! Somehow—in ways that remain shrouded in mystery—the pot of food was prepared and placed on the hearth and the family ate their normal Shabbat meal the day after the holiday!"

Meir always hated when Moses told this story. The boys would creep up on my husband hesitatingly—for by now Meir was a revered but distant figure, preoccupied with writing responsa and teaching only the oldest and most talented of students—and they would ask him what passages he found that allowed him to set the Law aside. Sometimes, when he was in a good mood and feeling expansive, my harried husband would joke with the boys, challenging them to find the passages on their own. More often, worn down by constant appeals for his wisdom, he would frown at them, chide them for their foolishness, and send them scattering back to the classroom. He would look upon the backs of their retreating heels and sigh. But he refused to ask Moses to stop telling that story for fear he might insult his son-in-law. So he was annoyed by it anew with every incoming class of students.

My Meir had many reasons for his short temper. A year after Chaya's second wedding, Rabbi Yechiel's son was thrown into prison on a trumped-up charge. It took all of Yechiel's skill of persuasion and his relationship with the royals of France to arrange for the boy to be set free. It was time, Yechiel wrote my husband, to leave Christian Europe.

He and his family and followers set off for Acre, in Eretz Yisrael, where the rabbi established a new school. He asked Meir to join him, but Meir could not face the idea of leaving his home and the *yeshiva* that was doing so well. Meir argued, in fact, against too many Jews emigrating to Israel. Their belief that the mere act of living in the Holy Land would save their souls, he told me, smacked too much of Christian sentiments. It was that philosophy that had sent so many Crusaders to engage the Muslims, creating nothing more than strife and bloodshed. He would write that the only ones who should go to Eretz Yisrael were those who could support themselves and had the resources to lead a holy life in the impoverished, war-torn country.

In truth, I was glad when Meir refused, for the thought of living anywhere but Europe frightened me. But with Yechiel's departure, my husband became the primary person in all of Ashkenaz invited to deliberate on matters of Jewish law and ritual. The letters poured in and my beleaguered husband woke earlier and earlier in the mornings, generally leaving our warm bed while the stars still shone to keep up with the volume of requests. The last thing I would do every night was leave his thickest mantle on the chair near the fireplace in the study, so he could wrap himself in its sheltering warmth in the light of earliest dawn.

The letters were addressed with a variety of titles, brimming over with the honor they paid him. Meir shook his head at those that named him "Chief Rabbi of Germany" or "Father of All Rabbis," and while his heart swelled to be called *Me'ir ha-Golah*, or Light of the Exile, he felt this was a title reserved for the revered Rashi or for Rabbenu Gershon, whose departed souls we honored by it. But he did not object to the abbreviation *ha-Maharam*, our leader, the rabbi Rav Meir—a distinction granted to notable rabbis, one he felt he just might have earned.

While Meir toiled early and late, my family settled about me. My Zipura suffered the loss of her husband in Barcelona to a putrid throat complaint he contracted while sitting up late talking to a Moorish doctor. After she completed her period of mourning, she prevailed upon her reluctant brother, who was studying in the academy there, to accom-

pany her home. It was while they were safely en route that we heard of a
new disputation taking place in Barcelona. King James I of Majorca had
convened a court of pious monks and bishops, and as many nobles as
could find seats for themselves, and demanded that Suesskind's beloved
teacher, Rabbi Moses ben Nachman, defend the Talmud against the accusations of Pablo Christiani, yet another apostate Jew set on earth to
bedevil us. My relief that my children were spared such a spectacle as I
had witnessed in Paris knew no bounds. When Suesskind arrived, determined to turn right around and head back, I refused to let him go.

"But I am in the midst of my studies there, Mama!" the strapping
young man protested, towering over me in the glory of his nineteen
years. "I cannot just leave off!"

My handsome son, whose glossy blond toddler curls had given way
to thick, untidy brown hair that he would push back impatiently, glared
at me when I refused to listen. Cutting off his complaints, I turned to my
exhausted daughter, who was clasping her only child, a timid little girl
whose arms were tightly wrapped about her mother's neck.

"Fermosa, do you want a special treat?" I asked the child. "I bought
you something with which to welcome you to Rothenberg. It is called
a *Schneeball,* a pastry shaped like a snowball! You probably have never
seen snow in Barcelona. You'll see snow here this winter. It's like ice falling from the sky!"

The girl nuzzled deeper into her mother's neck. "It's all right, Mama,
she will eat it later," Zipura murmured, rocking the frightened child.
"She is just tired."

"So are you, darling," I said, resting my hand briefly on Zipura's dark
head. "Take her upstairs and the two of you should lie down and rest. I
will bring you both a basin of soup, for perhaps we should wait a day or
two before we introduce little Fermosa to the schoolroom dining hall. It
can be overwhelming if you are not used to it!"

With a thankful smile, Zipura hoisted the little girl upstairs. I turned
back to my son, who stood there, waiting impatiently for me to pay attention to him. "Mama!" he cried.

"Yes, son?" I answered. "By the way, there is some business I want you to attend to while you are still in Rothenberg. A particular young lady your father and I want you to meet."

Suesskind blushed. We heard no more of his desire to return to Barcelona, particularly after he met Hannah, who soon became his bride. But the day we learned that Rabbi Moses ben Nachman had presented such an outstanding defense that the king allowed the Jews of Spain to keep their Talmud and only erase those passages that were offensive to Christians, Suesskind tugged at my sleeve.

"Did you hear, Mama?" he asked me, coming across me in the hallway outside the classrooms one morning.

"About the disputation in Spain? Yes, your father told me when he received the letter. You must be overjoyed." I wanted to reach out and stroke my son's unruly brown hair but knew he might flinch away from my touch. Since he was married, he was less willing to allow me to touch him. It saddened me, but I understood it, having seen it happen before to other sons and mothers.

"Don't you agree that Nachmanides has no equal anywhere in Europe?" he asked eagerly.

"In all of Europe?" I asked, my eyes resting on Meir's study door.

"Not counting Papa, of course," my son hastened to say.

Now a married man, Suesskind was content to finish his studies with his father and the many learned men who graced our academy. The young couple soon gave us a grandson, little Getschlik, followed by a string of little girls and then another son.

Zipura, too, married again. She did not want a scholar for a husband, she told Meir, no more husbands for her who endangered their lives with too much studying and late-night discussions. Despite his disappointment, Meir asked the *shadchan* to find a wealthy merchant who was eager to marry the daughter of a renowned rabbi. Zipura moved to nearby Hülserhof and gave us yet more grandchildren—another two boys and a darling little girl who, unfortunately, did not live past her second year.

Rachel and her husband, Binyamin ben Zuiskind, lived a few blocks away from us in cramped lodgings that were all the struggling couple could afford. They were not blessed with children of their own, for, like my mother, Rachel suffered as child after child died in her womb. Rachel mourned as Abraham's Sarah must have mourned, with cries to heaven railing against life's unfairness. But one day my wise husband put an orphaned child into her arms. Rachel clutched the babe to her and felt barren no more.

Thus it was that all of my children, who I feared would live so far distant from me, actually ended up in Rothenberg or nearby. While I did not consider myself old, one glimpse in the mirror or at my reflection in the river Tauber made me realize that my life was closer to its end than its beginning. I was fifty-five years old now, and my children's children—all thirteen of them—sought me out and called me *Großmutter*, begging me, in the age-old tradition, to sneak them special treats from my kitchen hearth. But Meir was still writing "may his life be prolonged" when he inscribed his father's name as part of his own—Meir ben Baruch. As long as Bruria and Baruch lived, we could not feel as though our own lives were dwindling to an end.

If mine were the story of a princess or even of a great queen, this is where I would end it. Surrounded by my children and grandchildren, my husband honored by the entire Ashkenazi world for his wisdom and judgment, my home comfortable, and my neighbors kind. The stories Jeanne had told me would have ended here, with their singsong conclusions of "happily ever after."

But mine is not such a story. And starting from the age of fifty-five, happiness would begin to leach from my life as milk from potted cheese.

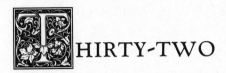

Thirty-Two

We decree that such Jews and Saracens of both sexes in every Christian province and at all times shall be marked off in the eyes of the public from other peoples through the character of their dress.
—CANON 68, FOURTH LATERAN COUNCIL, 1215

"I DON'T KNOW, SHIRA. WHAT DO YOU THINK?"

Meir turned to me. He was wearing the new hat, which I had sewn out of heavy yellow cloth stretched over a straw frame. It was cone shaped with a tall, peaked crown and a wide brim, topped by a round embellishment attached to a short, heavy cloth-covered stick. It sat unsteadily on top of his head, looking as though the least wind would knock it off.

"Does it fit?" I asked.

He turned to look again into the mirror he had borrowed from me. "Does it really look as strange as I think?"

"I've seen noblewomen wearing odder things—those triangular hats with filmy veils and two peaks. They call them butterflies. And the men with their sugar-sack hats . . . those tall ones that sit high on their heads, like logs. Or even peasant hoods with a high point and triangular scallops on the face. Try to think of this as just another type of hat. After all,"

I said, looking down at my sewing basket, which was filled to overflowing with yellow cloth, "everyone will be wearing them."

Meir shook his head, dislodging the hat. He removed it. Holding it in both hands, he glared at it. "We were doing fine without having to distinguish ourselves as Jews," he muttered. "Why are they forcing us to look like court jesters?"

The trouble started in Vienna in 1267, when the special Jew hat was first mandated. But the Rothenberg city council had just now decided to enforce it here. They called it the "horned hat," laughing that it was roomy enough for Jews to hide their horns. Looking at Meir now, I saw there would be no mistaking him as a Jew in the middle of a crowd. Despite what I said to reassure him, the hat looked ridiculous.

"How can I wear this on Shabbat?" he asked, putting the hat back on his head and staring gloomily in the glass. "If the wind knocks it off, what will I do?"

If the hat were blown off, he would have to stoop to pick it up, which was prohibited on Shabbat. I turned to my sewing basket.

"What if I sewed a strap so you can fasten it underneath your chin?" I asked. "Maybe something you tie or secure with a pin?"

He threw the hat at me, scowling. I said nothing, telling myself his annoyance was not with me but with the new law. I pursed my lips and picked up the hat, waiting. He thought for a long moment.

"Try it," he said finally, retiring from the room.

I sighed. Making the hat had taken me hours, working from a pattern the tailor in town created, based on a sketch drawn by the council in Breslau. The tailor couldn't possibly make a hat in time for every man in town, particularly not with our *yeshiva* and its nearly one hundred students. So we women had gathered for a lesson in plaiting the straw frames and rolling and stitching the complicated and ugly garment.

Frommet's hands hurt too much from what she called the old women's complaint to ply a needle. So she sat with her gnarled fingers in her lap and watched the tailor, suggesting how he might cut the cloth more economically. As we sat and stitched, our neighbor Trinlin, Chaya, and

Rachel gossiped about Zierele, a young woman who had married into the town a few years ago and who seemed marked out for ill fortune.

"They say she married at the full moon and that's why she's had such bad luck with her husband and family," said Trinlin. "Even the Gentiles know better than to do that."

"Everyone agrees that's why she lost her husband," said Rachel, eyeing the brim of the hat warily. She was trying to hem the cloth around the frame so it wouldn't unravel. "He left her with three children, none of whom were more than three at the time. That was two years ago. It was the middle child, the four-year-old, who wandered off into St. Jakobskirche."

"The church?" Chaya asked. "Father Franz is vicious when it comes to Jews. My neighbor, a Gentile but a good person for all that, says he reprimands her about her friendship with me every time she goes to church."

"He would separate us behind locked gates if he could," Frommet sighed. "Thank goodness not all Gentiles are like that."

"Yes, but this isn't the point," Trinlin said, impatient to discuss the source of Zierele's bad luck. "The latest trouble came when Zierele spoke German on the Shabbat instead of Hebrew."

Frommet shook her head at Trinlin's superstitions. "The child just left the house? Where was Zierele when he disappeared?"

"You always interrupt me—let me tell the story," Trinlin cried. "Zierele insisted on marrying at the full moon, clearly the act of a fool. Her husband decided she was too childlike to be a good wife unless he took charge. Someone told him to stomp on her foot when they were wed, because that would give him mastery over the household. Can you imagine? There you are on your wedding day, looking more beautiful than you've ever looked before, in front of your friends and family. And this man to whom you're handing your life—what does he do? He mortifies *and* hurts you by tromping on your foot!"

"I remember her weeping off in the corner," Frommet said musingly. "We were all upset for her. A bad omen for a wedding night."

Trinlin threw Frommet an annoyed glance, then ignored her. "The problem was, it robbed her of all good sense. Men don't realize when they sap a woman's will the kind of trouble it can cause. So she does something foolish, like speak in German during the Shabbat. I hear that's when she lost her best layer, the chicken that always laid two extra eggs every Friday morning. But even that's not enough misfortune for this poor soul. No, Frommet!" Trinlin said, flinging up a hand as Frommet opened her mouth again. "You be quiet and let me finish."

Frommet subsided, sinking back into her seat with a shrug and a laugh. I smiled quietly. How many times had I seen these two old friends snipe at each other, masking the affection they felt for each other? I was warmed at the thought of having spent so many years with such worthy women.

"So the husband dies, but the woman's left without common sense and the children, young as they are, take advantage. The oldest one is five now, and the next one four, and they're running around the town at all hours. Last week they sold their amulets and bought sweets with the pennies they earned."

"That's another bad omen," Rachel said, shaking her head and winking in my direction. I laughed inwardly. One of my girls' delights as they had grown and become women was listening to Trinlin's foolish stories. This one promised to be one of her best. We all settled down to listen, hands moving busily.

"So the four-year-old wakes up in the middle of the night and finds that without his amulet he's lost his shadow. He knows he would be cursed without it, so he goes off in search of it. He wanders all night. Toward morning, he sees the church and goes in to get warm. Maybe he thought his shadow made its way in there; who knows? Anyway, the priest is there, praying the dawn service, lauds, I think it's called. He sees the boy and takes him.

"Zierele wakes in the morning, becomes frantic at finding the boy missing, and goes out to look for him. She comes across dozens of people talking about this fatherless boy newly baptized at St. Jakobskirche and goes there to get her son back. But the priest won't let him go."

"Can the rabbi do nothing about it?" Frommet asked me. "I mean, aside from Trinlin's usual nonsense about losing shadows and chickens and marrying on the full moon, it does seem a shame that the priest stole the boy."

"Meir tried," I said. "He went and spoke with Father Franz. But the man had already shipped the child off to a monastery and said that he had been baptized and was now saved. Meir was terribly upset, but it happens all too often. And Zierele herself told me that it would be easier without the extra mouth to feed." I shook my head, my eyes on the hem I was stitching. "I didn't know Trinlin's story about Zierele's husband stomping her feet, but something certainly took that poor woman's wits. Her household is a shambles and the children are no better off than orphans. Not that I like the Church trying to steal our children!"

A bitter silence settled over us as we bent back to our sewing. As I grew older, I had hoped and prayed life would become easier for us Jews. My children and I had lived through so much—surely my grandchildren and their children might find it easier to observe God's commandments? But the opposite seemed true. Aside from the new regulations about the peaked hat, Meir had shown me a letter circulated by the famous churchman Aquinas, in which he wrote that Jews could not be treated as neighbors but should live in perpetual servitude. It was ideas such as these that gave clergymen like our Father Franz the boldness to steal and baptize our children or to come to our synagogues and preach sermons to us.

We ourselves had not been subject to a Christian service, but my father-in-law wrote that it had happened in Worms. The account of it stood on the table by our bed. As I reread it, the horror of it seeped into my soul.

The priest had just preached a sermon about the Jews' crucifying Jesus of Nazareth. A cry went up that the Jews should hear this sermon.

In minutes, one of the altar boys fetched a garrison of soldiers and the entire Christian congregation trooped toward the ancient stone synagogue.

The service was half-complete, each man possessed in his own world of murmured prayer, when the shadow of the cross fell over them. The priest stood in the doorway, soldiers at his back. The congregation drew back, frightened. The women shrieked and clutched their children to them. Baruch had been afraid that Bruria—old and sick though she was—might push forward and demand in her forthright fashion that the intruders depart. But the sight of men carrying pikes into the synagogue cowed even Bruria.

Behind the priest and the soldiers were dozens of the men and boys of Worms. They piled in, malicious intent on all their faces, eyes glinting in anticipation of the Jews' humiliation.

It was the sound of the cross that upset Baruch—the pounding of the stave of the heavy staff the priest carried as he made his way across the floor and up onto the *bimah*. Once there, he pounded it again, silencing the congregation's horrified and angry protests with the force of its slamming.

The priest pushed my father-in-law back with a fulminating eye. "I will preach the word of the Lord to you dog Jews."

A cheer rose from the spectators crowding the back of the synagogue. The priest smiled at them slyly and turned toward the stunned congregation to declaim: "I will show you the error of your ways. We will have conversions right here, right now. We will sprinkle the floor of this accursed spot with baptismal water, make holy what you have all made profane. We will not leave until we have preached the Word of God to you and made you see the errors you live by."

The sermon retold the crucifixion, piling guilt and shame upon the Jews. Baruch's elderly, shaky writing grew increasingly snarled with his agitation and I had to peer close to make out the last sentences. My eyesight is not what it used to be. "It is because we killed their god," my father-in-law wrote, "that they do not forgive us.

"Having seen the strong grip their enduring anger has on them," he added, "I wonder if they ever will."

It was something I had long contemplated, particularly after returning from the British Isles. There must be a way for both Christians and Jews to live together, peacefully, side by side, I thought, but as of yet, I had not found it. I shook my head, bending over my work again. My wandering thoughts had caused me to put down my needle and there wasn't time to waste. According to the city council, every Jewish male had to wear the hat by the end of the month.

———

In the days before the Passover holiday, we clean every stick of furniture, taking every item of clothing outside to shake it out in the fresh air. Our younger boys glory in the hunt for *chametz,* food made with leavening. I walk the hallways carefully, never knowing when a particularly enthusiastic youngster will come barreling around a corner, his cupped hands holding a crumb that he found in the bottom of his chest of clothing. The ritual of cleaning laid a balm upon my heart, breathing new hope that the harsh cold of winter and the grip of the Church upon our lives might lessen with the budding of new life.

Spring was slow to come in 1270. The harsh winter did not want to surrender to the lengthening days. Passover came early that year. We finished our spring cleaning shivering in the courtyard and more than one boy stopped to warm his hands over the fire we built to burn the *chametz.*

As we sat at the long tables bedecked in their pure white tablecloths, Passover platters shining before us, I allowed myself to feel relief that we had survived another winter. Unlike previous years, the community had lost only one boy this winter, Guta's son, who had died of an infection. While the mourning mother felt the loss keenly, she had several other children to console her. Now, bent back in the reclining position the Passover seder suggested, I listened as Suesskind's youngest son, all of three years old, lisped his way through the Four Questions. "Why is this night different?" he asked, and in my heart I answered: because we are all gathered here, under one roof, safe and sound—my children, my grand-children, my husband, and those of his students who did not make the long journey home for the holiday.

But in the days that followed, I discovered not everyone was safe. Messengers brought reports of blood libels in the towns of Weissenberg, Magdeburg, and Erfurt. Christians accused Jews of taking children and killing them, using their blood to make our *matzo,* the unleavened bread we eat during the holiday.

I recalled the appalled look on Father Anton's face as he described how the Jews of Lincoln had allegedly tasted young Hugh's blood, smacking their lips over its sweetness. They really believe these tales of terror, I thought, ice forming in the pit of my stomach. It was senseless to me that anyone could conceive of such horror for a religious purpose. But hundreds of Jews were massacred in their homes and synagogues because of these reports.

We did what we could to assuage the suffering. Meir and the other rabbis wrote letters of protest to the Pope and the emperor. We gathered food and clothing and dispatched it with our most trustworthy mes-sengers. We talked endlessly of how we would send the children away to protect them at the first inkling that the community was suspected. But we could not find a way to shield ourselves from harm.

Then, in Sinzig, when Jews gathered in their synagogue on Shabbat, the doors were chained and the synagogue burned to the ground. In my dreams, I heard the pounding on the exits as the congregation sought to escape, the wide eyes of the children clustered at the windows, the glass shattering but the bars holding them within. One night, the nightmares held me fast and refused to let me loose until the small hours of the morning. I woke in a cold sweat to find Meir lying next to me, looking at me worriedly.

"It was a bad dream?" he murmured. "You have been kicking and moaning half the night."

"Oh, Meir! What a nightmare!"

"If you tell me about it, it will fade," my husband said, reaching out with a caring hand to caress my graying head.

"It does not make much sense, but it was horrible, horrible," I said, shuddering. "Our house lifted up, spun around, and started down the street. We were trapped inside, running from room to room, trying to lean against the walls to stop it or steer it somehow."

"Shh," Meir said, pulling me back down so he could wrap his arms around me. He said nothing, but his look of compassion and his soft lips against my forehead soothed me.

I continued, "I looked for our children, I cried for Suesskind, Rachel, Chaya, Zipura . . . I couldn't find our children. I was frantic. Oh, Meir!"

He nestled me close, stroking my cheek. "Our children are safe, Shira. Their children are safe. Please God, may it remain so."

"It was so real!"

"Shh," he whispered into my hair. "It seemed real, but it wasn't. You're frightened by the reports of the killings. You've seen so much burning and blood yourself. So of course the news upsets you. I only wish . . ." His voice trailed off and a hard look settled on his face.

"You only wish?" I prompted him.

"Oh, my darling, if only I could protect our entire family. There must be a way. I must find a way."

I said nothing. I knew he could not safeguard us. No one could. The warmth of his arms calmed me, and I settled back to sleep. Even as I drifted off, however, I could feel him lying stiff beside me and wondered what he was thinking.

When I was younger, every day seemed an eternity. Summer afternoons stretched out, every second filled with the promise of an even longer one to follow. But now that I was growing older, the days spun past me, weaving themselves into months and then years so that one season melded into the other. I wondered once, to Meir, if it was the same for everyone, and he laughed and assured me he felt the same.

Frommet died and I mourned her passing as though she were my sister. I kept the shawl she had worn as a keepsake, storing it on the top of the chest that held my sheets. Every time I opened the heavy lid, the shawl reminded me of Frommet sitting in my kitchen, clutching it around her ample breasts. My stepmother passed away too, but Falaise was so distant that I did not learn of her death until nearly a year had elapsed. One of my half brothers finally wrote to me and my tears speckled the crackly parchment like phantoms of my memories of Mama Alyes.

My own passion for learning Torah and Talmud had returned, after years of setting it aside to tend to my family. My husband did not protest when Chaya and Rachel, their daughters, and some of their friends joined me around the table. We sat in the winter house, a set of smaller rooms where my family gathered and ate during the cold months to conserve our fuel. We studied together for only a few hours every week, but they were among the hours I enjoyed the most.

My grandsons were sent to distant cities to study, my granddaughters betrothed to scholars and merchants. I danced at their weddings and their *b'nai mitzvah,* my head spinning from the watered wine that was all my aged stomach could handle. My grandchildren, too, looked like small ghosts at times. In their upturned faces, I was forever seeing a feature or an expression that recalled someone who had come before— this one had Rachel's quick smile, that one Zipura's dreamy eye. I could see Suesskind's stubborn jaw in his sons, Meir's quick mind working in Chaya's granddaughters.

But amid the common round of life, bad news kept hounding us. When I thought back to my childhood, how the worst I had to worry about was the weight of the *rouelle* on my breast and the taunts from the town bullies, my heart sank as I realized how much more restricted we Jews had become. This feeling against the Jews was forming a noose about our necks. Soon after the massacres of the Jews in Germany, Chaya received a letter from one of her friends in Lincoln. The family had moved to London, and the woman wrote how town officials closed the main synagogue because the neighbors complained the prayers disturbed them. It was said the Jews' prayers had turned into evil fiends, battering the windows of good Christian folk, sneaking into open casements and causing all sorts of mischief. Banished from their synagogue, the congregation gathered at private homes to pray, Chaya's friend wrote, but even that did not placate the Christians. Finally, the bishop of London ordered the Jews to stop praying altogether.

"What shall we do, Chaya?" the young woman wrote. "Ask your father for us."

We shuddered to learn that more than a thousand Jews were massacred in Paris after another disputation, this one defended by Abraham ben Solomon of Dreux before King Philip, the French ruler they nicknamed "the Bold." The accounts were sketchy at best. The Franciscans, the archbishop of Paris, and other Church dignitaries were apparently swayed by Pablo Christiani's preaching to examine, yet again, the writings and teachings of the Jews. According to a French Jew who visited Rothenberg a year or so later, the Jews were offered a choice—to convert or to be killed. Not one Jew, our visitor said proudly, took the cross as a way to escape death. The bodies were piled high in the courtyards of Paris, he told an avid audience. I couldn't bear his graphic description of the corpses rotting in the sun. I fled the room for my garden, where I sat reflecting on my sweet memories of my early married life in Paris.

In our own country, the nobles elected Rudolph of Hapsburg as our king. We had lived for just over twenty years without a king, while the small baronies and counties of Germany and Austria—the old Holy Roman Empire—fought one another over who would have the largest portion at the table. I did not follow the intricate politics, but Meir worried about the new king. He gained the Pope's blessing, Meir noted drearily, by promising to mount a Crusade. We Jews know what Crusades can lead to.

But even more important than watching the new king take the throne and try to unite the squabbling German states was a death in Worms. For Baruch, Meir's long-lived father, finally passed away.

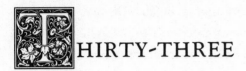

THIRTY-THREE

The Lord gave and the Lord has taken away;
may the name of the Lord be praised.

—JOB 1:21

WE ARRIVED IN WORMS AT SUNSET. I expected to find Bruria prostrate and despairing, but the doughty old woman was sitting up in her solar, waiting for us in her favorite high-backed wooden chair. Meir kissed her, the girls and Suesskind kissed her, but when I bent to do so, she batted me away with a quavering hand.

"You never loved either one of us," she said. "Admit it."

I reared back, alarmed. "I am sorry for your loss—Meir loved his father so much," I ventured.

The old woman hunched her bony shoulders. Her girth had fallen away over the years and her skin sagged over her body as though it missed the padding of flesh. "Meir had reason to love Baruch, for no son ever had a better father. He should have stayed here, in Worms, the way you've forced your children to live in Rothenberg or close by. But no, because of you, Meir lived in Paris and Rothenberg. Baruch always regretted his son chose to live so far away. So don't pretend to mourn him."

I looked over at Meir, my cheeks burning as though they had been slapped. My husband shook his head. "*Mütti*, you are not making sense," he told her, crouching down beside her chair so that his eyes were on the same level as hers. "Shira has been a good wife to me, a good daughter to you and to *Vater*. She mourns his death as much as anyone."

"I hate her," my mother-in-law muttered. "I've always hated her. And now that Baruch is dead, no one can stop me from saying it."

Bitter words rose to my lips. Remembering the circumstances, I bit them back.

"Shira, go downstairs," Meir said. "Children, go with her. I wish to speak with my mother alone."

I was halfway down the stairs when tears choked me. Chaya and Zipura tried to comfort me. Suesskind and Rachel went downstairs, where the rest of the family was waiting. There was Meir's brother, Abraham, and his family, who had settled in Worms to be close to Baruch. And Dolza, his sister, whose husband, Yoel ben Uri, had died several years ago. Several of Meir's cousins and uncles and other relatives had gathered for the funeral, all of them sitting around now, exchanging family news in muted tones as they waited for us to join them. Suesskind and Rachel were greeted with a chorus of blessings. By immediately launching into questions about the rest of the family, my two youngest children diverted attention from me.

The two older girls whisked me past the large room to the smaller quarters where Meir and I would sleep that night. I sat down on the edge of the bed, wiping away my tears.

"Mama?" asked Chaya after a long, strained moment while both girls looked everywhere but at me. "Why does *Großmutter* say such things to you?"

"Oh, darling," I sighed. "Your *großmutter* is half-right. I loved your grandfather almost as much as if he were my own father, but I never, ever liked Bruria." I glanced at the girls, who settled themselves on either side of me on the bed. Their composed faces showed me this was not a surprise to them. I hastened to add, "I had good reason, though. She disliked me before we ever met and tried to prevent my marriage to your father."

"Because of Nicholas Donin?" Zipura asked, studying the floor at my feet.

I felt a tingling of shock in my limbs that climbed up my spine into the base of my neck. I looked at my daughter. My eyebrows rose in surprise.

"When I lived in Barcelona, someone who had grown up in Paris told me that he was once in love with you."

"Nicholas Donin? The apostate?" said Chaya, half-horrified, half-fascinated. "The one who burned the Talmud in Paris?"

"I don't know how much you remember," I replied. "Do you recall I went to witness the disputation and was away for a few days?"

"Yes . . . ," said Chaya slowly, her finger tracing the pattern of the heavy quilt cover on my bed. "But I always thought that was because *Grandpère* had to testify and you went to the palace to be with him."

"Donin asked the queen to force me to attend," I said. "He was a student at my father's *yeshiva* when he asked me to marry him. I refused, but he . . . he remembered me." I took a deep breath. I felt awkward discussing these long-buried memories with my daughters. "He saw me in Paris once, the very day I was going shopping for my wedding feast with your *großmutter*. She saw us together and was horrified. She was unsure about me before . . . afterward, she never considered me fit to marry her son. Your *großvater* convinced her to let the marriage go forward. But she and I were never—"

Zipura put out a hand and clutched my forearm. "Mama?" she interrupted. "What ever became of Nicholas Donin?"

"Shira," said Meir at the door. "My mother wants to apologize to you."

Aghast, I glanced at Meir's stony face. His eyes opened wide for one hurt moment, then flickered shut. Zipura, sensing the tension between us, released my arm.

"Oh, Meir, it's a bad idea," I said, ducking my head down and glancing at him from under half-veiled eyelids. "Let her be."

Meir looked at me coldly. "I have not had an easy time convincing her that she owes you this apology, wife," he said. "Please do as I ask."

I rose, my limbs stiff both from the long carriage journey and from my unwillingness. "I'll go, but it's unwise, Meir. She's only saying what is in her heart. Her words don't hurt me anymore. And her apology won't be sincere."

"Let her tell you she is sorry anyway. No one will treat my wife as she just did," Meir insisted.

I moved past the girls as he turned away. "I will be downstairs with my family," he said. "Girls, come with me. Shira, please don't be long."

I passed by the large room where the family was gathered and made my way slowly up the stairs. But my daughter's question echoed in my brain.

What had become of Nicholas Donin?

———•———

The curse of Eve, our mother who wanted to know too much, sat heavily upon me on the journey home. I had stopped bleeding several years ago, but now, at sixty, my courses visited me one last time. It was as though my body wished to remind me of those days right after my wedding when I was denied my husband's touch. I sat in the corner of the carriage, as far from my grieving husband as I could, hunched over with cramps.

In her usual manner, Bruria had snapped out an apology to me and spent the rest of the mourning period ignoring me. I was content enough and left Worms knowing we would probably never see each other again. My husband, as stunned as I at the news of my bleeding, wondered aloud if this foretold something more dire. I shook my head.

"I am well, husband—I would know if my body were festering in some way. It is poorly timed, however. I wish I could console you with more than just words."

Meir smiled sadly as he leaned back against the cushions of the jolting carriage seat. We saw fertile fields and lovely green valleys through the small carriage window as we traveled past. "Thank you, Shira. It is hard not to be able to touch you, but perhaps God is forcing chasteness upon me as I mourn."

"You loved your father."

"I did. Who would not? He was a good man, a wise man. But what of you, Shira? Do you truly hate my mother, as she insists? I know you had no ill feelings toward my father."

I shrugged. "I have never liked your mother, but the feeling was— is—mutual. We both love the same man too much, perhaps."

Meir sighed, turning away from me. "At the next stop, I'll get onto the box with the coachman," he said, "so you don't have to huddle in that corner over there. We'll be home in two days."

We had traveled from Rothenberg with the children, but they had to leave several days earlier. We spent considerably more than the usual seven days of mourning in Worms. Meir wanted to tie up his father's affairs and settle his mother into a new, smaller home, where she would be cared for by a capable woman. Our carriage—a luxury we could easily afford, for we were wealthy as a result of our business dealings and the income from the *yeshiva* and synagogue—had made the journey back and forth to Rothenberg twice already.

Twisted by severe cramps, I remembered again how Eve wanted to know too much. She was cursed for her curiosity by God, and we, her daughters, suffer monthly as a result. As I was pondering this, the question I myself was curious about came out of my mouth. "Meir? What ever happened to Nicholas Donin?"

Meir looked over at me, past the bundles we had placed between us as a barrier. The look on his face was one of reserved resignation. "I wondered when you would realize I might know," he said. "Why did Zipura ask you about him, anyway?"

"Someone in Barcelona told her about Donin's ... *attentions* to me," I faltered. "She asked if he was the cause of your mother's dislike of me."

"It was a long time ago, you and Donin. You'd think I would have learned to approach the subject with less jealousy, wouldn't you?"

"Are you still jealous?" I asked, staring at my husband curiously, my heart pounding painfully in my chest.

"I am, Shira. What do you think of that?" His mouth twitched as though the confession half amused and half annoyed him.

"I don't know quite what to think," I said, trying to read him. It was true that I had always resented his lack of faith in my loyalty to him, that whenever Donin's name was uttered Meir had grown hard and cold to me. "It is not because you don't trust me, is it?"

"Have you ever done anything that would make me not trust you?" he asked, calm eyes studying my face.

I thought back to that summer afternoon so long ago in the charity hut, which remained unconfessed these many years. For a moment, I toyed with the idea of telling him about it. But better sense made me put that memory aside.

"I never have," I told him, and meant it.

"Then my jealousy must stem from me, not you," he said, looking down at his hands, which he held clasped in his lap. "And if you weren't afflicted, my dear one, I'd show you how much I have always loved you."

I sat back, thrilled by the passion in his deep voice. We may be old, I thought, and perhaps the children would be scandalized to think we feel so ardently about each other. But it was an abiding pleasure of my life that my husband remained enamored of me.

Our eyes met. The current of air that could always hold us entwined moved between us. With obvious effort, Meir looked away.

"Nicholas Donin," he said distastefully. "The man was not fortunate in life. His triumph over us in the market square in Paris was undoubtedly its high point. I understand he is embroiled in a controversy with the Franciscan order he joined—for some pamphlet he wrote opposing a decision of Pope Nicholas's. And his poor Italian wife finally obtained a divorce from him—she's been trying to get one for years. That's what I know. It does not seem like the man was ever intended for a quiet life. You should be glad your destiny was not tied with his."

I shrugged. "I called him an insect to his face, you know, and I hate him for what he did to us in Paris—and before Paris. Do you hate that I still wonder if by marrying him I might have changed the course of his life?"

"Yes," said Meir, looking out of the carriage window as we slowed to stop and change the horses at an inn yard. "I have to admit that I do."

THIRTY-FOUR

The person and property of the Jews as a group, and of every Jew
as an individual, belong to the sovereign and most particularly to
the monarch's treasury by rights of servi camerae.

—RUDOLPH I

THE NUMBERS OF JEWS KILLED for ritual murder charges kept
rising. There were ten in Mainz, twenty-six in Bacharach, sixteen in
Brüekerhausen. Every time we heard of more Jews accused, attacked,
and killed, we wondered how safe we were.

Nor was the blood libel the only bludgeon used against us. Following the interregnum—our kingless years—Rudolph levied heavy taxes
on us, heavier than most could bear. Faced with bankruptcy and fearing
more blood libels, hundreds of Jews began to leave their homes. They
would slip away in the night, abandoning homes and belongings, taking
only what they could carry, hoping to find somewhere more hospitable
to live. Meir and I talked about it late into the nights. Where could they
all go? Where would we go if we tried to leave?

In Paris, Philip the Bold once again ruled against Jews owning volumes of the Talmud and forbade synagogue repairs. In England, the

archbishop of Canterbury closed synagogues throughout the entire land. In Spain, the Jews were subjected to sermons preached over and over again specifically to convert them. The Jews who failed to surrender to Christ were put to the sword. Their blood flowed across the sunny cobbles of Madrid and Barcelona. The Europe we had known, our home for centuries, was becoming less and less welcoming.

Many of the refugees fled east, to the far reaches of Poland and the steppes of Russia. Others sought refuge in the Islamic countries. Still others—like Yechiel so many years ago—tried to find homes in the land all our hearts hungered for, in Israel.

One night we lay in our soft bed together, Meir and I, talking into the small hours. As the sun glimmered just below the horizon, both of us searched for excuses to stay.

"The trip would kill us both," I argued, nestling my head into my husband's chest.

"We are old but the children are not. Perhaps the children should go," he said, caressing my shoulder.

"I could not bear to lose them . . ."

"But if it meant their lives?" Meir retorted. "If they were to die here, if one day we were to wake up and find ourselves accused of murdering some child in order to make our *matzo*? You were in Lincoln when such an event happened. You know how it is the matter of an instant, how our lives are nothing more than guttering candles that can be blown out at any time."

"I cannot believe that," I murmured. "If I were to think that way, I could not live with it."

"We've never lived that way before," my husband agreed, the sigh that escaped his lips rising from the depths of his soul. "We lived through the burning in Paris. You pulled me from despair, making me realize I had to live, to help the world bear the pain of losing the Talmud. You helped our daughter recover from the loss of her husband, you raised our children and their children to respect our laws and live lives of honor and meaning. We have lived without fear or despair because of you, my brave wife. Our fortitude is—as the proverb states—the fruit of your hands, Shira."

I glowed for a minute at his praise but then felt sadness descend upon me again. "Except in dreams," I said bitterly. "I cannot prevent the dread in my dreams."

"Our dreams are one thing, our waking hours another." Meir was firm. "Let us talk about what we can do. The question is this: do we stay or leave?"

"Let me think about it," I begged. "I need time."

I walked through my house the next day just after sunset. Through the long front windows, the summer sky seemed to dip close to me, wrapping me in surprise at the stars poking through wispy clouds. I remembered a poem Meir had written once to amuse our young children, about the angels who watched over us. Meir's angels ran laughing from heaven's *mikveh*, damp footsteps stamped in sunset and summer rain, leaving tracks behind as twinkling stars. Where is that poem? I wondered. Undoubtedly it was buried amid the thousands of pages my husband had written over the years.

My daughters were busy clearing the dinner dishes from the long tables in the dining hall. We had spent so many happy hours in that room, every Shabbat punctuated by song and storytelling, every evening bringing its new discoveries to the young students, who peppered their beloved teacher with questions.

In a back room, Meir chanted from the Torah, spending some time with the youngest students preparing for their *bar mitzvah*. His voice, still melodious even while its richest resonance was lost to the years, rang out and helped their timid throats find the right pitch, the appropriate fervor, showing them how to climb up and down the scales of devotion.

I walked up the hallway and entered Meir's study. This was his sanctum. In the back of the room were the long tables where scribes would sit in careful postures, dipping their quills in the ink I prepared from gallnuts and vinegar. How often had I seen my husband slip into this study when he knew he could be alone? If I followed him, I knew I would see him pick out a volume of Talmud and cradle it in his arms. He would breathe in the sweet dust of its heavy bindings, remembering, as he and I would always remember, that summer afternoon in Paris.

How could we leave all this? The window stood open to catch the evening breeze and I could hear the faint rushing of the Tauber River beneath us. Just as I had played in the flax fields of Falaise, my children and grandchildren had camped out on the banks of the Tauber, dabbling their small feet on warm days, sailing bark boats that would disappear around the bend of the river as they chased them, yelling in delight.

We could not go, I decided. I was surprised to learn that Rothenberg was as much a home to me as Falaise or Paris had ever been, but it was so. And, it being so, I could not leave for the cold snowy plains of Poland or the windswept desert sands of Jerusalem. But before I could tell Meir that I had decided we must stay, we received news that changed everything.

———

The letter was sent by King Rudolph to the officials and burghers of Mainz, Speyer, Worms, Oppenheim, and the towns of the Wetterau. Meir received a copy of it from the grandson of Rabbi Judah ha-Kohen of Mainz, a distant cousin. Judah's grandson was one of the few Jews left in that city, for many had already fled.

As Meir slit open the seals that secured the letter, he was distracted by a sudden fight between two of the students. The shouts and catcalls could be heard throughout the house. We ran outside to find a small knot of boys egging on two of their number. They taunted them, trying to goad one into throwing the first punch. Luckily Meir did not need to intervene, for Binyamin was nearby. My son-in-law shouldered his way through the excited crowd and stopped the assailants.

My husband took both boys to one side to make them see reason. They were arguing about foolishness, about who had the better room in the *yeshiva*. They refused to stop spitting insults at each other, so Meir sent them both to their rooms, telling them they could not leave until they apologized to each other and to the entire *yeshiva* for disturbing the peace.

"It confounds me, sometimes, running a school," Meir said in disgust, returning to the stack of letters. He picked up his relative's letter again, standing in the cool breeze that came through the open window.

"They are just boys who have not yet lost their wildness," I said, looking up at him from my whitework. My eyesight no longer let me stitch the intricate embroidery I used to enjoy, but I could still do the rough hemming and sewing, leaving the delicate work for either Chaya or Rachel to complete for me.

But then I saw the look on his face and dropped the shirt I was making. "Meir, what is it?" I asked, pushing my chair back in haste and rising as quickly as my old woman's body allowed.

His entire frame shook as though he were in the grip of a tremendous anger. His eyes were like two black opals, shining dangerously in his white face, a flush of fury sitting high upon his cheekbones. His lips were drawn tight, his snowy beard twitching. I had seen Meir angry before. I had seen him in the depths of complete despair and frustrated beyond endurance. But I had never seen such an expression of utter fury on his face before.

He thrust the letter at me, speechless. I snatched it from him and read.

> . . . *since the person and property of the Jews as a group, and of every Jew as an individual, belong to the sovereign and most particularly to the monarch's treasury by rights of* servi camerae, *and since so many Jewish residents of your towns have chosen to flee beyond the sea without obtaining the king's permission for such a step, it is fitting and proper that the sovereign should appropriate the property these disloyal Jews have left behind. I hereby appoint the archbishop of Mainz and Count Eberhard of Katzenellenbogen to take possession of and to manage this property.*

In a note attached to the copy of the letter, Meir's cousin wrote:

> ... *the archbishop has already taken possession of some forty-*
> *five houses abandoned by our community and has stated in no*
> *uncertain terms that no Jews still living in Mainz are allowed to*
> *leave their homes. I fear they have set a guard upon us to ensure*
> *that we remain here. I urge you to leave Germany before Roth-*
> *enberg comes under similar guard, for living under these circum-*
> *stances is intolerable.*

I looked at my husband again. The grip of his wrath had lessened somewhat, but I could tell it would still be dangerous to speak unwisely to him. I feared for his heart. He was old and the shock was severe. So I said nothing, watching him breathe deeply of the fresh air wafting through the window, waiting as he strove to control his indignation and humiliation.

Finally, he spoke. His voice was quiet and even. "I need to write some letters, Shira. Can you fetch Suesskind and Binyamin and whomever else is available?"

"I will, husband, but you must talk to me first. What does *servi camerae* mean?"

He paced up and down the length of the room, his trembling fingers clasped tightly behind his back. "It is Latin. It means 'serfs of the treasury.' It means that we are nothing more than slaves to Rudolph, the same as the serfs who farm his land and raise his sheep and pigs and cows for him. But unlike them, what we raise—what Jews have always raised for the nobles who sought to bind them to them . . ."

"Money," I said, the word striking me like a blow. "He wants our money."

"He wants to suck us dry before letting the Church kill us," my husband said. "But I am not his serf and I will not submit to this. I am what I have ever been—a free man who was exiled from his homeland but who will not give up the rights of the freeholder. I am at liberty to come and go as I like and I am no man's serf. Not the archbishop's, not the baron's, not even that of King Rudolph of Hapsburg!" Meir stopped his pacing to grip my shoulders, hurting me a little in his careless vehemence. "Listen to me, Shira. I have sworn no oath of fealty. I am freer than a knight who binds himself to a lord or a king. My soul may be accursed in the eyes of their church but my body remains my own to dispose of as I please. And I please to leave Germany and to go where no man tries to imprison me by calling me serf!"

I reached up and touched his gnarled hands. I remembered the boy who had stood beside me in the snow. I could see the boy in the old man's eyes. I could see the fire and passion of my newly wed husband there, too. "I will fetch Suesskind and the others, Meir, and then I will begin what preparations I can."

"We will not be able to take much, Shira. It will be like leaving Egypt, when we couldn't wait long enough for the dough to rise. But if we are going to leave, we will all need to leave together, taking anyone who wishes to go with us. Anyone who is left behind . . ."

He didn't need to finish his sentence.

———◆———

It took us two weeks to prepare. They were weeks of whispered conferences, of glancing about to watch for spies. We debated where we should go. A group wanted to head east, toward Poland and Russia. Suesskind was one of their number and for a while my heart stood still, thinking that he might actually leave us, that I might never see my sweet child again. But in the end, his duty to his father prevailed.

Meir wanted to go to Israel. He reread Yechiel's letters, his accounts of how he had established a *yeshiva* in Acre. A final letter from Yechiel's son reported his father's death and how his sacred bones were interred in a graveyard on Mount Carmel. "This," Meir said to a sea of nodding men, the letter rustling in his hand, "is how a holy man should live at the end of his life."

He found me harder to convince. Poland and Russia sounded closer

to me, more familiar than the rocky, forbidding climes of Israel, torn
between the warring armies of the Crusaders and the turbaned Muslims. To help convince me, Meir brought out our much-thumbed copy
of Yehuda ha-Levi's verse and read to me the same poem I had once read
to him:

My heart is in the East, and I am at the ends of the West;
How can I taste what I eat and how could
it be pleasing to me?
How shall I render my vows and my bonds, while yet
Zion lies beneath the fetter of Edom, and I am
in the chains of Arabia?
It would be easy for me to leave all the bounty of Spain—
As it is precious for me to behold the dust
of the desolate sanctuary.

Slowly, for I could not do so quickly any longer, I walked through
Rothenberg early in the first week. I took note of the fortifications surrounding the city, the guard towers that Zipura had pointed out the
first day we had moved to the town. "They guard us from other knights,
other armies," my beloved husband had told the worried child, adding,
"That can't be bad." We had no idea then that it *was* a bad thing, I pondered, watching the thoughtless, bored young guards who were looking
for maidens to call out to and saw only a weeping old woman they could
safely ignore.

"'If I forget thee, O Jerusalem,'" I murmured under my breath, feeling the heavy, sweet sway of the words work their magic in me. By the
time I returned home, I was resolved to help my husband attain this one
last desire. We would live free in Jerusalem.

HIRTY-FIVE

On that day when my soul longed for the place of assembly,
I found nevertheless that a dread of departure seized a hold of me.
—YEHUDA HA-LEVI

THE PLAN WAS TO FIND a legitimate excuse to escape past the guard towers. Then we would travel, by both day and night, through various routes across the Alps into Italy. We would pretend to be Christian pilgrims, making our way to Rome to visit the holy city of the Pope. But our actual destination was the fabled city of Venice, where we could hire a boat to take us across the Mediterranean Ocean to the white sandy shores of Israel.

Pretending to be pilgrims was not a simple matter. None of us knew what was required. After days of debating back and forth, and almost abandoning the idea as not practical, Chaya came to Meir and me.

"My friend Gertrudis can help us, Papa," she said. "Her son made a pilgrimage several years ago. She still has the clothes he wore."

Meir and I looked at each other, alarm in both our faces. Gertrudis was Chaya's Christian friend and neighbor.

"Will she not betray us?" Meir asked. "She has a duty to her priests and her faith, just as you do."

"Not Gertrudis," insisted Chaya. "We have spent hours discussing such matters. You can trust her."

"If we can successfully pretend to be pilgrims, fewer people will question why such a large group is traveling abroad," I mused. "Christians live and die in one spot. Unless you are noble, or have a calling like Brother Anton, or are on pilgrimage, Christians who move about are instantly suspected of wrongdoing."

"Which are exactly the confines that Rudolph wants to impose on us," sighed Meir. "All right, Chaya. We'll have to take a chance. We'll talk to your friend."

The next evening, Chaya and Gertrudis slipped through the back door. Gertrudis was a red-cheeked, stout woman. Her flashing black eyes looked about eagerly, taking in every detail of our lives. We met with her in a windowless inner room. After greeting us, she put a bundle down on the table and opened it.

"This is what my son wore when he went on pilgrimage to Rome. If you wear clothes similar to this and carry a heavy stave, the authorities will automatically assume you are pilgrims," she said, pulling out a soft brown tunic and holding it up.

The clothes were quite simple. The long tunic was called a sclavein. Gertrudis told us that it could be brown or blue. A heavy pouch, pulled tight by a drawstring, was all the pilgrim was allowed to wear so he could carry his belongings. "If you have to refer to the pouch, call it a scrip," she said. Gertrudis couldn't bring us the stave, but she brought a sketch of what it looked like—a tall pole, taller than the person carrying it, topped with a round knob of wood or metal. Both staff and scrip were blessed by priests before the pilgrim set out on his or her journey—the scrip representing the poverty the pilgrim is supposed to embrace and the staff protecting him from the thieves and wolves often encountered on the way. I swallowed hard when Gertrudis talked about the wolves. I had remembered the threat of men on the road but had forgotten about the beasts.

"Is there not a hat?" Meir asked. "I've seen pilgrims wearing hats. And we Jews are enjoined to keep our heads covered."

"The pilgrim's wide-brimmed hat is a new fashion, Rabbi. My son did not wear one, but I have a neighbor who did. I can bring it tomorrow night. I'll ask her to borrow it because . . . because a friend is going on a pilgrimage." She let one hand linger on the bundle as if she were bidding it farewell, then pushed it toward us and turned away.

"Why are you doing this?" Meir asked. I was startled at the raw suspicion in his voice. "Your king wishes us to remain in Rothenberg, to deny us our right to move freely from country to country. Your priests would call you damned for what you do. Why are you helping us?"

Gertrudis grinned, not at all awed by his deep tones. "Kings, priests—they're all men, Rabbi. They call all women damned for something one woman did eons ago. I did not eat the apple myself, but I am supposed to be nothing more than some man's possession because Eve did. The priests think only two types of women exist—saint and sinner. I'm both—and neither. I am no man's possession, either."

Chaya and I looked at Gertrudis in open admiration. I could see Meir growing even more uncomfortable. He said nothing to contradict Gertrudis, however; he just thanked her for her help. He knew our safety depended on this fiery woman's goodwill.

With the clothes Gertrudis left behind, the picture of the stave, and the wide-brimmed hat she brought the next night, we were able to outfit our entire party in appropriate clothing. She told us that women wore a simple dress rather than the tunic. In addition, men and women both draped a mantle about their shoulders, which could be used as a cloak in cold weather and as bedclothes while sleeping on the road.

———

We all had to leave the same night, but we would choke the roadway and arouse suspicion if we all took the same route. So we planned three routes to the same spot. Meir's party was to travel through the cities of Munich and Salzburg into Italy. Suesskind's group would take a more circuitous route through Zurich, journeying through the Swiss canons as they traversed the Alps. Our third party would travel through the

Austrian section of the German Empire, making the crossing into the kingdom of Hungary and traveling from there to Italy. We would meet at the foot of the mountains, in the small town of Goerz, which bordered Slovenia and was part of the county of Gorizia. There, we thought, it should be safe for us to rest for a few days before completing the last lap of our journey to Venice.

I woke before dawn on that last morning. Meir was sitting up in bed beside me, his eyes fixed on the comforts of our solar. He caught me looking at him and laughed.

"For a man who is supposed to live for spiritual things, I will miss the luxuries you've surrounded me with," he said, putting an affectionate arm around my shoulders. "At least you will always be with me."

"And you with me," I said, nestling in his arms. My breath flowed faster as he stooped to kiss my shoulders, dipping lower to my breasts. He picked his head up and kissed me full on the lips.

"Shall we?" he murmured, his hands reaching for my hips. "It is still early."

I know the thought of passion in an elderly couple makes the young wince. As our bodies wrinkle and our hair grows white, our children think other parts of us wither and die, like unplucked fruit on the vine. But just as raisins taste even sweeter than grapes, our years of knowing each other's bodies helped us toward a tender climax. Our lovemaking may have been less frenzied than when we were young, but it was no less ardent.

When we were done, I fetched a basin of water and a soft cloth. We washed our hands and prayed. Then I took the cloth and dipped it in the water, wringing it out. I rubbed our bodies with it, making our pale flesh brighten as I cleaned away the residue of our lovemaking. We nuzzled briefly under the covers before reluctantly rising.

Making a final circuit through my house, running a hand over books, tabletops, candlestick holders, and all the other familiar household objects I would ever carry in my mind's eye, I could not help the tears from gathering. I recalled how Meir and the girls walked through that first day in Rothenberg, counting the rooms. This had been my home for more years than any other. Falaise might have been the home of my childhood and Paris the romantic and then tragic abode of my heart, but "Rothenberg" would be the place I would name whenever someone asked where I was from.

"Shira," Meir said, "it's time to go."

We walked together, hand in hand, to the carriage that would carry us for the first leg of our journey, which we would abandon after we transformed ourselves into pilgrims. We climbed in. Chaya and Zipura and their husbands were there already; we were to collect Rachel on the way. I gave both daughters a hug, lingering longest with Zipura.

"I'm glad you are coming with us," I whispered in her ear. "I was afraid you would not."

Zipura's lips pursed as she nodded toward Amnon, her husband, who was looking sourly out the window of the carriage. "He still thinks this is a bad idea, Mama," she murmured. "But Suesskind visited last night and told him what it would be like to be the only Jew left in the area. Amnon's not willing to face the torture chamber."

I shuddered. "No one should be." I patted her hand. "God willing, no one will have to."

Suesskind was traveling separately, leading the party taking the Zurich route. While I feared what could happen to him so far from us, I understood why it needed to be so. Meir had wanted Rachel's Binyamin to lead the third party, but I put my foot down.

"The girls travel with us or I don't go," I insisted.

The carriage pulled up at Rachel's door. She and Binyamin entered, along with her adopted son, Hirsch, and his wife and young child. It was a tight fit with all of us and I took the child I considered another great-grandson on my lap. Most of my other grandchildren no longer lived in Rothenberg, but Zipura's Gutleben and his family would join us on the road. Some of the grandchildren would meet us in Goerz. Others would remain in their own homes. My heart ached to think how the king's orders were breaking my family apart.

We pulled up at the gates of the city. Meir and I exchanged a glance. "Now we see," he murmured, "if *ha-Shem* wishes us to leave or not."

The guard's face appeared in the small window. "Going visiting? A fine day for it."

"It is, indeed," agreed Binyamin, forcing a hearty laugh.

"Well, off you go then." He waved us on.

The cobblestones rumbled beneath us as we drove under the stone gates and past the ramparts. I looked out the window as long as I could, watching the town's cathedral spire disappear beyond the horizon. Then I turned back around, facing my family. Rothenberg was in our past now, and our future—and the road—lay ahead.

HIRTY-SIX

Many of them will stumble; they will fall and be broken,
they will be snared and captured.
—ISAIAH 8:15

MY HEART ROSE AS THE RAMPARTS OF GOERZ, the town where we would meet the rest of our party, came into view. The Alps had been the part of the trip that frightened my husband and the other men most, because of the toll they knew the mountains would take on our party. Tempers had frayed as we made our way up the steep ravines and through the narrow passes, as cold seeped into our thin clothing and through the holes in our worn shoes. But none of the men had anticipated the effect the sheer beauty of the mountains would have on us all. Rounding a corner, we would break off from speech to marvel at God's grandeur. Before us were His mountain peaks, stretching as far as the eye could see, covered in a dusting of snow and rock, crags reaching up into the wide expanse of blue sky, summits often crowned with a soft covering of cloud.

I had expected the passage to be all snow and ice, but there were hollows in the mountains where meadows of blue and yellow and red wildflowers delighted us. Birds we had never seen before flew there and we saw small, mystical creatures that Noah must have taken on his ark but that were not numbered among the animals listed in the book of Genesis. We slept at night under skies that twinkled with thousands of stars, next to springs of the coldest, purest water known to man.

Even so, all we felt was relief as we made our way down the other side of the alpine pass. God watched over us, and we had not lost a single member of the party, though several of us were coughing and sick from sleeping out in the cold. But we hoped a night or two in an inn, sleeping in an actual bed—or, at least, a straw pallet—would work wonders for us all. We could not sing together as we strolled down the mountains to the small hills of Goerz, for our songs would betray us. But there was music in our hearts.

After weeks of nature's isolation, the city seemed packed and alive as we walked through the guard towers. Our pilgrim uniforms gave us instant access. "Ho!" said the guard genially. "You pick a fortunate week to stop in our small town, pilgrims. His Eminence the bishop of Basel is expected. He is on his way home from a trip to the Holy Father and stops here to pray in our church. You'll join us for worship."

We nodded and smiled, knowing we would avoid entering the church unless forced to.

The guard grinned back at us. "Pilgrims usually lodge in the Pilgar Inn, near the northwest side of town. Anyone can direct you."

We thanked him and made our way into the city. After the rocks and dirt of the mountains, the stones of the streets beneath our feet felt oddly regular. But as we walked through the city, I saw only filth and unkempt houses. Goerz seemed like a gray and sullen little town to me even before I had reason to hate it. I told myself the weariness of the journey was just catching up with me.

Because ours was the shortest route, we were the first of the three groups to reach Goerz. The plan was to wait for the others for a week, then move on if they failed to arrive. We hoped to arrive at Venice before the heat of the summer made that city unbearable. Our timing was not as good as we could have wished. It was the second of Tammuz, 5046, or, as the Christians count the dates, June 28, 1286. If all went well, we would reach Venice by mid-July and the shores of Israel by the early days of August. I knew it would be exhaustingly hot on our ascent to Jerusalem. I comforted myself, however, with the thought that the snow and ice of our years in Germany were forever behind us. Surely, I told myself, desert heat would comfort my old bones, the ones that suffered on wet, chilled mornings.

One of our two groups—sadly, not Suesskind's—joined us the following afternoon. Our reunion was bittersweet, for, unlike us, two of their party had perished on the road. One, a child of six, died as they traversed the narrow mountain ravine, tumbling down the sheer face of a cliffside after taking a wrong step. The second, an old woman a few years younger than me, simply failed to wake up one morning. We wept over their passing, and my heart went out to our third party—the one my son was leading—and prayed that they would arrive this day safe and sound.

We needed to purchase more food for the new arrivals. The girls had already walked into town, taking the dozen or so loaves we prepared that morning to the bakers to bake. I decided to stroll into the town center to find them, so we could shop together. As I was about to leave the courtyard gate, I heard Meir calling me.

"Do you want company?" he asked. "I cannot sit still any longer."

I reached out my hand and he walked up and took it. Our hands joined, we walked like a young couple through the courtyard exit and into town. We talked, softly, of the two we had just lost. The child—a little boy named Yitzik—was truly a tragedy. "The sages say that it is as if an entire world just perished," Meir sighed. "Who knows what the boy might have grown up to become? A scholar? A poet?"

"A good father and a good man?" I said, patting my husband's hand. "I am saddest for the boy's mother. Thank goodness she has several other children. I have never lost a child of my own, and please God, I never will. I cannot imagine it."

"Let us hope we will live a few years more, that once we reach Jerusalem we can see the children settled and happy."

"Amen, husband," I said, leaning briefly against his shoulder, feeling his warm body through his rustic tunic. In my mind's eye, we were young and just married again, moving swiftly on feet that did not hurt, holding our strong bodies upright.

We said little more. The twisting streets of the town were confusing. We had to ask directions twice. To this day I think back to that walk in strange surroundings, wishing we had not found our way. Just as we turned into the street where the baker's shop was located, we were startled by a sudden flurry of dust and noise.

"Stand aside for the bishop of Basel's cavalcade!" the cry went up. The townspeople stepped back close to the buildings so that the horses and carriages carrying the bishop and his party could pass. We shrank back as well.

The bishop appeared fond of ceremony. Several conveyances, including a long row of carts piled high with heavy chests, all flew his flag of green and gold. They rumbled through the streets. Outriders, wearing the dark green of the bishop's livery, protected the caravan. The bishop himself peered from a window in the lead carriage, smiling and waving and making the sign of the cross over the crowd. As they came toward us, the carriage slowed nearly to a crawl, as the street was so crowded.

I saw the bishop looking at us, noticing our pilgrim dress. I halfheartedly touched parts of my head and chest, but Meir, lips tight, simply stood back. I could see the bishop take in Meir's white face and long beard, noting the innate dignity of a man used to authority in his own sphere, despite his age and the shabby clothes that hung on his body.

"Make the sign," I hissed, grabbing his elbow in alarm. "The bishop is looking at you."

Meir shook his head. "The bishop will not notice an old man."

I felt something move in my breast, a kind of heaviness. I did not recognize it then as an intuition of danger, but I wished with every fiber in my being that we were not in that city, that we were on our way to

Venice, the city that held the ships that could transport us over the seas to safety. My heart—I told myself somewhat insensibly, my thoughts confused by panic—my heart is already in Venice. My body is merely trapped here, longing to rejoin my heart.

The carriages finally moved past. I was about to take a deep breath of relief when I saw him out of the corner of one eye. On the top of the last of the carriages, seated on the coachman's box, was a stocky, sour-faced man. He, too, wore the forest green of the bishop of Basel's livery. He was staring fixedly at Meir, his mouth slightly open. As the procession drove on in a cloud of dust, he swiveled around on his perch and kept his eyes focused on my husband.

I had not let go of Meir's arm. I squeezed it now. "Let's go," I said, pulling him away as quickly as we both could move.

———◆———

We waited just outside the baker's shop for the loaves to finish baking. The walk had tired us both, so we dispatched our daughters to shop for our increased numbers. They would return to collect us and the bread and we would all return to the inn together.

Meir sat back against a stone wall, his eyes half-shut. I did not want to interrupt his musing, so I settled down to wait. Exhaustion threatened to overcome me. The baker had set up benches in an arbor toward the rear of the building. We rested there, where the heat from the ovens would not disturb us. A bird warbled its summer song in the thicket of grape leaves overhead. The small green place felt very far from the city, even though it was only a few steps away. I felt myself relaxing, letting myself slip into sleep.

"I knew you were here!" said a small voice, and my eyes fluttered open to rest on Menachem, a young boy who had been in our group. "I wanted to tell you right away, Rebbetzin, that I just did a kind deed!"

"Did you?" I murmured, smiling at the boy's eager face. "You truly have earned the right to ascend to Jerusalem, then. What did you do, Menachem?"

The little boy pulled himself up, rocking onto his toes proudly. "A man in town asked me if the old man in our party was, indeed, Meir of Rothenberg. He said he had long wanted to meet the famous rabbi of Germany and couldn't believe his luck that he was here, in Goerz. I saw you both come here. So I told the man where he could find the Rav, in the baker's shop. Wasn't that good of me?"

I felt a sharp pain deep in my chest, radiating through my limbs. I struggled against the blackness that threatened to overwhelm me.

"What was the man wearing, Menachem?" My voice issued forth so faintly that I had to repeat the question before the boy heard me.

"He was all in green," the boy answered proudly.

"Meir," I said, frantically shaking him by the arm. "Meir, wake up!"

"What? What? Oh, Shira, I was dreaming such a wonderful dream about sitting in the shadow of the walls encircling Jerusalem . . . ," my beloved husband said. Then he saw my face and straightened up. "What is it?" he asked. "What has happened?"

There was commotion in the shop, the footfall of knights' boots. Peering past the child, I saw a small squad of men crowding into the bakery. I looked around, trying to find a back way out of the courtyard. But a high wall surrounded us on all three sides.

"We have to go . . . to leave Goerz," I said. "Someone asked Menachem here if you were—you."

The boy's face fell. "Did I do wrong, Rebbetzin?" he asked.

I put my hand out and patted his arm. "This is not your fault, child. You must believe that, no matter what happens."

The sound of heavy footsteps grew closer. Meir and I looked around. There was no way to escape. My husband stood, slowly, painfully. He stooped and kissed my forehead. "I have ever loved you, my Shira," he whispered. I blinked back tears.

The guards appeared at the back door of the bakery. They marched over to us, swords drawn, surrounding us in a half circle.

"Meir of Rothenberg?" one of them said. "By order of Count Meinhardt of Goerz, acting on information given to him by the bishop of

Basel, we are here to arrest you for fleeing King Rudoph I against his express commands."

"I do not recognize King Rudolph's authority in this matter," my husband said. "I am a free man who has sworn no oaths of fealty to Rudolph or to any sovereign king."

The knight shook his head. "You think he cares whether you are sworn to him or not, Jew? Come along, now."

I rose to accompany my husband, whispering a soft farewell to my daughters and son. But one of the other guards, having taken hold of Meir, pushed me back. "Not you, old woman," he said. "We don't want you."

"He is my husband," I cried out, moving forward again, terrified they might tear him away from me. "Where he goes, so do I."

"Not this time," the knight said brusquely. "Our orders are just for the rabbi."

"It is better that you do not come with me, Shira," Meir said soothingly. I wondered how he could be so calm. "The children will need you now."

"Where are you taking him?" I cried.

"He will spend the night in the dungeons of Count Meinhardt's castle," the captain said. "After that—I don't know. Come along, Rabbi."

I put my hands out and Meir took them in his. We clung together for a last moment, my heart beating so painfully I felt it might explode from my chest. I stared into his eyes and saw him blink back his fears, saw how he tried to convey his love for me and the children in his steadfast glance. Then the guard broke our grip and pushed Meir into the bakery and back out into the street. I staggered after them, watching as they marched him up the road and around a bend. Ignoring the curious faces around me, I blindly felt my way back into the garden. I fell onto a bench in a fit of weeping. Poor Menachem, beside himself at the consequences of his innocent deed, fell to his knees beside me and wept as well. I took his small face into my lap and cradled him against me.

"It will be all right," I murmured over and over, not believing my own words.

I heard my daughters screaming in the street. Not wanting to let go of the sobbing boy, not sure if my feet would even hold me upright, I sat and waited for them. They broke into the garden, flinging themselves down beside me, wailing, asking over and over again how this could have happened. We grieved together in the baker's courtyard for a long hour, clinging to one another, weeping until we felt empty and sore. Then we headed back to the inn to tell the others that we were discovered and our beloved Meir had been taken from us.

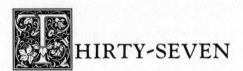

THIRTY-SEVEN

*You will not escape from his grasp but will surely be captured
and handed over to him. You will see the king of Babylon with
your own eyes, and he will speak with you face to face.*

—JEREMIAH 34:3

WE WOULD ONLY LEARN the particulars of what had happened
weeks later. We left the Pilgar Inn—where we were no longer welcome—
and found lodgings in a disreputable tavern in the poorest section of
town. The tavern was not large enough for our entire party, and we were
crowded and uncomfortable. Under such conditions, we decided we
could not all wait in Goerz for Meir's deliverance.

"He would have wanted you to set sail and find safety," I told the
assembled group the night Suesskind and his party found us, two days
after Meir was taken captive. "I will not leave Goerz until I know what
will happen to my husband, but the rest of you must go."

My children and their families, of course, stayed with me, as did a
few of Meir's closest students. The rest left us, bewailing the ill fortune
that forced them to abandon their beloved rabbi. In time, I heard many
of them decided not to make the crossing to Israel but settled near Ven-

ice instead. Some did set sail and we lost all contact with them. They might have flourished in that golden city on the hill we all longed for, perished at the end of a Muslim scimitar or under the hoofs of Crusader cavalry, or simply lived out their lives in piety and poverty. We would never know.

It was with infinite relief that I turned to my son to help me through the first weeks of Meir's capture. Suesskind was his father's son—learned, generous, just—but he was my son as well. His father's brilliance glittered just beyond his grasp, but he could be bullheaded and dig in, shaking out the truth by sheer determination. Suesskind hounded the count of Goerz through letters. He camped outside his residence day in, day out. The guards would chase him away but he would return, heedless of their swords and threats. Even so, it was nearly two weeks before Count Meinhardt agreed to grant him an audience. A slim hope kindled within all our hearts at the curt invitation. We tried to arm ourselves against disappointment by telling one another that it might come to nothing. My daughters and daughter-in-law and I waited for Suesskind's return, milling impatiently on the uncultivated piece of property in front of our lodgings, ignoring the stares and jeers of the passersby.

As soon as Suesskind walked into the tavern, we grabbed him by the arm and pulled him into a back room where we could talk undisturbed.

"It was a man by the name of Knippe who betrayed Papa," Suesskind said, frowning. "He was a student of Papa's while I was in Barcelona and you were in Lincoln, Mama. Rachel, probably, would have recognized him. Or Binyamin here."

"I might—though there have been so many students, one cannot remember them all. But if a Jew, why did he betray your father?" asked Binyamin.

"If he is the man I think he must be, he was wearing the livery of the bishop of Basel," I said. "That suggests to me—"

"An apostate," sighed Moses Parnes.

"Yes," I said, my heart chilled at the thought of yet another apostate wreaking havoc with our lives. "He must be."

We sat silent for a moment, each of us immersed in our own bleak thoughts. Then I asked Suesskind, "Where is your father now? Is he still in the count's dungeons?"

"No, Mama," he said. "He was moved twice already. Once to a prison in Wasserburg, an island in Lake Constance, and now to the great prison of Ensisheim, located near Rudolph's Koenigsbourg Castle. According to the count, he is probably still en route to Ensisheim."

"We will travel to Ensisheim ourselves," I decided. "We will appeal directly to the king. Find out what sum he wants as ransom. Perhaps they will let us see your father while we negotiate the terms of his release."

The journey to Ensisheim was difficult. We no longer concealed our Jewish identities. Several times we were turned from the gates of one city or another as we traveled through the southernmost reaches of the German empire. The Jews of these cities had fled from King Rudolph, unable to bear the weight of the heavy taxes. Those few who remained took us in, fed us, and sympathized with our grief for Meir.

It was on this trip that I came to realize how important Meir had become to the Jews of Ashkenaz. They quoted his pronouncements to me, many of the rabbis pulling out copies of his letters that they stored among their most prized possessions. Many told me how they followed his habits in prayer, reciting *kiddush* first and then washing their hands for the meal, reciting *"Adonai sifitai tiftach"* before the Amidah. My husband had touched the hearts of the communities of Germany in many ways, and they felt his loss keenly.

The trip was difficult for a different reason as well. For the first time in many years, I had to be careful about what we spent. We had grown wealthy during our years in Rothenberg but left most of our possessions behind in our flight from the king. The moment we departed, town officials seized our home, our school, and our belongings, handing our leavings over to the royal treasury. While Meir and I had never spent money recklessly, we had not denied ourselves comforts. As the small store of cash—already diminished from our trip—grew lighter and lighter, I became increasingly more anxious. What would we do when it ran out? And how would we afford Meir's ransom?

The hillsides and valleys of Alsace spread out before us, decked in summer flowers, a verdant odor rising from the ripening grapes. It was as beautiful as the area of Normandy where I grew up or the farms and hills surrounding Rothenberg. But the splendor of the summer days could not alleviate the constant heaviness of my heart.

As the town where my husband was imprisoned finally came within sight, I wasn't sure what I was supposed to feel. The dread that I had hoped would subside as we grew closer seemed to sit on my chest like a heavy, clawed beast. As we rounded a curve in the road, Rudolph's recently refurbished Koenigsbourg Castle rose before us, dominating the valley beneath. It was perched on the edge of a mountain, rising in pink- and gray-stoned glory, its ramparts bespeaking imperious power.

The town lay in a particularly lush area of Alsace. Jews lived in the nearby town of Wittenheim. We had sent word of our arrival and a messenger found us on the road, bearing a warmly phrased invitation. We were welcome to stay with them until we decided what to do.

Greeted by Rabbi Avner ben Shaul of Wittenheim, our party was placed—with tender care—into the abodes of several Jewish families. I remained with Suesskind's family at the rabbi's home.

"We have sent a delegation to the prison with food daily since the rav was incarcerated there," the rabbi told us. "The guards accepted our food, but all our attempts to see the prisoner were rebuffed."

I was relieved Meir had kosher food to eat but sighed to think no one had laid eyes on him since he was wrested from me in Goerz.

"However," Rav Avner continued more brightly, "we bribed one of the guards for an honest account of the rav's well-being. You will be glad to hear that Rabbi Meir is not being tortured any longer."

The idea that Meir had suffered torture made me feel faint. I groped my way into a seat. The rabbi's wife, Leah, watched me collapse and clucked her tongue at her husband in annoyance. She fetched me some cold, clear water from a nearby spring. I drank thankfully, waving away all of their cries of concern. My dizziness subsided.

"The great rabbi of Cologne has informed me that he will write King Rudolph personally," Rabbi Avner assured me. "You must not worry about Rabbenu Meir, Rebbetzin. He will be released shortly. I know it. God will protect him."

His wife ushered us all into the dining hall to eat. The food smelled and looked delicious after our makeshift meals on the journey. But I could not make myself swallow a morsel.

———•———

Months passed. Our emissaries to the king visited me to report on their progress. It seemed at first that it would simply be a matter of the amount of ransom—but then the king's agents stipulated that all of Jewish Germany had to agree to pay taxes to the king's treasury as part of any agreement. The rabbi of Cologne, Rabbi Hayyim ben Yechiel Hefetz Zahav, traveled from his city to negotiate directly with the king's representatives in Ensisheim. He then made the journey to the king's court to try to see Rudolph. But he was denied an audience with the king.

Rabbi Hayyim's community of Cologne told him they would refuse to abide by his agreements. They felt once they agreed they owed taxes to the king, the monarch would claim the right to tax them into poverty. I was indignant when I learned this.

"Do they care nothing about my husband's safety after all he has done for them?" I demanded of Rabbi Hayyim.

He patted my arm. "Rest assured, Shira, I have not given up. I will arrange the ransom so your husband is restored to you and to us all— and give him the freedom to travel where he will. But the communities of Germany must not bear the burden in taxes. I will keep looking for a way."

"I pray you find one, Rabbi. I fear I will die before I see my husband again."

"We are trying to get you in to see him. Take courage!"

Rabbi Hayyim and Suesskind were allowed to see Meir once only during these long few months—speaking to him through a small barred window in his jail cell. I searched Suesskind's face when he returned from the prison after finally seeing his father. The rabbi's family had kindly given us a room for our own use, and we sat there, my children and I, clustered anxiously around Suesskind. What I saw in my son's expression did not comfort me much. He had the same grave, pinched look his father had when worried. It didn't matter what loving messages the boy brought from his father or his assurances that Meir looked peaked but was not ill.

"He's just tired of being imprisoned, Mama," my son said, trying to comfort me, speaking to me with that impatient quality in his voice that the children sometimes used as I grew old. "And he's not a youngster anymore."

"Did you bring him the fresh clothing and the bread? The dried meat?" I asked, forgetting whether I had asked the question before or not.

"Yes, I did, Mama, I told you so. He was very grateful for them, for he was still wearing pilgrim clothes all these months later."

"I wish I could see him," I moaned, turning away to look mournfully out the window that faced Koenigsbourg Castle. "I am his wife; no one has a better right."

"I know, Mama," Suesskind said, putting his arm around me and hugging me. "He longs for you too; he said so."

As more weeks passed, we felt we could no longer trespass on the kind hospitality of the Jews of Wittenheim. So we moved to a small house of our own at the edge of the town of Sausheim. The rabbi of Cologne had arranged for a small but sufficient annuity for me during my lifetime and paid for the house out of collections made by Jews throughout Ashkenaz. "We consider it a holy duty, Rebbetzin," he told me when I demurred. "This is our way of honoring your husband until we can restore him to you."

The little house was not built for so many people. The third night after we had moved in, I escaped the hovering, loving presence of my family, saying I wanted to catch a breath of air outside. As I stepped off the back stairs, I saw Rachel and Suesskind walking together at a distance in the small garden. They were deep in conversation. Curious, I crept closer, keeping out of sight.

"It could be years, Rachel," Suesskind said to her, kicking the path as they walked up and down. "I've heard of cases where people have been held for ransom for more than a decade."

"We're all being held for ransom," sighed Rachel. She had a birch branch in her hand and was stripping it of its leaves. "Binyamin doesn't complain, but he is anxious to take up his life again."

"But what can we do?" Suesskind said. "I know exactly how he feels. But how could we leave Mama alone to deal with this? Besides, I am helping in the negotiations."

"Yes, but can that be your whole life? What would you do if Papa— God forbid—had been killed instead?"

The two of them had ambled to the edge of the garden. They leaned against a little green gate. There was a long pause between them as both stood deep in thought. Secluded by a thick hedge, I held my breath, waiting for Suesskind's answer.

"I didn't want to go to Israel, but Papa wanted it so much and it is a *mitzvah,* after all. What would I choose for myself, given total freedom of choice? Poland. New Jewish congregations are forming there now, and they need someone to lead them. Several new communities invited me to start a *yeshiva* there."

Keeping concealed by the shadows, I crept back into the house and sought my bed—the only place I could be alone, at least this early in the evening. I sat up, pulling a thin sheet to my chin, and thought long and hard. How could I keep them tied to me any longer? The children had given up enough of their lives during these tiring months. It nearly broke my soul into pieces to realize what I had to do. But two nights later I sat them all down in the little garden to talk with them.

"You must leave and go on—wherever you wish to go," I said, willing my face into the composed lines I had practiced in my little traveling mirror. "Go to Israel, to Poland, to some other country—it must be your choice. But you cannot stay here with me frozen in time any longer. Your father would be angry if I permitted it."

The children looked at one another. Their faces showed shock, alarm, regret—and relief.

"We could not leave you, Mama," Chaya protested. "You are so old and frail."

"I am old, child, but not frail. I can see to my own needs. And your father will be released soon enough and we will travel to Israel together, to die there. Our lives are over, children, no matter what happens now. Yours are still before you."

"I am negotiating on Papa's behalf," insisted Suesskind.

"Rabbi Hayyim and I spoke about this last night, Suesskind. He says you have been indefatigable in pursuing your father's freedom but that what will follow now will require months of discussions over small articles in the agreements. He tells me such legalese is best left to those not personally involved. I think he's right. Besides, your papa would want you to find yourself a synagogue and a congregation and a school to continue his work of hastening redemption and preparing for the Messiah's arrival." I turned to the girls' husbands. "That is the job he would ask all of you to do, in whatever way you can, whether it be through teaching or through charity. It is our best answer to King Rudolph and the others who want to see our lives stopped because of their pronouncements."

There were tears glistening on the girls' cheeks—and not just the girls. Binyamin reached over and gave me a warm hug. "Mother Shira, truly we cannot leave you here alone," he said. "It would break Rachel's heart. And mine."

I reached past him to smooth my Rachel's hair. "Binyamin, I must say to my girls what Naomi said to Ruth and Orpah long ago on that plain in Moab: 'May God deal loyally with you, as you have dealt with the dead, and with me. May God grant you that you may find rest, each of you in the house of her husband.'"

"Yes, Mama," sobbed Chaya, "but do you remember how Ruth then responded to Naomi?"

"Of course," I said, glancing warmly upon my firstborn, the baby of my heart. "Who could not remember? She said: 'Entreat me not to leave you, or to return from following after you. Wherever you go, I will go; and where you lodge, I will lodge; your people shall be my people, and your God my God.'" I made myself smile then, stretching my lips and my cheeks painfully thin, hoping my expression made me look certain of my words. "But, my darling, I ask you to do something much harder. I ask you to go and live—live your life apart from me."

"Someone *must* stay with you, Mama," Zipura cried. "The others still have work left undone—teaching, working with a congregation—but my husband and I have nothing but ourselves to offer. We can perform acts of charity here in Sausheim as well as anywhere else in Europe. I will stay with you."

Relief flooded through me. While I strove to act as I thought my husband would want me to act, my heart was torn to shreds at the thought of losing all my children. I turned to Zipura's husband, the man who had left his entire store of wealth behind him in order to follow Meir to Israel. He had done so unwillingly, I remembered now. "Well, Amnon? What say you?" I said. "My daughter cannot make this decision for your household."

He came forward and took Zipura by the hand. It warmed my heart to see real affection pass between them. "In fact, Mother Shira, she can," he said. "For we have already discussed it. I am going to begin my travels about Europe again, building up trade in a small way. I will be able to bring you news of your children wherever they settle. Zipura will stay here and tend to you—and, please God, to her father when he is finally released."

There was much more weeping to be done and we all talked into the night. But in the span of a few weeks, I bid farewell to all of my children but my Little Bird. Suesskind went to Poland, attaching himself to a congregation there. Chaya went north to Bohemia, Rachel south to Spain. They wrote of their new homes, of the good work they did, of how their own children were thriving. Their letters warmed my cold heart.

But *ha-Shem* would not allow me a frozen heart forever. Rabbi Hayyim came to me one afternoon, more than a year after my husband was imprisoned, to tell me that he and several other rabbis would be permitted to visit Meir the next day—and I would be allowed to go with them.

———

I rose early the next morning and fetched a basin of water to clean myself. Using a soft feather, I cleansed the creases of my face. The woman who looked back at me in the glass was a stranger. I had been old before they had taken my husband from me. Now I felt ancient.

I dressed in spotless white linen, putting a coif about my hair. I sat outside as the fitful winter sun rose in my garden. The ground, hard as iron, covered the life that slept protected underneath. A harsh wind snapped in my face and brought some color to my cheeks. I laughed at my vanity and told myself the difficult journey to the prison would probably undo all my hard work. What was I thinking, primping my body to look like the young girl my Meir had once loved? It was with trembling fingers that I wrapped my cloak around my shoulders and sat down to wait for Rabbi Hayyim to fetch me.

We traveled to the prison in an open cart. Speaking loudly to be heard above the rumble of the stones beneath our wheels, Rabbi Hayyim told me that they had finally reached an agreement with the king about Meir's release but that Meir himself had refused it.

"What in the world is he thinking?" I asked, dread and anger forming a knot in my stomach.

"I don't know, Rebbetzin. This is what we are going to find out. But the king's emissary was clear. Rabbi Meir thanks us for our efforts and prefers to remain in prison. It's a mystery."

"Indeed," I said bitterly. "How long will it be now?"

"Before we reach the prison? Just another few minutes. He will be so happy to see you."

"And I him," I said, my heart pumping like a child's in my breast.

The guards of the prison all looked grim, their scabbards worn at the front of their link metal tunics so they could quickly grab their short swords. The doors of the immense gray-stoned prison were heavy. A guard was ordered to winch it back, using an enormous chain that looped around a heavy pulley. The shriek of metal against metal set my teeth on edge.

We passed through five stations. At each, a guard examined our papers, counted the number of people in the cart, searched our bodies and our belongings. My womanhood was disregarded by these flint-eyed knights. I was flustered at the feel of a man's hand groping my arms, legs, and more intimate parts, but I set my teeth and bore it.

At the fifth station, we left the cart behind. Accompanied by an armed escort, we were hustled into the depths of the prison. Finally, after what felt like a journey to the earth's inner kingdoms, we reached Meir's small cell. The man standing guard in that corridor pulled out an immense iron key and opened the heavy oaken door. He swung it open. My breath coming in anxious gasps, I pushed to the front of the group. The rabbis, sensitive to our reunion after so many months, pulled back and allowed me to make the last few steps alone.

"Meir!" I cried, my eyes struggling to adjust to the dimness of the room.

"Shira?" came a faint voice from a chair and table in a corner. "Shira?"

The man at the table rose and shuffled forward. I could barely make out his body, but his movements were those of a man who had been sick or hurt badly. With a sob, I rushed into his arms. For a long moment we clung to each other, both crying, our tears mixing as he kissed every inch of my face he could reach—my forehead, my eyelids, my cheeks, my throat. Then our lips met and we hung on as though each of us were trying to absorb the other into their body.

Finally, Meir broke our embrace, stepping backward and holding me out at arm's length. "Oh, my wife," he said, his voice crackling with emotion. "I had given up hope of ever seeing your dear face again."

"And I of seeing yours," I said, laughing and crying at the same time. "Oh, Meir, I have been so miserable about you—without you!"

"You are well, my Shira? You look worn and thin. And the children? Where are the children?"

The rabbis entered and Meir turned from me to greet them. But as he hugged each of his visitors, his eyes kept returning to my face, as if to assure himself that I was not an apparition. I smiled and nodded at him, eagerly feasting my eyes on his countenance. He was so pale! So thin! Noting how the bones stretched his cheeks, I hastened to empty the basket of food I had brought with me. There was a goodly store of cake and bread and pottage and even a cold chicken stew.

"What of the children?" Meir asked again. I explained how I had dispatched them to their own destinies. He sighed and nodded, particularly when I recounted Rachel and Suesskind's conversation in the little garden. He heard me without interruption. When I finished, he pressed me for details. Where was the house? How had I afforded it? Who was taking care of me? All of his concern was for my welfare. My heart swelled with love for this remarkable man who sat in the bowels of a prison and worried about his wife.

But our time was limited and Rabbi Hayyim finally stepped forward. "We must interrupt, I'm afraid, Rabbenu Meir," he said. "We have been allowed to see you so that we may plead with you. Why have you refused to allow us to pay ransom on your behalf? You must see that you cannot remain here. We must have you restored to us."

Meir turned and reseated himself on his chair, pulling me close beside him. As there was only the one chair, I kneeled down and kept my hand tucked into his. The rabbis arranged themselves in a loose circle around us. My husband sighed, looking up at them.

"I insisted on seeing the entire agreement before I would concur, Rav Hayyim. You have been tireless on my behalf and I thank you. And the rest of you as well," he said, nodding at the other rabbis, who smiled and bowed. "But I cannot accept."

"You must," said another of the rabbis. "We will not allow you to refuse."

"Do you think I do not want to be freed from here?" my husband asked, a thin edge of despair creeping into his voice. "It is the thought I wake with, the thought that accompanies me into the lands beyond sleep. I wish with all my heart to be free. I think, sometimes, that I will die here, immured in this place. Every time I think that, some part of me dies a little bit."

"So let us free you," Rabbi Hayyim cried. "It is inconceivable that the great Rabbi Meir of Rothenberg—the Maharam—should be penned in here like a common criminal!"

"But if you free me—what then? What happens next, Hayyim? The next time King Rudolph goes off to war or marries off a child and feels his purse pinching him? He plucked me from my congregation, took me from my family, and placed me in this prison by force of arms. If I give in to him and allow you to pay the ransom—and the sum is utterly ridiculous for such an old man—what will happen next time? Will he put you in jail next? Or you? Or you?"

As Meir spoke the words, he pointed at one and then another of the rabbis. The sudden suggestion made them rear back. I could see dread dawning in their eyes as they looked about and noted anew how miserably my husband was housed.

"So you will stay here for the rest of your days?" Rabbi Hayyim asked, his shoulders sagging.

"I fear that is my fate," Meir said, his voice growing deeper with resolve.

"Do you want to kill me?" I gasped, unable to stop myself.

He reached down and put his arms around me. "Oh, Shira, darling. You have been so brave through all our tribulations, my own *eshet chayil*—my woman of valor. But I cannot allow the communities of Ashkenaz to hand over twenty-three thousand marks to Rudolph on my behalf! Besides the principle of the matter, it is an obscene amount of money."

"There are twelve communities already raising the sum needed," Rabbi Hayyim said. "We do so with joy in our hearts that you will be restored to us."

"Oh, if it were only the money!" Meir said in exasperation. "But Rudolph wishes us to agree that we owe him our fealty, so he can raise taxes with which to enrich his war coffers. He would use our hard work and sweat and danger to pay for his building of churches and his royal fetes. I cannot permit that, Hayyim! He would restrain us in our homes—as he is already trying to do—and claim us as his slaves. And after he frees me, he will find another to imprison, and then another. No, I prefer to be the only prisoner Rudolph keeps chained behind locked bars. By my not giving in to him, the rest of you shall remain free."

"But . . . you cannot stay here for the rest of your life, Meir! Look at how they are forcing you to live!" I cried.

Meir smiled down at my distressed face. "I have had months and months to look about this tiny cell, wife. You cannot tell me about a lump in the straw that my body has not found, about a mouse in the walls who has not ventured out to eat the crumbs I leave. I have no light and my eyes fail, I have no books and my heart fails. But I will not leave this prison as a man sworn to Rudolph. I will not let the communities be sworn on my behalf."

Meir looked around. I saw the wretchedness—the rustic table and chair, the thin straw pallet, the bucket in the corner where he was forced to relieve himself, where the stink of his own body hovered. Then I looked at his face. Rather than the set, white look of desolation, it was smiling and brave and unwavering. I looked at him and wanted to wail, gnash my teeth, and cry "What about me? What about my loneliness without you?" But I saw the answer in his face. He would not leave unless the king capitulated. And the king would not.

"Can we not at least make you more comfortable?" I whispered. "Perhaps the guards would accept a small stipend for us to be allowed to visit you, to have your students come and see you again. To let me visit regularly. And bring you books."

Meir's face brightened. "I would welcome all of those things, Shira. It would lighten the burdens of my soul to be allowed to read again, to see my students again. And to see you—Shira, of all I have longed for, it is you that I think of most."

He held me close. I wished the world would retreat and leave us be. But it was not possible. All too soon, the guards came to fetch us. As we left, I glanced backward to see Meir turning himself to the table, picking up a crust of bread, and carrying it, with a shaking hand, to his mouth. In that moment I knew I would dedicate the rest of my life to bringing my most beloved husband succor and comfort whenever they would allow me to visit him in prison.

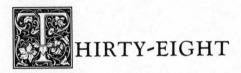

THIRTY-EIGHT

The Rock will console you compensate you for suffering
restore you from captivity . . . raise you up from degradation.

—MEIR BEN BARUCH

I GREW SHAMELESS ASKING FOR MONEY on Meir's behalf. The sum of twenty-three thousand marks—an amount so vast that it took my breath away when Rabbi Hayyim mentioned it—was ever in my mind when I asked for charity for the prisoner. In contrast to that enormous sum, I spent perhaps a few hundred marks on small comforts for him over the years. But they made a difference.

We were able to have him moved to a better cell, one with a slit window that let in a tiny amount of natural light. I paid to have his soil bucket removed three times a day so that the stench never became overwhelming. I bought a new table and several chairs for him, so he could sit with students and scholars who came to study with him. And come they did. They sat with him for hours on end, reading to him when his own eyes failed, writing responsa for him when his hands ached and he could not hold the quill. His injury from his youth often flared up in the damp cold of the prison cell, and it annoyed him not to be able to write. My own handwriting was growing shakier, but I forced my trembling fingers to form careful letters whenever he asked me to serve as his scribe.

My husband and his students studied together. The prison corridor rang with argument and counterargument, with hymns of praise to *ha-Shem*, with thoughts that ranged from the ridiculous to the sublime. I made sure that Meir's cell was isolated enough from the other prisoners—Christians all—so that no one could hear to complain when these enthusiasms bubbled forth.

I liked to think that if his study sessions were the light of his otherwise gloomy existence, my visits were the warmth. We would sit together for hours, recollecting our youth, the infancy of our children, their triumphs and tragedies as they grew older. I brought him news of recently born great-grandchildren, the many letters from our children and grandchildren. We would say a *Shechiyanu* for every moment of family joy.

There came a day when he had news for me. I entered the cell that morning and put down my basket—filled, as always, with good food and clean linen—and could see he was tentative, peering into my face uncertainly. My heart started to beat faster. I finally could stand it no longer. I placed the last loaf of bread on the table and turned to him.

"What is it?"

He smiled at my intuition. "Good morning, my Shira. My students visited me yesterday and they brought me news of your old suitor."

My heart sank. He pulled out a letter and, with trembling hands, unfolded it.

"This is a copy of a letter from Jacob ben Elijah, a rabbi in Venice. Nicholas Donin was condemned by the Pope for writing a tract criticizing his fellow Franciscans. He was stabbed and killed by the knight of a baron who could not stand his canting and preaching one moment longer."

Meir handed me the letter. I wiped a single tear that refused to be blinked back and turned to my husband with a sigh.

"Can you mourn such a man?" my husband asked quietly. "Such a sinner?"

I sat silent for a moment, deep in thought. "My father once compared him to the *beryonim* of old, the troublemakers that Rav Meir"—I glanced over at my husband—"prayed would die. It upset me that such a wise man wished for someone's death, no matter what wrong they had wrought."

Meir said nothing, looking closely at me.

"When I studied the passage with my father, I remember being delighted that Bruriah convinced Meir to pray for their repentance, so their sin would be no more," I continued. "What would Nicholas Donin's life have been like without his sin, husband? It is that life that I mourn."

———•———

The years passed, tranquilly if not happily. Through Meir's students, we received infrequent news of new atrocities. My husband would rage against them from the confines of his cell, sometimes furious, sometimes despairing. I wondered what Chaya felt when she learned that King Edward I had expelled every Jew from England, allowing them to take only what they could carry. My own neighbors, Gentiles all, often sang the song of the Host and the Jews, how blood poured forth from it and would not be stopped, how the Jewish couple tried to do everything they could to destroy the Host but could not. Hearing the gruesome lyrics set to music always made me shiver. Yet my neigbors always treated me well, no matter how many malicious songs they sang about the Jews.

In fact, my reputation in Sausheim remained unsullied despite my religion. I became known as the lady in white because of the light-colored linen and fine woolen clothing I liked to wear. After all, how could an old woman whose house was always spotless, who sat in her garden and could quote passages from scripture, threaten anyone? I did not seek to heal the sick, for I had no skill with herbs and potions. But if someone were in pain or in need, I would be there, with my little basket, knocking on the door and trying to help.

As I grew less and less able to care for myself, Zipura lived faithfully by my side in our small home. Her husband visited infrequently. His modest success in business this second time around secured a future for my daughter. As Zipura cooked and cleaned, I spent hours outside in my garden, walking its gravel paths ever more slowly. Or I sat for long hours in the small arbor that recalled my happiest years, the days in Paris before the burning.

As for Meir, he was as comfortable as we could make him. "We all live in prisons, both of our own making and those made for us, Shira," Meir told me once, close to the end. "I would never have chosen this cell or this conclusion to my life. When Moses led us out of slavery into the Promised Land, he could never have pictured that his people would end so far distant, in an exile that threatens to dwarf our years in Egypt. But I am not a slave, for I chose not to be one. I am imprisoned and reviled for my faith, but I won't accept serfdom as my ultimate fate."

His words made me shudder. It was a cold morning and the cell was dank during the dark months. I clung to my husband, trying to find a warm spot in his arms. "I fear we have years of suffering before us, husband. Not you and I, for we are old and growing ever closer to our final days. But our children and their children. And their children."

Meir's eyes clouded. "I am a scholar, not a prophet. I cannot predict the future. But if you are right—and it seems that you may be right— somehow I feel certain we will endure. Look what you and I have already survived. We have suffered loss and heartache, but we are still here. Our children learned this from us and their children learned it from them. Someday, perhaps, we will move past the fear of the Gentiles. Someday, perhaps, they will understand that we wish to do nothing but live in peace with them, worshipping as we want and must."

I thought of the village priest who had visited me two weeks ago, announcing as I let him through the door that his intention was to convert me. I had not told Meir of the priest's visit. I would not. I had fed the priest a meal at my table and we had talked of spiritual matters for many long hours. When he left, his head and shoulders drooped.

"I came full of fire and passion for your soul, Frau Shira, and I depart bereft."

I remained silent. I could not content him. I feared we would never content the Gentiles, who saw us as strangers in their midst, unbelievers and heretics. But the man sat at my table and ate my bread, and for a while, a short while, we were able to discuss the things that mattered to both our religions. I hoped that Meir was right. Maybe someday—a day long distant, perhaps—there would be peace between us.

———◆———

One April morning, the first day with a promise of warmth in the air, Rav Hayyim brought me the news of my husband's death. After he left, I went outside to sit in the garden. I felt empty, drained of feeling. I could hear Zipura weeping inside. In a few minutes I would go in and comfort her. My heart went out to the others, to Chaya, Rachel, and Suesskind, and to their children. I knew all of Ashkenaz would grieve for my husband, the man who refused to buy his liberty, preferring instead that his people remain free.

At my feet was a small flower, a narcissus, nosing its way up to the light. I crouched down next to it, brushing back the soil from its half-closed petals. A verse from the book of Job came, unbidden, to my lips: "'Man that is born of a woman is of a few days and full of trouble. He comes forth with a flower and is cut down, he fleeth also as a shadow and continues not.'"

I felt very light, very warm. The day seemed to be turning unseasonably balmy. I rose and walked to a small bench, set back among the small bushes that bordered my garden oasis. "Meir," I said, wanting to hear his name form in my mouth. "Meir."

My head felt too heavy. I wanted to lie down. I felt myself sink onto the bench. Another verse rose to my lips, from the Song of Solomon:

"'My beloved speaks and says to me: "Arise, my love, my fair one, and come away; for now the winter is past, the rain is over and gone. The flowers appear on the earth; the time of singing has come . . . """

There was more but I found I could not speak. I smiled as I thought of my life, my husband, my children. I remembered Meir telling me how we would endure. Slipping farther down, I let myself close my eyes.

UTHOR'S NOTE AND ACKNOWLEDGMENTS

I DON'T REMEMBER the first time my mother told me I was descended from a famous rabbi who lived in Europe in the 1200s. While I enjoyed the allure of family heritage, I never asked her to delve into the specifics and did not even know my ancestor's name. But when I probed my family tree to uncover the truth of a completely different event, I stumbled upon a reference to Rabbi Meir ben Baruch of Rothenberg, the Maharam. Living in the twenty-first century, I did what any curious historical novelist would do. I Googled him.

What I discovered was fascinating. I had never known that in 1242 an apostate Jew named Nicholas Donin, having been excommunicated by the chief rabbi of Paris, convinced the Pope and French royals to burn every copy of the Talmud in a Paris market square. My ancestor, Rabbi Meir ben Baruch, was among the witnesses. Meir was a Talmudic student who, like his contemporaries, spent his youth traveling from *yeshiva* to *yeshiva* throughout the area of Europe known as Ashkenaz—

which then was situated primarily in France and Germany. Meir was so moved by the tragedy that he composed an elegy to the Talmud, *"Sha'ali Srufa,"* or "O You, Who Burn in Fire," which today is included as one of the liturgical laments in the annual Tisha B'av service that mourns the tragedies of Jewish history.

I learned how, years later, Meir ben Baruch settled in Rothenberg, founded a Jewish seminary, and became known throughout Europe for the wisdom of his responsa, letters written in response to Talmudic questions. As I did some of my research online, I found that Meir would often be quoted as a source to resolve even modern-day questions. There's good reason for this. Meir lived at the end of the so-called silver age of Jewish scholarship, the period in which Jewish scholars in Germany and France corresponded to address questions of Jewish ritual and law. During his long life, Meir witnessed ever-increasing restrictions against the Jews, mandated by clergy and nobles, and carried out, often with tragic results, by Crusaders, peasants, and townspeople. He distilled many of these regulations to their day-to-day usage, writing, for instance, that it behooved Jews who were afraid the wind would blow off their clumsy "Jew hats" on the Shabbat, when they were prohibited from picking them up, to fasten them with a strap. Meir exhibited a tremendous amount of modern common sense for someone who lived during the 1200s!

At the end of Meir's life, Rudolph I of Hapsburg took the throne. Rudolph sought to enslave his Jews by naming them *servi camerae,* "servants of the [royal] chamber." Meir recognized the danger in complying with the king's ruling and fled Germany together with his followers. But on his journey to Israel, Meir was recognized and captured. As commonly occurred during the Middle Ages—think of Richard Lionheart as just one example—Meir was held for ransom. But part of the price for Meir's freedom was accepting Rudolph's decree of the Jews' status. Meir refused to countenance his people's enslavement and remained in prison for the rest of his life.

I had felt Meir's influence on the Jewish people long before I was aware that it originated with my ancestor. At every Shabbat service, we rise to honor God, to "open our mouths to declare Your glory." That part of the service had always resonated with me and I was thrilled to learn that it had been Meir who introduced it.

Yet I struggled to bring Meir to life. It was not until I created Shira—a wholly invented character—that I felt I could encompass the man's fascinating life. Meir, a product of his age, was strongly opposed to a woman stepping foot into a congregation of men. By pairing him with a curious and intelligent wife, herself raised in a rabbinical household, I felt I could infuse the domestic side of Meir's character with vitality. I also could use the character of Shira to incorporate a fictional love triangle—Shira's relationship with Nicholas Donin—into the plotline, adding a secondary emotional layer to Meir's hatred for the man.

In addition, Shira's existence allowed me to explore yet another of the dark chapters of Jewish history. While the Little Hugh episode occurred during Meir's lifetime, he lived far distant from it. But as I researched the time period, this horrific tale of a boy drowned down a Lincoln well and the resulting wave of anti-Semitic feeling that swept through England took possession of me. Knowing that the Jews—unlike their Gentile neighbors—traveled widely during the Middle Ages both for study and trade, I sent one of the family's daughters to Lincoln so that her mother could visit her there.

There was much that I did not originally know about Jews during this period of history that would eventually find its way into the manuscript. While Christians were suspicious of anyone who did not believe in Jesus and the Crusades gave knights and townspeople an excuse to persecute them as infidels, I was surprised to learn that the Church itself officially protected Jews, granting them special status as witnesses to the miracle of Christ. But such protection presupposed that the Jews were willing to stagnate as remnants of the late biblical age. When it became widely known that Jewish scholars instead had embarked upon a rich and varied tradition of learning, embodied in the Talmud, which continued long after the time of Christ, Christian rulers and Church officials were appalled. Up until this period Jews had enjoyed a semblance of autonomy and independence, but as the truth about the Talmud became known, new humiliations were heaped upon them. A cycle of distrust and persecution became the lifestyle of the Jews in Europe as they sought temporary refuge in different countries, only to have their peace punctured by other restrictions that often culminated in dreaded pogroms.

I consulted too many sources to name but grew to depend upon some in particular. These included Israel Abrahams's *Jewish Life in the Middle Ages* and Leonard B. Glick's *Abraham's Heirs: Jews and Christians in Medieval Europe.* I drew heavily from Avraham Grossman's *Pious and Rebellious: Jewish Women in Medieval Europe* and Elisheva Baumgarten's *Mothers and Children: Jewish Family Life in Medieval Europe* for my knowledge of how Jewish women lived their lives. I also consulted Susan L. Einbinder's *Beautiful Death: Jewish Poetry and Martyrdom in Medieval France,* particularly the chapter dedicated to Meir's elegy. For information about the Paris disputation and the burning, I am grateful to Alan Temko's "The Burning of the Talmud," a poignant article that appeared in *Commentary,* and Judah M. Rosenthal's two-part "The Talmud on Trial: The Disputation at Paris in the Year 1240," which appeared in *The Jewish Quarterly.*

But foremost among the books consulted was Irving R. Argus's *Rabbi Meir of Rothenberg,* a two-volume collection of Meir's writings and scholarly essays about his life and responsa that gave me enormous insight into the man and rabbi. This book proved highly elusive. If I began my research on Meir with a Google search, I owe my possession of these invaluable volumes to eBay and a persistent and caring husband, who hunted it down for me. Steven, thank you.

There are many other people who supported me as I wrote this novel and whom I wish to thank. My writing group critiqued several portions of the book, and some of its members—Caprice Garvin, Sondra Gash, and Elaine Denholtz—undertook the task of reading the full manuscript. Kathy Harris and Beverly A. Jackson also read the entire book and offered invaluable advice. So too did my sons, Geoff and Alex. My most faithful reader, my sister, Sipora Kreps, read several versions and gave me boundless encouragement.

Rabbi Robin Nafshi was kind enough to offer a rabbinical perspective, correcting many anachronisms and mistakes in theology. She also reviewed and amended the glossary that appears at the end of this book. Any errors that remain are my own. Rabbi Don Rossoff offered me midrashic tales to include and Rabbi Mary Zamore studied Talmud with me, helping a newcomer to this aspect of Judaism take her first tentative steps.

Carol Plumm-Uci's suggestion that I set my alarm for four thirty A.M. to carve myself out a slice of writing time amid family, full-time work, and other obligations helped me bring the book to completion and it was through her recommended course of action that I was able to traverse the intimidating process of finding an agent. That agent, Judith Riven, proved to be everything I could have ever wanted—professional, capable, resolute, and responsive to even my most naïve questions. Maggie Crawford, my editor at Pocket Books, was the type of editor I feared had vanished from the publishing scene—thorough and thoughtful in her editorial comments, refining the novel and readying it for publication. I am grateful, too, to the Pocket publicity team, Jean Anne Rose and Ayelet Gruenspecht, who are working in conjunction with my publicist, Carol Fass, to Simon & Schuster's Director of Adult Marketing, Wendy Shenanin, and to my most careful copy editor, Aja Pollock.

I only wish my mother had lived to read this novel inspired when she told me how far back our family tree stretches. I dedicate this book to her, to the Ruttenberg and Shidlowski families, who are descended from Rabbi Meir ben Baruch—and to the woman who actually was Rabbi Meir's wife, whose silent life I was privileged to imagine.

LOSSARY

Adonai sifatai tiftach u'fi yagid techilatecha—The opening line of the Amidah or the standing prayer: "Eternal God, open my lips, that my mouth may declare your glory." Originally uttered by King David, asking God for repentance after his sins with Bathsheba.

"Adon Olam"—"Lord of the World," a liturgical hymn sung during various services.

aleph-bet—The Hebrew alphabet.

Amidah—"The Standing Prayer," recited three times a day.

aron hakodesh—"The holy ark" containing the scrolls of the Torah.

Ashkenaz—Originally a term to describe the regions of medieval France and Germany where Jews lived. Eventually this came to encompass all of Western Europe.

Avodah Zarah—A Talmudic tractate (chapter) dealing with laws pertaining to Jews living among Gentiles.

ba'alat brit, ba'aleh brit—Godparent, godparents.

"Baba Batra"—A Talmudic tractate (chapter) that deals with a person's responsibilities and rights as the owner of property.

bachurim—Lads, young men.

Baruch atah Adonai elohainu melech ha'olam—The formulaic beginning of virtually all Hebrew prayers: "Blessed are You, Eternal our God, Ruler of the Universe . . ."

bat—Daughter of.

beit midrash—Study hall.

ben—Son of.

"Berakhot"—A Talmudic tractate (chapter) that primarily addresses the rules regarding the blessings and prayers.

Be-reshit—Genesis.

beryonim—Troublemakers.

bimah—A raised platform in a synagogue from which the Torah is read.

brit, brit milah—Covenant of circumcision.

b'ruchim ha'chatan va'kalah—"Blessed be the groom and the bride."

b'shert—A soul mate. According to the Talmud, it is predestined whom a man will marry before he is born.

b'tulah—Virgin.

chametz—Food made with leavening, which cannot be eaten during Passover.

chazzan—Cantor.

cherem—Excommunication from the Jewish community. The most severe of the type of bans that were used to enforce Jewish observance; *cherem* meant expulsion for an indefinite period and was only invoked when an offender had been repeatedly warned to repair his or her ways.

cholent—A long-cooking stew, usually made with meat, potatoes, beans, and barley. Because it can simmer for a long time on low heat, this is a favorite Sabbath meal.

chuppah—A canopy traditionally used in Jewish weddings, symbolizing the home the couple will build together.

dam betulim—Literally, "blood of virginity." Hymenal bleeding.

Eretz Yisrael—The land of Israel.

eruv Tavshilin—Preparing a cooked food prior to a Jewish holiday that will be followed by the Sabbath. Normally, cooking is allowed on Jewish holidays (as long as the fire is created before the Sabbath), but only to be eaten during that day, and not for consumption after the holiday.

esha moredet—Rebellious wife.

eshet—Wife of.

eshet cha'yal—Woman of valor.

foetor Judaicus—(Latin) Jewish odor.

galut—Exile.

"Gittin"—A Talmudic tractate (chapter) that deals with issues of divorce.

goyim—Non-Jews.

Hag samech—"Happy holiday."

ha-Shem—Literally "the Name," a phrase used when one wishes to mention God, whose name is not to be spoken aloud except during prayer, according to Jewish tradition.

Havdalah—"Separation"; the ceremony marking the end of the Sabbath and the beginning of a new week.

herei at m'kudeshet li b'taba'at zo k'dat Moshe v'Yisrael—"With this ring you are consecrated unto me according to the Law of Moses and Israel." Traditional vow stated by a groom at his wedding.

kashrut—Jewish dietary laws, requiring, among other restrictions, a total separation of meat and dairy foods and the prohibition of pork and shellfish in any form.

kavvanah—Intention or concentration.

Kiddush—The blessing recited over wine to sanctify the Sabbath or a Jewish holiday.

"Kiddushin"—A Talmudic tractate (chapter) that deals with the initial stage of betrothal and marriage.

Leili Brit Milah—The evening festivities before a circumcision.

mazel tov—"Good luck"; used colloquially to wish someone well or to offer congratulations.

mechetzah—A partition that separates men and women during prayer.

Megillah—The scroll that contains the story of Esther, read on the holiday of Purim.

melamed—Teacher of Hebrew and early Bible and Talmudic studies.

mezzuah (pl. mezzuzot)—A piece of parchment (contained in a decorative case) inscribed with specified Hebrew verses from the Torah and affixed to the doorways of a house.

mikveh—Ritual bath designed for full-body immersion of both men and women to achieve ritual purity.

mishloach manot—Gifts of food and drink given to friends and relatives as part of the Purim celebration.

Mishnah Torah—Maimonides's comprehensive code of Jewish law. Also known as the *Yad Hachazakah*.

mitzvah—Literally, a "commandment." Used also to refer to a good deed.

mohel—A man specially trained in circumcisions and the rituals surrounding the procedure.

Nazarene—A generally derogatory term for Christians, derived from Jesus's hometown of Nazareth.

ner tamid—The eternal flame that burns above the ark inside a synagogue.

neshamah—Soul.

niddah—Impure. Generally, a woman is considered *niddah* when she is menstruating or has menstruated without completing the ritual requirements, including a visit to the *mikveh*. During this period, men and women are prohibited from having sexual relations. Some couples also refrain from touching, passing objects, and sleeping in the same bed.

niddui—A lesser form of excommunication, usually set in seven-day spans.

pareve—Food that can be eaten with both milk and meat meals.

pashidah (pl. pashidot)—Small cakes for the Sabbath.

"Pirkei Avot"—A tractate (chapter) of the Mishnah composed of ethical maxims of the rabbis.

p'ru v'rvu—"Be fruitful and multiply." From Genesis 1:28.

Rav—The formal expression for "rabbi."

rebbetzin—A rabbi's wife.

responsa—Written questions and answers, generally about practical matters, derived from the period following the redaction of the Talmud. The responsa added to a body of legal literature (Torah, Mishnah, and Talmud); legal codes came after the responsa to help the Jews understand which laws governed when there were conflicts.

shadchan—A matchmaker. During the Middle Ages, the *shadchan* was generally a man.

shalom bayit—Household peace.

shamash—The bailiff of a synagogue.

Shavuah ha-Ben—Literally, "the week of the son," a celebration before the circumcision.

Shechiyanu—The prayer celebrating special occasions. The prayer's

English translation is "Blessed are you, Lord our God, Ruler of the Universe Who has kept us in life, sustained us, and brought us to this moment."

Shema—The most important prayer in Judaism, it is recited twice daily: "Hear, O Israel: the Lord is our God, the Lord is One."

shiduch—A wedding arrangement. During the Middle Ages, the father was responsible for making a match for his sons and daughters.

shiva—Mourning.

shofar—A ram's horn, sounded on Rosh Hashanah.

simon tov—A good sign.

Ta'anit Esther—The Fast of Esther, which takes place from dawn to dusk on the eve of the Purim holiday, to commemorate the three-day fast of the Jews of Persia who were saved by Esther's heroism. If the Fast of Esther falls on the Sabbath, it is observed on the previous Thursday.

tallith—A prayer shawl with knotted fringes worn during morning prayers.

talmid (pl. talmidim)—Student.

"Toldot Yeshu"—A derogatory medieval account of Jesus from the Talmud, used since the ninth century by those antagonistic to the Jews to create hostility against them.

Torah she b'al peh—The oral Torah. Tradition claims that when God gave Moses the written Torah on Mount Sinai, Moses also received a companion Torah *she b'al peh* that he used to teach to the people of Israel. According to the sages, this was the origin of the Mishnah and the Talmud, which were added to over the years.

tzedakah—Charity.

tzin'ut—Modesty.

"Vikuach"—Literally, "Disputation," this was the Jewish account of the disputation between Nicholas Donin and the rabbis. While I have attributed this account to Shira, historically it was authored by Joseph ben Nathan Official.

Yad Hachazakah—Maimonides's comprehensive code of Jewish law. Also known as the Mishnah Torah.

yeshiva—Jewish seminary where students learn Torah and Talmud.

Yeshu—Jesus.

yetzer ha'rah—Evil inclination.

ABOUT THE AUTHOR

MICHELLE CAMERON discovered the inspiring story of Rabbi Meir ben Baruch while exploring her family tree. She lived in Israel for fourteen years and served in the Israeli Army. She currently lives in Chatham, New Jersey, with her family. Visit her website at www.michelle-cameron.com.